Missing Pieces Series

COLLECTION

N.R. WALKER

Copyright

Cover Art: Covers by Combs
Editor: Boho Edits
Publisher: BlueHeart Press
Missing Pieces Series © 2020 N.R. Walker
Missing Pieces Collection © 2021 N.R. Walker
Missing Pieces Collection Print © 2022 N.R. Walker

ALL RIGHTS RESERVED:

No part of this book may be reproduced in any form or by any electronic or mechanical means, including information storage and retrieval systems, without written permission from the author, except for the use of brief quotations in a book review.

This is a work of fiction, and any resemblance to persons, living or dead, or business establishments, events or locales is coincidental. The Licensed Art Material is being used for illustrative purposes only.

WARNING

Intended for an 18+ audience only. This book contains material that is intended for a mature, adult audience. It contains graphic language, and adult situations.

TRADEMARKS:

All trademarks are the property of their respective owners.

MISSING
pieces
SERIES COLLECTION

PIECES OF YOU
PIECES OF ME
PIECES OF US

PIECES OF *you*

MISSING PIECES SERIES
BOOK ONE

Chapter One

JUSTIN

DALLAS SLID a mug of coffee on the kitchen bench in front of me. "You'll need to take the van today," he said, nodding to the overcast and dreary day.

I sighed. "Thanks," I mumbled before taking a sip. I was unsure if that order was coming from my boyfriend or my boss. Though that was probably unfair. Dallas was both boyfriend and boss, and we'd never had a problem with blurred lines before. I was just in a pissy mood.

I wasn't in a bad mood, exactly. I just wasn't a morning person. The rainy weather didn't help, considering I was a mobile bike mechanic, which meant I'd be working in the rain today. I loved my job, and I loved Dallas. I just didn't love mornings. Dallas squeezed my arm and fought a smile as he walked out of the kitchen.

I met Dallas when I was twenty-five. I'd not long moved back to Newcastle from two years in Darwin. The best motorbike mechanic shop in town was looking for a new mechanic, and I was a perfect fit for the job. They wanted a dedicated, hard-working KTM expert, and that's what they got. I was looking for work and certainly wasn't actively looking for a boyfriend, but along with the perfect job, I found a guy who was a perfect fit for me.

He was tall and gorgeous, with brown hair and a jawline of

scruff and piercing hazel-grey eyes. He was also the strong and silent type who never said much. He was hard-working, strict but fair, and everyone respected him. He was also kind and gentle, had a quirky sense of humour, and would do anything to help anyone. It helped that we shared a passion for bikes and that neither of us minded grease-stained fingernails and the permanent smell of oil on our skin.

Being gay and a mechanic was hard enough. It never occurred to me to look twice at a guy at any shop I worked at. Typically, mechanic shop breakrooms had calendars of naked women and guys who bragged about scoreboards of bedrooms and weekend football.

But not Dallas, and not his shop. He was different. And when I first started working with him, I'd thought I'd imagined the way his gaze would linger just a beat too long or how he'd stop and smile . . . because there was no way—no freaking way—he could look at me like that.

I hadn't been there long when Davo, another mechanic and a good mate of Dallas' asked me if I had a girlfriend. I'd laughed it off, shaking my head, not wanting to give my sexuality away, but then he'd asked if I had a boyfriend.

I'd frozen, and somewhere in the workshop a spanner had hit the concrete floor.

"It's okay," Davo had said, smiling a little too much. "I mean, we're cool with it here. Aren't we, Dallas?"

I'd shot Dallas a look over where he was picking up his dropped spanner while I was trying not to freak out and wondering how best to deny everything.

"Course it's fine," Dallas had mumbled, glaring at Davo before turning back to the bike he was working on.

Davo had laughed and walked away, finding something amusing, and I had tried not to dwell on it. But I knew guys who'd been bullied or, worse, bashed at work when they'd been outed. That afternoon at knock-off time, I'd been cleaning up in the breakroom when Dallas had come in. I hadn't noticed everyone else was gone, but the shop looked deserted.

I'd thought for sure he was about to fire me. Or jump me and hold me down while everyone took turns in kicking the shit outta me. But he'd looked troubled, awkward even, had scratched his beard, and swallowed hard. "I uh . . ." He'd let out a breath. "I just want you to know that if you're gay, that it's okay. I mean . . ." He'd shook his head. "Jesus."

"I'm not," I'd lied.

"Because I am," he'd said at the same time. He'd stared at me. "Oh." He'd frowned, and I'd regretted seeing the hurt in his eyes.

"Oh, um... Shit," I'd stammered.

"You okay?" he'd asked, putting a hand on my shoulder. His hand was huge and so warm, it had burned through my overalls. "Wanna breathe for me?"

I remembered sucking back a breath, putting a hand to my forehead. "Yeah, thanks. I thought . . ."

He'd taken his hand back and leaned against the sink, casual as ever. "You thought what?"

"I mean, I'm out. People know . . . I'm gay, that is. I just don't advertise it, especially at work because sometimes . . ."

"Sometimes people are arseholes."

I'd nodded quickly. "Yeah. Was Davo . . . ?"

He'd grinned. "Davo's fine. He's a mate of mine. The guys here know, and hell, most of my clients too. They don't have a problem with me. Well, if they do, they're too chickenshit to say anything."

I'd smiled at him and he'd stared that hazel-grey stare. My stomach had flipped, and he'd given me a crooked smile in return. And that was the beginning of months of too-long looks, shy smiles and off-the-charts sexual tension. Until Davo and Sparra called us into the breakroom and told us enough was enough. They were done with the tiptoeing and the breath-holding and how antsy I was and how pissed off Dallas was. "You're both not leaving this room until you sort it out," Davo had said, slamming the door behind him.

Dallas didn't want to have a relationship with a staff member, because lines got crossed, he'd said. I'd nodded because I understood, that made perfect sense, and I wasn't keen on shacking up with the boss either. He'd nodded and I'd nodded, and for a few long seconds, we'd stood, trying to breathe, like there was no oxygen in the room. He'd licked his lips, and holy shit, those eyes . . .

I'd taken one step closer before I even knew what I was doing, and he'd crossed the floor and had hold of my face and his tongue in my mouth before I could think.

But I didn't need to think . . .

Because I just knew.

"WHAT'S GOT YOU SMILING?" Dallas asked.

I was still staring out the rain-splattered window. "Just remembering our first kiss."

Dallas laughed and put his empty cup in the sink. "Fucking Davo. Still takes credit for that, you know."

"Oh, I know. He tells me all the time."

He stepped in close, lifted my jaw, and planted a soft kiss on my lips. "And I still thank him." His phone buzzed and he groaned. "First one for the day."

It had just gone six-thirty. I nodded and took a mouthful of coffee. "Gonna be a day of it, I'd say."

He glanced to the weather outside the kitchen window and nodded. "I'll go restock the van."

"Be down in a sec." The 'commute to work' was a single flight of stairs because we lived in the flat above the mechanic shop. Well, Dallas owned the building, and that included his business and his home. It was a two-bedroom unit that wasn't about to win any fancy-living awards, but it suited us perfectly.

I finished my coffee and pulled on my boots, gave Squish the cat a scratch behind his ear, pocketed my phone and keys, and pulled the door locked behind me.

By ten to seven in the morning, I'd finished loading up the van with Dallas when he handed me his high-vis raincoat. "Dunno if it'll keep you completely dry," he said as the rain poured down outside.

"If I come back soaking wet, will it be asking too much for

the boss to get me out of my wet uniform? You know, being a work-safety thing and all."

Dallas gave me my favourite smirk. "Nah, the paperwork's a bitch."

My mouth fell open, making him laugh, and he gave me a quick kiss just as Davo ran into the shop with his coat pulled over his head.

"It's pissing down," he said. He pulled his coat off with a grin, then shook the water off himself like a dog.

Sparra followed in not far behind him, dripping wet. "Good weather for ducks, ay."

"Yeah, you lot have a really awful day here in the fully-enclosed, dry shop. I've already got a call out," I said, holding up my PalmPilot.

"Uh, make that two," Dallas said, looking at his phone. He thumbed something on the screen, then the second booking popped up on my screen.

"Great," I grumbled. "You lot enjoy your second cuppa. I'll be out in that." I nodded toward the deluge blowing in through the open roller door.

Davo and Sparra laughed and flipped me off as they disappeared into the breakroom. Dallas shook his head, smiling. He fixed the collar of my coat and kissed me. "Be careful."

"Always."

He smirked at the rain. "I'll, uh, I'll have the report filled out by the time you get back."

"Report?"

"For the wet clothes," he murmured, his voice full of gravel and promise.

I laughed as I got into the van. First stop was Glendale, so it wasn't far, maybe fifteen minutes tops with this rain. I put the wipers on full bore, cranked the heater up so the windscreen didn't fog up, and hit the road.

It was supposed to be just another ordinary Tuesday in a very ordinary life. A day of work, some laughs with the boys at the shop in the afternoon, maybe a jog after work. Or if this rain hung around, maybe Dallas and I would curl up on the couch with Squish and watch some TV, then fall into bed and make real slow love till late.

Completely ordinary, completely mundane, and completely wonderful. It was all I'd ever wanted and never dared dream to have. Until I met Dallas and he made every wrong in my life right. It was ridiculous how happy I was. Even when I woke up grumpy in the mornings, he still smiled at me and he still loved me, no matter what.

Life was damn near perfect. Actually, there wasn't one single thing I would change if I was given the chance. Not one thing.

I sat in a line of traffic waiting for the lights to turn green. The rain had eased a little, though the taillights in front of me were still refracted by the water and the lights. Cold Chisel came on the radio, so I turned the volume up and began to sing along to "When the War Is Over." Dallas and I didn't exactly have a song, but if we did, this would be it. A song about learning to live again; a true classic Aussie anthem about life.

Life . . .

It's funny how they say your life flashes before your eyes just before you die. Or that there is profound clarity the moment before your life ends.

I had none of that.

As I was following the slow line of traffic through the inter-section, the light still green, and just when Jimmy Barnes was about to belt out his part of the song, I heard the sound of screeching brakes and honking horns. I just happened to look out my window at the truck aquaplaning straight for me. It was jack-knifed and sliding and coming so fast and in slow motion at the same time.

No, there was no life flashing before my eyes, no profound moments of clarity. As the grille of the truck came at me, my very last thought would have been funny if it hadn't been my very last thought.

Oh, that's just fucking great. The song's just getting to my favourite part.

I waited for the sound of impact, to hear the breaking glass and twisting metal. I waited for the pain. But it never came.

Chapter Two

DALLAS

I CHECKED the clock at ten to nine. Two minutes since I checked it last. Justin hadn't checked in yet, and he always checked in. His first job should've been finished ages ago.

"He'll be fine," Davo said, catching me clock-watching for the twentieth time. We'd been working on a bike together at the far end of the shop. "He'll drive in any second now lookin' like a drowned rat, bitching about the rain. You watch."

"Hmm," I grunted, not feeling his confidence.

"Uh, Dallas? Boss," Sparra called out with an edge to his voice.

Davo and I turned just as two uniformed officers walked in. My blood ran cold and my stomach soured. "Can I help you?" I asked.

"This is Forty-four Carney Road?" one of the officers asked.

"Yes, that's right."

The other officer spoke. "We have this as the address of a Mr Justin Keith."

My knees almost buckled. "That's right. He lives upstairs with me." I swallowed hard and my lungs felt far too small.

"You're Dallas Muller?"

"Yeah, that's right." I was trying real hard not to freak out. "I'm his boyfriend. And his boss. We live together. Is everything okay?"

Maybe it was my tone or the flat-out panic in my voice, but the first cop took pity on me. "There's been an accident, Mr Muller. We're going to need you to come with us."

Accident.

"Is he . . . ?" Fuck. No, they didn't take their hats off. Cops take their hats off if it's real bad news, right?

"He's been taken to John Hunter. The vehicle he was driving was T-boned by a truck."

I didn't hear much after that. My legs didn't want to hold me up anymore and the air got real thick and heavy . . .

I remember seeing the look of horror on Davo and Sparra's faces. Davo took my keys, told me he'd look after the shop, and helped me get into the cop car. I don't remember the drive to the hospital. I just remember trying not to vomit. And trying to breathe.

The two officers escorted me straight through the emergency department and I found myself in a waiting room. The foul hospital smell clung to the back of my throat, and one cop handed me a plastic cup of water with a look of pity and the other cop came back with a woman in scrubs.

"This is Dallas Muller. He's the boss *and* boyfriend of the patient from the vehicle accident."

"His name's Justin Keith. We live together," I said numbly.

She looked at me, at my dirty overalls and my grease-covered hands. "Does he have any family?"

Oh fuck.

"Um, not really. His mother doesn't care about him," I whispered. "His sister lives in Sydney. I can try to get her number. It'd be in Justin's phone, in the van, maybe. He had his phone with him when he left this morning. Is he okay? Please . . ."

She didn't answer. "Does he have any allergies?"

"Uh, no. I don't think so." My hands began to shake and my eyes burned. "I'm sorry, this is all a bit much to take in. Where is he? Can I see him? Please. Please."

She had weary eyes, I noticed. She put her hand on my arm. "Mr Muller, he's in surgery. His right arm is broken, and he has multiple fractures in his right leg . . ."

I nodded. "Okay." Arms and legs were okay. They could be fixed, more or less.

"Mr Muller, there was also some head trauma. I don't know the extent and I won't speculate, but he's in the best hands right now."

I didn't hear much after that. There was something about MRI and CT scans and something else about not knowing for a few hours yet, but the room began to pulse and spin and the nice officers sat me back in a chair. Even they left after a while, and hospital staff came and went, but I sat in that waiting room for I don't know how long. The chair was probably uncomfortable but I never felt a thing.

An eternity later and Davo and Sparra arrived, peering cautiously around the wall. "Oh, there you are," Davo said. "They said you were up here . . ." His frown deepened. "What do you know?"

"Nothing much," I answered, my voice sounding rough. "He has a broken arm and leg, and there's some head trauma. He's in surgery. He's been in surgery for fucking hours."

Sparra handed me my phone. "You left that at work."

"Thanks, mate."

"I know it's a bit early but we were so worried. I locked everything up and fed Squish," Davo said. "And don't you worry about nothin', Dallas. I'll open up in the morning and take care of everything. You just worry about him, 'kay?"

I nodded, overwhelmed with gratitude for these two and fear for my Justin. I swallowed back tears. "What time is it?" I asked as I checked my phone. Shit. It was after two o'clock in the afternoon.

"The accident's been on the news and everything," Davo said gently. "There are photos of the van. Fuck, Dallas. It don't look good. They're saying it's a miracle he survived."

I stared at the black screen on my phone, not daring to see any news, any reports, or pictures. My heart couldn't bear it. "He got hit by a truck."

Davo nodded, his mouth a thin line, his eyes full of sorrow. "It went through a red light. The brakes locked up, apparently, and it just slid right into him. There was nothing Justin coulda done."

I shook my head, feeling all kinds of hollowed out. "Fuck."

Just then, a doctor came in, and when he saw us, three rough-looking mechanics, he smiled. "Mr Muller?"

I stood, and Davo and Sparra stood beside me. "Yeah, that's me. How is he, doc? Is he okay?"

His smile died, but there was kindness in his eyes. "He came through the surgery and they're taking him through to recovery."

My breath left me in a whoosh and I almost sagged with relief. "Thank fuck." Sparra patted my back, and I willed myself not to cry.

"He's not out of the woods yet," the doc said firmly. "In fact, we won't know the extent of his injuries until he wakes up. He took quite a blow, the impact resulting in a subdural haematoma. We operated to relieve the bleed and the pressure. His arm has been reset, but his leg will require some surgery, though our main concern right now is his brain. They won't operate on his leg until his brain injury is stabilised. There is some swelling, which we're monitoring, but Mr Muller, brain injuries are complex. There can be lasting damage that may affect him for the rest of his life. We won't know the extent until he wakes up."

I nodded, still numb. "But he survived. Everything else we can live with."

He gave me a sympathetic smile, and I didn't know if he pitied my naivety or if he liked my optimism. But I had to believe Justin would be okay.

He just had to be. Because the alternative was incomprehensible.

"Can I see him? Please?"

The doc gave a nod. "Just for a minute. He won't be awake for some time, so a quick visit. Then you might as well go home and get some rest yourself."

"I'm not leaving," I replied. Wild fucking horses . . .

He gave a nod like he expected me to say exactly that. "Come with me." He shot a glance to Davo and Sparra. "He'll be a few minutes if you want to wait here."

They both nodded, and I followed the doc through the double doors and down the hall. He stopped near a blue curtain. "He'll be in Intensive Care at first," the doc said, his voice low. "But I'll see you tomorrow and hopefully we'll know a lot more."

The doc was gone then, and a nurse took his place. She pulled back the curtain and I almost couldn't look.

Jesus, how did this even happen? How did he leave just this morning, smiling as he bitched about the rain, and now here he was in hospital?

It felt so surreal.

Until I saw him.

He was bandaged . . . everywhere: his arm, his head. He had tubes and so many monitors, and his face—God, what I could see of it—was banged up and bruised. He looked far too pale and there was dried blood smeared . . .

Christ almighty, nothing in the world could have prepared me for seeing him like that.

He was impossibly still, and Justin was never still . . .

The nurse put her hand on my arm. "Two minutes. Then we're taking him to the ICU."

I nodded, I think. I couldn't seem to move. My feet felt welded to the floor. I had to make myself move closer, mechanically and heavy, to the left side of the bed. I reached for his hand, though it had tubes taped to it. It was cold and it didn't feel like him at all. I held his fingers, and it took me a second to realise why it felt so foreign.

Because he never threaded our fingers like he always did. He never moved to touch me back like he always did. Even in his sleep, as soon as he felt me near, he would curl into me or squeeze me.

But this time he never moved.

Hot tears spilled and I sobbed back a breath. "Justin, baby. It's me. You're gonna be okay. I'm here."

The right side of his body had obviously taken the brunt of the hit. His arm was wrapped from his shoulder to his fingers, the bedding was held off his right leg; I was grateful I couldn't see it. And though his head was bandaged, I could see his right eye was swollen, and there looked to be stitches above his eyebrow. His cheek was purple, his jaw marked, and he had small cuts and nicks all over, from the shattered glass, I guessed.

The left side of his face wasn't so banged up, but his eyelid was purple. His beautiful eyelashes fanned out, casting delicate shadows on his pale cheek. A cheek I'd touched a thousand times.

He was so still.

The nurse appeared at my side. "I'm sorry. Time's up. We need to take him."

"I just got here. It's not two minutes yet."

She gave me a curt smile. "Rasida will show you out. You can see him again in the ICU after three o'clock."

I didn't even have time to argue because a swarm of scrubs came in and wheeled Justin away. A short woman with a kind face smiled up at me. "Come with me," she said, leading me back the way I'd come. "I know it's scary right now, but they're taking him where he needs to be." She continued to talk in a smooth, calming tone as we walked, not that I heard much of anything. Then we were back in the waiting room and Davo and Sparra both shot to their feet when they saw me.

"Ah," Rasida said. "Get him something to eat and a juice or a soft drink. He can come down to the ICU after three o'clock." She held up three fingers, then patted me on the back but spoke to Davo. "You take him now."

They nodded and she left, and then they looked up at me. "Is he . . . ?" Davo started. "How was he?"

I shook my head, not able to speak. My eyes burned and a tear escaped, but I quickly scrubbed it away. "He doesn't look too good," I tried to say.

Sparra squeezed my shoulder. "He's not the only one. Come on, she said to feed you."

I put my hand to my stomach. The thought of food made me nauseous. "I just need to sit down," I said, my voice still not working right.

I found myself sitting in a chair trying to take deep breaths. Sparra was gone, but Davo was beside me, his expression grave. I had to tell him something. "The whole right side of his body took the worst of it," I managed. "He looked dead. I thought he was dead."

"He'll get better," Davo said, patting me gently on the back. "You know how stubborn he is. He's too pigheaded to die."

I laughed, though it sounded more like a sob. I wiped my face. "He sure is stubborn."

Sparra appeared then, holding a packet of rice crackers and a can of lemonade. "Found a vending machine," he said, holding them out to me. I tried to wave him off because the last thing I wanted to do was eat. "Boss," Sparra said. "You look green. If you want to see Justin again today, you need to not be sick. They won't let you near him if you're fucking green. Now eat."

I stared up at him in shock, and Davo did too, until he laughed.

"What I mean to say," Sparra added, "is that you probably should eat something, please. That doctor-lady said you should too. So here."

He was still holding them in front of me, so I took them. I had to sip the lemonade to wash the cracker down, but after the first stayed down, I had a few more and half the lemonade, and I did feel a bit better.

Davo stood up. "Come on," he said, nodding for me to stand. "It's almost three. You can see him again soon."

"I don't know where the ICU is," I admitted as I got to my feet. At least my knees weren't so wobbly now.

Sparra stood with me. "Then we'll find it."

Ten minutes later, I stood outside the ICU. "Don't worry about the shop," Davo said. "We got it covered. You just concentrate on him."

"Yeah, and tell him to hurry and get his lazy arse back to work," Sparra added with a smile. Then he nodded, more serious. "And you tell him to get better soon, 'kay?"

I gave a nod. "Thanks, guys."

I went through the door and was met by a clerk who threw twenty rapid-fire questions at me. No, I wasn't family I was his de facto. We live together. Yes, boyfriends. Next of kin, his normal doctor, private health insurance details, Medicare info, sign here . . .

"I just need to see him," I said and was eventually, after an eternity, taken to one nurse in particular.

"Ah, you're his partner," she said warmly. She walked me to bed five. "He's all settled in for now. You can hold his hand, talk to him."

She didn't have to tell me to be quiet. The room was like a tomb. It was cold and there was nothing but the sound of beeps and respirators, and I didn't dare look at any of the other beds. I just sat by his side and took his hand. I marvelled at how our hands matched: rough, calloused, our oil-and-grease-stained nails. We each had cuts and bumps on our fingers. These hands worked hard for our money, but they also loved and caressed and touched . . . I knew his hands, how they felt on my body, how he loved to hold hands . . . I brought his knuckles up to my lips, closed my eyes, and cried.

Two days later—two days of nothing but sympathetic looks from doctors and nurses, two days of listening to every beep, every blip, every heartbeat, when hope was starting to fade— Justin opened his eyes.

Chapter Three

"Hey," I whispered, real low. My voice croaked from disuse.

Justin's left eye closed, then half opened again. His right eye was still swollen shut, but this was the first sign of life in two days. Surely it meant he was waking up.

"Hey," I tried again. "You're okay. You're in hospital. I'm right here, baby."

His eyelid slowly closed again and, this time, stayed closed. His nurse today was Naomi, and she was quick to check all the machines he was hooked up to and write everything down. She smiled at me. "Could be a good sign."

Could be?

"I'm sure it is," I said, touching the side of Justin's face. "If you need to sleep, baby, you take all the time you need. I'm not going anywhere."

Naomi did something to the machines and took a printout of some kind with Justin's folder. "Keep talking to him," she said.

"Talk to him? About what?"

"It doesn't matter. Just keep it nice and calm. I'm sure he likes the sound of your voice."

I sat back down and took his hand again. I wasn't game to take my eyes off his in case he opened them. "Uh, so I called your sister. She's gonna come up next weekend," I began. "She texts me for updates every day. I think she told your mum. I'm not sure though. Hopefully it might make your mother pull her head out of her arse."

Naomi quirked an eyebrow at me and smiled. "Sorry. I didn't mean to hear that."

"It's okay. His mother's . . . not very nice."

"Lucky he has you," she said with a wink before heading back to the nurses' station.

"Of course he has me," I whispered to Justin. I stared at his face, his beautiful, bandaged and swollen face. "They've done more scans on your brain and they're happy there's no more bleeding, and the swelling's gone down but there's still some bruising. Doc said he's still not sure of what effect the extent of the damage will have on ya, but he did say you'll have a cracker of a headache for a long while. He's one of the best brain doctors in the country, apparently, so he knows his stuff. He said brains are complex and delicate, and yours took a helluva hit. There was a fracture in your skull and a bleed that shut off some blood to one part of your brain."

I was just rambling, all out of order, trying to remember everything they'd told me. "Your arm was broken up near your shoulder and in your forearm. They told me the name of the bones, but I can't remember it. The one near your elbow, is that the radius? I dunno what they called it." I squeezed his hand. "Your leg isn't too good, but nothing they can't fix. They just want to worry about your head first. Your leg'll need surgery, apparently. They must have you on some pretty good drugs if you can't feel it. But they said maybe an operation tomorrow, depends how you fare today. They're more worried about your head than your leg." I kissed his knuckles. "Just one day at a time, baby. That's all you can do."

I didn't tell him that the doctor had said he might never fully recover or that he might have some permanent brain damage. Or that he might have lost the ability to speak or walk properly. Or that we had to face the possibility that his life would never be the same. He might need a full-time carer; he would likely need all kinds of therapy for years. He might never regain consciousness.

Except he just did. For a fleeting moment, his eye opened. He was still in there. I knew it.

I knew it was the doctor's responsibility to prepare people for the worst. I understood why. But I was ready for the worst. Whatever issues we had to face, we'd face together.

I kissed Justin's hand again and held his fingers to my cheek, closed my eyes, and sighed. Together forever, I repeated to myself. Together forever.

I took a moment and began again. "Anyway, Davo and Sparra have been a godsend, if you can believe that. I mean, they've always been good blokes, but they've really stepped up and looked after the shop for us. I haven't been to work at all. You were always saying I needed to take some time off." I couldn't even smile. "Davo's been taking care of everything. I only go home to shower and sleep. Pretty sure the nurses here are sick of my face. Squish misses you too. Not as much as me, of course. I know I bitched a lot about you hogging the blankets, but Justin, I'd do anything to have you back in our bed. I miss you so much. So any time you want to open those pretty eyes, you just go right ahead."

Justin's doctor appeared with Naomi at his side. "I hear someone opened his eyes."

I nodded. "Just for a second. He blinked, real slow. But that's good news, right?"

He smiled and walked to the other side of the bed. He leaned over Justin and lifted his eyelid, peering into his eye with a penlight. "It can be, yes," he said.

"I mean, it's a sign that there's something going on in there, isn't it?"

The doctor gave me one of those patronising I-can't-say-because-I-don't-want-to-get-sued smiles. "We're still taking it one day at a time. His vitals are good. He's strong and healthy."

I sighed at his noncommittal reply, and after he finished looking at screens and printouts, I wasn't disappointed when he left.

The next day, Justin opened his eyes again. This time he kept them open for a few seconds. He didn't seem to focus on anything, and I tried to keep him with me. "Justin," I said, getting to my feet. I held his hand. "Hey, it's me, Dallas. You're okay. I'm right here."

His eyes closed slowly again and he slipped back to the comfort behind his eyelids.

The day after that, the nurse told me he'd opened his eyes a few times during the night, and I took my usual seat beside him and held his hand with a smile.

With hope.

I spent the morning reading to him, just page after page of quiet, soothing words. I even read the article on the new and improved Yamaha, which he would have hated, and maybe part of me wanted him to wake up just to tell me that KTMs were a better bike. It was an argument we'd had a thousand times, and truth be told, I probably would have agreed with him if the playful bickering wasn't so much fun.

"Whatcha reading to him?" Naomi asked as she pressed buttons on a screen.

I held it up so she could see the cover. "It's just the monthly motorbike magazine he subscribes to," I replied.

She grinned. "That's sweet."

Then Justin squeezed my fingers. "He squeezed my hand," I blurted. And when I looked over, his eyes were open. Still heavy-lidded but open, and more focused. "Hey," I whispered. "Justin, you're okay. You're in hospital. I'm right here beside you."

He blinked, and I thought his eyes would stay shut. But they opened again.

"I'll go page the doctor," Naomi said.

"You were in a bad car accident," I said. "But you're gonna be okay." I didn't know if that was the truth, but I wanted to reassure him any way I could.

He opened his mouth but no sound came out, then he slow blinked again. His eyes focused on me, but they were hazy, distant. He slow blinked another time, but on the next blink, his eyes stayed closed.

Forty minutes later, he opened them again. He seemed to focus better and was more alert. He opened and closed his mouth again. "Justin, can you hear me?" I asked. I stood and leaned over him so he could see me. "You're okay. You're in the hospital."

This time, his doctor and Naomi both arrived and there was another doctor with them as well. They took over and I stood aside, letting them do their thing. All the while, my heart was in my throat.

They asked him questions, not that he answered in words—he mostly grunted and squinted—but they were clearly happy with this development. This was progress. No matter how small.

Then Naomi was in front of me. "Okay, we're going to be taking him down for more scans and tests. It's almost rest time anyway, so why don't you come back after three."

"Oh, sure. Okay." I nodded, though I certainly didn't feel like leaving him. I checked my phone. It was almost midday, and rest time was one till three. Three hours . . . What the hell was I supposed to do for three hours?

Naomi patted my arm, clearly seeing me struggle. "Go home. Get something to eat. Have a nap. You've been here more hours than me this week, and that's saying something." She smiled. "We'll take good care of him."

So that's what I did. I went back to the shop, happier than I'd been in five days. I walked in carrying a bag of burgers and chips from the old takeaway shop a few blocks down.

Davo grinned when he saw me. He left the bike he was working on and stood in the middle of the doorway. "That smile has to mean good news."

"He opened his eyes."

"Well, I'll be fucking damned." He turned and yelled into the shop. "Hey, Sparra. Jusso opened his eyes!"

I held the bag up. "I bought us some lunch."

It felt good to smile again. After what had been the week from hell, I was beginning to wonder if I'd ever smile again. But there in the winter sunshine, sitting around with Davo and Sparra, listening to them talking shit and laughing, it was cathartic. Justin was in the best hands he could be in, and I fully expected to get back to the hospital at three o'clock and hear good news.

And I was smiling when I walked back through the ICU doors. I wanted to hold Justin's hand, look him right in the eye, and reassure him he was gonna be fine.

Except I didn't get the chance. Justin's curtains were drawn and his doctor met me at the station. "Mr Muller," he said, his face unreadable. "I'd like to go somewhere to chat in private."

And I knew then, why he'd never said that Justin waking up was a good thing, why he never liked to give hope prematurely.

Because sometimes hope was the wrong thing to give.

He sat me down in a small room with awful yellow walls. My blood was pounding in my ears and my stomach was bubbling. Then he got straight to the point. "Mr Muller, when did Justin live in Darwin?"

"Darwin?" I shook my head. "Uh, like five years ago. He's from here originally. Went to Darwin for a few years but moved back to Newcastle five years ago. Why?"

"Hmm, five years . . ." He nodded like that made sense, but then his brows furrowed. "Have you heard of retrograde amnesia?"

"Amnesia? Like in the movies?"

There was that smile again . . . "I'm afraid it's not much like the movies at all. Unfortunately, it's not that simple."

"Is he talking? Does he not remember who he is?"

"He is talking, yes. Mostly just yes and no, which is a good sign, cognitively. There was no way to know just how much damage had been done or if he would be able to speak at all."

Okay, well, that was good, right? But amnesia? "I thought amnesia was not knowing who you are," I said, and as soon as I heard the words out loud, the penny dropped. "Oh."

The doctor nodded. "Justin remembers who he is. But he thinks he lives in Darwin. He believes he's twenty-five." He frowned. "Mr Muller, there's no easy way to say this. He doesn't know who you are."

Chapter Four

JUSTIN WAS SLEEPING when I went back into the ICU, and I was kind of glad. The hope I'd felt earlier was long gone, and in its place was a hollowed lump of dread.

The doctor said it could be temporary. Most cases saw a marked improvement in the days and weeks and months after the initial trauma. But he made it very clear that sometimes the memories never returned.

"The only true test is time," he'd said.

He'd begun to tell me other things, like what to expect and what it all meant, but I think he knew it was too much. I'd zoned out.

He doesn't know who you are.

He doesn't know who you are.

I sat by his bed and took his hand. It was warm in mine and I threaded our fingers, relishing in what might be the last time I held his hand for God knew how long—if ever. He was asleep, so I told myself it was to comfort him in his dreams, but I knew all too well it was for my benefit, not his.

And I told myself that it'd be okay. That his memory would come back in a day or two and we could concentrate on getting him better. That he'd remember me, and he'd remember us. I had to believe that. It wasn't hope. It was survival. Because he was my entire world. There was simply no other option.

I wouldn't give up on him.

I don't know how long I sat there like that, for minutes or hours. But he groaned and his eyelids slowly opened. He swallowed and groaned again, and I could only assume he was more with it because it sounded as though he was feeling every injury. Even with the drugs they were giving him.

He turned to me, and those beautiful, familiar eyes met mine. Those eyes that had shone when we'd laughed and burned when we'd made love. And now there was nothing . . .

No recognition, no spark. Only exhaustion and wariness.

He pulled his hand from mine. I'd forgotten I was holding it.

"Hey," I said weakly, trying not to let the hurt show. "I'm glad you're awake."

He slow blinked again and his lips parted, and his mouth worked like he was thirsty.

"Would you like some water?"

He hummed and gave a small nod, which made him wince.

"Naomi?" I said, going to the nurses' station. "Can he have water? I think he's thirsty."

She inclined his bed so he was sitting up a bit and gave him small sips of water, and he sagged back on the bed with another groan. He licked his lips and blinked, all in slow motion.

"Head hurts," he rasped slowly.

"You were in a car accident," I said. I wasn't sure what I should be telling him . . .

He frowned. He looked so different sitting up. His head was still bandaged across his right temple and the corner of his right eye, though the eye was still swollen shut. It was now purple and black, with mottled red splotches. The angry red mark on the right side of his jaw was still visible under his scruffy beard. His left eye was bruised and there was a cut across the bridge of his nose.

He looked like fucking hell.

And I hadn't seen the wound underneath those bandages yet. The doc had described what he'd done, so I could only imagine it, and it was no wonder his head hurt.

His right arm was still bandaged from his wrist to his armpit, and his leg was still broken. They'd stabilised it, of course, but they wouldn't risk surgery until they knew more about his brain activity.

"Head hurts," he said like he hadn't just said that. His words were a slow drawl.

"Would you like me to get the doctor?"

"Hmm." He slow blinked again, then his eyes drew to me. They were flat, empty, and confused. "You the doctor?"

My heart squeezed to the point of pain, and it was so sharp, the pierce of it took my breath away.

Naomi intervened, stepping in front of me and pulling the blanket up across his belly. "The doctor will be here soon," she said smoothly.

There was a long pause. "Head hurts," he mumbled.

"I know. We'll lie you back down now and you can close your eyes. That will help. Want another sip of water?" she asked, putting the cup to his lips. He sipped the drink without lifting his good hand, and his eyelids drooped heavily. He was asleep again before Naomi got the bed fully reclined.

She fixed his blanket again, then turned to me. "He's very confused, and that's to be expected." She put her hand on my arm and met my gaze. "Don't take it personally. I know that's easier said than done, but he doesn't mean it. Sit with him while he sleeps."

I nodded, numb, except for the burn behind my eyes.

But I sat, and he slept.

***

THEY OPERATED on Justin's leg the next day and they moved him to the neuro ward the day after that. He slept for most of it and would wake up and say that his head hurt. I would offer him sips of water and put the cup to his lips, and he would look at me with the same blank stare he gave the nurses and doctors. There was zero recognition.

They changed his head bandages and I saw the scars and staples for the first time. The side of his head was shaved, and there was an L-shape of staples from his temple down the back of his head. He had stitches above his eyebrow, which looked minor compared to the whopping surgical scar on the side of his head. His right eye was still badly bruised, but the swelling was starting to go down.

I fed him some beef broth, of which he managed just a few mouthfuls, but at least it was something. "Have you had enough?" I asked.

"Yeah," he murmured. "Thanks, doc."

I almost dropped the spoon, and my heart broke into a thousand tiny pieces.

TIME SEEMED to pass in a weird void. I had no idea if it was fast or slow. The only hours I kept were visiting hours. That's all there was. He was getting better, apparently, but he kept calling me doc. It broke my heart every time.

The thing about the neuro ward, as opposed to the ICU, was that he could have other visitors. And I'd just finished pushing the over-the-bed table away when Davo and Sparra arrived. They were escorted by a nurse who told them they had five minutes only.

They'd both showered after work, looking all kinds of nervous. And then they saw Justin.

Davo paled and Sparra took a small step back. "Oh," Davo said. "Thought we'd come visit." He looked at me, then, with a panicked look in his eyes. "He's, um . . ."

Justin looked at them, then looked at me. He was squinting again, a sign I now recognised as pain. "Can lights off, doc? Hurts m' eyes."

"Sure thing," I replied. I flipped the switch above his bed and he closed his eyes, quickly falling into sleep.

Davo and Sparra both stared at me, so I gave them a nod. "Wanna go for a walk? He'll be out for a while now."

They nodded woodenly, and both gave Justin a cautious once

over before I led them out. I made it to the waiting room before I took a breath. "Holy shit," Davo said. "He looks . . ."

"Like he got hit by a truck?" I offered, trying to smile. I was also fighting tears. "He thinks I'm a doctor. Which is pretty cool, right? Means I look smart."

"Fuck," Sparra whispered. "Dallas, I'm sorry, man."

Davo nodded. "We thought we'd just come and visit him. Sorry. I shoulda checked first."

"No, you should visit. You're mates of his. He won't remember you now, but he might remember that you visited. Later on, in a coupla weeks or whatever. He'll remember that you came to see him."

"How you holding up?" Davo asked quietly. "We haven't seen ya since the other day, and it was good news back then . . ."

"I'm okay. I should have called or texted. Sorry. I've just been here. And I can't deal with much else right now. I've just dumped the shop onto you both. Sorry."

"Hey, it's okay. We got it all under control," Davo said. "Don't worry 'bout nothing. I put your mail on your desk though; you might wanna get that in case there's something important."

I nodded.

"Everyone knows about Justin," Sparra offered gently. "All the customers. They've been calling. And they all said to tell him to get better soon."

I managed a teary smile. "That's real nice."

"How long since you ate last?" Davo said, studying my face. He didn't need an answer. "Come on, let's go find the cafeteria."

A toasted sandwich and a cup of tea later, I felt somewhat better, though exhaustion started to catch up with me. I hadn't been sleeping well, at all. I'd tossed and turned all night, hugging his pillow in our very empty bed.

"So what'd the doc say?" Davo asked.

"He's got two plates and a bunch of pins in his leg, nineteen staples in his head, six stitches." I swallowed hard. "He, uh, thinks he's twenty-five and still living in Darwin."

"Fuck," Sparra breathed.

"The neurosurgeon said there was damage to the memory bank of his brain, and there's no way of knowing yet how bad it is. If he'll ever remember again, or even if he can even make new memories yet. Things like the name of his nurse, or if he just ate." I shrugged. "It's early days. And he sleeps a lot. Apparently that's common with a brain injury. I have a lot of information they've given me about what to expect. Things like exhaustion, real bad headaches, temper, confusion, anger. But he could remember everything when he wakes up tomorrow. Or next week. Or it could come to him in dribs and drabs over the next few weeks or months." *Or not at all* . . . I sighed then and tried to speak with a conviction I just didn't feel. "I mean, they weren't even sure if he'd be able to speak or communicate at all, and he's doing that just fine."

Davo shook his head sadly, but then he met my gaze with determination. "He'll be just fine. You watch. It might take a little while, but like I said, he's too stubborn to let a fucking truck stop him."

Sparra nodded. "Yep. And I know Jusso will do everything he can to make you happy. He'll come back to you, Dallas. His brain might have forgot, but this in here—" He thumped his heart. "It won't forget."

And with that, the tears I'd been trying not to cry fell like rain.

I ARRIVED AT THE HOSPITAL, just like every day since the accident, the second they opened the doors to visitors. Justin was sitting up in his bed surrounded by three doctors in white coats. His neurosurgeon, Doctor Anderson, smiled at me, though I had no idea who the other two were.

"Morning, Mr Muller," Doctor Anderson said. "These are Doctors Simeon and Chang. Justin's going to start some physiotherapy today with Doctor Simeon, and Doctor Chang is a cognitive recognition specialist. You'll be seeing more of them and less of me now going forward. They'll both need to speak with you at some point."

I gave them a nod, but honestly, I just wanted to see Justin.

"Hey," Justin said. "I know you."

And my heart stopped. Hope ignited like a forest fire in my chest. "You do?"

He smiled, slow and hazy. "Yeah. You were here before."

"I was, that's right." Come on, Juss. One more step. One more step . . .

"Are you a doctor?" he asked.

My heart sank, and I couldn't bring myself to speak.

Doctor Anderson stepped up, though I didn't hear what he said.

Doctor Chang led me toward the nurses' station, out of earshot. "That was rough for you," she said kindly. "I'd like to say it gets easier, but I'm not sure it does."

I shook my head, unsure of what to say to that and feeling very overwhelmed.

"My name is Julia Chang," she said. "I work with people who live with amnesia, and with their families and loved ones, helping to navigate the effects of traumatic brain injury. I'll be working with Justin, and you, from now on as he moves to the next stage of his recovery."

"Okay."

"Doctor Anderson said Justin has no close family and you'll be his primary carer? Is that correct?"

"Yes."

"I'll be working with Justin today to try and establish the extent of his amnesia, and I want you to be there. Do you think you can do that?"

"Yes."

"It won't be easy, and he may say things that are upsetting to hear."

"Like when he keeps calling me his doctor?"

Her eyes softened. "But he recognised you today from yesterday, and that is a good sign." She smiled. "That tells me he has the ability to make new memories, and that is very good news."

Of course it was. I knew it was. I was just still hurting over the doctor comment. "Okay."

"But first, we need to establish a basis from which to move forward. What we tell him as fact will be the foundation from which he can start."

I frowned. "I don't know what you mean."

"We cannot plant memories in his mind. It is best if he can remember on his own. But if he asks questions, we need to be honest in the facts without giving him our own opinions and experiences. It's not as easy as it sounds," she said. "Retrograde amnesia is the loss of facts and experiences but not the skill or the ability. He's a motorbike mechanic, yes?"

I nodded. "Yes."

"Right, so he won't remember if he owns a motorbike or when he bought it. But he will remember how to ride it."

My mind was beginning to spin. "Okay."

"And we need to be united in what we tell him. He will begin to feel very overwhelmed and very lost and confused. We need to give him information he can anchor to, okay?"

"Such as."

"Things like where he lives, where he works. Who he's in a relationship with."

"Oh . . . I didn't think I could tell him that. I didn't want him to freak out . . ."

"We need to tell him this truth and show him photographs, or videos if you have them." She frowned but gave a nod. "If you were married, we would tell him without question. The fact you live together and he has no one else makes this case unusual. If we do not tell him in hopes he remembers on his own, yet he goes to live with you, it just raises more questions, more confusion, and untruths and lies. And that would be detrimental to his recovery and to his trust. Trust is critical here, so we must tell him the truth." Her eyes bored into mine. "But Mr Muller, you should prepare yourself . . . he may reject the idea, of you, of your relationship. You will need to give him all the space he needs, and you cannot pressure him. It will not be easy for either of you. Hard and sad for you, but terrifying and confusing for him."

I swallowed hard. "Okay."

"For the next few weeks and months, everything in your life is going to be about him and his welfare. You're going to have to put his needs above your own for a while. Your wellbeing is important, don't get me wrong, and you'll have support as well. But these next few steps are critical to his recovery, and he has to be our primary focus."

"Doc, since the day I met him, my life's been about him. That ain't gonna change any time soon."

Doctor Chang smiled, and I was pretty sure she wanted to say something like "You have no idea what you're in for" or "Naïve looks good on you." But the truth was, there wasn't anything I wouldn't do for him. I was all too aware just how much everything changed the day of his accident and how it would all change again once we told Justin some truths.

But we couldn't move forward if we weren't brave enough to take that first step.

"Are you ready?" she asked.

I nodded. "Yes."

"JUSTIN, can you tell me where you are?"

"Hospital," he answered after a second, and his words were slow.

Doctor Chang sat on one side of his bed; I sat on the other. We'd explained we were going to be asking questions. The truth was, the doc would be asking. I would just be sitting in. She wanted me to be a part of his recovery, but I was to remain impartial. I had to answer directly, without personal input.

"Do you know why you're in hospital?" Doctor Chang asked.

He paused and concentrated. "Car accident?"

"Do you remember the accident?"

"No." He shook his head. "Someone told me."

"Who told you that?"

He frowned. "Don't know."

"You were in an accident. The van you were driving was hit by a truck," she said plainly. "You took a hard hit to your head, and you're having trouble remembering things."

He gave a small nod. "My head hurts."

"Do you know which city the hospital is in?"

"Darwin."

My heart squeezed, but Doctor Chang continued like that was an expected answer. "Justin, you're in Newcastle, New South Wales."

He squinted as though he was trying to join invisible dots. "I don't live in Newcastle anymore. Moved away."

"You moved to Darwin when you were twenty-three, and you spent two years there. Then you moved back to Newcastle."

"Why?"

"You grew up in Newcastle. Do you remember that?"

He gave another small nod, though somewhat delayed. "Yeah. I went to school there. Got my apprenticeship. I worked at, uh . . ." He swallowed hard. "Newtown Road . . ." He squinted as though he couldn't quite grasp the details.

"Do you know how old you are?"

He stared at her for a long moment. "Um, twenty-five."

My heart gave another painful squeeze.

The doc put the motorbike magazine in front of him and he smiled at the cover. It was a photo of a KTM dirt bike and its rider sliding in mud. But then the doc put her finger in the top corner. "Can you read this fine print here?"

The truth was, we weren't sure about the cognitive damage done to skills like reading and writing, if he could read at all, or what the words would mean to him if he could.

He leaned forward a tiny bit, squinting at the issue date of the magazine. It was the newest one, the most current. It took some time to process, but we knew the moment he had. He shot a look to Doctor Chang, then to me. He could read it, all right. And the confusion in his eyes told me he understood.

"Justin, you turned thirty this year."

He shook his head. "No, didn't."

The doc showed him a photo on my phone. "Do you recognise this person?"

It was taken at his thirtieth birthday party, and the photo was of him with his arm around his sister. He blinked. "'S Becca."

Oh, thank God. He remembered her, at least.

"That's right," Doctor Chang said. "And this was your thirtieth birthday."

He swallowed hard and looked away from the photo. The doc handed me my phone with a nod. She was about to get to the hard part.

"Justin, do you remember anything about the people you might have dated?"

His eyes flashed to her then, full of fire and caution. "I uh . . . no . . . I'm not seeing anyone."

Again, my heart burned.

"Do you remember any of the men or women you might have dated?"

There it was. The word *men*.

His jaw bulged and he closed his eyes. His sexuality had been such an issue for him when he was younger, and I could only assume he remembered *that* all too well. It wasn't until he met me that he really accepted being his true self.

"You have a troubled relationship with your mother because she never approved of you being gay. Is that right, Justin?" Doctor Chang pushed gently.

He flinched, even with his eyes closed. After a deep breath, he opened his eyes but didn't look at us. "She doesn't . . . she never . . ."

"There's absolutely nothing wrong with being gay," she whispered, touching his hand. "You're safe here, and you've got some amazing friends here in Newcastle who love you just the way you are."

His gaze shot to hers. Then he looked away and licked his lips. "Don't remember . . ."

"Do you remember Dallas?" she asked, gesturing to me.

Justin glanced at me, then back to her. "He was here before. He works here, I think. I don't know . . ."

God, the ache . . .

"He doesn't work here. He's here to see you, Justin."

Justin swallowed hard but didn't say anything, and I didn't dare breathe.

"Justin, you live with Dallas. You live with him, and you work together. You're both motorbike mechanics at his shop in Wallsend, Newcastle."

He looked to me then, startled, disbelieving. I felt like I could vomit.

"Dallas is your boyfriend, Justin. You've been together for four and a half years. You live together."

He shook his head. "No."

Doctor Chang took my phone again and showed him the photos we'd agreed on. Me and him laughing, me and him holding hands, cuddling on the couch, kissing . . .

His expression didn't change. If anything, the only noticeable difference was the tiredness that seemed to settle over him. His blinks became suddenly slower, as though his eyelids had quickly become too heavy to keep open. He licked his lips but seemed to have difficulty in swallowing. "Don't remember . . ." He frowned and a tear escaped the corner of his eye. "Don't remember any of . . . what you're telling me . . . I can't . . ."

"It's a lot of information to process," Doctor Chang said gently. "I can see you're tired."

He closed his eyes, his face a bruised and swollen mask of sadness.

"I'll be back again tomorrow and we can talk some more."

He didn't reply. He was already asleep.

Doctor Chang turned and gave me a small smile. "That's step one."

Only a million to go.

"Tomorrow we'll see if he's retained anything we've discussed today."

Christ.

I tried to nod, to speak, to acknowledge her somehow, but I was too busy trying not to cry.

JUSTIN WAS STILL ASLEEP when I left at the end of morning visiting hours, and I had absolutely no idea what to expect when I returned.

Would he even want to see me? Would he ask me to leave? Would he ask me a hundred questions?

Would he remember the conversation at all?

One good thing that came from Justin's session with Doctor Chang, was that he knew he was gay. He'd had a real rough time in his teen years, and he'd struggled a lot. His mother rejected him when he was eighteen, and he'd fought hard to be true to himself.

It was hard enough for him to endure that once. The thought of him having to relive that a second time was torture.

So if there was one good thing I could take away from this morning's session, it was that at least Justin knew that about himself. There was so much of his life missing, but that fundamental truth was still there.

He was awake when I got there after his rest time was over. He was propped up in bed, and the blankets were pulled back off his right leg so I could see it properly for the first time. It wasn't bandaged fully. The scars would need to heal first. There was a reddish-purple line of staples on the outside of his thigh and one down his shin.

It looked painful.

He saw me and pulled his table closer, like it was a shield. But then stopped himself and he swallowed hard, then winced.

I tried to smile for him but was sure I didn't quite pull it off. "Hey. Is it okay if I come in?"

He stared at me for a long, heart-stopping moment, and I was certain he was about to say no, but he gave a small nod. "I um . . . I can't remember your name . . ."

There was that pain in my heart again. My eyes burned but I blinked it all away. "My name is Dallas. Dallas Muller."

"Dallas," he whispered, like he was trying the word for the first time. Maybe he was hoping it would ring some distant bell. It clearly didn't. He shook his head.

I noticed he hadn't eaten much of anything off his plate. The fact he was eating actual food was a good sign, but his sandwich sat untouched, and a plate of diced fruit salad looked like it'd been pecked at. "Food's no good, huh?"

He made a face. "Not hungry."

"That sandwich has tomato on it," I said, trying to sound cheerful. "I'm sure I could bring you something that you actually like, if you want."

He considered that for a drawn-out few seconds. "Do you know what I like?"

Shit. I had to phrase things so carefully. "Well, the doc probably wouldn't be too happy, but if I happened to bring in some KFC at dinner time and accidently leave it on your table, you might not mind."

He looked at me then and his lip quirked, and I thought for a heart-splitting second that he might actually smile. But no, he didn't. "I might not mind."

I put the bag I was carrying on the seat and pulled out some magazines. "I thought you might like to read through these." I slid the four latest dirt bike magazines onto his table, pushing his discarded food tray to the side. The truth was, he'd read these magazines a dozen times, but he wouldn't remember that. And at least with the dirt bike magazines, he could just look at the pictures if reading was too much of a strain.

He eyed them and gave a nod. "Uh, thanks."

"No problem."

He looked at the bag I'd brought with me for a bit and made a face, so I picked it up. "I brought myself an iced coffee on the way here," I explained, taking the brown plastic bottle out of the bag. They were our weekend treats when we got groceries. Full of caffeine and sugar, Justin loved them. I honestly hadn't brought it for him—he'd been so reluctant to eat anything, I didn't think he'd want anything with milk in it. But he looked twice at it, and his eyes shot to mine.

I had no idea if he remembered it, if it triggered anything, or if he just wanted it. But it was the first time I'd seen any kind of recognition since he woke up. "Iced coffee," I said, holding it out to him. "You want it?"

He stared at me in that slow-processing way he did now, then opened his mouth to say something before deciding not to.

I twisted the lid off the bottle and smiled at him. "I won't tell the nurses you had a sip if you don't." He wasn't supposed to be having caffeine but a tiny sip wouldn't hurt…

He gave the smallest of nods, so I gently put it to his mouth and he had a small sip. He tasted it for a long few seconds before he swallowed. But then he hummed and closed his eyes, and the left corner of his mouth ever so slowly lifted upward.

I could have just about burst with happiness. I wanted to weep from the force of it.

Such a small step. A tiny, tiny step. But, oh my God, it was worth it.

"I'll keep it here for you," I said quietly.

He opened his eyes. Well, his left one. His right one was still badly swollen, though it was looking better every day. "I like that," he murmured. "Iced coffee."

"Yes, you do."

He closed his eyes again, though he seemed peaceful. I wouldn't want to assume that he was happy I was there, but he was okay with me being in his room, and he hadn't asked me to leave, which I took as a good thing. So I sat in my usual seat, grabbed one of his magazines, turned to page one and started reading it aloud.

Chapter Five

ALMOST TWO WEEKS after his accident, his sister, Rebecca, arrived to see him. She'd caught the early train up from Sydney on the Saturday, and I met her at the entrance of the hospital, to save her trying to find her way through the wards. She looked bone-tired, like all single mums who worked two jobs, but she was relieved to see me. I greeted her with a kiss to the cheek.

"How is he?"

"He's okay. He's working with the different doctors every day, like the physio and the neuro specialists."

"He still can't remember?"

"No. He may never regain those years, but we're hopeful."

She stopped walking. "He doesn't remember you at all?"

I shook my head.

"Christ, Dallas. That's gotta be hard."

Hard, awful, excruciating, heartbreaking . . . "I'm just grateful he's alive."

She frowned. "Sorry I couldn't get away sooner."

"What do you mean, you couldn't juggle two jobs and two kids to hike a couple hundred kilometres at the drop of a hat?"

Her face softened, and she gave me a sad smile. "But still . . ."

"Like I said to you when it happened, he wasn't in any shape to see you anyway," I explained. "But he's getting better every day. He can see out of both eyes now."

"Oh God."

I brightened for her. "Come on. I told him I was going to find you. He was excited about you visiting, so we better not keep him waiting."

I took her bag for her, and together we walked to Justin's room. "Ugh, I hate hospitals," she mumbled as we got closer.

Yep, even after all these days, all the hours, I never got used to the smell. It was cloying and awful. The neuro ward was quieter than most, and darker. Most patients here had noise and light sensitivities, Justin included.

I stopped her at the door. "He doesn't do too good with loud noises or bright lights. His headaches are bad, and he has aphasia, which is trouble remembering some words. But if he asks questions, be honest. He knows he has amnesia but it's confusing, so if he mentions anything that doesn't quite gel, we need to gently steer him back on course."

"Okay," she whispered, then took an unsteady breath.

I nodded to his room. "He's waiting."

I'd explained his injuries to Rebecca before, but nothing quite prepared you for seeing your loved one in a hospital bed all bandaged and bruised.

The bed was slightly inclined so he was kind of sitting up. He had his injured leg out from under the blankets again, his lines of staples on full display. The matching scar on his head was bandaged, and I was thankful Rebecca didn't have to see that. But the right side of his face was now a horror show of black, purple, green, and yellow. His right eye was open. Though it was bloodshot, he thankfully still had vision.

He'd had tests on his vision and hearing, focusing on the right side, where the most damage was, and the docs were pleasantly surprised to find all circuitry was still intact. Though when the doc had shone a penlight in his right eye, Justin had puked on him as thanks. He said it felt like the light pierced his brain and the pain was unbearable. He'd shaken and moaned, curling in on himself, and it was a short, sharp reminder of his injuries.

But yeah, while I knew it was bad, I was so used to seeing him lying in bed all banged up that I'd forgotten the shock it was for others. Rebecca put her hand to her mouth and got all teary. "Holy shit," she cried.

Justin looked at her, then looked again. His smile was wide. "Becca?"

She went to him and hugged him carefully, and she fussed over him and he stared up at her like he couldn't believe what he was seeing . . .

And it occurred to me, like a jolt to the heart, what the difference was.

He remembered her.

He was, for the first time since he woke up, seeing someone he remembered, seeing someone he knew.

And it wasn't me.

I was no more than a stranger that he was polite to, like his nurses and doctors.

And all of a sudden, the room felt too small, too hot, and it was much too much. I put Becca's bag down by the chair. "I'll just let you catch up," I said to no one in particular. I didn't know if they heard me. I simply slipped out of the room and made my way back to the main entrance.

I needed air.

Just ten minutes. I just needed some fresh air in my lungs, to take some deep breaths and clear the swirls panicking in my mind. I knew he didn't remember me. I was very well aware. It shouldn't have come as such a surprise, but I guess seeing it with my own two eyes was different.

I stood outside and leaned against the wall. It was a little overcast; the air was cool and the sun was warm on my skin. I closed my eyes and concentrated on my breathing until I no longer felt like crying or screaming.

I need to get my shit together. I was in this for the long haul, for however long it took. Every nurse, every doctor had told me a thousand times there would be hurdles and setbacks, and some days would be nothing but backward steps.

But this wasn't a setback for Justin. This was a milestone for him. He finally remembered someone from his past, a face, a name, memories, recognition, dots that finally joined on their own. Justin finally got matching pieces of the puzzle that was his past.

I needed to recognise that and be happy for him. I needed to find Doctor Chang and tell her of this breakthrough. Because that's what this was. What did she tell me? All those days ago? That everything was about him, it needed to be about him. This wasn't about me. How could it be? I needed to remove my pain, square it away for another day, for a conversation with a therapist or someone . . .

I needed to be there for Justin, and I had a sense of urgency to get back to him. So I called past the cafeteria, using coffees as an excuse for my disappearance. I even bought a small decaf cappuccino for Justin. I added sugar and asked for it to be lukewarm so he didn't burn his mouth.

One thing I had noticed over the last week was how he no longer paused to think if something might be hot or cold. It was just food or drink, and he would simply put it in his mouth. Not that he ate a great deal, and not that hospital food was ever scalding hot, but cups of tea sometimes were. And he would quite often take a sip without giving it time to cool, which had made him reluctant to drink any tea or coffee at all.

I knocked on the door to announce my arrival, with a tray of takeout coffee cups in hand. Rebecca was sitting in my usual seat, holding his hand. The tears were gone, and Justin looked tired. His blinks were slow, but he looked happy.

"Anyone for coffee?"

"Oh, you're a doll," Bec said, taking hers. "Thank you so much."

I pulled Justin's table over and sat his coffee in front of him. "I got one for you too. It's not too hot, and I got them to add some sugar."

He blinked up at me and gave a slight nod, making no attempt to lift his left arm, so I held the cup to his lips and he took a small sip. "'S good."

"It's proper coffee," I said, giving him as big a smile as I could manage. He didn't need to know it was decaf. "How does your arm feel? Can you hold the cup?"

He'd been working on some weakness in his left arm with the physio. There was nothing broken or sprained with his left arm, but brain injuries did strange things to bodies, and sometimes he wouldn't even attempt to use it. His broken arm, apart from being broken, was understandable. But there was nothing actually wrong with his left arm, and the physio had told me to encourage him to use it, which was why I asked him.

He looked at his arm and raised it heavily onto the table. "Yeah," he said. "'S all right."

I held the cup for him while he grasped it and stood ready as he slowly lifted it to his mouth. He took a sip and put the cup back down all without incident, just a little slower than usual.

Bec watched on, then her gaze flickered to mine with a flash of sadness before she smiled back at her brother. "I was just telling Jussy that I spoke to our mother. Nothing's changed there." She gave me a pissed-off raised eyebrow before smiling back at Justin. "And then I was telling him about the girls."

Their mother had always been horrible, so I couldn't say I was surprised. But the girls were a much happier topic. "Oh," I said, giving her a meaningful look. "Have you got any recent photos of them on your phone? I'm sure he'd love to see them."

She clued in and quickly pulled out her phone. "Oh, sure." She showed him the screen. "This was Phoebe's costume for book week."

His eyes shot to hers. "No. She . . . That's not . . . she . . . walking . . ."

Bec looked to me for help. "Justin," I said gently. "Phoebe is six now."

He looked at me, then at Becca, then at the screen. "She is?"

"Yep," Bec said, teary again. "She had her birthday just two months ago. You sent her a *Frozen* backpack and lunchbox."

His eyes went wide. "I did?" God, he'd spent an hour trying to pick the right one . . .

Bec nodded. "And she loves it." She swiped to another photo. "And here's Holly playing soccer."

Justin looked at all the photos Bec showed him of the girls over the last few years. He shook his head in disbelief, and while he was clearly exhausted, there was a deeper understanding in the sadness.

Bec put her phone away and cupped his face. "You okay, Jussy? Do you need to sleep?"

He slow blinked, almost not opening his eyes again. "Tired."

"We'll let you get some sleep," she said, looking to me again.

I nodded. "It's almost rest time anyway. We'll be back at three. Just like always, soon as they open the doors, I'll be here."

"And Bec?" he asked, trying to open his eyes.

She put a hand on his arm. "I'll be back too."

He sagged then and succumbed to sleep. I fixed his bed so he was lying down flat, pulled up the blanket, and moved the table out of the way. Then I led Becca out, and neither of us spoke until we reached the cafeteria.

I ordered us some toasted sandwiches and more coffee, and when I sat opposite Bec, she shook her head. Tears threatened to spill but didn't. "He's um . . . He's . . ."

"He's doing much better," I offered.

"He really doesn't remember."

"No. But he remembered you, and that's a good thing. And the girls. He *remembered* them. He hasn't really remembered much since he woke up. He's been taking in what we tell him, but today it was like a light went on. And that's a real good thing." I sighed. "And honestly, I think seeing the photos of them was good for him. Hard, but good. We can tell him he's no longer in Darwin and we can say he's missing some years, but I don't think he ever really understood. He doesn't remember me at all, so I'm not a gauge of time for him. And you might have aged a little, but not that he would probably notice too much. But the girls . . . last he remembered, Phoebe was still in nappies and now she's in school. That's a big change."

Bec nodded and chewed on her bottom lip. "Do you think he'll get better?"

I sighed and turned the coffee cup in my hand. "I asked the brain doc that in the beginning, and she said better wasn't the right word. Will his body heal? Will his leg and arm mend? Yes. Will his brain? We don't know. Will Justin ever be who he was before the accident? No." I put the cup down and pushed the half-eaten sandwich away. "Brain injuries change a person forever. Even if he remembered everything tomorrow, he'd still have headaches and dizziness and issues with light and noise. Even if he comes good and is right as rain for years, ten years from now he might still have setbacks and bouts of headaches, or one day wake up with slurred speech. We just don't know. But we do know this is a long-term thing."

She got teary again. "Thank God he has you. This can't be easy for you, and I'm sorry I can't be more help."

"It's not easy," I admitted. "But I love him."

She reached over and squeezed my hand. "And he loves you. From the second he saw you, he did. You should have heard how excited he was when he first told me about you. He was head over heels in love from day one. He will remember that. I know he will."

Now it was me who got teary. "I hope so. If not, he'll just have to fall in love with me all over again." I tried to smile, to laugh it off, but couldn't manage it. Because what if he didn't? "And if he doesn't . . . Well, I'll do whatever he needs to be happy. Because that's what you do when you love someone, right? You'd do anything to make them happy. Even if that means letting them go."

A tear ran down Becca's cheek and she wiped it away. "It wasn't just *his* world that got turned upside down by a truck that day, was it?"

I shook my head but couldn't answer until I was sure my voice would hold. "No. Not just me, either. The boys at the shop are covering for the both of us. Davo's basically running the whole place. I'd be lost without them. Justin doesn't remember them at all either."

She took a deep breath. "Is there something we can do to help him remember?"

"We can't plant any of our memories in his head. We can just show him things and hope he remembers on his own."

"Like the photos of the girls."

"Exactly."

"Have you shown him photos of you and him together?"

"Some, just on my phone. A few days ago," I replied. "I was going to get some printed. They have a kiosk thing, but I couldn't figure it out and I ran out of time."

She brightened. "Where's the kiosk?"

"Just down the road. Why? Do you know how to use them?"

She smiled, grabbing her bag. "Sure I do. We'll print them off, then he can look at them all day long. He will remember you, Dallas. I know he will."

WE GOT BACK RIGHT on three o'clock when the doors opened for visiting hours again. Matt, the nurse, gave me a smile. I was familiar with most of the staff on the neuro ward now, and they knew me. "Brought him lunch again," he said warmly, nodding to the bag I was holding. Then he gave me a wink. "Can't say I blame him for not wanting hospital food."

"Is he awake?" I asked.

"He was about ten minutes ago. Physio's been in. Wants him up on his feet tomorrow."

"That's a good thing, right?"

Matt smiled. "I'd reckon so."

Justin was awake when we got there. He was frowning at the menu in front of him on the table. "Hey," I said softly as we walked in.

He looked up and gave me a small smile, but then he saw Bec behind me and he gave her a real smile. I pretended it didn't burn all the way through and put the bag on his bed near his leg. "I brought you a juice and a water," I said, putting them on the table. They were the pop-top kind so he didn't have to worry about unscrewing lids, and I'd already removed the seals. "And one of these."

It was a lunch snack box that was full of things he could pick at: grapes, salted pretzels, cheese cubes, and some crackers with a small tub of hummus. I'd bought him one before, and it was the most he'd eaten in a while.

He inspected everything I put in front of him, then he looked at me. "Thanks," he said politely before searching for his sister.

I stood back and let Bec in closer. "Whatcha got here?" she asked, sliding the menu closer. "Do you need to fill this out?"

"Think so." He stared at the sheet of paper and frowned. "Don't know what I like. And I read the . . . but I can't remember . . . And I can't hold the pen too good with this hand." He lifted his left hand and let it fall back beside him.

"Would you like Dallas to fill it in for you?" Bec asked.

I went to the right side of his bed and turned the menu around to face me. "It's a bit hard to write with your left when you're right-handed," I said casually. "What about some toast and tea for breakfast, and I'll bring you in an iced coffee when I get here?" They had decaf ones and it wasn't like he'd know the difference . . .

He gave a nod.

"And for lunch, if I order the sandwich but I bring you something, then you can choose which you feel like the most."

He nodded again. "I like this," he said, slowly reaching for the snack box I bought him.

"Then I'll bring you one every day," I said, making a mental note to call into the supermarket on the way home. It'd be cheaper if I made it myself and brought it with me. Now that he was actually eating food . . . "And for dinner," I continued. "They have fish or cottage pie, so I'll put the cottage pie." I was going to add "because you don't really like fish" but stopped myself.

Justin picked at his grapes and pretzels and cheese, then reached for his water. I was tempted to get it for him, to help him drink it, but thought it must have been bad enough not being able to tick boxes on a menu. The least I could let him do was take a drink by himself. As long as he was comfortable moving his left arm, I was comfortable in letting him.

"So, Jussy," Bec began. "I wanted to show you some more photos. You think you're up for that?"

"Hmm," he agreed as he sipped his water. Then he ate

another grape. Food he could hold in one hand and pick at was definitely the way to go.

Bec and I had agreed that the photos would be best coming from her. He remembered her, he knew her, he trusted her. She stood up by his arm and held out the first photo. We'd mixed a few, from her phone and mine, so there'd be some faces he recognised. "Here's you and me at your birthday dinner last year," she said. "You and Dallas came down to Sydney and stayed with me and the girls for the weekend."

"And here's you with both Phoebe and Holly," she said, showing the next photo. The girls were in their pyjamas, tackling him on the couch, the three of them laughing.

He squinted. "That's really them," he murmured, shaking his head like he couldn't believe it. Not that he didn't believe her, just that he didn't believe he was missing so much time.

Bec nodded. "And here's one of Dallas and the girls." In this photo, Phoebe had her arms around my neck, and I was holding a laughing Holly under my arm like a football. We thought it might be good for Justin to see that I was part of his missing pieces. His nieces knew me, they loved me. They called me Uncle Dallas . . .

"And here's you at work," she said, moving to the next photo. It was a picture of him sitting on a client's brand new KTM dirt bike. They'd called into the shop to show it off, and Justin just had to sit on it and take it for a bit of a ride through the shop and out into the car park. His grin was almost from ear to ear.

His eyes shot to Bec. "That mine?"

"No," I answered for her. "It was a client's bike. He brought it in to show you. Your bike is a bit older than that."

He looked up at me. "Have a bike?"

"You do, yes. A 2016 KTM 450 SX-F. There's a photo in there."

His smile widened. "KTM?"

"You wouldn't own anything else." The truth was, he'd always wanted one. It was his dream bike, and for his thirtieth birthday, I bought him a new second-hand one.

But more on the photos . . . I pointed to a guy in the background of the photo he was holding. "That's Davo. He came in to see you last week."

Justin frowned and shook his head. He didn't remember him.

The next photo made my heart thump against my ribs. It was a selfie, of me and him, our arms around each other. I was smiling at the camera but he was smiling at me. "Here's you and Dallas. Goofing off on the couch by the look of it," Bec said fondly.

We'd just got home from the footy and it was freezing. I was set to cook dinner, but he wanted pizza and he'd pulled me onto the couch, tickled me, and kissed me until I gave in. It was one of my favourite photos, and the memory of how that night had ended in bed . . .

Justin stared at the photo, like really stared at it. "I don't . . . Don't remember . . ." Then he looked up to me. "Sorry."

"That's okay," I replied when it was obviously very, very not okay. "It's not your fault."

Bec moved on to the next photo. "Here's you at the beach. Two years ago?" she asked me.

I nodded. "Yep. We went up to Halliday Point for the weekend."

He frowned again, and I wondered if it was too much. The doc said it was okay—— good, even—— to show him photos, but that frown and the line between his eyebrows kind of told me he'd had enough.

"Wish I could 'member," he mumbled, closing his eyes.

Bec gave me a sad smile and put the photos on his table. "It's okay, Jussy."

"No 's not," he replied. When he opened his eyes, they were teary. "Missing so much. I wish could . . . but it's just not there. It feels like I'm . . . like it's all some . . . joke. Except for my arm and my leg and m'fucking head hurts. God."

I wanted to touch him, to pull him into my arms and hold him and tell him everything would be okay. I wanted to kiss the side of his head and rub his back while he slept . . .

But I couldn't even hold his hand.

I had to clamp my mouth shut and my hands were fists at my side. "It'll get easier," I whispered.

He wouldn't look at me, and that probably hurt more than anything.

Bec took his left hand. "Jussy, I know it's hard right now. It's okay to be scared. And to be pissed off that everything you know was taken away from you. But you gotta know how much you are loved. Me and the girls, we love you. And Dallas loves you so much."

Justin screwed his face up, then winced, and tears escaped.

And I still couldn't touch him, I couldn't fill in the blanks for him. But I could tell him the truth. "I do love you, Justin," I said, ignoring the burn in my eyes and the lump in my throat. "I know that must seem strange to you right now. But I won't give up on you. You're not alone in this. I'll be with you, however you need me. I don't expect anything from you. I just want you to be happy and healthy. That's all."

His face twisted as if in pain, and another tear escaped. "So tired," he said with a groan. "Hurts."

Bec put a hand on his arm and kissed his temple. "Go to sleep. I gotta get going if I'm gonna catch my train. But I'll call you tomorrow."

He opened his eyes slowly, exhausted. "'Kay."

"Love you, Justin," she said.

He almost nodded but fell asleep.

Bec wiped her tears away, and when she looked at me, she had that fierceness that was obviously a family trait. I'd seen it in Justin's eyes a thousand times.

"He will remember you," she said, her bottom lip trembling. "He will remember how much you love him. I know he will."

Chapter Six

Doctor Anderson finished asking Justin his usual round of questions, then took one look at me and frowned. "You need to look after yourself too," he said. "Not sleeping?"

I shook my head but plastered on a fake smile in front of Justin. "I'm fine."

He sighed, because this was obviously a conversation he had with the loved ones of his patients all the time, but his expression was kind. "Do I need to remind you that you can't look after him if you don't look after yourself?"

"No, I got that, thanks."

He clapped me on the shoulder just as two other doctors arrived. "Okay, Justin," the physio said. "We're gonna get you up and on your feet today." Justin had been doing exercises from his bed, leg bending, that kind of thing. But they needed to wait because of his head. Vertigo and a fall or severe headaches and nausea were serious issues with brain injuries. But they reckoned he was ready, so . . .

Justin glanced to me, then swallowed hard. "I don't know."

The physio was undeterred. He explained what he was going to do in a no-nonsense voice that gave no room for argument; how he would stand on his left foot for three seconds and they would hold his weight. First they sat him up and let his head catch up with the movement; then they gently lowered his feet to the floor and let him sit like that for a few minutes.

He was already pale, but he kept searching for me, which made me happier than it should've. I gave him an encouraging nod each time. Because if he could do this, we were one step closer to going home.

One small step.

"Okay, Justin, on three."

"One."

He looked up at me, scared but determined.

"Two."

He took a deep breath.

"Three."

They lifted him and he stood on his left foot for one second, two seconds, but then his head fell forward and I shot to him as if to catch him. But he was well supported, and they put him back on the bed. He was white as a sheet now, sweat beaded on his brow, and he was breathing heavy.

"You did great, Justin," the doc said. The neuro and the physio both fussed over him for a bit and left the nurses to get him comfortable again. I thought he might vomit, but he didn't.

Soon enough it was just me and him. He had his eyes closed, though he had a bit more colour. A tear ran down to his temple. "You did real good," I whispered.

"Head hurts," he breathed.

He looked so helpless, so fragile, that I couldn't help myself. I had to comfort him somehow and let him know he wasn't alone. I took his hand in both of mine. "You're okay, Justin. You're not alone. Everything will be okay."

Another tear escaped, but he squeezed my fingers and never let go until sleep relaxed his grip.

SOMETHING HAD CHANGED for Justin when he woke up. He was different toward me. The polite smiles once afforded to a stranger were now something else. I didn't want to overthink it, but the look he gave me was something closer to how he'd look at a friend.

And that was a pretty big fucking deal.

I must have dozed off in the seat beside him, listening to his peaceful breathing, only to be woken up by a machine beeping. I jolted upright to find a nurse at one of his machines, changing something. "Didn't mean to wake you," she said apologetically.

And Justin smiled at me. "Was wondering if you'd wake up."

I rubbed the crick in my neck. "I didn't mean to fall asleep, sorry."

But he was still smiling. Not quite like he'd smiled at his sister, but different to how he smiled at the nurses and doctors.

I didn't want to question it. I didn't want him to stop it or second guess himself. I'd take anything he could give me, and if that was a slight quirk of his lips, I'd gladly take it.

I checked my phone for the time just as his lunch tray was delivered, but he took one look at the plate of mixed sandwiches and frowned. "Here, I'll swap you," I said, taking his sandwiches and producing the packed lunch I'd made for him. It was similar to the ones I'd bought for him—a container split into sections for different snacks—but I added a few things I knew he liked. Well, things he used to like. Like some of those soy crisps and the sweet and salty popcorn, along with some grapes and cubed cheese, and I even threw in a few M&M's. Things he could pick at with one hand, that didn't require a great deal of chewing, and things that didn't crunch too loud in his head.

I took the sandwich and began to eat it, and he did the same, using his left hand slowly, but using it nonetheless.

"The doc said you're not sleeping," he said between mouthfuls. It wasn't posed as a question, but it kind of was.

I finished chewing and swallowed. "Uh, yeah."

He was quiet for a while, lifting some popcorn to his mouth and chewing methodically. "Because of me."

Jesus.

I certainly couldn't say it was because I hated sleeping alone and how I missed him most at night. How I missed the way he searched for me, even in his sleep, and how he'd wrap himself around me like a freaking koala every night. It used to annoy me sometimes, and now I missed it so much it hurt. "I'm just worried, that's all."

He frowned as he ate a grape, and I gave him all the time he needed to process what was said, and perhaps what he was trying to say. "Sorry I don't remember you," he said.

I tried to smile for him but gave up. "It's not your fault."

"Wish I did," he said, so quietly I wasn't sure he meant to say it out loud. When I met his gaze, he was looking right at me. "You're here a lot, and Becca liked you, so you gotta be all right."

My heart felt like it could burst, and I almost cried. Instead, it all came out as a laugh. "Yeah, I'm all right."

"You're not exactly . . ." He squinted at me. "I can't think of the word." He shut his eyes. "Why can't I think of some words?"

You're not exactly . . . *I'm not exactly what? Jesus, don't leave me hanging on that.*

"It's the aphasia," I said gently. "It means you have trouble with some words some of the time. It's random."

He sighed and opened his eyes slowly, suddenly looking tired. "It's like my brain is bogged, ya know? Like the wheels are spinning but the back wheel can't . . . hold." Pretty sure *hold* wasn't the word he wanted, but I didn't correct him. His right eye closed and I wondered if his headache was getting worse. "Like the things I want to see are all misty."

That was the most he'd said to me, the most honest he'd been with me since his accident. I smiled at him, a proper smile, no faking or trying. An actual fucking smile. "That makes sense. And it's still early days yet. The mist might clear and you'll be able to see."

He looked from me to the snack box. "And if it doesn't?"

"Then we find new ways. We work on different things."

"We . . . ," he said softly.

Oh hell. What if he didn't want that? What if he didn't want me to be a part of his life anymore?

I opened my mouth to say something—say what, I had no clue—just as a nurse came in. "Visiting time is up. You'll have to come back after three."

I nodded woodenly, sure if I moved too fast, I'd splinter into a thousand pieces.

What if he didn't want there to be a *we* or an *us*? What if his life, after this, didn't include me?

"Hey, can I ask you something?" Justin said to the nurse.

"Sure," she replied, walking in closer.

"What's the word . . . I can't think of the word for pretty but not. Opposite of that."

"The opposite of pretty?" she clarified, eyeing me cautiously.

"Yeah. There's a word. Not ugly. That's not the word . . . Jesus, why can't I think of the word."

"Unattractive?" she hedged, clearly not sure where he was going with this. I had no clue either.

"Yes. That's it," Justin said excitedly, but I could see he was tired. "I wanted to say he wasn't unattractive. That's the word."

"What?" I asked, confused.

"You," he said, a lazy smile on his lips. "I said you weren't exactly unattractive."

Oh.

Oh.

"Oh!" I barked out a laugh. "Right. Um, thanks?"

The nurse laughed, probably relieved, but tapped her wrist in a time's-up fashion as she walked out.

I could not believe he said that to me! I had absolutely no chance of trying to hide how happy that made me. "You're not exactly unattractive either, you know," I said. "I'll be back after three."

I left him then, feeling on cloud nine. It wasn't that he thought I was good looking, that even with no memory of me whatsoever he still thought I was good looking. It was that he smiled at me like he was comfortable with me, that I wasn't a stranger. And how he spoke to me about how he was feeling and what it felt like to not be able to remember things . . .

I was still smiling when I got back to the shop. Davo looked at me and then did a double-take. "Holy shit, is he . . . ? Did he remember something?"

"Nah, not really," I said. "It was just a good morning. It was small." I held up my fingers, barely a centimetre apart. "But I saw a glimpse of him today. Justin's still in there."

"For real?"

"He said something funny, and he kinda said he thought I was good looking."

Davo's grin widened. "Yep. That sounds like him all right."

I laughed, and so help me God, it felt good to actually laugh. "I mean, it could all be different when I go back, and he might be having a real shit afternoon and not want me in his room when I get there, but this morning was good. And I'll take all the small steps forward I can get."

"Speaking of a real shit afternoon," he said, still grinning. "That pile of mail on your desk isn't getting any smaller."

I gave a nod, and after neglecting my business for two weeks, went into my office.

JUSTIN WASN'T in a shit mood when I went back. He was just tired. Physio really took it out of him, but he never really complained. The docs had said that we could expect outbursts of anger and misdirected rage, as was common with brain injuries, but I had yet to see that in him.

He wasn't the type to get angry before his accident. Actually, he hated aggression and confrontation, so maybe I shouldn't have been surprised that there were no bouts of temper. Not to say there wouldn't ever be . . . I knew all too well that frustration made people lash out, but Justin was more inclined to retreat into himself. He wouldn't sulk, but he went quiet, trying to figure stuff out in his head—and now, well, his mind wouldn't cooperate.

"You okay?" I asked.

"Dunno," he mumbled. "Tired."

"Physio sucks, huh?"

He almost smiled. Almost. "Yeah. Doc said m' arm's getting better. And I'll be up on my feet again. Every day now."

"Oh, that's good, right?"

He made a face. "Was talking about going home."

Oh . . . Going home. There I was excited by the prospect, and he didn't even know if he had a home.

His gaze shot to mine before going back to his leg. "Yeah."

I pulled the seat closer to his bed so he could see me without having to turn his head. "Hey. You have a home."

"Do I?" He shot me a look. "'Cause I don't remember it. The last I remember was a shitty unit in Darwin, but that's not right anymore, is it?"

"No, it's not. You have a home here, in Newcastle. It's above the workshop, the mechanic shop. You have a place to go home to, where all your stuff is. And Squish."

He glanced at me then. "Squish?"

"Our cat."

He frowned. "*Our* cat . . . ?"

Fuck. "Sorry. *The* cat." My frown matched his.

"Sorry."

"Don't apologise." It wasn't his fault he didn't remember anything. He shouldn't have to apologise.

He let his head fall back on the pillow and closed his eyes with a long sigh. "I don't like being here," he whispered. "But at least it's . . ." He screwed up his face, trying to search for the right word but settled on a bit of a shrug when the word wouldn't come. "I know here. I don't know anywhere else but here."

I couldn't even tell him it would still be nice, though, to be surrounded by his own things because he didn't remember any of it. "Did the doc say when you might be leaving?"

"Week or so, maybe," he replied. His eyes were barely open and he was mumbling. "Said because of you. Look after me. Help recovery quick."

I covered his hand with mine. "Go to sleep, Juss. I'll be here when you wake up."

He took a deep breath in and was already asleep before he exhaled.

Going home . . . He was almost ready to go home. Was that too soon? For him?

For me?

What if I wasn't good at being someone's carer? What if he took a fall because I'd done something stupid like left the bathmat on the floor? What if he couldn't cope with the stairs?

What if he didn't want to live with me?

Certain Justin would be asleep for a while, I left him and went in search of his nurse, who pointed me in the direction of one of his doctors. She was just finishing up with another patient, and she smiled when she saw me.

"You look worried," Doctor Chang said, meeting me in the corridor. I knew she wasn't the expert on this in particular, but she'd spent so much time with us over the last week or so . . .

"Justin mentioned going home? How do I get ready for that? What if I suck at it?"

She smiled warmly. "I need a cup of tea. Come sit with me."

I followed her to the small break room and waited as she filled two cups with hot water, threw a teabag in each, and handed me one. Apparently I was drinking black tea now.

She sat in one of the chairs and waited for me to sit next to her. "Okay, first things first. Justin's doing well. All things considered, it could have been so much worse."

I know that. Jesus, I know that.

"His recovery is going well, and yes, we can think about him going home soon. Another week or even a couple of weeks." She sipped her tea. "But there are many things we need to do before then. Occupational therapist first. They will go to your house and suggest changes to make life easier for him."

I let out a relieved breath. "Okay, good. We have stairs."

She made a face. "Also, Justin needs to prove he can walk assisted, with crutches or some kind of mobility aide. Crutches might be difficult until his broken arm is healed. So yes, home is on the table, but he has some hard work to do yet." She looked me right in the eye. "He will have a lot of ongoing medical appointments and will need full-time care in the beginning. Help with bathing, using the toilet. It's not easy. And a home nurse will visit daily for a little while, but the bulk of responsibility will fall on you."

"Okay." I nodded. "That's fine."

She smiled and sipped her tea again. "The photos were a good idea. He was looking at them when I arrived today."

"He was?"

"Yep. He was looking at the photos of you both, but you in particular."

That made my heart do crazy things. "Oh."

She smiled at me. "He said you must be a kind person because you visit every day and you bring him iced coffee and food that he likes."

God, her words almost made me cry. "He said that?"

"And that you looked really worried after he tried to stand up for the first time, and that you held his hand when he cried."

I barked out a laugh and had to wipe my nose with the back of my hand. "I can't believe he said that." I took a shaky breath and shook away the tears. "I worried he wouldn't want anything to do with me when he woke up. Or even any day I walk into his room. I mean, he could say thanks but no thanks, couldn't he? He's not just missing memories of me, but he has no emotional attachment to me either. And that scares the hell out of me."

She stood up and stretched her shoulders. "He's trying to get the pieces to fit. Not the old pieces," she said. "But the new pieces in this new, confusing puzzle. He's trying, and that's a real good sign. There are no guarantees, of course. But he *is* trying."

She left me alone with a promise to see me again tomorrow, and with a heavy sigh, I took the awful cup of tea back into his room and waited for him to wake up.

THE DAYS that followed were much the same. Physio, both lying down and standing on his left leg and getting used to being upright. His head still got the better of him and he was dizzy and nauseous, and he was still tired as hell. But he was improving. He was almost using his left arm all the time, and his aphasia and slurred speech were only more pronounced when he was tired.

He had more CAT scans, more MRIs, and they modified his

pain meds, and he had to take an entire pharmacy of pills every day.

But he *was* improving.

He smiled when I got there every morning. Which might have been only for the iced coffee I brought with me, but it was a smile nonetheless. He was eating more and his bones and scars were healing well, and by all accounts, his army of doctors was happy with his progress.

When I arrived with his iced coffee in hand, his bed was rumpled and empty. The bike magazines and photographs were spread all over his table; he'd obviously been looking at the photos again. He looked at them quite often, sometimes flipping through them like a deck of cards, sometimes studying each one.

A nurse I didn't know came in and began stripping his bed. "Uh, excuse me, but where is Justin?"

I mean, his things were still here, but he wasn't, and he'd never not been in here before . . .

"He not have a good night," she said in broken English. "They take him."

I turned her words over in my head. "Take him? Take him where?" *Don't panic, Dallas. It's probably nothing.* I tried to make my voice as calm as possible. "I'm sorry. Where did they take him?"

"Oh, hi, Dallas," Donna said. She was another nurse that I'd become quite familiar with. She looked after Justin a lot. "They've just taken him for a shower."

I almost buckled with relief. "Christ, why didn't she lead with that?"

Donna chuckled and helped remake the bed. They were like a pit-crew, taking efficient to a whole new level. Donna straightened the room up as the other nurse took the dirty linen to a huge hamper at the door. "He won't be long, I'm sure."

"Did he not have a good night? The other nurse said . . ."

"Apparently not."

"Was it pain? Did he try and get up by himself?"

She shook her head. "Nightmares," she whispered. "And if

the nightmares aren't bad enough, he jolted awake and strained his arm."

"His right arm? The one he broke?"

She gave a nod. "He was okay, but a shower will help freshen him up. I'd imagine he'll be happy to see you."

"Yeah," I said, not feeling her confidence.

She gave me a sly smile. "He watches the door for you, you know."

"He does?" *Was I smiling? Or was my face as stunned as I was?*

She finished tidying with an amused smile. "He won't be long."

I slumped in the chair, trying to get my head around everything I'd just learned. If they were showering him, his arm must be okay. But the nightmares . . . that was new. Well, it was new to me.

Did he dream of the accident? Because he had no memory of that. But I could only imagine the scream of tires, twisted metal, and shattered glass. I'd seen photographs of the van and how they'd had to cut him out . . . Was that what he remembered?

I shuddered at the thought.

Movement at the door pulled me to my feet. Justin came through in a wheelchair, his right leg propped up out front. An orderly was pushing him, and his doctor followed him in.

"Hey," I said, taking in the sight of him. He looked all shower-fresh, and he was clean-shaven. He was obviously tired, but he smiled when he saw me. That familiar smile... "There you are."

The orderly and I helped him onto the bed, and I fixed his pillow for him and pulled the blanket up. It took him a second to catch his breath. "Hey," he murmured back.

The doctor propped Justin's pillow and Justin gave a nod. "Okay. No physio today, as long as you promise to keep using your left arm and move your left leg a bit for me, okay?"

Justin nodded slowly. "'Kay."

The doctor then looked at me. "Lots of rest today. I'd even go so far as to say maybe cut the visit short this morning and just come back this afternoon."

I opened my mouth to speak, but Justin spoke first. "He stay." He closed his eyes. "He can stay. Please."

Oh my God.

"I'll stay," I whispered, running my hand down his arm and taking his hand. "I'll stay right here."

His fingers squeezed my hand a little and his breathing evened out. He was already asleep.

The doctor sighed. "Make sure he rests."

"I will," I promised. "Doc? Did he say what the nightmares were about?"

The doctor looked to Justin, who was very much asleep, then back to me and shook his head. "He doesn't know exactly. Just darkness and fear."

My heavy heart sank to my feet.

"It's not uncommon," the doc said. "It wasn't the first time, and I can assume it won't be the last."

I nodded, and the warden scooted my chair over so I didn't have to let go of Justin's hand before they left me alone with him. "It's okay, baby," I whispered. "Whatever comes at us."

He didn't stir, not even a little bit, for most of the morning. I held his hand and studied his beautiful face. His bruises were mostly gone now, the cut above his eye had healed nicely. The hair where they'd shaved his head was growing back, hiding the L-shaped scar.

His dark hair, sun-kissed skin, his long eyelashes, his gently parted lips . . . He really was beautiful. And I hated that his independence had been taken away from him. I hated that his life had been turned inside out because of the truck, because of the rain, because of someone else. I hated that he was scared, and I hated that I couldn't fix everything and give him back what had been taken away.

It wasn't fair on him. He did nothing to deserve this shitty blow. And, selfishly, I hated that this had happened to me, to us. We'd had the perfect life, and in the blink of an eye, it was gone.

Deleted.

For Justin, it was as though it had never happened. The life we'd had, the love, me, us . . . completely erased.

The actions of someone else had taken it all away. I wanted to be mad, to find the truck driver and show him the damage he'd done, but I didn't have it in me. I just wanted Justin to be safe and loved. That was where my energy and focus had to be.

Sometime later, I was reading one of his bike magazines aloud to him when I felt eyes on me. ". . . The subframe is longer, and the swingarm has a longer adjustment slot. The most obvious change is that the bodywork is different . . ."

I glanced up from the page to see Justin smiling sleepily at me. "Keep going," he mumbled.

"I'm only reading the KTM articles, just so you know. Don't want you getting mad at me for filling your head full of Yamaha specs."

The corner of his mouth quirked upward, and I continued to read aloud to him, my voice deliberately soothing and melodic. Eventually his eyes opened and stayed open, and he watched me as I read through more of the magazine.

It warmed my heart, and I could only hope it did the same to him.

Eventually he tried to sit up a little, so I fixed his bed for him to be more upright. "Oh, I almost forgot," I said, handing him the iced coffee. "It's not super cold, but it'll be fine."

He sighed after the first sip. "Thank you."

"Had a rough night, huh?"

He grunted some kind of response, then said, "My brain is misty today."

He'd said before that his mind was misty, and I wondered if he meant foggy. It didn't matter. The message was clear. "The doc said you'd need rest today."

He slow blinked and gave a nod, and it was like we'd gone back two weeks in his recovery. They'd said his recovery would feel like two steps forward, one step back, and we'd had so many steps forward that this stumble felt huge.

I rubbed my chin and smiled for him. "You shaved. Looks good."

He almost smiled again. "Didn't. The guy did."

The nursing staff did it . . . "Well, he did a good job."

He slowly reached his left hand up to his face, then let his hand drop back down. He took another slow sip of his drink, then his eyes closed. "Read more? Like your voice . . ."

He liked my voice . . .

So I chose a different magazine and started at the beginning, pretending he couldn't hear the tears and hope in my words.

HE WAS BETTER the next day, almost like he hadn't had a bad day the day before. And two days later, his recovery seemed to be back on track.

He'd obviously had a better night's sleep, and his morning physio wasn't horrible. He was bending his leg okay and lifting his bandaged arm, and he was able to stand for a bit. He even put the foot of his injured leg on the floor.

"I liked the chair," he told Doctor Chang. "With the . . ." He scowled. He pointed to the door. "With the . . ."

"The wheelchair?" she asked.

"Yeah. Wheelchair."

"You liked being out of this room, being mobile and seeing other people, and getting out of this room?" she asked. "Did I mention getting out of this room?"

Justin's smile almost became a grin. "Yes."

She was serious then. "Do you think you're up for it?"

"Dunno. I want to try." He swallowed hard. "Can I try?"

She gave him a fond smile. "I think so. When do you think you'd be up for that?"

"Today. Now." It was the first time we'd seen him excited for anything. It was hard to ignore.

The doc made a face. "I'll have to see if there's a warden or a nurse—"

"I'll take him," I said.

She looked at me then, and there was humour in her eyes.

"You two aren't planning some great escape, are you? You're not gonna make a run for it?"

Justin smiled up at me, and I grinned right back at him. "We could . . ."

"But you won't," Doctor Chang said, stern but with a bit of a smile. "I'll see what I can find."

Two minutes later, she reappeared pushing a wheelchair. Together, we helped Justin out of bed and into the chair. She got his leg propped up and properly supported, and I put a blanket over him. She gave us a list of instructions and warnings, but soon enough, I was pushing him out of his room.

I'm pretty sure I out-grinned him, but he was so much happier. "How about we go outside? It's sunny but it's not too hot, and there's a courtyard we—"

"Yes."

I chuckled and made our way to the exit. I ignored the way people stared at him, at the scar down the right side of his head, or how his right leg and right arm were clearly injured. I wanted to say, "Yeah, take a good look. This is what happens when half your body gets slammed by a fucking truck," but I thought better of it. I was proud of him for surviving, for coming this far.

I wheeled him out into the courtyard. There were flower beds and grass and a tree at the far end, but we only went to the grass. As soon as he was in direct sunlight, he closed his eyes and let his head fall back and let out an almighty sigh.

"Feel good?"

"So good." He smiled upward. "Never knew I'd miss this."

I wheeled him as close to the grass as I could. Then kneeling at his left side, I lifted his foot.

"What are you . . . ?"

I pushed the footrest up and gently lowered his good foot to the grass. "Can you feel that?"

"Oh."

I grinned up at him. "Feel good?"

He nodded. "Thank you."

He spread his toes a little and wiggled his foot in the grass, like he was planting himself in the earth. After weeks spent in a clinical ward, where everything was sterile and disposable, I imagined it felt amazing.

I parked my arse on the grass, stretched my legs out, leaned back on my hands, and turned my face to the sky. "Feels good, huh?"

"So good."

I chanced a look at him and found him with his face still turned skyward, a small smile at his lips. Christ, he was . . . everything to me.

Neither of us spoke for a bit and I wondered if he'd fallen asleep, but then he said, "The doctors gave me options for a home," he murmured quietly. "When I go . . . leave."

I sat upright, my heart strangled in my chest. "What?"

"Guess they had to. Needed to know I had options. But I told 'em I had a home." He brought his head forward and his eyes drew to mine. "You said I had a home?"

"You do." I nodded earnestly, trying not to let my panic show. "You do have a home."

"And a cat," he said like it was utterly absurd.

"Squish."

He nodded and then his face screwed up, a mix of pain and sadness. "I don't remember you," he whispered. "From before."

I swallowed hard, dreading what he was about to say. "I know."

He stared at me for a long, heart-stopping moment. "I wish I did. But I don't."

I tried to speak, but no words would come.

"Hey," he said, making me look at him. "It hurts you. I can see that."

I nodded again but didn't trust my voice to speak, if I could speak at all.

"But I trust you," he said quietly. "I dunno why."

I gave him a teary smile. "You used to say that before. That you felt safe with me. I know it was never easy for you to trust me. You had a shit time with guys in Darwin."

"I remember that."

"You moved back to Newcastle and said you weren't looking for a relationship, but then . . ." I let my words trail away.

"But I felt safe with you."

I nodded. "Yeah."

"Still do. It's hard to . . ." He squinted. "I forget my words . . ."

"It's hard to explain?" I guessed for him.

"Yeah. Explain. It's hard to explain. I don't know you, but I want to. I trust you. And there's . . ." He made a face. "Shit. My words."

"Take your time," I said gently. "There's no rush."

"The sun is starting to hurt my eyes," he said, squinting his eyes closed.

I jumped up. "Okay, then let's get you somewhere else."

I fixed his footrest and wheeled him back inside, and we just walked slowly for a bit. "Want to check out the cafeteria?"

"Sure."

"Just tell me if you've had enough or if you want to go back," I said, not wanting him to overdo it. We'd only been out for half an hour, but still. "How's your headache?"

"'S okay."

When he said okay, he meant ever-present, never-subsiding, skull-crushing pain. The drugs took the edge off, of course, but it was always there. I could tell when he hurt in particular, as his right eye would sag a little or he'd squint more often.

"Did you want something to eat or drink?" I asked as we neared the cafeteria.

"Um . . . I dunno."

"What about some fries? Just a small one, between us. Then I better get you back, or Doctor Chang will send out a search party."

He seemed happy enough as we waited for our order, but his blinks were getting a little heavy. "People look at me," he said.

"Maybe they want to see a guy who survived getting hit by a truck," I said jokingly. "He's pretty great."

He smiled but it faded fast. "Don't feel it."

"Well, you are." I leaned in closer. "And fuck anyone who

stares. They don't know what you've been through or how far you've come."

That earned me a small smile, but then our fries came and he savoured the first taste. "Real food."

I laughed. "If the doctors asked, tell them I bought you salad." He'd lost some weight in the first two weeks after his accident, but he was starting to fill out again. The iced coffees probably had something to do with that.

"Calm," he said.

"What? Calm, what?"

"The word I couldn't say," he replied. "Before. I lost the word. Calm, that's it."

"What's calm?" I couldn't remember . . .

"You. Me. You make me feel calm. I trust you. I dunno why. But I'm calm when you're here."

I had to swallow the lump in my throat. "Thank you."

"So when I go home," he said, slow blinking, almost asleep. "I go with you."

Chapter Seven

FOR THE NEXT FEW DAYS, Justin wanted to escape his room in the wheelchair and I was all too happy to oblige. He had the staples in his leg removed, he did his physio, and he was eating more. He still became exhausted easily, he still forgot some words when he was tired, and he still had splitting headaches. The doc said these things could, and probably would, take weeks or months to abate. Maybe even longer.

And that was okay with me. I was here for the long haul. I was in it for forever before his accident, and I wasn't the type to quit when things got tough. Certainly not when he needed me the most.

When I got back to the hospital after the mandatory midday rest period, he was still asleep. He'd been looking through the photos again because they were in a messy pile, and the deck of cards I'd brought in for him was on his table as well.

Each and every visit was different, and I never knew what I'd be walking into. Would he be in a good mood? Would he be unwell? Would he be angry and frustrated or sore from pushing himself too hard? Would he be more tired than usual? Or would he be itching to get out of his room again?

Him being asleep, or dozing at least, wasn't too unusual. Exhaustion and constant tiredness were common after a brain injury, and I thought nothing of it. I planted my backside into my seat and answered a few emails on my phone that I hadn't got to yet.

Justin began to stir . . . No, not stir awake. He was still sound asleep. He was having a nightmare. He began to twitch and mumble in his sleep, slow at first but then urgent and a little scary. His face etched in pain and his body jerked, his mumbling growing frantic.

He was going to hurt his arm or reopen the scars on his leg.

I took his hand. "Hey, Justin," I soothed. "Hey, baby."

He jerked again and groaned as though something hurt. I stood up and put my hand to his cheek. "Jusso, it's okay. Wake up. I'm here with you."

His eyes shot open, wild and unseeing, until the pain kicked in and he moaned as he sagged back on the bed. "It was just a dream," I whispered. "You're okay. You're safe here."

He let out a shaky breath, his eyes closed, and he shook his head. "Fuck."

I gave him a few seconds to take some deep breaths and collect himself. "Just a bad dream," I murmured.

When he was calmer and breathing easier, I asked, "Do you remember what your dream was about?"

His fingers gripped mine and I noticed his strength was definitely returning, and after a long while, he shook his head. "No."

I suspected he might have nightmares about the accident, and I didn't know if I was disappointed that he still couldn't remember it or if I was glad he couldn't.

I wanted him to remember something.

Anything.

He kept his eyes closed while he concentrated on his breathing, and he eventually let go of my hand so he could sit himself up a bit more. "Hurts when I get like that," he mumbled.

"All tense?" I asked, and he nodded. "You jerked your injured leg and your broken arm. That has to hurt."

He made a face. "Yeah."

"Can I get you anything? A drink of juice or water? Did you need me to get the nurse?"

He shook his head and closed his eyes again. "Just sit with me."

There he was again, saying things to make my heart go crazy. "Of course."

He was quiet for a long few moments, and I sat beside him with my hand on his arm. "I don't like the dreams," he said eventually. "I dunno if it's my brain remembering something. It's hard to know what's real."

I frowned, my heart hurting for him. "Can you remember the dream? Maybe I can help shed some light . . ." I didn't know what else to say.

He turned his head slowly and stared at me. "Not really. It's like I'm falling. It's dark. Nothing is . . ." He licked his lips and sighed. "Kinda feels like I'm gonna die."

I slid my hand down his arm and took his hand, threading our fingers. "That sounds awful. I wish I could make them stop. The dreams, that is. It's probably just your brain trying to process what it's been through. Hopefully they'll stop or become clearer."

He almost smiled. "Hopefully. I have another dream too, but I can't quite remember . . . It's hard to know what's real."

"Is there anything you remember from that one?"

He closed his eyes as though he was trying to recapture it. "I don't know."

"That's okay. Don't try to force it." I could see it was an uneasy topic, so I changed it. "So, the occupational therapist came by," I said. I'd told him the appointment was today but didn't expect him to remember the details. "To check the flat and see if we'd need to change or fix anything before you come home."

"Oh yeah? What'd they say?"

"Everything's fine. Except for the stairs. The flat's above the shop. The mechanic shop, so the stairs are gonna be a pain until your leg is better. Just means you'll have to go slow, one step at a time. But everything else is fine. I thought the shower might be a pain for you, but she said it was great. I mean, it's only a two-bedroom unit, and it ain't too fancy, but I guess simple is good. No trip hazards or nothing, so that's good."

He nodded slowly and his brow furrowed a bit. "Stairs . . ."

"Yeah, Davo and Sparra were gonna try and rig up some kind of crank seat, like with a really big bike chain, and if they used an old two-stroke motor . . ." I shook my head. "I think the lady thought they were joking."

He did smile at that. "Davo and Sparra. I know them, right?"

"Yep. You've worked with them since you came back to Newcastle." I took the pile of photos and found the one of them and pointed each of them out. "That's Davo, and that's Sparra."

"Is that his name? Sparra?"

"Nah, his last name is Bird. Tony Bird is his real name, but apparently when he was in high school, Bird became sparrow, and well, sparrow became Sparra."

Justin's smile widened. "And I like them, right?"

"You sure do. They're great guys. Davo's basically been running the shop for me. I'll owe him a few cartons of beer, I reckon."

Justin's eyes met mine. "You don't have to come in every day."

"Yes I do," I replied. "Of course I do. I don't want to be anywhere else. Unless you'd rather I didn't, but I'll be here until you say otherwise."

He rested his head on the mattress, but his gaze never left mine. He just stared for a while, and I wanted so bad to lean in and kiss him. I wanted it so, so bad. But those days were gone . . .

"Sucks that you gotta look after me," he mumbled. "Like I'm a kid or something."

"It won't be forever. You'll be up on your feet in no time." I put my hand back on his, which he didn't seem to mind. "And it's no hassle. You don't owe me anything, no apologies, nothing. I do this because . . ." I paused because I almost said something that maybe he wasn't ready for. But then I realised maybe he needed to know. "Because I love you, Justin. Years ago, I made a promise to you to be by your side through whatever life threw at us. I know you don't remember, but you don't have to. Because I remember. And I'll be by your side for as long as you'll have me."

He stared for a few heartbeats and he opened his mouth to speak, just as there was a soft knock on his door.

It was two uniformed police officers, oblivious to the moment me and Justin were having, and the first had a clear plastic bag with them. "Sorry to interrupt," the first cop said. He offered Justin a smile. "You're looking a lot better than the last time I saw you."

Justin stared blankly, then he looked at me. I shrugged.

The cop explained. "I was one of the first on the scene of your accident. I helped get you out of the van."

I got to my feet and offered my hand to shake. "Thank you."

"Had some personal items from evidence I thought you might like returned." He held the plastic bag out to me. I could see it was Justin's wallet and his phone and what looked like some papers and a logbook, so I put it on Justin's table. "They were in the van at the time of the accident. We don't need them, and I thought I'd save you the trip down to the station."

"Uh, thanks," Justin said.

He'd been questioned very early on but, of course, couldn't remember anything. Those first few days, he really wasn't in shape to be questioned at all.

"Still can't remember anything?" the second cop asked. It wasn't meant to be callous, but Jesus Christ, some empathy wouldn't have hurt.

Justin gave a small shake of his head. "No."

I gave the second cop a curt smile. "He can't remember anything from the last five years. Not one thing."

"Yeah, sorry," he replied sheepishly.

"What happened to the driver?" Justin asked.

Whether it was because Justin spoke slow and a little slurred or the first cop felt bad or not, I couldn't be sure, but he seemed to take some pity on Justin. "He wasn't injured, if that's what you mean. There was dashcam footage, and he returned a negative for drugs and alcohol. It's been ruled as an accident. His brakes locked up in the rain. There were a lot of witnesses." His voice softened, like he slipped out of police-mode. "He's actually pretty shaken up about it, and he's very sorry. He wanted to come see you but was advised against it. He knows you were badly injured."

Justin slow blinked, and I could almost hear his brain catching up with everything the cop just said. "He can come see me," he said. "I don' mind."

"You sure?" I asked Justin.

He gave a nod, but he closed his eyes and sighed.

I looked at the policemen and tilted my chin toward the door, and they followed me out. "He gets tired real easy," I explained quietly. "And today hasn't been a great day."

"Sorry," the first cop said, and I believed him. He seemed genuine and I liked him. "For what it's worth, I'm glad he made it. I had my doubts when I first saw him in that van, but he's obviously a fighter."

I nodded, unsure if I was about to cry or laugh. "Thanks for coming by," I managed.

"I'll let the driver of the truck know," he said. "He's an older guy, been driving trucks for forty years and never had so much as a parking fine. He's really struggling, mentally and emotionally."

He's not the only one, I thought.

"Anyway, I'll pass on the message but will be sure he gives adequate notice of a visit," he said. "Who knows, it might help them both."

I nodded. "Maybe. Mornings are better. He's not so tired. And tell him no flowers on the neuro ward," I added. "The staff wouldn't let them in anyway, so just to save him the money . . ."

"I'll be sure to pass that on," he said. "Thanks again." He clapped my shoulder and they left, and I went back into Justin's room.

I thought he was asleep, but his eyelids opened slowly. "They go?"

I smiled. "Yeah. Said to say thanks." I sat back next to him. "If you don't want that truck driver here, if you change your mind, you just let me know."

He sighed and looked wearily at me. "I dunno . . . I think I need to see him. Dunno. My life was okay up to . . . what I remember last. Then it's gone. Like blank. Like a puzzle with no pieces. I need any pieces I can get."

I let out a long, sad breath and gave his hand a squeeze. He gripped my fingers and held my hand, and I relished the feel of his skin against mine, the warmth of it that seeped through to my core, because I wasn't just holding his hand—— he was holding mine.

"Looks like they brought you your wallet and phone," I said eventually, nodding toward the bag on his table.

He reluctantly let go of my hand and reached for the bag. He opened it with one hand and tipped the contents out. He took his phone first and pressed the button on the bottom. It was dead, unsurprisingly. "Screen's cracked," he noted.

"It was cracked before the accident," I said. "You dropped it on the concrete floor at the shop."

He huffed. "Course I did."

"I can bring your charger in tomorrow," I said. I would have offered to take it home and charge it overnight, but I didn't want him to think I'd delete anything . . . not that I thought he would think that, but I didn't want him to wonder or question. I wanted to be as transparent as I could be.

He took his wallet next, opening it and sliding his licence out. He inspected it, and I supposed it must have felt like he'd found something from the future. But it was his photo, our address, and the date. He took out the bank card, his Medicare card, other membership cards, but he clearly didn't recognise them. He pulled out the two twenty-dollar notes and shrugged. "Should probably give this to you," he said. "For the iced coffees."

I laughed as he slid something else out of his wallet. It was a photograph, and one I'd forgotten was in there. It was of him and me with our arms around each other, dressed up in our good jeans and shirts, smiling at the camera. He stared at it and stared some more. He frowned and shook his head, clearly drawing a blank.

"We were going to a concert," I said quietly. "I got you tickets to see Birds of Tokyo for your birthday, two years ago."

His gaze went to mine. "I wish I could remember . . ."

"I know you do."

He shook his head. "No. I really do." He thumbed the photograph. "It's like I'm looking at a stranger. Like I'm looking at photos of people I've never met. Even me. I don't recognise me in this . . ." He frowned again, his eyes teary. "I look so happy. And I don't remember . . . I feel . . . cheated. Like this was taken away from me." A tear escaped and he wiped it away with the back of his hand and stared at the photo. "All I ever wanted was . . . this."

"And you have it," I replied, swallowing back my own tears. *What else could I say?* "I'm not going anywhere, Juss. We can get back to this. If you never remember anything, it's okay. We'll make new memories. You're very loved by everyone. You'll have it again."

He closed his eyes again, tears beading on his eyelashes. "I want to remember," he whispered.

"I know you do."

His eyes stayed closed and his breathing deepened. I thought he'd gone back to sleep, but when I tried to let go of his hand, he gripped it tighter. "Stay. Talk to me. I like your voice."

I couldn't help but smile. "I like your voice too."

He smiled and ducked his head, but then he slowly rolled onto his side to face me. Something he rarely did because of his injuries, but I helped pull his pillow under his head to support his neck more and waited for him to get comfortable.

"Did you want me to read to you?" I asked.

"No," he whispered. "Tell me how we met."

Oh.

My heart danced around in my chest and I damn near could have cried. Somehow I held it together enough to speak. "You applied for a job at my shop. Of course I hired you because you're one of the best mechanics I'd ever seen. You'd just moved back from Darwin and you were keen for the work." I smiled fondly at the memory. "You were also scorching hot and funny. You were kind and gentle-natured, and apparently I used to not be able to speak around you. Davo took the piss out of me for months, because every time you walked in, I was utterly useless. But I didn't know if you were into guys, and I had this 'don't get involved with workmates' policy that I'd managed to abide by for a decade."

Justin's eyes were heavy-lidded, but he was smiling.

"And anyway, Davo reckoned you'd been checking me out, and one day when we were both there, he asked you if you were seeing anyone, a girl or a guy. I could have killed him," I said with a laugh. "But anyway, you said you didn't have a boyfriend, and he said something like, 'Oh, that's a coincidence because neither does Dallas.' Like he just put it all on the table in front of us, ya know?"

Justin kept smiling.

"Then after more weeks of us dancing around each other—not being able to be in the same room as each other, basically—Davo locked us both in my office and told us the sexual tension was unbearable and we weren't coming out until either one of us quit or we finally made out."

He slow blinked. "He locked us in your office?"

I nodded. "Yep."

"One of us didn't quit, did we?"

I shook my head slowly. "Uh, no." My laughter became a sigh. "We didn't come out of my office for a while either."

He made a happy sound. Though his eyes were closed now, he was still smiling. "Davo sounds like a good guy."

I chuckled. "He reminded us all the time that we owed our relationship to him. When we decided on the boyfriend thing, then again when you moved in with me, and again when we decided to become cat-dads and keep Squish. Now that I think about it, Davo's actually been a bit of a dick about it, to be honest. But yeah, he's a good guy."

He never opened his eyes, but he seemed so peaceful, happy even. "Tell me more," he mumbled. And I would have, but he was already asleep.

<h1 style="text-align:center">Chapter Eight</h1>

THE NEXT DAY I arrived with Justin's phone charger and plugged his phone in while he took his first sip of iced coffee. It was gonna take a little while for the battery to come to life, but he didn't seem to mind. He was in a good mood today.

He'd been going through his daily exercises, and he said he'd even been up and peed by himself. He was proud and I was chuckling when there was a knock at the door. Amy, the nurse, appeared and came in hesitantly. "Justin, there's a gentleman here to see you. Apparently he'd asked if he could see you and you said yes. He was driving the truck," she said with a frown. "If you don't want to see him, that's okay. I'm sure he'll understand."

"No, it's okay," Justin said. He looked at me, his eyes asking something I couldn't read. "You'll stay?"

"Yeah, of course. If you want me to stay, then yes."

He let out a breath and nodded at Amy. "I'll bring him in," she said before disappearing out the door.

"You sure?" I asked Justin.

He swallowed hard. "Yep. I don't know why, but I think I need to do this." But then he held out his hand to me and I was stunned for a second, wondering what he might have meant or wanted, but when I slid my hand over his, he clasped onto it.

Of course it made my insides all warm, but there was no time to savour it. An older man with grey hair and grey eyebrows stepped inside, wringing his hands. He looked on the verge of tears, and I'd wondered if he'd slept at all. "Good morning," he said. "The name's Jimmy Litchfield. I was . . ." His voice broke. His eyes were glassy. "I was driving the truck that hit your van. I just wanted you to know how sorry I am, and how . . . well, yeah. How very sorry I am."

I turned to Justin and he squeezed my hand. "Hey, Jimmy, I'm Justin."

I stood up and let go of Justin's hand so I could offer my hand to Jimmy. "I'm Dallas," I said without adding a title or point of reference to my being there or holding Justin's hand. The fact was, Justin and I weren't really boyfriends anymore . . . I mean, my heart still thought so, but my brain knew I couldn't be boyfriends with someone who didn't know me. "Please come in," I said to Jimmy, gesturing to the other side of the bed. I sat back down and took Justin's hand once more.

"The nice policeman said I could come see you and that mornings were best," Jimmy said. "I've been . . . I've been a bit of a mess since the accident." He then gestured to Justin lying in the hospital bed. "Not as much as you. That's not what I meant. I just meant . . ."

"It's okay," Justin said. "I get it."

"I can't stop thinking about it, and I don't sleep much anymore," Jimmy said. "It was an accident and the truck locked up on me. I hit the water and just aquaplaned straight into ya." He frowned deeper than I thought possible. "I can still see your face as I was coming for ya. I tried to stop . . ."

"I don't remember the accident," Justin said.

"The policeman said you lost your memory," Jimmy said.

"Five years," Justin said quietly. "Like someone just erased it."

"That's just awful," he said, getting teary again. "I'm real sorry. I know sorry don't mean much."

"Yeah it does," Justin said. "It helps that you came to see me. I need as many pieces as I can get."

Jimmy nodded, but I doubted he understood what Justin meant. "And your leg and arm . . . ?"

"Yeah, got myself some hardware," Justin said, looking at his leg with the brace. "New suspension rig."

Jimmy managed a smile. "Can see that."

"And my arm's not too bad. Looks worse than it is." Justin put his head back and managed a smile. "Head's not as hard as I thought it was though. Well, the thick skull was finally good for something, but the inside got . . . shook a bit."

"Despite all his injuries," I added, smiling at Justin, "we were still very lucky."

Jimmy looked at me then, and he saw our hands joined. It took him a second to recover, but he did it well. "My wife drove me in today. I'm still not good behind the wheel," he said. "Bit too jittery, since the accident, that is. And I'd be lost without her. Real good woman. And I'm glad you got someone here with you too. I can't imagine if you didn't have someone." He was teary again and got choked up. "My granddaughter married a nice girl. Real smart and takes good care of my girl, and that's all I ever wanted for her. So I just wanted you to know. That I don't care about this." He waved at our joined hands. "I voted yes to marriage equality because it's a good thing." He grimaced as though he was horrified at his verbal diarrhoea.

Justin snorted quietly, then turned to me, his eyes wide. "Wait. Marriage what?"

I laughed and gave his hand a squeeze. "Marriage equality. I'll explain that later." Jimmy looked all kinds of confused, so I clarified. "He can't remember that. The last five years is gone."

"Oh, sorry," Jimmy said, frowning again. "I guess . . . the last five years, right."

"There's a lot he needs to get caught up on," I said, smiling at Justin.

Justin nodded. "Sounds like it." Then he lifted his head up. "Wait. Did the Knights win a premiership in the last five years?"

I laughed, and Jimmy broke out in a grin. "No, son," he said. "You haven't missed that."

Jimmy stayed for a few minutes more, and he really was a nice old fella. He genuinely felt terrible, and the cops were right. Both Justin and Jimmy needed this. Jimmy needed to know that Justin was okay, and Justin needed to see the human aspect of the accident that took so much from him. Not to blame anyone, but to see that it was an accident and nothing more. And maybe that feeling of disbelief, that awful doubt, the not knowing that was now Justin's reality, might get a little closure.

I walked Jimmy out and saw him to the end of the ward. "Will he be okay?" Jimmy asked. "He talks slow. Did he used to talk like that, you know . . . before?"

I shook my head. "No, he didn't used to talk like that. But he's getting better every day. He doesn't forget words too much anymore, and he's really improving. The docs said he's real lucky. He might not ever remember the last five years though," I answered.

"Well, at least he has you. I'm glad he remembers you."

I tried to smile. "He, uh, he doesn't remember me. Not from before. He only knows me as the guy who hasn't left since he woke up."

Jimmy stared, and this time a tear did escape. He blinked and wiped at his face. "I'm so sorry. I never was one to pray, but I've been asking the good Lord to watch over him."

I was the least religious person on the planet and Justin was one step behind me. "I'm really grateful for that. You keep those prayers coming, okay?"

He nodded and wiped at his face again, just as an older woman wearing a blue sundress came down the hallway. Jimmy saw her and he began to cry again. Her face softened and she took his arm. "Thank you for seeing us today," she said. "It means a lot to my Jimmy."

"No problem." They turned to leave, but I didn't want to end it like this. This poor man was really struggling. "Hey, Jimmy," I called out and waited for him to turn. "We have the bike shop, Muller's Mechanics on Carney Road."

"I know it."

"Well, that's us. I'm Dallas Muller." I gave him a smile. "How 'bout you give me a call in a few weeks and I'll let you know how he's getting on. Or you could even drop by and see him, but call me first."

It felt strange to be making plans for weeks or months ahead when I didn't even know what tomorrow would bring, but it felt right.

"I'd really like that," Jimmy said, finally smiling. "I'll do that." He gave a determined, thankful nod, and I'd like to think I gave him some light in what had been a dark few weeks for him.

I watched them walk away, and with a deep sigh, I went back to Justin's room. He was on the bed, of course, but he was lifting his sore leg, doing his exercises. "His wife met us in the hall," I said.

"He was a nice fella," Justin said.

"He was. He's a bit upset. I think it did him good to see you," I said. "How do you feel now?"

"Better, I think." He shrugged his good shoulder. "I'd be pissed if it was a drunk driver or a stolen car or something. Or if he didn't care. Ya know? Like if he changed my whole life and didn't give a fuck." Then he grimaced. "Sorry. Do we swear?"

I laughed. "Ah, yeah. We do. Probably too much. Just not in front of customers."

Justin smirked. "Got it."

"But you feel better now that you've met him?"

He nodded and chewed on his bottom lip for a bit. "I didn't want the accident . . ." He cleared his throat. "The nightmares I have. The darkness and the fear. I dunno if it's my brain trying to show me the accident, to tell me what went wrong, ya know? But now it's not so scary. It's just a nice old guy whose brakes locked up in the rain. It wasn't . . ."

I frowned. "It wasn't what?"

"It wasn't death driving that truck."

I stared at him.

"That sounds stupid, sorry," he added quickly. "I dunno why I think that. It's just a stupid dream."

I took his hand in both of mine, sitting beside him. "Hey, it's not stupid. It doesn't sound stupid. It sounds pretty fucking real, if you ask me. It's no wonder those nightmares scare the shit out of you. And I'm sorry you've carried that around with you."

He sighed, frowning. "Maybe now I've met the driver, it

won't be so bad."

I nodded. "Let's hope so."

I was going to ask if he had the nightmares every night, or even about the other dream he'd mentioned, when there was a light knock at the door. "Ugh, PT time," he mumbled.

While Justin was expecting his physical therapist, instead he was met by his other doctors. Doctor Chang gave him a big smile. "Good morning," she said cheerfully. "I have some good news!"

"Uh, okay," Justin hedged, unsure.

"I think you're ready to go home," she said. "The last MRI and tests came back and I'm happy with the results, and Doctor Anderson is too. We still want to run a few more physical tests, but I think we can move onto the next step in your recovery. And that involves going home."

Justin was speechless, and I couldn't work out if it was a good speechless or a bad one.

"When?" I asked.

"We want to see how he goes with some mobility aids today, and all things going well, you can bust him maybe even tomorrow." She went on to explain a few things about home care services and whatever, but my concern was Justin.

I took his hand. "Hey," I said quietly. He looked at me. "Are you okay with that? With going home? Do you think you're ready?"

He swallowed hard. "I want to be ready," he replied. "But I . . ."

He was scared. Not just about being on his own, but he was scared about leaving with a man he didn't really know.

"How about this?" I said, trying to be braver than I felt. "We'll get you home and settled in. The home care nurse will come by every other day, and if you'd prefer to stay somewhere else, you just have to tell them. And we'll figure it out. No pressure, okay?"

He let out a breath and looked to his lap. Then he nodded. "I want to leave here, but I don't know what or where home is."

Doctor Chang intervened. "Going home will be a huge adjustment for you, and you can expect to be off-kilter and feeling a little lost and confused. It's not going to be easy, but I think you're ready for it. I wouldn't suggest it otherwise."

Then the occupational therapist stepped closer to the bed. I hadn't even noticed before but she was wheeling some kind of scooter thing that had four small wheels, a bike seat, and handlebars like the scooters the kids of today rode. "This is a steerable seated scooter," she said, then she proceeded to sit on it and prop her right foot up on a footrest above the front wheel. "You can steer with one hand and propel yourself with your left foot."

She wanted Justin to try it. Crutches were no good because the cast on his arm went up to his armpit, and a wheelchair wasn't much use when he couldn't use his right arm to help push himself. But this scooter with a seat should be good for him and would hopefully allow him to reclaim some of his independence around the flat.

He sat himself up and gently lowered his right leg to the floor. He took a few moments to let his head catch up with being upright, and when he was certain he was ready, we helped him onto it. The doc put his right foot up onto the footrest and allowed another few seconds to let him find his equilibrium. He leaned his bandaged right arm on his lap, but he gripped the handlebar with his left like a pro.

"We might be able to rig up a motor," I joked. "Just a two-stroke, or a Peewee 50—"

The two doctors and one nurse all spun to yell at me. "No!"

But Justin laughed. He actually laughed, and so help me God, he looked at me and my heart soared.

Doctor Chang could see it was a joke, and I was pretty sure she liked seeing Justin happy, but she was still a doctor. "It's a mobility aid, not a motocross bike. There will be no modifications to the scooter. Are we clear? Accidents are one thing, but I charge double for stupidity."

"No modifications," I said with a grin. "Got it."

All jokes aside, they helped Justin move the scooter, standing either side of him in case he fell or became dizzy. But he could do it, and his smile when he turned around in the hallway told me everything I needed to know.

He was ready.
He was coming home.

———

WHEN I CAME BACK after the lunchtime rest period, he was scrolling through his phone. He put it down on his lap when I came in and gave me a look I couldn't quite decipher. He looked tired, but there was something else . . . I held up the overnight bag. "Clothes for going home," I said, putting the bag by his bed.

"Thanks," he said, but he chewed on his bottom lip like he wanted to say something but didn't know how.

"Hey," I said gently. "Everything okay?"

"Yeah, just." He picked his phone back up. "Just looking through this."

"Find anything?"

"Well, lots. Nothing I remember. But you're in here. A lot, actually."

I sat in my seat and gave him a smile. "Photos, I take it. And texts."

He nodded and scrolled, though I couldn't see the screen.

"Is that weird?" I asked.

"A bit," he answered. "Like I'm reading texts between strangers. I should . . ." He sighed. "I should feel something, but I don't. Not like that. It just makes me feel sad."

"Sad?"

"Because it's all missing. This life." He turned the phone around, and I could see a text conversation. He read it aloud to me. "You: *Still at Coles?* Me: *Yep.* You: *We're out of milk.* Me: *Okay.*" He looked at me then. "It's just so . . ."

"Boring? Unromantic?" I prompted.

He snorted. "I was gonna say nice. Like it's so real life and normal."

I smiled because that was true. But it was also kinda sad because all he'd ever wanted was normal. He'd never wanted anything fancy or a high-flying, dramatic romance. Just a boyfriend to be at home with. Sure, we had our own romance, but we were two blokey blokes whose idea of together-time was riding and fixing motorbikes. "It was."

He scrolled some more. "And here," he said, showing me the screen. "Me: *Hey babe, running late. Be home soon.* You: *Okay, drive safe.* Me: *Want me to get KFC for dinner?* You: *Do I get a choice?* Me: *Nope. KFC it is.* With a laughing face."

I chuckled. "You like KFC."

He sighed as he stared at the screen. "And the photos."

"Oh . . ." I made a face. "Were there any nudes? I probably should have paid more attention to the photos you kept."

He turned the phone around and showed me the screen, giving me a flat stare. "I can't see if we're fully naked in this, but that's me on a bed and I think that's your arm, and I'm fairly certain I know what we're doing."

I laughed, my cheeks heating. "Uh, yeah. I took that photo. I was telling you how hot you were when we—" I cleared my throat. "—when we made love, and I took a photo to show you. I didn't know you kept it. You were supposed to delete it."

He let out a breath. "I take it I still . . . I mean, I always liked to . . ." He shook his head. "Never mind."

"If you have any questions, about anything, I will do my best to answer you. I'm trying to keep my emotional response out of it and just answer with facts so I don't colour the information with my experience. Which isn't easy." I shrugged. "But don't be embarrassed. You can ask me anything. I'm trying to help you."

He made a face. "I was just going to say that I always liked to . . . bottom," he whispered, "and from this photo . . ."

"If you're asking if you bottomed and I topped, then ah, yeah. You did."

His cheeks were red. "Well, at least that's something that hasn't changed."

I laughed, but I didn't want to dwell on the sexual side of us. I didn't want him to feel pressured, and if—if, one day—it ever happened again, it would happen when he was ready. "Any other photos?"

He sighed again. "Lots. There's a lot of bikes. That also hasn't changed. There's pictures of a cat being all cute and shit."

I chuckled. "Squish."

"How did we get him?"

"We found three abandoned kittens at the shop. You made a bed for them and left food out for the mum cat, but she never came back. So you started feeding them and looking after them. Davo and Sparra thought you were crazy, but you were determined. Anyway, you had the vet check them over and you found homes for two of them, but no one wanted the black cat. Bad luck or some bullshit. Not that it mattered because there was no way you were giving him up anyway. We kept saying you should have called him Shadow because he was always one step behind you, but you called him Squish."

"I named him that?"

"Yep. You kept saying you were gonna squish him if he didn't get out from under your feet."

Justin smiled. "That's kinda cute."

"It's totally cute. He misses you," I added. "Squish does. He yells at me when you don't come through the door with me."

Still smiling, he went back to his phone. "There's a bunch of pictures of those two guys, Davo and Sparra. Mostly goofing around. It's a mechanic workshop, so I guess it's where I worked too?"

I nodded slowly. "Yep. That's the one."

"And there's pictures of you and me, but mostly you, and even of the cat that's in a house. The walls and furniture are the same."

"That's the flat above the workshop," I explained. "That's where you live."

"Thought so." He scrolled through a few more photos. "Are there any posters in our flat?"

"Posters?" I shook my head. "Like wall posters? No, we weren't big on decorating, if that's what you mean. Why, do you remember something?"

"I don't know. I see something in my dream. I think it's a poster."

"A poster of what?"

He made a face. "Of a Harley Davidson. So weird, I know.

But it's hard to focus on and I'm not sure."

I shook my head slowly. "No, sorry. Was there one in your place in Darwin?"

He shook his head and frowned, then let the phone screen go dark and laid it on his lap, resting his head back on the pillow. He let out a long sigh. "You know it's weird, but I know how to use a phone, and I remember how to ride a bike, but I can't remember where I live or who I live with. I can't remember my friends, but I can remember how to make my nan's spaghetti. The doc gave it some big fancy name, but to me, it's just weird."

It was called procedural memory function, but I didn't need to rub that in his face right now. The name wasn't the important part of this story. "It is weird, Justin. The skills are there, like how to do stuff, but the facts and info are gone."

He nodded. "Yep. Doc told you too, huh?"

I smirked. "Yep."

"She said going home can trigger some memories." Justin's speech was getting slower, a sure sign he was tired. "Like if I see the cat, I'll get *bam, bam, bam*, flashes of me getting the cat, feeding the cat, cuddling the cat. She said sometimes that happens, but not always."

"Well, we can hope."

He slow blinked. "It's like right there. In the mist. But right there."

"What's right there?"

"Memories," he mumbled. "Everything. Like I can almost touch 'em but can't."

He could barely keep his eyes open, so I took his hand, and the familiar warmth was incredible. "Have a nap, Juss," I whispered. "You need all the rest you can get. Got a busy day tomorrow."

His eyes stayed closed but he gave a small smile. "Leaving."

It stung a little that he didn't say 'going home,' but to be fair, it wasn't home to him. But I was going to do my damnedest to make it his home again.

"Yeah, baby," I whispered, knowing he was already asleep. "Leaving."

Chapter Nine

When I arrived the next morning, Justin was sitting up on the edge of his bed, showered and dressed. I'd chosen some loose track pants for him, thinking they'd be easier on his leg, and one of his favourite shirts. He looked so different in normal clothes rather than the hospital garb he'd been in for the last three and a half weeks.

"Morning," I said, unable to hide my excitement. "How are you feeling?"

He smiled. "Okay. Nervous."

"I'm nervous too," I admitted.

"You are?"

"Sure. I'm nervous that I might not be the best home care person and you'll hurt yourself because I did something wrong."

"Like what?"

"I dunno. Leave the bathmat on the floor and you'll trip over it and smack your head on the tub. Or that the stairs are gonna be too much for you. That kind of thing."

Or that you'll realise you don't want to live with me anymore . . .

"That makes two of us," he murmured.

"You're worried that I'll be a bad home carer?"

He snorted. "Uh, no. I'm worried that you *have* to be my home carer, that you'll get sick of having to babysit me."

I went to him and stood in front of him, putting my hand on his shoulder. "I'll never get sick of it. You're not a burden, and you're not a hassle. We'll get through this. It just means you'll have to put up with my terrible cooking for a bit."

He almost smiled. "Thanks." But then he took a deep breath and met my gaze. "I mean it. Thank you. You don't have to do this, like you could have bailed, but you didn't. I could have had no recollection of my life before the accident and be homeless. But you stuck by me."

My hand burned to touch his face, to cup his cheek so I could kiss him softly. Of course I couldn't, so I pulled my hand away. "I wouldn't be anywhere else." He smiled but looked away. A line formed between his eyebrows. "How's your arm feel? Is that shirt okay?" I'd chosen one with loose short sleeves.

He looked down and lifted his arm out a little. "Yeah, thanks. It's fine. They re-bandaged it. Doc was happy with it."

"Good. Did they say when you can leave?"

"Just waiting for the doc to come by. She's got papers and pills, that kinda stuff."

"Okay. Did you eat already? I put your iced coffee in the fridge at home. Thought it might be something to look forward to."

He smiled more genuinely then. "Thanks. Yeah, I had some toast."

I pointed my chin at the scooter seat thing. "Wanna give it a whirl? I mean, we gotta get used to it with just me helping you."

His smile widened. "Okay. Yeah, okay."

I wheeled it so it was in front of him and put the brakes on, then went to his left side and took his arm. "So," I said. "All your weight on your good foot. Ready?"

He gave a nod, his face etched in concentration. "Yep."

He stood, and holding him with one hand, I manoeuvred the scooter back so he could lower himself onto the seat. We wobbled a bit but we held steady, and I lifted his right foot up onto the footrest. I looked up at him to find him grinning. "We good?" I asked.

"We're good." He was panting a little, but he'd come so far from the first time he'd used this.

Yes, we were. We were gonna be just fine.

"Oh, I see someone's keen?" Doctor Chang said from the door. She was smiling, holding a folder and a white paper bag.

"Oh," I said, feeling like a kid getting in trouble. "We just thought we'd see if we could get him onto it without another significant head trauma incident."

The doc stared at me but Justin laughed, and she relented with a sigh and a bit of a smile. "Well, I'm glad there was not another traumatic brain injury. Because one is enough." She put the folder on Justin's bed and asked him to wheel over. She showed him his release forms, every prescription he needed, an itinerary of all his follow-up appointments, exercise and physio stuff, and a booklet journal for him to document anything and everything. She then showed us his pill schedule, which was an entire freaking chemist full—pills for pain, anti-seizure, anti-inflammatory, anti-coagulants, and whatever else— and I was so glad it was all written down. She closed the folder. "It's a lot of information."

I nodded but gave Justin an encouraging smile. "We got this. Once we get home and find our own routine, we'll have it down pat."

Doctor Chang gave me a fond look. "Yes, you will."

A nurse came in with a wheelchair. "Your ride, sir."

"Can't I leave on this?" he asked Doctor Chang.

"Sorry. Hospital policy."

"I'm more of a fall-risk when I get out of the chair and onto this thing," he tried.

"Mr Keith," Doctor Chang said. "Please humour me."

He sighed. "You know, I can remember high school. And being called that reminds me a lot of high school."

I laughed and Doctor Chang shook her head. "You two," she said, rolling her eyes.

But like a good boy, I helped Justin transfer to the wheelchair, and the nurse took him out to the station to say a round of good-byes. Doctor Chang stayed beside me. "He was very lucky in that accident," she said quietly. "It could have been a lot worse than what it was. But it's not all going to be easy. There's going to be hard roads ahead."

"I know," I said. "But we've got this."

"He's lucky to have you," she whispered before she met my eyes. She breathed in deep and gave me a watery smile. "I wish I could tell you he'll regain his memories, but I can't."

I gave a nod. I knew this too; if he hadn't regained anything after six months, it wasn't likely he ever would. "Yeah. We'll just have to make new ones."

She looked at me like she was trying to figure something out. "You can't be shaken, can you?"

I almost laughed. Because, Jesus, this whole accident had shaken me to my core. "Quite the opposite actually. But what choice do I have? He might not remember me, but he needs me. And I love him."

She nodded, her eyes glassy. "I wish every one of my patients had a you."

The nurse wheeled Justin back to us. He looked up at Doctor Chang. "Well, Doc. It's been fun."

"But you can't wait to leave me," she said, joking. She nodded toward the exit. "Well, you can't get rid of me that easy. I'm walking you out."

I put Justin's overnight bag on his lap and the nurse stood aside so I could do the honours. Doctor Chang took charge of the scooter thing, and with a double-check that he'd got everything from his room, and after far too many days, we finally walked out of the neuro ward.

As we made our way through the hospital toward the exit, the doc asked us what we had planned for our first day of freedom. "Oh," Justin said with a frown. "I dunno. Probably not much."

"Well, I thought I might get Justin propped up on the couch in front of the flat screen," I said. "There's a Motocross special on Foxtel right now."

He looked back up at me, his grin wide. "Hell yes."

Doctor Chang laughed. "I should have known." Then she stopped at the doors to the outside. "Well, this is as far as I go."

We got him out of the chair and onto his scooter, and she looked at us both. "You're gonna do great, Justin. One day at a time. You have all the info, but if you need anything, you can call. And I'll see you in one week for your first appointment."

She waved us off and I slung the overnight bag over my shoulder. "You ready?"

He inhaled deeply and swallowed hard. "Yep." Then he shrugged his good shoulder. "Well, there's Motocross and iced coffee waiting for me, so yeah."

I laughed, and we made our way toward the car park. It was slow going, and I made sure I walked on his right side so I could catch him should he get dizzy or fall. He didn't though; he just went at his own pace.

But then he did the strangest thing.

We got to the entrance and he saw my blue ute and headed straight for it.

I stopped walking, which made him stop. "What's wrong?" he asked.

"Justin," I whispered. "Which car's mine?"

"The Holden ute," he said, scowling at me like I was an idiot. But then he realised . . . His eyes went wide, his mouth slack. "How did I know that?"

I laughed. "I don't know."

His eyes were comically wide, and he was smiling but stunned and probably confused. "Did you tell me that?"

"Nope."

"Was it in the photos?" he asked.

"I don't think so," I answered. I mean, I couldn't be absolutely certain, but I was pretty sure there weren't any pictures of my ute. "We never talked about it."

"How did I remember that?" he asked, then looked back at the ute. "How did I know you drove a piece of shit Holden when you could have bought a Ford." His eyes darted to mine. His chest was rising and falling hard, and I couldn't help it.

I burst out laughing. "You told me a thousand times that I should've bought a Ford. We joked about it for years."

He opened his mouth and closed it a few times, though he

looked a little scared. "I know that. I know that argument. I remember it. Not saying it to you, but just that it was a thing."

I did put my hand to his face this time. I couldn't help it. "You remembered something. Jussy, you remembered something."

His eyes began to swim. "I remembered something."

I had to swallow back my tears. "You did!" I swiped his cheek with my thumb, relishing in the touch for the briefest moment before I pulled my hand away.

"I remembered your car," he whispered. "I just saw it and I knew it, like I'd seen it a thousand times, that it was yours. I mean, I didn't really *remember* it, I just knew it. Like I knew my sister when I saw her. Or how I knew I liked iced coffee."

"But this is better than that," I said. "Because I only bought my ute four years ago. You couldn't have known from before. Not that you knew me when you were in Darwin, but the car is kinda new. You remembered something from within the time you lost, Juss."

He nodded slowly, then put his hand to his forehead. "I did."

I put my hand on his shoulder. "Your head feel okay?"

"Yeah, I think," he said, distractedly. "Headache's still there."

The headaches were a constant. It was only their severity that changed. "Let's get you home."

I helped him into the ute and got his seatbelt sorted, then put his scooter and bag into the back, strapping them in. I got in behind the wheel and buckled up and put the key in the ignition. He had his eyes closed, almost squinting. "You okay?" I asked again. "With being in a car?" I wasn't sure if the accident had affected him on some subconscious level.

He must have been thinking the same thing. "Uh, I think so . . ."

"I'll go slow. If you need me to pull over, just say so. Home is just ten or fifteen minutes away. So it's not too far."

He nodded and I could see he was clearly tired. I turned the radio off to eliminate noise, backed the car out, and slowly made our way home. It was mid-morning, the sun was shining, there was hardly any traffic, but I was hyperaware of every vehicle around us. I had no idea how he'd react if someone pulled into traffic too fast or braked too hard. Thankfully, the trip was incident-free.

I pulled the ute into the driveway and drove around the workshop into the backyard. It was where we sometimes parked to unload groceries and stuff because it was closer to the back stairs. I shut the engine off and gave Justin a smile. "Here we are."

Davo came out of the workshop, wiping his hands, and Sparra followed him into the sunshine. "Here he is!" Davo cried. Davo knew Justin couldn't remember him, but Davo was determined to treat him like he always had.

"They've missed you," I said quietly before getting out. I went around the front of the ute and opened Justin's door, then got his scooter ready, putting it beside the ute. "Okay, getting into the ute wasn't too bad," I said. "Now let's see about getting you out."

He sat side-on, lifting his right leg, and gently lowered it to the ground, but he couldn't quite get leverage with his left arm to help propel himself upward.

"Here," I said, offering my hand. He took it and we slowly got him onto his feet. He smiled with a hint of pain and exhaustion.

Justin looked at Davo and Sparra. "Hey. Um." He made a face as though he was embarrassed. "I'm Justin."

"We know who you are," Davo said, his grin firmly in place. "But I'm Davo, and this is Sparra. It's real good to see you up and about, mate. And this one here—" He pointed his thumb at me. "—hasn't stopped smilin' since there was talk of you comin' home."

"Ugh, thanks, Davo," I said, trying not to blush. "Haven't you got work to do?"

He just laughed, and Sparra added, "Heard him vacuumin' and everything. He hasn't been that nervous since you two first hooked up."

Davo whacked Sparra with the back of his hand. "You're not supposed to talk about that," he whisper-hissed at him.

I sighed. "Seriously, guys."

But Justin chuckled. "Nah, it's okay. Don't sweat it."

I turned to face him. "You wanna hit the couch and watch some Motocross, maybe rest for a bit?"

He nodded. "Yeah." But then he looked at the stairs. "Oh."

"Uh, yeah. Did you want to sit on your scooter for a bit?" I suggested instead.

He shook his head. "Nah. I'm up. If I sit down, I'll be down for a bit. Let's do this."

I handed the scooter and my keys off to Davo. "Can you carry that up for us, please, and hold the door open?"

Davo grabbed it and jogged up the stairs, unlocked and opened the door, and waited.

We got to the bottom of the stairs and he could stand, holding the railing easily enough. If he could use his right arm properly, he'd have no trouble using the railings like crutches, but his arm wasn't up for that. He managed two stairs and looked up to the top as though he was looking up at Everest. "Jesus."

"I have an idea," I said, behind him. "You can say no if you want . . ."

Justin half-turned to eye me. "What?"

"I could put you over my shoulder. It just might make you dizzy, that's all."

"Over your shoulder?" he asked.

"Well, yeah."

"It wouldn't be the first time," Sparra said, then grimaced. "Ah, sorry."

Justin shot Sparra a quick look. "It wouldn't be?"

Sparra gave me an apologetic look, but then he turned back to Justin. "Well, no. It was the State of Origin a few years back, and you backed Queensland and took a shot of Bundy for every try they scored, and anyway, they won by forty points and you were shitfaced. You were gonna sleep down here but Dallas weren't havin' none of that, so he carried you caveman style up the stairs."

Davo laughed. "You spewed upside down all the way up. Funniest shit I ever saw."

I couldn't help but laugh, because that night had been hilarious. But Justin was flagging. His blinks were slow and his words were too. If we left it any longer, he would be taking a nap in the workshop. "What do you reckon?"

"Don't fancy putting my head down, to be honest. Like upside down. Leg pain I can deal with, head pain not so much."

"Yeah, okay, sorry. Good point." I should have known that, but I was glad he spoke up with what he was comfortable with.

"I can do this," he said, more determined this time. He took a deep breath and steadied himself.

I stood behind him, ready to catch him should he fall. "I got you."

He held on to the handrail like crutches, and bearing as little weight as he could on his injured leg, he made one step. Then another, and another. It was slow going, but he was doing this. And so help me, he was determined.

"How's it feel?" I asked, my hands at his waist.

He grunted as he lifted his right leg up to the step he was standing on. "'S okay," he said, panting. "You just wanted to check out my arse, didn't ya?"

Sparra laughed. "There's the Justin we know!"

I laughed at that but kept a hold of him as he made the final step, then helped him onto his scooter. He was breathing hard but he was smiling, clearly pleased with his progress. But he looked exhausted.

I propped his right foot up and helped him push inside. "We're gonna get you to the couch, okay?"

He nodded.

I took his left arm and helped him onto the sofa. I pressed the button that lifted the foot recliner and he settled back with a few rough breaths. He had a line of sweat along his brow. I propped him up with cushions, making him as comfortable as possible.

"How's your head?"

He winced at that and shook his head a little.

I turned to Sparra, who was looking a little uneasy. "Sparra, his black bag in the back of the ute, it's got his meds in it."

He took off and was out the door, but Davo stayed and appeared with a glass of water that he handed to Justin. "You gonna puke, Jusso?" he asked. "I'll get ya a bucket."

Justin shook his head. "Nah. Head hurts though."

I put my hand to his face and let him lean against me a little. "I'm sorry. But you're here now. We'll get you settled in and you can nap in front of the sports channel."

He nodded just as Sparra came back in with the bag. He handed it over, then he and Davo both gave me a nod and slipped out the door.

I got Justin a pain pill and knelt down in front of him. He swallowed the pill without question, a testament to his pain, and let me take the water. "Today was a big day, yeah? But that was the worst of it. It'll get easier every day. Though I reckon me and Davo might work on that motorised seat up the stairs for ya, huh?"

He half-smiled, but his eyes drifted closed and he slept.

I fell back onto my arse and sagged. I knew Justin was exhausted, but I was too. The last four weeks had come down to this. Every mile of hell we'd trudged through came down to Justin finally coming home. And now he was here.

I felt the mountain I'd been trying to move finally budge. We had a long way to go, sure. But he was home. The weight I'd been carrying had lifted a little and its reprieve took the wind out of me.

I was so relieved, so fucking tired, I didn't even have the energy to get up. I simply lay back on the floor in a heap in front of the couch and closed my eyes.

Chapter Ten

I woke up with a start, wondering where the hell I was and why my neck hurt like a bitch. Was I on the floor?

"Looks like someone's awake," a warm voice said. I turned, my neck protesting loudly, to find Justin still lying on the lounge. But now he had a lump of purring Squish on his chest. Squish had his eyes closed, looking all kinds of contented, and Justin smiled at me. "He certainly knows me."

I sat up, groaning as all the kinks and knots made themselves known. "If I ever fall asleep on the floor again, kick me and tell me to get up."

"You were zonked right out. Figured you must've needed the nap."

I squinted at the clock. Shit. I'd been asleep for two hours. I heaved my sorry self to my feet. "You hungry? I'll make us something."

"Anything that's not hospital food would be great."

I stopped because I had intended to make us a sandwich each, but that was probably the last thing he felt like. "Want pizza? It is your first day out and all. We should have something to celebrate."

"Oh my God, yes." He groaned. "I want the filthiest, greasiest Domino's pizza ever."

I laughed because that was such a Justin thing to say, and gave Squish a pat. He opened his big yellow eyes and gave me a look of proud disdain. "I told you he was coming home," I said, giving the cat a scratch under his chin.

"I woke up like this," Justin said. "He must have found me and decided I looked comfy."

"He's missed you," I murmured. I met Justin's eyes. "I know you don't remember being here, but it's real good to have you back."

He kinda smiled, a bit confused and a bit weirded out by the looks of it, so I changed subjects. "Barbeque Meatlovers, right?"

"Yes, please."

I found my phone and thumbed the app and simply clicked on our last favourited order. My card was already connected; I hit confirm and slid my phone onto the coffee table. "It says thirty minutes."

He squinted at me. "You ordered it already?"

"Yep. They have an app now, on your phone. Makes it super easy."

He frowned. "There's a bunch of shit on my phone I don't know what the hell any of it's for."

I gave him a smile. "We'll get you caught up."

"I sent Becca a text," he said. "Told her I had my phone back. She replied like ten times, so that's something that also hasn't changed."

I snorted at that, then thought of something. "Hey, when you're ready to get up, I can show you around. Bathroom," I said, then the one I'd been dreading . . . "And your bedroom."

He began to sit up, pissing Squish off. "Sorry, little dude," Justin said. "But yeah, the bathroom would be good. I need to pee."

I showed him the button that retracted the recliner and I wheeled his scooter closer. "How's your leg? You gave it a bit of a workout earlier."

"It's okay now," he said, transferring himself to his scooter easily enough. "Those pain pills don't muck around."

He lifted his right foot up onto the footrest and took hold of the handlebar with his left hand. I was certain the pain pill helped immensely, but it was also amazing what a nap did to his energy levels.

"Okay, so you know how I said the unit was kinda basic," I began. "Well, this is the kitchen, dining, and lounge room."

And it was. The unit was basically a large rectangle above a mechanic's shop. One half of the rectangle was the living space, with the kitchen along the end wall and corner, a small dining table, and a three-seater couch facing a big flat-screen TV. The other half of the flat was two bedrooms and a bathroom. That's all there was to it.

I walked to the small hall and he wheeled himself behind me. "Bathroom is here," I said, opening the first door on the left. "It's pretty big. Shower, toilet. Washing machine and dryer are in there too, and the linen cupboard." Then I pointed to the door at the end of the hall. "That's my room," I said, not wanting to dwell on that. So I quickly opened the door opposite the hall. "And your bedroom is here."

He peeked inside at the double bed and nodded slowly. "Gotta use the bathroom first."

"Need some help?" I cringed, but it had to be asked.

"Nah. Be okay."

"Okay, sure. I'll just leave you to it," I said awkwardly, walking back out to the living room. I picked his bag up and slid it onto the couch for him, cleaned the kitchen bench, again, then checked inside the fridge and pantry for what groceries we'd need—— anything to keep myself busy.

Finally, I heard the toilet flush and the sink tap turn on and shut off, then a minute or two of silence. I was going to ask if he was okay, but the door opened and he scooted slowly across the hallway until he was staring into "his" bedroom.

The thing was, it was *our* room. It had been our room for five years. But I couldn't expect to sleep in his bed now. We weren't "together" like that anymore. And the very last thing I wanted to do was freak him out or pressure him.

He'd just had his whole world upended. He needed to feel safe here, and if that meant I had to move into the spare room, then so be it. The shitty pull-out sofa bed would be my bed for . . . well, possibly forever.

He wheeled himself into the room, and with a quiet sigh, I left the kitchen and followed him. "This is nice," he said. He was sitting on his scooter just inside the doorway. It was a basic room with a heavy wooden-frame queen-sized bed and a large window that faced the back of the workshop. The walls were a light grey, doona was dark blue, and there were two bedside tables with old touch lamps I'd had forever. We never needed anything fancy. We weren't the fancy type.

But I'd cleared out my personal things, things like my phone charger and most of my clothes. "Uh, that door is the wardrobe."

He scooted to the left side of the bed—his side—and touched the bed cover. His eyebrows knitted and he shot me a look.

"What's up? Do you remember something?"

"I dunno," he whispered. "Not a memory. Just something I know."

"What is it?" I asked, my heart in my throat.

"I don't know," he said, a confused and frustrated line between his eyebrows. "It's familiar, but it's not. I don't know how to explain it. Like I know this is my bed, but I can't remember exactly."

"Like how you knew my ute when you saw it."

He nodded. "It's weird. I mean, it's good. I guess. Like knowing what colours are in a painting but not knowing what the picture is. It doesn't make much sense, but it's something."

It made me smile. "It *is* something. And that's two somethings on the first day. That's pretty good."

He was quiet for a long moment. "You said this was my room."

I nodded.

That confused look was back. "Did we . . . We were together? Before the accident?"

I had to clear my throat. "Um, yeah."

"But we didn't share a room . . ."

My mouth was suddenly dry. "I didn't think you . . . Actually, I thought you'd be more comfortable if I took the second room. Some privacy, you know, for when you need space to chill out or just for some alone time, given everything you've been through."

He was frowning at me, and I couldn't bear the weight of his scrutiny.

"We shared a wardrobe," I said. "I mean, the clothes. Shirts, sweaters. After a while we couldn't remember who owned what and we just wore whatever was clean, basically. So if you find something and you want to wear it, go right ahead. Except the Newcastle Knights stuff, that's all yours."

He managed a smile at that. "Who's your team?"

"Bulldogs."

He stared blankly at me.

"Do you not remember them?" I asked because that was well outside of the last five years. The Bulldogs had been around forever.

"Yeah, of course," he said. "I just thought you were a decent guy, and now you tell me you're a Bulldog supporter? I thought I had better taste in men. What the hell happened to me in the last five years."

I laughed because that was such a Justin thing to say. He'd taken the piss out of my footy team since the day he found out. I'd worn an old Bulldogs jersey one day and he'd laughed till he almost cried. He was a Knights supporter to the bone, and we'd ribbed and jibed each other for years.

"Well, your taste in men is just fine," I said with a smile. "Your taste in football teams, not so much."

He chuckled, his eyes bright and happy.

"Dallas?" Davo called out. It sounded like he was at the bottom of the stairs. "Pizza guy's here."

"I'll get it," I told Justin. "Wanna get us something to drink from the fridge?"

He nodded and I went down to collect the pizzas. When I got

back, Justin was sliding two cans of lemon soda onto the table, then he scooted back to the kitchen and began opening cupboards. He found plates, and I was going to help him but wanted him to do things on his own. I knew Justin—the old Justin—and I knew if he needed help, he'd ask for it.

He put the plates on the table and scooted back to the cupboards. "Where the hell are the glasses?"

I chuckled. "Cupboard above the sink, to the left."

It meant he'd have to stand up, so I put the pizzas on the table in case I needed to grab him in a hurry. He put his right foot on the ground and stood up, reaching to open the cupboard. He had to duck his head back a bit so it didn't hit him, but he kept his balance and put one glass on the counter, then another, then slowly sat himself back on his scooter. He stacked the glasses and held them in his left hand, then scooted back to the table.

He'd done it. All by himself.

And from the smile he wore, it was easy to see he was pleased with himself.

I forced myself not to smile at him and pointed to the cupboard. "You uh, left the cupboard open."

He snorted. "Don't push your luck."

I laughed and pulled out a seat next to him, then opened the first pizza box. "Your Meatlovers," I said, sliding it closer to him. "And my chicken and pineapple."

He stared at me, wide-eyed. "Okay, what the hell? Chicken and pineapple? How were we together?"

I burst out laughing. "Just shut up and eat yours."

He laughed as well, and for a fleeting moment, it was like nothing was different, like nothing had changed. The way he looked at me, all happy and laughing, made me giddy. It felt a little like the first time all over again.

Like when we'd just got together and everything we did was new. When just a glance from him was enough to make my belly flip. When his smile and his laugh wrapped themselves around my heart.

It was just like that, though somehow maybe, possibly, even

better. I valued it now, like truly knew how much that was worth, and I'd never take it for granted again.

———

I CARRIED the empty pizza boxes down the stairs to the recycling bin and walked into the workshop. Sparra saw me first. "How is he? You're smiling, so I guess it's all good."

"He's back on the couch watching Motocross, but I reckon he'll already be asleep. He was struggling to keep his eyes open after a belly full of pizza, so I left him to rest. He still needs to sleep a lot."

"How's he settling in?" Davo asked, walking over as he wiped his hands on a rag.

Pretty sure my smile answered for me. "He's good. He remembered my ute this morning, and he remembered the bedroom. Nothing huge, and more just kind of knowing than remembering, but that's pretty damn good. The doc said coming home can trigger stuff."

"That's awesome," Davo said, his grin wide.

"He's still the same, isn't he?" Sparra said. "Like his sense of humour is just the same."

I nodded. "Yeah. He's still the same." All the doctors had warned me about possible personality changes that some people had after a brain injury, but Justin was still the same sweet, funny guy he'd always been—and for that, I was so grateful. "He took the piss out of me for having a Holden and for having pizza with pineapple. And for being a Bulldogs supporter."

They both laughed at that. "Same old Jusso then," Davo said.

"Yep. Anyway," I said. My cheeks were starting to hurt from smiling so much. "Thought I'd tackle that pile of paperwork on my desk. You guys need a hand with anything?"

"Nah," Sparra said. "Not today. I'm just finishing up on the Yamaha; should have it done by this arvo. But we've got the Williams' Kawasakis coming in tomorrow."

Davo nodded. "Four bikes. Drive chain and transmission,

brakes. Nothing huge and we can handle it if you need, but if you're gonna be around . . ."

"I'll be here," I said. "You guys have been a godsend. I really appreciate everything. I hope you know that."

Sparra looked like he'd swallowed something sharp; he never was too good at compliments, but Davo gave me a nod. "Any time, mate."

Feeling better than I had in weeks, I went into my office and sat down at my long-abandoned desk. I'd managed to get through some of the urgent stuff over the last month but I was way behind. Knowing Justin was safe asleep upstairs, and with a note by his phone to call me if he needed me, I took a deep breath and started with the top of the pile.

Two hours later my phone beeped with a message. *You here?*

I quickly thumbed out a reply. *Just downstairs. You okay?*

Yeah.

The little text bubble appeared, then disappeared, and then nothing, as though he wanted to say something but stopped himself. I pocketed my phone and ducked out of my office and through the workshop and took the stairs two at a time.

Justin was sitting up on the couch, still a little sleep rumpled. "Hey," I said. "Everything okay?"

He squinted one eye. "Yeah. Just woke up. You weren't here."

I sat on the coffee table in front of him and handed him the note. He read it and frowned. "Sorry. Didn't see it."

"Don't apologise," I said with a smile. "I'm never far away, okay?"

He nodded. "Guess I'm not used to being alone."

I switched from the coffee table to sit right beside him. I took his hand. "Hey. You're not alone. I'll always be around. And during the day, on the rare occasion I ever have to duck out or go run an errand, the boys are downstairs. They'll come straight up."

He looked uncomfortable, embarrassed even, and licked his lips as though his mouth was dry. "They're not you."

I squeezed his hand and fell against the back of the sofa, sitting side-on, looking right at him. The fact he wanted me around made me happier than it probably should have, but his needs were bigger than my ego, and I needed to remind myself of that. "It's been a crazy day, huh? New place, new everything."

He nodded and closed his eyes, clearly still tired. "Took a bit to remember where I was." His fingers tightened on mine. "The only constant thing in my life since I woke up . . . is you."

My heart squeezed to the point of pain. "I'm not going anywhere."

He was quiet for a bit. "Nothing makes sense," he whispered eventually, then opened his eyes to look at me, his dark eyes imploring and so, so familiar.

"What doesn't make sense?"

"I can't remember anything. Like I have everything up to a point, then it's gone. It's just blank. Like I'm trying to remember something that hasn't happened yet."

I squeezed his hand. I didn't know what to say to that but I could at least show him I was listening.

"I can't explain how it feels," he said. "I just woke up and you weren't here and I wasn't sure where I was for a second. Kinda scared me, that's all."

"That's understandable," I whispered. I threaded our fingers and held his hand in both of mine.

"Nothing here is familiar," he mumbled. "But it kinda is. It's hard to explain. I can't remember this place, but it feels right. Like, I feel like I belong here, even though I've never been here before. It's so hard to explain. I'm sorry. I keep talking shit. I just woke up. Guess I'm a bit misty."

"It's okay, Juss. You don't need to apologise. But thank you for telling me how you feel. I'm glad you feel you belong here. This is your place, your things."

He smiled tiredly. "I need to piss. Again."

I snorted out a laugh because apparently this was who we were now. "Okay then, let's get you up."

He groaned. "God, this sucks. Everything's a freaking chore."

I pressed the button on his recliner and the footrest slowly went down and straightened him upright. "It's gotta be a drag for you. Nothing's easy anymore."

He moved cushions out of the way. "Nope."

"It'll get easier every day though," I said, now standing in front of him. I held out my right hand to his left and widened my stance. "Okay, you ready?"

He nodded, took my hand, and I gently pulled him to his feet. He was putting more weight on his right leg but he could only do it for short bursts, but he came to his feet and my hand automatically went to his waist. He was standing up, our bodies so close, our faces so close.

It took my breath away and he chuckled, like he knew exactly the effect he had on me. "Hi," he said gruffly.

I swallowed hard and took a small step back, stepping out of the trance. "Hi." I pulled his scooter closer and helped him sit on it. "Are you dizzy?" I asked.

When he didn't answer, I looked up from where I was helping his right foot onto the footrest to find him watching me. "Nah. Not dizzy."

"You okay?"

He smirked, that cheeky smile where only one half of his lips curled upward. "Yeah. I'm all good."

"Okay."

He scooted himself into the bathroom, and as soon as he was out of view, I walked to the kitchen and put my hands on my knees and finally sucked in some lungs full of air. God, Jesus freaking Christ. Did he even realise he was flirting? Was he even flirting? Did he remember just what that smile did to me?

No, Dallas. He doesn't remember...

The toilet flushed and I stood up straight and got my breathing and stupid heart rate under control.

He scooted out slowly and bypassed the couch and came over to where I was. "Would you mind if I grabbed a bottle of water?"

"You can have anything you want," I replied. I opened the fridge door so he could see inside it. "Anything in the fridge or pantry, or whatever. You don't need to ask." I took a bottle of water out and handed it to him.

"Thanks. Kinda stupid that I need to keep drinking water when taking a piss is a two-man job."

I laughed at that. "Your kidneys will thank you."

"Maybe I could ask the doc to put that catheter back in." He rolled his eyes. "So, you going back downstairs? I mean, to work?"

"It's just paperwork. I can bring it up here if you'd rather have the company."

"No, 's okay." He swallowed and tried to smile. "I'm good now. And you're like two seconds away."

"Sure?"

He nodded. "Sure."

"Okay, well, I better get back to it. I need to get this paperwork done today. They need me on the floor tomorrow and I should get these bills paid. I haven't exactly been around much."

Justin frowned. "Yeah, of course. Sorry. You must . . . be really behind." He turned and backed the scooter up.

"Hey, Jussy," I said gently. He stopped and gave me a sideways glance, so I walked over and stood in front of him. "It was my choice. My priority was you, and I have absolutely zero regrets. I would choose the same again, without hesitation."

He met my eyes. "Still sucks for you though."

I gestured broadly to him. "Not as much as it sucks for you," I said, and he conceded a smile. "No one asked for this. It's not anyone's fault. The universe just handed us a really shitty deal, that's all. And we'll do whatever it takes to get through this. That's what we do. Okay? No guilt, no regrets."

He rolled his eyes. "Are you like some kind of perfect guy? Did they bring out a perfect guy in the last five years that I don't know about?"

That made me smile. "I'm far from perfect. Just you wait till you see how stubborn I can be."

"Like a mule in molasses," he whispered. I stared at him and he gave me a second look. "What?"

"You used to say that," I replied. Whether it was something he used to say before he knew me, from a time when his memory was intact, I couldn't be sure.

"My nan used to say that," he said, but then he shook his head. "Sorry."

"Don't ever apologise."

He searched my eyes for a beat too long, then sighed before he slowly scooted back to the couch. He threw his water bottle on first, then manoeuvred himself onto the sofa, slowly, but by himself, just as Squish came out from the hall. "I wondered where you went," Justin said as he pressed the recline button. Squish jumped on his lap, purring loudly, and they got comfy.

"Can I get either of you something before I go back downstairs?" I asked as I put all the remotes and his phone by his hand.

"Nah, we'll manage, thanks." He gave me a genuine smile. "Thanks. But me and Mr Squish are gonna watch something. Maybe there's a documentary on mice or fish he'd like to watch."

I laughed. "Okay, well, I better leave you to it. I'll just be another few hours, unless I get sick of looking at numbers and decide I should be watching mice or fish with you two."

He was settled in, so I went back downstairs and Davo saw me. "You left in a hurry. Everything okay?"

"Yeah, he's fine. But we could take bets how long it is before he goes batshit crazy with boredom."

Davo laughed, but Sparra obviously overheard. He came over. "My nan had her hip done and we took her jigsaw puzzles and crossword books." He shrugged. "She loved them."

"That's not a bad idea," I thought. His OT had suggested things like that.

"Nah," Davo said. "There's something better than that, and we have a few that need doing too."

"What is it?"

"Puzzles he'd actually be interested in doing. We've got those two old 125 engines that need full rebuilds. All the seals and manifolds need replacing, missing bolts and washers. Cleaning, tuning."

I grinned at him. "That *is* a puzzle he'd like." Those old engines had come off wrecks and had been sat in a corner for years. We were gonna get around to fixing them sometime, just to resell or use on a rebuild. But they needed work and it was time we never made a priority for. "I love that idea. But I might suggest a jigsaw puzzle first. Then when he's sick of doing them and needs to get out of the flat before he goes crazy, we can suggest the engines. His cast comes off next week, so that might be good timing. Give him something new to do, to break the monotony. Because knowing Justin, while he needs the rest and while he gets tired a lot, he's gonna be climbing the walls soon."

Chapter Eleven

I was nervous about Justin's first night at home. He'd got himself changed into some boxers and a T-shirt and brushed his teeth while I cleaned up after dinner. I'd made a chicken salad, after all the crap we'd eaten, and Justin ate it happily, apparently oblivious to my nerves.

The night before he came home from hospital, I'd slept on the sofa bed in the spare room—now my room—because I'd remade his bed with fresh sheets. And while I was excited and grateful to have him home, sleeping in separate rooms wouldn't be easy for me. It was stupid, but it somehow confirmed that things were different between us now.

But giving him a safe place to recuperate was my priority. He certainly didn't need the confusion and pressure of our relationship—a relationship he didn't remember—while recovering from a traumatic brain injury, and I felt like an arse for even thinking about it.

So when he got himself back onto the couch, his leg elevated and his arm supported, he changed the TV channel. "What did you want to watch?"

"I don't mind," I answered, wiping down the sink. "TV shows all suck, but there might be something on Netflix."

He stared at the remote for a while, and when I walked over, he handed it to me. "I dunno how it works," he said, his voice slower and a little slurred. It was always worse when he was tired, especially at night. I took the remote and he gave me a weary smile as he patted the seat right next to him. "Can you sit wi'me?"

"Of course I can."

I sat beside him, not touching, but after a few seconds, he wiggled over and leaned against me, his head on my shoulder. "'S okay?"

"Yeah, of course," I whispered, not trusting my voice for anything more. "You feel okay? How's your head?"

"Mmm, 's okay."

He would have to take his pills before bed, so he couldn't really take anything just yet. We'd organised all his pain meds on an app for his phone and allocated them into those dispensers with each day marked on it, and I'd put the remaining pills in the cupboard above the fridge. We'd marked down all his appointments for the next week on the calendar in the kitchen and in our phones, and during the afternoon he'd written in his journal how he felt about being home and the things he'd 'remembered.' Though as he said, he didn't remember them exactly: my ute and the bedroom. He just knew them. His writing hadn't ever been great, he was certainly never going to win a neat-handwriting award, but it was a bit worse now.

It was crazy how one huge change was made up of a lot of little changes. There were so many things that were different.

But this, us sitting on the couch together like this, was so very much the same. There was always some part of us touching. The *old us* had always curled up on the couch together. It would seem the *new us* did too.

It wasn't easy because I was trying to separate the two versions of us, to give him the space he needed to heal. This Justin needed to be the one to decide if he wanted an *us*, not me. It didn't help my heart at all when he reached over and took my hand.

I was going to ask if he was okay, but his eyes were closed. He wasn't asleep yet, but he was peaceful, and if he needed to hold my hand to help with that, then I wouldn't ever object.

I told my heart to wait, to be patient, and to give him all the room and support he needed. Because if I was being truthfully honest, I needed it too. Having his head on my shoulder, his hand in mine, helped me heal too.

Would it ever become anything more? Only time would tell.

I had hope though, and my heart clung to that like a lifeline.

After a little while and before he fell asleep, I got his pills for him and a glass of water. He used the bathroom again and scooted into his room. He went to his side of the bed and pulled the covers back, but he was too tired to haul himself up and onto the mattress from his seat so I helped him stand and sit on the edge of the bed. He lifted his leg in carefully and lay down. "Oh yeah. This better than hospital bed," he mumbled, half-coherently.

I pulled the blankets up and resisted the urge to lean down and kiss his forehead. Instead, I swiped my thumb across his forehead and his eyes drifted closed. "Night, Justin. I'm really happy you're home," I whispered.

He hummed something I couldn't understand because he was already asleep. So I watched the rise and fall of his chest for a few seconds until Squish jumped up onto the bed and curled himself in close to Justin's side. "You watch him for me," I said, and Squish replied with a purr.

I left his bedroom door open and the bathroom light on, in case he needed it during the night. But I closed my door because I didn't want him to see that it wasn't really a bedroom. It had a sofa and an old desk with a printer that had stopped working long ago. I crawled onto the sofa bed, the protesting springs loud in the quiet flat.

I hated that I was in here and he was in there, but I was just happy he was home. Day one was done. Doubting I'd get much sleep, and with one ear listening for any sounds from Justin, I closed my eyes anyway, and the next thing I knew it was morning.

I HAD the kettle boiling and was buttering toast when Justin came out of the bathroom. He was squinting his right eye the way he did when his headache was particularly bad. Without a word, I grabbed his pillbox thing and set it on the table and poured a glass of water from the tap. "Here, have this," I said as he scooted over.

He downed the tablets without a word, so I knew it was bad. I put a plate of toast in front of him and he gave me a nod.

I squeezed his shoulder gently. "It'll make you feel better." His shoulder was tight under my fingers. "You're all knots. Want me to massage that out?" I asked as I lightly kneaded his shoulder and neck.

He dropped his head and groaned, his eyes closed. "Ugh, that's good."

"Didn't sleep too well?" I asked.

He shook his head. "No."

"Was something wrong?" I asked, moving my massaging fingers to his right shoulder. I was more careful on this side, but the muscles in his shoulders and neck were painfully tight. "Were you uncomfortable? In pain? Feels like you were tense all night."

"No pain," he answered slowly. His head was still down as he enjoyed the massage, but he obviously wasn't going to elaborate.

"Well, if it's something I can fix, like if you need a heater or a fan, just let me know. Or keeping Squish out; I was worried he'd choose your sore leg to use as a pincushion."

"Nah, he's okay," Justin said quietly. I let go of his shoulder and he hummed. "Feels better already, thank you."

"No worries," I said as nonchalantly as I could. "Want some coffee? Kettle just boiled." I'd bought some decaf for home because that was what we drank now, and it didn't even taste that bad. It was just one more small change we'd had to make.

"Mmm, please." He bit into his toast and I went about making two decaf coffees. It was quiet while he ate, and I made more toast before sitting down at the table next to him. "I had nightmares again," Justin said. "Thought they might have stopped . . ." He finished with a shake of his head.

"Maybe we could ask the doc for something to help you sleep," I suggested. "You can't be waking up with your shoulder that bad. It's not doing your arm any favours." Not to mention how bad the lack of sleep was to someone with a brain injury.

He sipped his coffee. "Hmm. Maybe. I think yesterday took more out of me than I realised."

"It might take a few days to get over it," I said. "You know, getting hit by a truck will do that."

He managed a bit of a smile, and his right eye wasn't squinting now. I assumed his morning meds had kicked in. But he needed a day on the couch, or back in bed even. "I need to shower," he said, frowning. He very clearly hated being so dependent.

I just shrugged like it was no big deal at all. "Then let's get you showered."

The rules were no showering alone. Not that I had to be in there with him, but I needed to be close by should he get dizzy or fall, and the door could be ajar but should never be locked. We put the waterproof cover over his arm and he swore he was fine to get out of his boxers by himself, though that did earn me a smile.

The water started and I stood out in the hall like a fucking pervert. I never peeked; I never even wanted to. I just needed to hear if he was sick and to be close by if he fell. I kept expecting to hear the dull thud of his head hitting the glass shower screen if he did fall.

Of course he was fine. I heard the occasional mumble about something to do with hot water and another one about the smell of shampoo. That one made me smile.

Once I heard the water shut off and him mumble something about the towel, I let out a huge sigh of relief. And happy he wasn't a fall-risk, I left him to it.

I pulled the living room blinds half-closed so it wasn't so bright for him. I put a tray on the couch next to him with a bottle of water, some fruit, and a packet of those soy crisps he liked so much.

He scooted out of the bathroom wearing a pair of shorts and nothing else. "Feel a bit better?" I asked.

He gave a bit of a nod and made his way to the couch. He

manoeuvred himself onto it with some effort today. He really must be feeling ordinary. "Hey, Dallas?"

I turned at my name. It had been so long since I'd heard him say my name ... "Yeah?"

He pressed the recliner button. "Could you get me a blanket or something, please?"

"Yeah, of course," I said. I pulled out an older blanket from the linen cupboard and settled it over him. I made sure the remote controls and his phone were beside him. "I'll just be downstairs. I'm five seconds away, that's all. You call me or text me if you need anything, okay?"

He nodded but he made no attempt to turn the TV on. He simply closed his eyes. "Thank you."

I couldn't help myself this time. I leaned down and kissed the top of his head. "You're welcome."

HE WAS asleep when I checked on him at ten o'clock, though his water was half gone and he'd attempted some grapes and a banana.

The TV was on at lunchtime, the volume low. It was replays of football games from the 80s, something that didn't require much thinking. Certainly no plot to follow and no references to the world in the last five years. Justin was staring at it blankly, but he gave me a smile when I walked in.

"Feeling better?"

"Yeah. A bit. I'm still really tired."

"Then you can take it easy for as long as you need."

He gave a pointed nod to the table. "What's that?"

"Jigsaw puzzles," I replied. "Sparra brought them in this morning. Said they were just collecting dust and thought it might give you something to do when you're feeling up to it. Just for something different to do."

He smiled at that. "Okay."

"You hungry?" I asked. "I was gonna make some toasted sandwiches. Ham, cheese, and mustard. Want one?"

"Sure."

The thing with Justin was that he was always agreeable. Mostly. He was so easy to get along with; nothing was ever an issue. But what I'd noticed with his injuries and how they'd affected him was that he would agree to almost anything. Want me to put on a movie? Sure. Want a sandwich? Yep. Magazine? Okay.

It was as though he had no capacity for thinking, for countering, or questioning. Because if he didn't want a sandwich, it just meant I would follow up with more questions, which would require more thinking. If I'd asked him what he wanted on his sandwich, he'd probably just shrug.

Obviously when he was exhausted, all he could do was just go with the flow.

I sat next to him on the couch and offered him a triangle of sandwich, which he took and ate half of. "What're you working on today?" he asked.

"Some Kawasakis. We have a client who has four of them. He and his three kids all ride, and they're heading off on some camping trip for a few weeks where they ride through bike trails. They get full services done every year."

"Sounds fun."

"Oh, for sure."

He was quiet for a second. "Will I ever ride again?"

Oh, God. My heart hurt for him. "Course you will," I said. "Just need a bit of time first."

He nodded and ate another small bite. "Doesn't feel like it today."

"Do you have any pain?"

He gave a gentle shake of his head. "Nah. Just all misty. And really tired."

"Want to go back to bed? Might sleep easier there."

"Hmm," he said, making a face.

I took that as a no.

"I'll just stay here," he said. "Don't want to sleep all day and not be able to sleep tonight."

"Good point," I said as I finished off my lunch. "Can I get you anything else? Need to use the bathroom?"

He seemed to think for a bit. "I could pee."

"Okay then," I said brightly. "Let's get you up."

I stood in front of him and took his hand, pulling him slowly to his feet. I gave him a second to let his head catch up with the change, and when I went to pull away, he held onto my shirt. He put his forehead on my collarbone. "Stay," he whispered.

I didn't dare move. I didn't dare speak. I even tried not to breathe. But my arm moved without my permission, going around him, slow and measured, and as soon as my palm touched his back, he sighed into me. Then he leaned his face against my chest and settled against me. His body, his warmth.

He was everything.

And I remembered a long-ago conversation. He'd once told me when he was younger and struggling with his sexuality, struggling with finding guys who would treat him right, he never had anyone. And all he ever wished for was someone to hold him and tell him that everything would be okay.

He said it would have saved him years of hurt—trying to fill a void left by his mother who hated that he was gay, and trying to find that salvation in men who all treated him like crap—if he'd only ever been held and told that everything would be okay. He'd told me once it wasn't until he'd met me, after I'd held him and promised him things would be okay, that he believed he was even worth loving . . .

My heart burned for him now.

I held him tighter. "It's okay, Juss. You're gonna be just fine," I whispered. "Everything's gonna be okay."

He breathed in deep, as though he was trying to absorb my words, and let out a shaky breath. He was leaning against me, too tired to hold his own weight, and I held him a little tighter. I rubbed his back, feeling him relax under my touch.

"I got you," I murmured against the side of his head. "It's all gonna be okay, Jussy."

He took a few moments to breathe before he sighed and

pulled away. "I really need to pee." He gave me a sad shrug. "But thank you."

"Any time." I put my hand to his face, thumbing just under his eye. "Any time, Justin."

His eyes flickered with something. Was it uncertainty or insecurity? I wasn't sure. It was gone so fast. I pulled my hand away and dragged his scooter over, helping him onto it. He went into the bathroom and I cleaned up after lunch. I replaced his tray with fresh water and fruit and rearranged his cushions for him. I also put his journal beside his seat and the notes from his physio. Not that he *had* to use them, but if he wanted to, he could. He came back out and had obviously splashed water on his face.

"Feeling okay?" I asked.

"Yeah. Better now," he said, managing a bit of a smile.

"Hugs are a pretty strong medicine," I said. "Any time you need one, just ask."

He made a face and chewed on his bottom lip. "We used to do that? Before, I mean?"

I nodded. "Yep. Sometimes you'd have a bad day and I'd hug you until you felt better."

He gave a thoughtful nod. "Seems right. You're good at it, so I guess you had to do it a lot."

I laughed. "Only as required."

He smiled as he transferred himself onto the couch. He seemed happier, and as he pressed the recliner button and his feet slowly came upward, he said, "I don't know whose idea it was to get these push-button recliners, but I'd like to thank them."

"Uh, we actually argued over them."

He shot me a look. "We did?"

I nodded. "You thought it was a waste of money. The ones with the pull handles were cheaper, but I wanted these."

He shook his head, disbelievingly. "I was an idiot. These chairs are great."

I barked out a laugh. "No you weren't. You were cautious with money, that's all."

He pulled his blanket up a bit. "Well, I'm glad you won that argument."

I smiled at the memory of the first night we got that couch. He was still kinda mad about the waste of money, sitting in the same seat he sat in right now, and I'd straddled him on my knees. I pressed the button and we slowly reclined. He'd laughed as I kissed him, and we made out and ended up making passionate love for hours. He never complained about the cost again.

"Me too," I replied. "The day nurse will be here in an hour. Pretty sure it's just a check to see how your first day home went."

"'Kay," he said.

I left him and went back downstairs, and when the nurse arrived, I took her up and introduced them. She asked me about the meds and I showed her everything, but I left them to talk. If he had any concerns, in particular about me, he'd feel more comfortable if I weren't there. But she came back down a short time later, saying everything was fine—his exhaustion was expected after coming home—and that he was resting again.

Me and the boys finished up on the Williams' bikes and had some very happy customers. It was, all in all, a good day. It felt good to be back on the floor, surrounded by familiar sounds and smells of the workshop and to finally be productive at work, but I was glad to call it a day and go check on Justin.

When I walked in, he was sitting on his scooter at the table doing a jigsaw puzzle. "Hey," I said, smiling at his improvement.

"Hey." He frowned at the pieces on the table. "Thought I'd try one of these. But it's not going so well."

I walked over to the table. He'd chosen a beach scene puzzle. "Oh, look at that! You're doing great!" He had all the pieces turned over the right way and he had some colour sorting thing happening and had started to form the border. Putting my hand on his shoulder was such a natural thing for me, to touch him, to show affection, and I pulled away, hoping he wouldn't think too much about it.

When I risked a glance at him, he was blushing a little. His eyes were definitely brighter, so I deduced his headache had lessened. "Thanks."

"I was thinking of having steak and mashed potato for

dinner. Maybe some green beans and honeyed carrots. What do you reckon?"

"That sounds really good," he said. "What about . . . what about if I help you with dinner, then maybe you could help me sort out some of these pieces?"

I grinned at him. He was feeling better, and he was sounding more like Justin. "Perfect."

HE SEEMED to enjoy helping me cook, which was nice. It was like old times to me, but it was new for him, and if his smile was anything to go by, he liked it. I think he actually liked being helpful more than the cooking itself, but I'd take his happiness in whatever form it came. I cut up all the steak for both of us so he wouldn't have to attempt it with his clunky cast, and we ate on the couch with the TV off.

He was happier as he ate, affording me small smiles between bites. He liked the nurse, said she was nice, and asked me about the bikes we'd worked on and what we had to do tomorrow. I explained the jobs we had booked in and he listened intently. I asked him if he wanted to venture out tomorrow at all, and he made a face. "Dunno," he replied. "I'll see how I feel. I would like to, but if I need another day of rest . . . I don't want to feel like I did this morning again."

"Fair enough. And I'm really glad you know when to say no. Oh, and your PT is the day after tomorrow, so maybe another day of taking it easy would be good."

"Does she come here or do I go there?" he asked. "She comes here, right?"

"For this one, yes. She comes here. Next week you have two appointments at the hospital though."

He made a face. "That sounds like fun."

I laughed quietly. "Well, getting your cast off will be worth it. And we could get KFC on the way home, or we could swing past the beach if you want or go to the movies? Anything you want to do."

His gaze darted to mine, and his cheeks went pink again. "What, like a date?"

And just like that, my heart rocketed around in my chest. "Uh, sure. If you're up for a date, then yes. I'd like that very much."

He gave me that shy smile he used to wear a lot when we first got together, when he was interested but unsure of putting his heart on the line. "I'd like that too. But dunno what I'll be up for after a long hospital visit."

"That's a week away. You'll be amazed at how much better you feel in a week," I said, trying not to grin too hard. "Anyway, we can have other dates before then that won't knock you around too much. We can watch movies here, do a jigsaw puzzle together. Oh my God," I said, just realising something. "You get to watch *Game of Thrones* for the first time, all over again."

He snorted out a laugh. "Game of what?"

"*Game of Thrones*. A TV show we watched every week, religiously. We have it on Netflix so we can have date night marathons, if you want?"

He smiled, easy and genuine. "I'd like that."

"And we can re-watch every sporting grand final for the last five years. Footy, ice hockey, surfing world championships . . . the list is endless."

"So having the last five years deleted from my mind isn't all bad, right?" he said, trying to smile.

"Well, we need to look for the positives, right? And if doing things again for the first time with you is one of them, then yeah, I'll take it."

He frowned a bit and his eyebrows furrowed. "Did we have a first date?"

"Sure we did. Want me to tell you about it?"

He nodded.

I took his empty plate with mine and slid them onto the coffee table for now. "Well, we had our first kiss in my office, which I told you about."

"Davo locked us in there," he added.

I laughed. "He did. Anyway, so we kissed, and it was incredible. Which kind of sucked because it was the middle of the day and we both had so much work to get done. So yeah, we were a bit handsy, but we needed to cool it and get through to knock-off time. Which we did, by the way. Even though Davo complained the tension was worse by four o'clock." I let out an embarrassed laugh and ignored the heat in my cheeks. "Davo and Sparra left for the day, but you hung around, and I asked you to come upstairs with me."

"Wow, you moved fast," he said with a grin.

"To talk. I asked you upstairs to talk."

He raised a disbelieving eyebrow at me.

"I did, I promise. Actually, as soon as we got through the door, I said, 'Uh, we need to talk,' and you said, 'Well shit, that doesn't sound good,' and you told me later you were worried that I was going to fire you. Which, God, I never would. But anyway, that kinda made the point of the whole need to talk. We needed to put down some professional-slash-personal boundaries and decide how we were going to work this. We both agreed that work was a priority, in the beginning, and we wouldn't let anything else between us become an issue in the workplace."

He nodded. "Sounds fair."

"And we agreed that one-night things weren't our style so we agreed that some actual dates would be fun."

He smiled.

"Then we almost broke my dining table making out on it."

His eyes went wide, his jaw slack. "No . . ."

I laughed. "Yep. Your bodyweight it could hold. Mine on top of yours, not so much."

His grin matched mine. "We did that?"

"Yep. It was old and needed replacing anyway. The legs went on it in the end."

He sighed loudly. "I wish I could remember that."

Me too, Jussy. Me too.

"But that wasn't really a date. I mean, we did eat . . . later that night." I cleared my throat, embarrassed at saying this stuff out loud. "But the next weekend I took you out for dinner. We went to La Mensa, an Italian place, which we went back to a dozen times. I brought you back here afterward, and you kinda never left."

He stared at me. "From one week? I never left?"

I laughed. "Nope. You rented a place when you moved back from Darwin. But it was kinda small and it wasn't great, and you didn't have much because you sold it all so you could move back here. It's cheaper to buy new furniture than it is to pay to move it all a few thousand miles."

"Yeah, true. And what I had in Darwin wasn't worth much anyway," he said. "I can remember Darwin just fine. Like it was just a few weeks ago."

I took his hand. "I know, Jussy. It all must seem strange to have someone explain this all to you."

"It is." He nodded, but his hold on my hand tightened. "But tell me, what happened next?"

"Your lease agreement was coming up on where you were, so you gave notice and moved in here with me. I think we'd been seeing each other for just a few weeks. It was quick and people probably thought we were crazy. But we just . . . clicked."

He leaned his head against the back of the couch but he never took his eyes off me. "I, uh . . ." He shook his head and laughed. "This is so weird. Because I don't know you. I mean, not really. But you know everything about me." Blush coloured his cheeks. "I'd like to, I'd like to get to know you, that is. And I'd really like to go on a date with you."

I laughed, my heart so full it felt like it would burst. I took his hand and squeezed it. "I'd really like that too."

He laughed too, but then he looked right into my eyes and it really felt like he was seeing me for the first time. "But you should know something before we start dating."

My heart skipped several beats. "Oh yeah, what's that?"

"Well, apart from the brain injury and amnesia, which sucks, I also have a broken arm and a leg with a new internal suspension system," he said with a smile, and it made me chuckle. "I'm a bit of a mess, actually. Just so you know what you're getting yourself in for."

I squeezed his hand again, and now that we were 'officially

dating' I turned his hand over and kissed his palm, then held his hand to my face. "I know what I'm getting into, Juss. And I can tell you, without any doubt, that you're worth it."

He smiled tiredly at me as he gently scratched my beard. "I like this."

"You've always liked it. I shaved it once and you hated it."

A slow smile caught his lips and he slow blinked. "Sounds about right."

"You're tired," I whispered. "Why don't you go get ready for bed and I'll tidy up in here."

He sighed. "Hate not being able to do stuff."

"I know. But it'll get better. I know it seems slow to you, but I see improvements every day."

"Today sucked."

"Well, today sucked because yesterday we did too much. We know now that reaching your limit isn't worth it. But I reckon tomorrow you'll be as good as gold."

"Hope so. Got a date with a real hottie tomorrow night."

I laughed. "Is that right?"

"Yep."

"That's a coincidence," I said, smiling. "Because I do too."

He looked at me, his brow creased, his face sad. "You do? But . . ."

I laughed and rubbed his arm. He was obviously too tired to process sarcasm, another change since his accident. "My date is with you, Juss. You're the cutie I have a date with."

"Oh." He shook his head and laughed. "Sorry. Tired."

"Come on," I said, standing up. I held out my hand and pulled him to his feet. We were barely an inch apart and he put his forehead on my chest again and sighed.

"You do good hugs," he mumbled.

So I wrapped my arms around him again, holding him tight and breathing him in. He was heavy against me and I rubbed his back. He let out another sigh, long and loud, and then he got heavier. "Okay," I said, waking him up. "You need some sleep."

"Jigsaw puzzle," he mumbled.

"We can do that tomorrow."

I helped him onto his scooter and he sighed again, his eyes heavy-lidded, but he got himself to the bathroom. I took our plates back to the sink and had the washing up almost done by the time he came back out. He took his night pills and I helped him into his bed. He was using his leg more, but with only one arm and being so bone-tired, it was all too much.

Squish joined him as soon as I had the covers pulled up and I left the two of them sleeping. I finished cleaning up and put everything away, and I never stopped smiling.

He wanted to date me. He wanted to go on actual dates, and he wanted to know more about me. He liked holding my hand and he liked my beard. He blushed like he used to when we first met, when we were first together, and he was nervously excited about being with me.

And that gave me butterflies.

Actual tummy jitters. I was so happy, I went to bed excited for what tomorrow might bring.

BUT THEN, somewhere in the dead of night, a scream woke me up. I shot bolt upright in bed, wondering if I'd dreamed it . . . But then a gasp and sob echoed from the room across the hall.

"Dallas? Dallas, please."

Chapter Twelve

I FLEW OUT of bed and into Justin's room. He was sitting up on
the bed with his left hand on his head, and he was breathing hard.
"Hey," I whispered.

He looked up at me. His eyes were wide, even in the dark
room. He shook his head. "Dream."

"Oh, baby," I said, going to him. I sat on the edge of the bed
next to him and put my hand on his arm. "You're okay."

He sobbed and sniffled. "Stay. Please?"

"Of course," I said. I went around to my side—or rather,
what had been my side—and slipped in under the covers. I slid
over and urged him to lie back down and gently pulled him into
my arms. He came willingly, snuggling into me just like he used
to do. His head was on my shoulder, and his plastered arm was
heavy on my chest but it felt good. The weight of it was comforting. I rubbed his back and whispered sweet nothings into the top
of his head.

Justin's ragged breathing evened out, and in no time at all, he
was out like a light.

He slept soundly, like he hadn't slept that good in weeks. It
was a deep, heavy sleep, and I smiled at the ceiling. I knew that
this meant different things to us. It was purely to comfort him,
but God, it was a comfort to me too.

Our breathing synced, the rise and fall of our chests, our

heartbeats . . . I closed my eyes, relishing in this most wonderful feeling.

The next thing I knew, it was morning.

I WAS up before him and thought it would be best if he didn't wake up and freak out that I was in his bed. I slipped out from under the covers and pulled on a shirt, then went and made us some breakfast. I carried the tray of decaf coffee and toast into the room and he stirred awake.

"Morning," I said, unable to keep from smiling.

"Mmm," he said, trying to wake up.

"Breakfast in bed today," I said.

He sat up, leaning against the headboard, bleary-eyed. "Oh, morning."

"How do you feel?"

"Good." He looked to my sleep-rumpled side of the bed. "Oh. Sorry about last night."

I slid the tray onto the bed. "Don't apologise. It was fine. I, um, actually, I slept like the dead."

He hummed. "Me too. I slept all night. Apart from the nightmare . . . but when you were here, it was . . . good. Best sleep ever."

I handed him a coffee. "Do you remember the nightmare?"

He shook his head. "Nah. It's just darkness and falling. It's awful." He sipped the coffee and sighed. "But I dreamed the other dream again, I think. Afterwards. I dunno. Not much makes sense in my head. It's hard to tell if it's a dream or reality. If I'm remembering something or if it's just a dream."

The other dream? "What was it?"

He made a face. "The poster dream."

Oh, that's right. The Harley Davidson poster.

"I dunno. It's like a sign or a poster, I think. Whether it's just a dream or if I saw it one time, I dunno."

I chuckled and bit into a piece of toast. "Dream of bikes often?"

He laughed quietly and put his cup down and picked up a slice of toast. "Not really. This Harley poster is a repeat though."

"You've dreamed of it often?"

He nodded as he chewed and swallowed. "I thought there might be something like it here. It feels like it should be at home. Is there a poster in the workshop?"

"Nope. There's a KTM poster, which you put up. And a Yamaha one the rep gave us to match your KTM one as a joke. And just some bike calendars and promo posters for tyres and stuff. But no Harleys. We've been to a few trade shows though. Maybe you saw something there. The doc said what comes back to you could be random."

He shrugged it off. "Something not random would be good." He washed the last of his toast down with a sip of coffee. "God, I wish I could cut this cast off. It's itchy as hell. I'm just about done with it. Do we have any saws downstairs? Angle grinders?"

"You're not using an angle grinder on your arm."

"A hacksaw?"

"I'm going to go with a hard no on that one too. I'll drive you to hospital and you can beg them to take it off before you try to use power tools."

"Today?"

Shit. He was being serious.

"If you want."

He took another mouthful of coffee and seemed to consider his options. "Do you think they'll take it off for me?"

"I think they will if I tell them you want to use an angle grinder on it."

He smirked, then it faded. "Shit. I have the nurse and physio coming today."

"We can ask them if you're ready to have it taken off. If they say yes, then we can go tomorrow."

He sighed. "I just want my body back, ya know? I don't want the cast or the scooter thing anymore. I can deal with the amnesia —well, I can't but I don't have much choice—but if I could just walk to the freaking bathroom, that'd be great."

"It's frustrating," I said.

"Beyond that."

"Well, hopefully the doc will say yes to taking the cast off. The last X-ray was good and you've had no pain."

He eventually smiled. "You always know what to say."

"No I don't," I admitted. "Not always."

"I think you do. Like just now when you said you'll make more coffee and toast while I go pee. That'd be great, thanks."

I laughed at that. "Message received and understood." I took the tray from the bed and went back to the kitchen to start on more coffee and toast while he got himself to the bathroom. When he came back out, he used his scooter, of course, but he was using his right leg more and more, which was a good sign. His eyes were bright and he was happy.

A complete one-eighty from the day before. It was amazing what decent sleep could do.

He took his pills, ate the toast, and took a long sip of coffee. "What time are my appointments again?"

"Physio at nine, nurse at ten." It was just seven-thirty now.

"So, I have enough time to come downstairs for a bit first?"

"Oh, sure. Do you think you're up for it?"

"Yep."

"You don't think it might be pushing your luck after how tired you were yesterday?"

"Nah. I feel really good today. Probably best I've felt since I woke up. From the accident, I mean. Not woke up this morning."

I snorted. "Yeah, I gathered that."

"And anyway," he added, "if I get too tired, you can carry me back up the stairs."

"Is that right?"

"Yep."

He was in such a good mood, I didn't want to dampen it with my worrying. "Then I better go get showered and get ready for work."

When I walked back out, dressed for the day, I saw he was dressed too but he'd also washed up our few breakfast things. "You didn't have to do that," I said, nodding to the sink.

"I want to. I need to do my share. What I can do, at least."

"Well, thank you. I appreciate it."

He beamed, then took a steadying breath. "Okay. I want to see the workshop and some sunshine, and I have about an hour before my first torture appointment."

I went to the front door and held it open. "Then let's do this."

He stood at the top of the stairs, holding onto the railing while I took his scooter down to the bottom, then I went back up to the second step from the top. "Right. One step at a time."

He did the first few steps, slow and somewhat awkwardly. "Ugh. Going up's so much easier."

"It's okay. We got this," I said, keeping my hands on him. He took another step, then another and another, and finally he was at the bottom.

His grin of accomplishment was beautiful.

He got back on his scooter and put his right foot up on the footrest, and I unlocked the huge roller door and lifted it up. This place had once been a regular mechanics so the roller doors were wide and tall enough to let a truck through. I went inside, flipped the lights on, and unlocked the matching roller door at the front of the shop. I unlocked the padlock on the front gates and opened them wide, and when I went back inside, Justin was sitting on his scooter in the middle of the workshop.

He had his eyes closed and his serene smile damn near took my breath away.

"I know this smell," he said.

Every mechanic's shop smelled of grease and oil, tyres and exhaust. It permeated every surface. "Smells like work to me."

He chuckled but shook his head. "No. I know this smell, Dallas." He swallowed hard and looked down toward the office. "And I know that's my station. And I know there's a fridge in the breakroom with a scratch down the door. And I know there's an old radio on the bench in the corner and it gets better reception when it rains . . ." He put his hand to his mouth. "Oh my God, I remember."

He remembers . . .

He shot me a look, his eyes wide and a little watery. "I remember this."

I went to him and cupped his face in my hands. "You remember it." My voice was a whisper. "Baby, you remember."

"I remember."

I had to stop myself from kissing him. I wanted to, God, how I wanted to. I was just so happy I could have cried! I dropped my hands and looked around the workshop, trying to see it through his eyes. "What else do you remember?"

"I don't know. Nothing really. Just bits and pieces. And it's not really a memory. It's just that I *know* where my station is. I *know* about the fridge and the radio. I just know."

"That is so awesome," I said, because it really was. All these tiny pieces of the puzzle would eventually help form the picture of his missing years. The fact I wasn't yet any of the pieces stung a little, I couldn't lie.

He remembered this place. He remembered my ute. He remembered tiny pieces of our lives.

But he didn't remember me.

Justin scooted down to the office, peeking in, then he looked in the break room. He grinned when he saw the fridge with the scratch. "How did it get scratched like that?"

So he remembered the fridge and the scratch, but he didn't remember being with me when we bought it.

"Bought it like that. It was one of those clearance sales of damaged stock. They couldn't sell it at full price, but there's nothing wrong with it. Apart from the scratch."

He scooted back slowly, looking at the different work stations: his, Davo's and Sparra's. Being down here obviously made him happy. Eventually his eyes went to our bikes, and more importantly, to his. His wide gaze shot to mine, and he grinned. "Is that mine?"

"Sure is."

He scooted over to it and touched the tank, the seat. "Holy shit."

"You'll ride again," I said. "One day."

He nodded. "One day." Then he looked around, searching for something. "There's no poster of a Harley."

"What?"

"The Harley Davidson poster I see in my dreams. It's not here. I know you said it wasn't, but I thought there might be something . . . It just feels so familiar, like it's something I see all the time."

Before I could question him on that, Davo drove into the yard. He and Sparra got out, bickering about something on the radio as they walked in. "Heyyyy," Davo said as soon as he saw Justin. "Look who finally decided to turn up for work." He offered him a left-handed bro-shake, and Justin laughed as he took it.

"Sorry, had some time off," Justin said. "Apparently. Like five years or something."

We all laughed, and Sparra shook Justin's hand too. "Good to see ya up and about, mate."

"Yeah, feels good," he said, still smiling. "Hey, have either of you guys got an angle grinder or an electric saw?"

I snorted. "Juss, you can't cut your cast off with a power tool."

Davo laughed. "Well, we *could*." Then he sized up Justin's arm cast. "Just how fond of the arm are you?"

I snorted. "Exactly my point."

Justin laughed, but then he tapped the cast with his knuckle. "It's driving me crazy. My arm is so freaking itchy."

"My brother used to shove Mum's knitting needles down his to scratch his arm," Sparra said. "We don't got no knitting needles, but I reckon a welding rod might work."

Davo brightened. "Or what about a long reach screwdriver? They're heaps long and skinny."

I shook my head but couldn't help but laugh. I guessed this was what happens when a group of mechanics tries to find solutions for an itchy arm stuck in a cast. It made me happy as the three of them went off in search of something resembling a knitting needle for Justin to scratch with under his cast. They weren't just workmates, but they were his actual mates, and he needed them.

All the pieces of the puzzle, Dallas. Not just the pieces of you.

Turns out the long reach screwdriver was a bit bulkier than they'd first thought, and the welding rod was a no-go as well.

"Here," I said, holding up a pro-lock tool. "Try this."

Sparra laughed. "Ah, when in doubt, use the slim jim."

Justin grinned as he scooted over to me. "Break into cars often?"

"Not since I was a good-for-nothin' teenager, no," I admitted. "Now I keep it in case someone locks their keys or their kid in a car."

He shoved it down the top of the arm cast and groaned. "Holy shit, that feels so good."

"We have a winner!" Sparra cried.

But I was still stuck on Justin's groan and the look of bliss on his face. God help me . . .

Davo nudged me with his elbow. Bastard never missed much. "Work to do," Davo said as he walked off, still smirking.

Right, yes. Work.

Davo called out, "Jusso, you're with me."

I opened my mouth to object, but Justin gave me a grin before he scooted off after Davo. Sparra clapped my back. "You snooze, you lose," he said with a shit-eating grin. "You get to help me. I got that seized-up Honda to pull apart."

So for the next little while, I helped Sparra with that while keeping one eye on Justin. Davo had him holding some boxes. I heard Davo say, "You're not useless. You still got one good arm," as he piled on another box. I might have objected, but Justin's smile told me to shut my trap.

"He's better today," Sparra said quietly.

"Yeah. He got some decent sleep. Makes a helluva difference." I looked over to Justin and Davo, who were now both in front of a bike Davo was working on. It was an old Yamaha in for an overhaul, and Davo was talking about something to do with the front forks. "He remembered a few more things," I said to Sparra. "Just little things, but it's something, at least."

"Oh man, that's awesome!" he said, his enthusiasm trailing off. "That's a good thing, right?"

I shook my head in some attempt to clear the self-centred funk. "Yeah, it is. It's great."

"But?"

"But nothing."

"But it weren't about you," he whispered, more insightful than I'd have given him credit for.

"It weren't about me," I said, just as quietly. "Which shouldn't matter."

Sparra just kept right on working, trying to get a spark plug out. "Dallas, he's been over there with Davo for three minutes and he looked back over here for you about ten times already." His gaze went from the spark plugs over to Justin and back again. "Make that eleven. He's still yours. No memory loss gonna change that. I never did see what he gone fell in love with you once for, and now he's about to do it twice."

I laughed at that, but Sparra's words—as blunt as he was—really hit me hard. I kept my back to Justin and Davo. "Has he been looking over here?"

Sparra shook his head and cranked the handle of the spanner, straining to get it to budge. "Does Davo need to lock you both in the office again?"

I snorted. "Ah, no. Probably not."

Just then, a car pulled into the yard and Justin's physiotherapist got out. "Jusso, you're up."

He scooted over to the open doorway. "Oh good. My dial-a-torturer is here."

She laughed at that but gestured to him, up and down. "But look at you. Shouldn't you be taking it easy?"

"I'm not working or anything," he said. "And I've only been down here for about thirty minutes."

She rolled her eyes like she'd heard it all before. "So, we upstairs?"

"Yep. This way," he said, leading her through the workshop to the back stairs. I followed them, of course, because he was going to need me on the stairs. He stood up at the bottom, holding onto the railing, and I carried his scooter up before darting back down to help. He managed the stairs well though; going up was much easier than down. And his PT watched on like it was a test, which it probably was.

But he got to the top without too much effort—a vast difference since his first day—and he scooted inside. He didn't need me to stay so I left them to it, and she was already asking him a whole bunch of questions by the time I got out of earshot.

We had a delivery truck arrive with boxes of parts, and I figured it was a good time to run through a quick stock count. A short while later, I heard a female voice ask where I was, and Davo appeared with Justin's PT in tow. I put my clipboard down. "Oh, you're done already?"

"Yeah, he's had enough of me for today."

"Is he okay?"

She laughed. "He's doing great. He managed the stairs perfectly. Which I told him I wasn't too happy about but made him promise that he'd never attempt them, up or down, by himself."

"Yep. I told him that too. Did he tell you that his coming-home day wrecked him? He was so tired yesterday. He only kinda come good yesterday afternoon, but he's been great this morning."

"Yeah, he said that. I told him he should rest all afternoon. He said he would try." She rolled her eyes at that. "But he's been doing his exercises, which is good, and the jigsaw puzzle was a good idea. I've given him new exercises, and if he gets the cast off tomorrow— and that's a big if—he'll need to work on that arm."

"He asked about getting his cast off?"

"Oh yes."

"Did he tell you about the angle grinder?"

"The *what*?"

I snorted. "He wanted to take it off with an angle grinder, but I said no."

"Well, thank God for you," she said with her hand to her heart. "Keep him away from power tools, and I'll see you both next week. You keep looking after him and he'll be right as rain in no time at all."

Smiling at that, I waved her off and I wanted to go check on him but didn't even get to the bottom of the stairs before another car pulled in. It was his nurse, so I showed her upstairs too. Justin was getting a bottle of water out of the fridge when we came in. After seeing he was fine, I headed back to the door, but Justin called out, "Dallas? Can you stay?"

"Sure," I said, not really knowing why he wanted me to stay. But when I sat beside him, he was quick to take my hand. "You okay?" I asked.

He nodded but glanced toward the nurse, who was still getting out her equipment. She checked his meds and his journal, took his blood pressure, his temperature, shone her little light thing in his eyes and ears. She sat on the coffee table and asked him a whole bunch of questions about how he was handling being home, all while writing everything down.

She checked the movement of his fingers on his plastered hand, checked over his injured leg, and was happy with how everything was progressing, physically. He was exactly where they expected him to be, if not a little further ahead.

"Headache?" she asked.

"Yeah, it never really goes away. Just get used to it, I guess. I don't like taking the pills, but I can tell when they're wearing off."

"Any nausea with the headaches?"

Justin shook his head. "No."

"Good." She smiled. "And in your journal, you said you've had some memory triggers?"

"Well, yeah. More today, just this morning, so I didn't write them in yet. But it's hard to explain. It's not like a memory with anything attached to it." He licked his lips and squeezed my hand, and I knew this was what he needed me here for. "It's just things I know that I know. Like I knew Dallas' ute when I saw it. I knew it was his. But there were no flashback scenes of us driving anywhere, or being in the ute at all. I just knew it was his. And I knew the fridge in the break room had a scratch down the front. I didn't see it, I knew before I looked in there. But there was no memory of it, I just knew it was there."

"Okay, that all sounds perfectly normal," she said gently. "I'm not a neurologist but I work with a lot of traumatic brain injuries, and what happens for one person will differ to the next. You should definitely speak to your doctor though."

"So why is it stuff that doesn't matter?" he asked. "I never cared about the fridge before. I never cared about the stupid old radio, but I knew it was in the corner, and I knew it got crap reception unless it was raining outside." He shook his head. "Why do I remember useless shit like that?"

"Some people say that the beginning of regaining memories is like poking pinholes in a dark fabric, letting tiny circles of light in. Little ones at first, and there's no saying what comes through the holes. Sometimes it seems irrelevant, like you said, but you are recovering some memories. Some people don't even get that."

He sighed. "I know. I just . . . I guess I hoped . . ." He looked at me, frustrated and sad.

"I think he wants to know why he can't remember me?" I offered gently.

Justin's face crumpled. "It's all I want. Just something. I don't care about the goddamn fridge. I want memories of you," he said, his expression so vulnerable. "And I want to feel what goes with it. That's the hardest part. It's not just losing the memories. I lost the feelings as well, and I want that back."

"Oh, Juss," I said, putting my hand to his face. "We'll get back to that. You fell in love with me once, what's to say you can't love me twice?"

His eyes welled with tears. "God, that is so unfair to you. I hate how unfair it is to you. Every time I say or do something that makes you think I've remembered more, you get a look in your eyes, like hope. And to see it fade out when you realise I still don't remember you, it just fucking kills me. It's like a light going out, every time. I wish I could remember. I want to, so much. God, you have no idea." He was mad, about as pissed off as I'd seen him. I wanted to reassure him, but he needed to vent and get this out. He deserved that.

"And you know what?" he said. "It's unfair to me too. I hate that it was taken away from me. Not just my memories, but who I am. Who I was. Who *we* were, Dallas. I want memories that mean something. I want memories that I can feel. Instead, all I get is a nightmare where everything's black and I'm falling and that scares the shit outta me, or some weird Harley Davidson poster that I need to find. I can't explain why, but it's important."

"I'm sorry," the nurse said. "A poster?"

Justin nodded. "It's so stupid. But I see this poster and I feel it in my chest. Like right here." He put his hand to his heart. "Like it means something to me I can't explain. It means the world to me and I can't even describe it, but I can feel it."

"Try describing it," I said. "Tell us what you see. Maybe we've seen it somewhere."

He wiped at his eye and shook his head. "It's a Harley Davidson poster, or at least I think it is. The poster with the logo, but in my dream there's no words. Nothing in my brain makes sense. The tighter I try to hold it, the more it disappears."

I squeezed his hand. "Oh, baby."

The nurse was scrolling on her phone. She turned the screen toward us. "Like one of these?"

He scanned the pictures of different Harley Davidson posters, shaking his head. "No . . . no . . . no." Then he froze. "That one. With the wings."

She tapped on it and made it bigger. "This one?"

He nodded quickly. "That one. With the wings. What does it mean?"

I looked at the picture, then looked at Justin, and . . . holy shit. It felt as though the world had stopped turning. I laughed and then had to bury my face in my hands so he didn't see me cry.

"Dallas, what is it? What's wrong?" Justin asked. "You know what this means?"

I dropped my hands, not caring if I fucking cried in front of them. I simply didn't care. I began unbuttoning my shirt to some very strange looks from both the nurse and Justin, but I pulled my shirt off, then pulled my T-shirt over my head so they could see my chest.

Or, more importantly, the two huge wings tattooed across my chest.

Justin stared at the tattoos, then his wide eyes met mine. "It's you. Oh my God, it's you." He burst into tears and put his hand to his mouth. "I remember you. My heart, all this time, oh God . . ."

I pulled him in for a hug and he cried against my chest for a second until he pulled away and pushed my arm. "You didn't tell me you had this tattoo!"

"I wasn't about to be half-naked in front of you. And you told me your dream was of a Harley Davidson poster!"

"I said it didn't make sense. Don't blame me, my brain got scrambled, remember?"

I burst out laughing, so relieved. So very relieved.

He remembered something about me.

I put my hand to his face, so desperate to kiss him. To feel his familiar lips, his mouth, to hold him, kiss him, taste him . . .

Until the nurse cleared her throat.

"Oh," I said, pulling my hand away. I swallowed hard and shook my head. I had to wipe tears from my face. "Sorry."

"Don't apologise," she said, smiling. "If only every home visit was like this." She got to her feet and started to pack up. She told us to keep doing everything we were doing, to keep writing down in the journal every day, and to call if anything changed.

Just as she got to the door, I remembered something and followed her. "Uh, sorry. The cast. It's due to come off next week. Can he have it off sooner? Please? Like tomorrow?"

She gave Justin a stern look. "If he promises to wear the collar and cuff."

I baulked. "The what?"

"Collar and cuff. It's a sling to support the upper arm bone from the shoulder down."

"Oh." I made a face, because boy, collars and cuffs had a completely different meaning. "Thank God, I thought you meant—"

She raised her hand. "I know what you meant." She gave us a

wink, told Justin to rest well, and promised to see us next week. Then she was gone.

I closed the door, and when I turned to face Justin, he was standing up. He took some very tentative steps toward me without the scooter, without any assistance. He was slow and trod gingerly on his sore leg, but he was determined.

He came to stand in front of me. I held his good arm, taking some of his weight. He trailed his fingers across my tattoo with the barest of touches. It sent a shiver through me. "I remember," he whispered. "Not you, exactly. But I remember something. I remember these tattoos. And I remember how you made me feel. And I don't know you the same as you know me, but my heart does. This is the only memory I can feel." He looked at me with tears in his eyes. "My heart remembers you."

I ran my thumb along his cheek and gently lifted his chin and oh so slowly pressed my lips to his. His lips were soft and warm, his taste familiar. He closed his eyes and leaned into me, letting himself be held. And even though we'd kissed thousands of times, this was our first.

Our very first kiss all over again.

Chapter Thirteen

JUSTIN

Finally something made sense.

Finally.

When I first woke up in that hospital, everything hurt. Every part of me. Even with the drugs, my brain still registered pain. It was muted and simmering, but it pulsed under the surface. Pain like you cannot imagine.

My leg, my arm, my chest, but my head.

Wow.

The pain in my head. It was bewildering.

I don't remember the first few days. It all passed in a blur of excruciating pain and nausea, dizziness, vertigo, beeping machines and the cold, metallic hum of drugs.

Then things came back to me in ebbs and flows. The doctors, the nurses, that warm, strong hold on my hand that kept me tethered to reality.

I knew who I was. My name was Justin Keith, I was born in Newcastle, New South Wales, but now lived in Darwin, Northern Territory. I was twenty-five years old.

Except I wasn't.

Apparently.

At first I thought they were joking. Until the doctors became serious and started running more tests and they brought me newspapers that showed the date five years into the future, which was a pretty cool trick.

Except it wasn't.

Apparently.

And all the while, there was that guy who I saw all the time. He was sexy as hell, had brown hair with a tint of grey at his temples. He had dark circles under his blue-grey eyes, and there was a bleakness to him that told me this was all real.

I was thirty now, apparently.

I'd moved back to Newcastle almost five years ago and I worked as a mechanic. That made sense because I *was* a mechanic, and I hadn't been having the best time in Darwin, so that wasn't so hard to believe.

But how the hell was I thirty?

How did five years just disappear?

It felt like someone had written my life on a whiteboard, then wiped the last five years off. I had zero recollection. Zero knowledge, zero connection.

And that was the hardest part. The emotional disconnect. I had no emotional attachments to anything or anyone that had been part of my life in the past five years. I couldn't remember them, like they'd never existed. How could I feel something for someone who never existed?

They told me that handsome stranger was my boyfriend, which might have been the craziest part of the whole nightmare, because how the hell could someone like me jag someone like him? But no, not even just boyfriend, but live-in boyfriend. Oh, and he's my boss too.

I didn't know him, not the first thing about him, but I could see how sad he was and how hopeful he'd get, or a hint of light in his eyes before it faded away when reality dawned.

No, I didn't know him.

But I liked him, and I trusted him. I couldn't explain why, I just did.

Could this have been some Jason-Bourne-type plot to play evil mind games with me? Well, it was highly unlikely. But no. Not Dallas.

He was big and burly, but he was gentle and kind. His smile made my days in hospital bearable. My days were filled with tests and physio, pain and more pain. My nights were filled with strange dreams, which at first were heavily medicated, but as the doses decreased, the weirdness increased.

The falling nightmare was dark and awful, filled with fear and the unknown. My therapist said it sounded like symbolism for the accident and not knowing what the future might bring. I wasn't convinced. It was just fucking falling and darkness to me. And it was a fresh hell every time. You'd think you'd get used to it, but no.

My other dream was different. It was a pair of wings. But it was misty, like my mind, though it wasn't swirling around the wings. It was covering them, as though my mind wasn't ready to show me the whole picture. I was certain they were the wings from the Harley Davidson vintage ads I'd loved as a kid. At least, that's what they reminded me off. That was all I had to go by.

But it was how they made me feel . . . that was the strangest part. Just like the falling dream was fear and a screaming heart rate, the wing dream was comfort and safety. It was love. Which made no sense.

My therapist jumped straight onto the wings-equal-religion train, and how the warmth and safety I felt might have been me wanting to reach out to God. I told him I had amnesia, not delusions. It wasn't symbolic of heaven or angels . . . I knew that.

"There must have been a poster at my home or work," I'd said, and it was plausible enough.

But there were no such posters in the flat or at work.

Because Dallas had them tattooed on his fucking chest. And my beacon to him, my warmth and safety, had been right in front of me the whole time.

I wasn't kidding when I said I wanted to know him, to date him. I wanted it more than anything. Me coming home from the hospital had proven that. He'd been amazing. He gave me independence when I needed it, and he helped me when I needed it. He was considerate and kind and funny, and he smelled so good . . .

And he was my Harley Davidson poster. He was my wings dream, what my heart yearned for. What my heart was trying to show me.

And all those weeks wondering why I couldn't remember him or what he meant to me were over. Because now I knew.

I walked over to him, limping and slow, but so help me God, I was going to do this on my own. I stood in front of him and traced my fingers over the wings I'd seen in my dreams. *I knew these tattoos.* I looked up into his blue-grey eyes, and my heart . . . my heart knew.

"I remember," I whispered. "Not you, exactly. But I remember something. I remember these tattoos. And I remember how you made me feel. And I don't know you the same as you know me, but my heart does. This is the only memory I can feel." I took in his handsome face. "My heart remembers you."

My heart remembers you.

He took my face in his hands and kissed me, tender and sweet, but with emotion he could barely contain. When he broke the kiss, he pressed his forehead to mine, his eyes closed. "Oh, Justin," he breathed. "My heart remembers too."

"You're a really good kisser," I whispered. I was giddy and excited and so fucking relieved. It made him laugh.

He thumbed my cheek and scanned my face, settling on my eyes. "That's not the first time you've said that to me."

"I'd like to do more of it, if that's okay?"

He grinned. "That's very okay."

But as he brought his lips to mine once more, I stopped him. "Uh, wait."

"What's wrong?" His expression quickly worried. "Is it your leg? Headache?"

"No." I took his hand and laced our fingers, unable to stop my smile. "I know this is going to sound weird, considering we live together and considering what I assume we've done . . . in the bedroom." God, that was awkward to say out loud. "But I'd like . . . I'd, uh . . ." I sighed. How could I ask this of him? When he'd already given up so much? "My entire life got thrown upside down. Everything I thought I knew is different now, and . . ."

One corner of his mouth curled upward. "You want to get to know me first."

My cheeks flamed. "Am I that obvious?"

"Obvious, no. But I know you, Juss. And when we first got together, you wanted to know me first."

"I thought you said I moved in with you just weeks after we first kissed."

"You did." He laughed. "And it was an intense few weeks. But you said you'd had enough of shitty men and one-night stands."

I nodded. "Those I remember." Hurt flashed in his eyes. Because I remembered them and not him. "Sorry, Dallas. I know that's not fair on you."

He shook his head. "Don't apologise. It's not your fault. There are pieces of you that are a part of me, and I'll help you find them. I promise you, Justin. I don't care how long it takes. I'll wait until you're certain. I'll wait forever if I have to."

"I don't think it'll take forever," I said, marvelling at the square angle of his jaw, the warmth in his eyes. "Our first date tonight will be a good start."

His grin widened and he let out a laugh. "That sounds good to me."

"You don't mind? I mean, we live together and I'm guessing we've gone further than kissing before. I mean, I still have that photo of me and we're very clearly doing a lot more than kissing in that photo."

He chuckled and gently lifted my chin, kissing me chastely. "I don't mind one bit. You know what's better than getting to do all that for the first time with you? It's getting to do it all for the first time again."

This time I slid my hand along his jaw and brought his mouth to mine. He tasted like a long-lost summer day, something I was so very familiar with but couldn't exactly recall. He was strong and warm, and he felt so right. "Okay," I said, breathless. "I need to sit down."

The concern was back. "Do you feel okay?"

"I feel great," I said as he helped me back to the couch. "But it's been a helluva morning and I'm kinda beat."

The tiredness was the worst part. Well, probably not the worst part—there were a lot of worst parts. But I never knew bone-tired was actually a real thing, but damn . . .

When I was reclined and comfy, he pulled his shirt back on. He laughed at my pout. "I'll come back up and check on you in a bit."

I nodded. "Okay."

He sat down beside me and took my hand. He lifted my knuckles to his lips. "You remembering my tattoos means so much to me. If you remember nothing else, I won't mind. But you remembered this, and that's all I need."

"I just remember how it made me feel," I told him. "When I woke up, I didn't know what or where home was, except those wings kept coming back to me. They felt familiar when nothing else did. Like home."

His eyes were glassy and he put my palm to his cheek and let out a shaky breath. "Thank you."

"You okay?"

He nodded and laughed at himself, blinking back his tears. "I'm gonna let you get some rest, and I'm gonna plan the best first date ever for tonight."

I hummed out a sigh. "Our first date." Then I corrected. "Sorry, our second first date? Our first date all over again? I don't know what to call it. My brain gets slow when I'm tired."

He leaned down and kissed my forehead. "I know, baby. Get some rest. I'll just be downstairs. Call me if you need me."

I smiled and it took a second for his words to process. "Like it how you call me baby. And I like second first dates."

His smiling face was the last thing I remembered seeing before sleep stole me again. I stored it away in my mind, in my heart. I never wanted to forget him again. I finally had a piece of the puzzle. Just one single piece, but what a piece it was. That piece was Dallas. No, I didn't have any old memories of him, but I liked the new ones. Was I mad that those memories were stolen from me? Sure. Probably more sad than mad. But I couldn't do a damn thing about it. There was no point in expending energy I didn't have on things I couldn't fix.

And anyway, I looked forward to making more memories. New experiences. New memories.

Starting now. Starting new.

PIECES OF *me*

MISSING PIECES SERIES
BOOK TWO

Chapter One
JUSTIN

THE MIST WAS thick and heavy, surrounding me and swirling through me, weighing me down. It clung to my bones and made it hard to move. Heavy and tiring, and impossible to see through. If I could just see past it, through it, if it would just clear a little, I'd be able to see . . . All the answers were in there, the life I'd had, everything I'd known, was shrouded in mist . . .

Until the wings came into view. Like they had before in every other dream. Hard to recognise at first, so much was missing. But they shone a little brighter now, the mist swirled and danced around the wings, and I tried to get to them faster. I needed to be closer, and the mist began to clear. I reached out and touched the wings. I'd never been able to touch the wings before . . . This was new, and I was closer than I'd ever been.

Then the mist was gone.

The wings were soft under my palm. A heartbeat boomed under my touch, scaring me. Calling me home.

I startled awake with a name echoing through my head.

Dallas.

And for a brief moment, I could feel his warmth, his strength. I could smell his scent, taste his kiss . . .

Then it was gone.

I closed my eyes, trying to grasp what was left of that dream, trying to recall every detail, but I couldn't. The dream I'd had many times had changed now I knew what the wings were. What they meant, and why they felt like home. When I had no idea what home even was, those wings resonated in my heart.

I understood now why that stranger who sat by my bed in the hospital, who never left, felt so familiar. I didn't know him, I'd never seen him before, but for some reason I trusted him. When he'd held my hand in hospital, it felt . . . right. It felt new, but somehow familiar.

And now I knew why.

Sure, I'd seen the photos of us together, and I'd read the text messages, but they never sparked any feeling apart from sadness, because I couldn't remember, and I longed for what the two guys in the photo had. I had no emotional connection to those pictures. I didn't recognise him in those photographs, and I didn't recognise who I was in them either.

But somewhere in my brain, in the mist and blank confusion, was a pair of wings—a memory—that had been trying to tell me since the accident that the man by my bedside was my home.

I'd had snippets of memories, of things I knew, but this one was a big one. This one had feelings behind it. Safety, comfort, strength.

Like he'd said, if that was the only thing I ever remembered, he'd be happy with that. And I kind of agreed with him. I mean, I wanted all my memories back, but that one was a real good place to start.

I pressed the incline button on the couch and sat up, giving myself a few seconds to adjust. I hated how my body and my mind were no longer in sync. How it took a few seconds for things to register, like there was a two-second telecast delay. And the worst part was that I knew I was talking slow. I could hear it, but I just could not kick my brain into second gear. Everything I did was slow. How I thought, how I spoke, how I moved.

It was just how I was now.

I hated it, but there was nothing I could do about it. Sure, it was frustrating, but I just didn't have the energy or the brainpower to be angry about it. There were a lot of things my mind wouldn't let me do. A lot of things I knew I should care about or ask about, but I just . . . couldn't. I didn't have the capacity for it.

I could remember what it was like to be thinking about twenty different things at once, to worry about things like work and money, but now my mind had none of that noise.

There was only mist, and haze, and a whole lotta blank.

At least my bladder still had a direct line to my brain. With a sigh, I sat forward on the couch and got myself onto my scooter. I used the bathroom, then sat in front of the jigsaw puzzle for a bit. I got some more of it done, which felt good. It was slow-going like everything else, but it felt good to accomplish something. Progress was progress, one piece at a time.

Dallas came up for lunch and he was all smiles when he saw me at the table. "Hey, you."

My belly did a little somersault, and the pleasantness was a nice change from the confusion that I'd been shrouded in. "Hey."

He came over and put his hand on my shoulder. It was warm and there was a gentle strength in his touch. "Getting more done, I see. It's looking really good."

I didn't know why his approval meant a lot to me. I smiled up at him. "Thanks."

"I'm gonna make myself a toasted sandwich. Want one?"

Food. Did I want to eat? I thought about my stomach and if it was hungry, but I couldn't really tell. If Dallas was eating, then I probably should too. "Sure."

He set about getting the toaster thing out, then bread and other stuff from the fridge. I left the table and scooted over to the kitchen, and remembering where the plates were, I put two plates on the counter.

Dallas grinned at me. And instead of making a fuss about me doing stuff, he talked about the bikes they were working on: one was a simple service, one needed a new brake line, and another was having the forks replaced because the guy had stacked it hard in the national park up north. "Sorry if the noise down there is disturbing you," he said. "Did it wake you up?"

I had to think . . . "Nope. Didn't hear anything." Had I

heard anything? I knew how loud mechanic shops could get with motors kicking over every so often, things banging and clanging . . . How could I not hear that? I was right above it . . . "Haven't heard anything."

"Well, good," Dallas said. "I wondered if we were disturbing you."

I put two bottles of water on the counter, trying not to think too much about me not hearing loud noises outside. "It's weird," I said. "My head is blank most of the time. Like really misty and empty, but it's full. There's no more room. I can't think about stuff because all the space is taken up by mist. That probably doesn't make sense, sorry."

"It makes perfect sense," he said, that kind smile ever-present. "It's probably a good thing you can't hear it. Especially Sparra's singing."

I smiled at that and Dallas slid the toasted sandwiches onto the plates, then took them to the table, careful of the jigsaw puzzle. "Let's see who gets the next piece."

I carried the waters from the counter as I scooted over and Dallas sat next to me and slid a plate in front of me. "Careful, these'll be a bit hot. Might want to leave it for a bit."

"'Kay." I picked up a puzzle piece and slotted it into place.

Dallas gasped. "You cheated!"

I laughed. "Did not." I had all the same colours put together. "I've just been looking at it longer."

He grumbled and picked up a piece but couldn't get it to fit. "Oh, this is bullshit," he said with a chuckle.

I sorted through the pieces near me and gave it to him. "Try that."

It slotted straight in and I laughed. "Okay, you win," he said, giving me a full grin. "So I was thinking about this date tonight."

Date . . . oh yeah. "Our second first date."

"Yep. I was thinking we could order some Chinese food for dinner and start watching *Game of Thrones*, make some popcorn, and maybe if I'm real lucky, we could hold hands."

I was smiling at him, that giddy feeling was back. "Hold hands, huh?"

He chewed on his bottom lip, looking all kinds of cute and happy. "How does that sound?"

"Good." I know he said a few things—Chinese food and TV —but one stuck out more than the others. "I like holding hands."

He laughed and picked up his sandwich, then nodded toward mine. "These are fine to eat now."

"Okay." I took a bite, and it was good. I liked mustard and it was helpful that I didn't have to tell him what I liked, because if I tried to think too hard about what food I liked and didn't like, I couldn't name them. Everything was harder when I was tired, and I was tired all the damn time.

I wanted to try harder, though. I wanted to be better. I just needed to try and wade through the mist and make sense of what lay beneath it.

"Oh, and I called the hospital," Dallas said between bites. "Eight o'clock tomorrow you can get your cast off. Arranged it so it's before your appointment to see your PT doctor and Doctor Chang."

Ugh, more appointments, but at least I was finally getting rid of the cast. "Thank you. I can't wait to have it off." I looked down at my arm. "I want my body back. I hate not being able to . . ." What was the word? I couldn't quite find it. ". . . move and stuff."

"Tomorrow you'll be new and shiny." Dallas' smile became a frown. "Though tomorrow's gonna be a pretty full-on day. Lots of appointments and walking about. Will you be okay with that?"

Probably not, but if Dallas was with me . . . "You'll be there, right?"

"Of course." He stood up and rubbed my shoulder before taking his plate to the sink. "I wouldn't be anywhere else."

He sat back down at the table but looked through the puzzle pieces while I ate my sandwich. Everything I did was so damn slow. And it never fazed him one bit. He never made an issue that I took so long to eat or talk. He was just so great about everything.

"A-ha!" he said, slotting a piece into place. "I got one."

I smiled as I chewed, and without really meaning to or without thinking about it, at least, I reached for his hand. I just wanted to hold it, apparently. And he laced our fingers with a grin and proceeded to look for another puzzle piece.

He stayed for a bit longer, and I really loved having him here. His warmth and his scent and his hand in mine, it settled something in me. The confusion in my head was calmer when Dallas was there, and I knew he'd look after me and he'd make sure everything was okay. I knew he couldn't stay with me all day, but it was good to see him, to be with him.

"Well, I better get back downstairs. I told the boys I'll be out all day tomorrow," he said. "So I better get as much done today as I can." He leaned down and kissed the top of my head and headed toward the door.

"Dallas?" I called out. Damn my stupid brain . . . In the three seconds it took for me to stop him, he was almost gone.

He turned. "Yeah?"

I pushed my scooter out from the table and stood up. "Can I . . . ugh, can I have a hug?"

He crossed the floor in a few long strides and collected me in a crushing hug that was everything I needed. God, it felt so good. He was a good six inches taller than me and much stronger, so he could just wrap me up and, my God, he just made everything so much better. It was like he transferred some of his strength to me, which was ridiculous, but I felt stronger after he hugged me. Some of his calmness settled over me.

That shit was like a drug.

I breathed him in and would have stayed right there forever if he didn't pull back. There was concern in his eyes. "You okay?"

I nodded, smiling now. "You give the best hugs."

He chuckled. "You can have one any time."

"Good."

He was warmth and strength, and I fit against him just right. His hands were big, his skin rough and calloused and divine. When he cradled my face, I couldn't help but lean into his touch.

He studied my eyes for a long moment before he pressed his lips to mine. Just quick, but soft and warm, and his beard tickled my chin. "I better go back downstairs," he said quietly. "Call me or text me if you need me, okay?"

"'Kay."

I took my plate to the sink and washed up the few things we'd used. It wasn't much, but I wanted to help as much as I was able, and it probably wasn't the best job. Washing up with one hand, and my left hand at that, wasn't easy. But I got it done and felt better for it.

Then I parked my arse back on the couch and picked up my journal. Writing with a full-arm cast was bad enough, and even I could tell my writing was bad, but I managed to write down what I remembered about the wing dream and about Dallas' tattoos. I wrote down that I knew about the fridge and the radio downstairs, and I wrote down that I'd had another nightmare.

But then I also made a list, trying to write it as neat as possible, of the things I wanted to remember to talk about. Things I knew I should talk about but didn't really have the capacity to. I figured if I made a list, then when I was actually able to, I could ask. I wanted to be better for Dallas, and for me too. But I wanted to get better—I wanted to have the life the old me had in those photographs with him. I wanted that. And that meant I needed to think harder, to try harder to get my life back.

But the whole time my mind just kept going back to Dallas.

And in an attempt to find some answers, or maybe in hope that I'd see something that would open the locked vault of my memories, I got myself back onto my scooter and went to the end of the hall.

Dallas' bedroom.

Chapter Two

DALLAS

Account overdue.

Past due.

Insufficient funds.

I sighed and stared at my laptop screen. Between the guilt and shame was an overwhelming sense of drowning. Even when I'd first started my business, I'd never had money worries. Not like this. Now bills were coming in that I couldn't pay, and orders weren't delivered because I couldn't pay upfront, so I was swapping money between accounts, playing cat and mouse with debtors and creditors just trying to keep my head above water.

I typed out another quick email asking my case manager to please chase up the workers' compensation and insurance claims. It had only been a few weeks since we'd filed the paperwork, but our workload had lessened to almost half, yet the bills had never stopped coming.

I'd never kept anything from Justin before, but he couldn't know about this. It would only add to his stress and be detrimental to his recovery.

I closed my laptop and sighed. I'd promised Juss some Chinese food for dinner, so I added that to my growing credit card debt and shut my office door.

After Davo and Sparra had gone, I locked the workshop up, padlocked the front gate, and carried the Chinese takeout up the stairs. Despite the worry about money, I was excited for tonight. A night on the couch in front of the TV probably sounded lame to anyone else, but it sounded kinda perfect to me.

All the little things I once took for granted were now like pockets of gold. Watching TV, curling up on the couch, holding hands . . .

I would never take them for granted again.

It had very nearly all been taken away from me, and now I knew its true value, I'd never discount anything ever again.

The loungeroom was empty, so I put the Chinese food on the kitchen counter and saw the bathroom door was open. "I ordered dinner early," I said. "So I didn't have to leave again."

No reply.

I walked to the bathroom and peeked inside, half expecting him to be at the basin or peeing or something.

He wasn't.

Trying not to panic, I turned to his bedroom. Maybe he'd gone for a proper lie-down, but his bed was empty.

I called out louder this time. "Juss?"

It was then I noticed the door to my room was ajar. *What the hell?*

I peered in, almost afraid of what I might find, my heart in my throat. But there he was, asleep on my bed.

Oh, Jussy.

My heart was doing all kinds of crazy things, trying to calm down after almost having a panic attack but filling with love and sadness. Why my bed? Had he needed to be close to me?

I quietly sat beside him and put my hand on his arm. "Hey, Juss."

He stirred awake, drowsy and confused at first, until he noticed me. "Oh, hey."

"You okay?"

"Yeah, why?" He sat up and looked around. It clearly took him a few long seconds to remember. "Oh."

"Were you looking for me?"

"No, I . . ." He shook his head. "I didn't mean to fall asleep. I want to be better. For you. And I thought maybe if I saw your things, I might remember . . . But I was tired."

I slid my hand up his arm. "You want to be better, for me?" I shook my head. "Juss, you don't have to do anything for me."

"I want to." He squeezed his eyes closed and scrubbed his hand over his face. "I want to be better."

"It'll take time," I whispered, taking his hand. "And baby, we've got time."

"Do we?"

I nodded. "All the time in the world."

He sighed and looked around the room. "This isn't your room, is it?"

"Sure it is."

"I mean, you said it was your room, and you said I needed a private room."

He was frowning, so I clarified, "I didn't want you to feel pressured, that's all. Bringing you home to share a bed with a man you didn't know kinda felt wrong to me."

He looked at me then, smiled, and shook his head. "There's no bed in here."

"There's this," I said, patting the thin mattress we were sitting on.

"It's a sofa bed, not a real bed."

"You slept on it okay."

"It smells like you."

I smiled at that, and he threaded our fingers. "You can take naps in here whenever you like."

"It's a small room," he said, looking at the desk, the old printer, and the very lack of anything else. There was no room for anything else. I had to step over the sofa bed to get to the desk. "It's not a bedroom."

He didn't say anything about the small pile of clothes folded on the desk that I was using as a dresser, or my joggers under the desk. "It does me just fine."

"Does it make you sad?" he asked. "To sleep in here?"

Jesus. I wasn't prepared for this conversation. I lifted his hand to my lips and kissed his knuckles. "No, Juss. I'm glad to have you home. That's enough for me."

He was quiet for a minute, and I let him get his thoughts in order. "What time is it?"

"Almost six. I had some Chinese food delivered already. You hungry?"

"Uh, sure." Then he smiled. "It's our date night."

I chuckled. "It is. Here, let me help you up." I stood and held out my hand. "Where's your scooter?"

He took my hand and put his feet on the floor and slowly stood up. "I left it in the hall. There wasn't enough room in here."

I hadn't even noticed it; I'd been in such a panic to find him. But he took a few steps on his own, with me holding onto him, and he walked to the door. I was grinning at his progress, at his determination. "How does that feel?"

"Okay. Weird. Sore. But good." He held onto the doorframe. "Feels good to be up."

"Well, just don't overdo it," I said, grabbing his scooter. "Or you'll end up back at square one."

He sat on his scooter and sighed. "I shoulda stayed upright. I need to pee. Now I gotta get up again."

I chuckled. "Well, I'll leave you to do that and go sort dinner out."

By the time he came out, I had dinner on the table, careful of the jigsaw puzzle, of course, with two cans of lemon soda and two empty wine glasses. I also had the lights down low and two candles lit on the table.

He stopped and stared; a slow smile tugged at his lips. "What's this?"

"A date," I replied. I felt a bit foolish, actually, but I wanted to do something special. And corny, because Justin had always liked corny. No, we weren't fancy, and no, our wine glasses weren't expensive crystal, and the candles were just the old ones I had in case of a blackout. But all Justin had ever wanted was a guy who made him feel special, and given the circumstances, this was as special and as corny as I could do. "Our second first date. This isn't too corny, is it?"

He grinned as he scooted over to the table. "This is great." Then he laughed. "I can't believe you did this."

I poured the drink into his wine glass. Alcohol was out of the question, given his brain injury, so a non-caffeinated soft drink it was. "For you, sir," I said, taking my seat.

He was still grinning as he sipped it. "Did you do this before?" he asked. "I mean, did you do this for me before?"

"Candle lit dinners? No, actually, I didn't. This is a brand-new memory for you. A first." We'd had nice dinners at home before, plenty of times, but I'd never lit candles and used wine glasses with Chinese food before. "I should have, though. I should have done it all the time, and now I can't think of one single reason why I didn't."

Justin's smile became something else. Happier, a little shy, and somehow just for me.

It set the butterflies in my stomach to full flight. I wiped my hands on my thighs and let out a laugh.

"What?" he asked, a faint blush on his cheeks.

"Just you." I shrugged. It was scary how it had almost been taken away from me and I never wanted to ever take it for granted again. But I didn't want to dampen our date night with constant reminders of his accident. "You're just really cute, and I like seeing you happy."

He laughed it off with a roll of his eyes, embarrassed. So I eased up on the compliments and dished out the food instead. I'd ordered his favourites, but nothing too spicy, and there would be enough leftovers for tomorrow.

"I didn't mean to fall asleep in your bed," he said on his way to taking a sip of his drink.

"Oh, that's okay. Don't think anything of it." The truth was, it was kinda nice that he was thinking about me and trying to make sense of our relationship when I wasn't there. He was trying to fill in so many blanks. "Is there anything you wanted to know about me?"

"Well, yeah," he said. "Everything. I don't know anything

about you. Not really. I know you're nice. And kind. And I know I trust you, and I like you," he said, then cleared his throat. He made a face and his blush deepened. "Like, I *like* you. You give the best hugs that heal something in me, so I'm guessing my heart knows the real you, so I should probably get my head caught up."

I stared at him, almost not believing what he was saying. It made me so ridiculously happy that I wanted to pick him up and twirl him around like some stupid romance movie. Instead, I gave his hand a squeeze before I shoved food into my mouth so I didn't grin like a crazy man.

He wanted to know everything, and considering this was his first date with me, I started at the beginning. "I was born in Singleton, went to school there. Got a mechanical apprenticeship when I was seventeen; couldn't get out of school fast enough. Moved to Newcastle when I was nineteen and finished my apprenticeship at Yamaha."

He made a face as he chewed and swallowed his mouthful. "Yamaha . . . shame."

I laughed at that. "Sorry it wasn't with KTM."

He smirked. "I knew you couldn't have been *that* perfect."

I chuckled at this side of him. This was the old Justin. The Justin who joked and took the piss out of me every chance he got. "I have two older brothers, Dean and Mark; they both live in Singleton still. I don't talk to them too often. My mum died when I was eight and my dad remarried when I was thirteen. No one really liked the fact I was into guys, and no one really cared too much when I left town."

He put his fork down. "Oh, Dallas, I'm sorry."

"Don't be. It's what made me who I am today. I decided the best revenge was success, and I own my own business, I own this place. It's not the Taj Mahal, but it's mine. It's more than what they have."

He reached over and took my hand, and frowned. "My mother doesn't like me either."

I squeezed his fingers. "I know, baby. But you've got Becca and the girls, and you've got me. And I've got Davo and Sparra.

They're like my brothers. We get to make our own family and I'll take that any day over a shitty biological one."

He nodded. "Did we . . . was that something we had in common?"

"Yeah. One of a lot of things, but it's something we both understood."

"What else?"

"What it was like to be a gay mechanic," I said. "It's not an industry that is all too tolerant of that kind of stuff. And other gay guys, in clubs and stuff, never really stuck around. Guess they didn't like oil-stained hands or something."

"Do your customers know about us?" he asked. "I mean, did they know we were . . . ?"

"Our regulars know. If it bothered them, they'd have gone somewhere else, I guess. But just the typical customer, nope. None of their business, really."

His smile was kinda sad, and he was staring at our joined hands on the table. "You know, I like a mechanic's hands. Your hands. The grease and . . . it gets into the nails and the skin." He turned our hands over and looked at my nails. "They're not pretty. They're banged up and rough, but these hands work, and they fix things, and that's pretty great."

I stared at him in the flicker of candlelight and my heart fell a little more in love.

"You're looking at me like that again," he said. He took his hand back and picked up his fork—I kind of forgot he only had one hand to use—and he ate some more food.

"Like what?"

"Like you know me . . . like you like me." He made a face and stabbed a piece of plum chicken with his fork.

"Does that make you uncomfortable? I'm sorry. I don't mean to. I just . . . can't help it sometimes."

He smiled around his mouthful of food. "No, I don't mind." He met my gaze. "It's better than the sadness. I didn't like that much."

"Sadness?"

"Yeah, at the hospital. You used to look sad when I didn't know who you were."

"I never was much good at hiding the way I feel."

He ate some more. "Did I like that? That you couldn't hide the way you feel? Pretty sure that I'd have liked that."

I chuckled. "Yeah, you liked that. Even if we had a fight, you'd tell me afterward that you'd prefer to know and not have the mind games."

"Did we fight often?" he asked with a frown.

"Not really. Usually it was over stupid stuff, like dishes or laundry or not replacing the empty toilet paper roll. Stuff that really doesn't matter at the end of the day. We never had any major disagreements."

He surprised me by laughing. "Toilet paper?"

I chuckled, considering he almost died and we wasted precious moments arguing over fucking toilet paper. "Crazy, huh?"

He smiled as he ate. "Tell me more about you."

"Like what?"

"I don't know. I can't really think of questions. What would people on a first date ask?"

I took a long sip of my drink. "Well, let me see . . . My favourite colour is blue. Favourite food is a big dirty burger from the takeaway shop down the road. Never was a big drinker, but if the boys were having a night, I'd probably have a Jack and Coke. I like watching the footy; I'm a Bulldog supporter as you know."

He groaned. "So bad."

I laughed. "I like the Sydney Swans in AFL, the Newcastle Jets in soccer."

"Those are okay. I can deal with those. But the Bulldogs . . ."

I rolled my eyes and smiled as I ate some Singapore beef. "And when the Bulldogs played the Knights, we'd have a bet. It was usually just like washing up for a week or a foot massage, something like that."

He grinned. "So, how many times did you lose that bet?"

I pouted. "Shut up."

He laughed at that. "See? I can lose five years and I still know the Knights beat the Dogs."

I pushed my plate away. "We won a few."

He gave me a happy smile, then nodded to my meal. "Do I like that?"

"Try it."

He pierced a piece and hummed as he ate it. "I like that. I've never had that before, have I?"

"Yep, you have."

He frowned. "I don't remember it. It's weird that I've done things, eaten things, lived a whole life that I can't remember."

"It must be very weird," I replied. "And I can't pretend to understand what it's like for you. But I'll help you, and if you have any questions or want to know anything, I won't ever lie to you."

He met my eyes and smiled. "Thanks. It can't be easy for you either."

"I dunno," I replied, giving him a nudge. "I get to do it all again with you. I get a second chance to make everything better."

He seemed to think about that for a long moment. "What would you do different?"

"Well, I certainly won't be arguing about toilet paper, I can assure you."

He smiled. "Glad to hear that."

"I won't sweat the small stuff. I'll appreciate the little things and I'll never take a single day for granted."

He studied me. "The accident scared you," he said. It wasn't a question.

"Terrified me." I tried to smile. "Terrified me."

"It musta sucked. Sorry."

"Not as much as it sucked for you," I said, getting to my feet. I rubbed his shoulder, then began to clear away the table. "Want to go get comfy on the couch? This'll just take a second."

"Sure." He scooted a plate to the counter. "Um, I know you said something about watching a TV show . . ."

"Yeah, but we don't have to."

"I just can't concentrate too much, sorry."

"That's okay. You can choose what we watch. I don't mind at all."

By the time I finished cleaning up, Juss was on the couch flipping through the sports channels so I blew the candles on the table out and joined him and Squish on the couch. Again, I sat close but not too close and within a few moments, he'd wiggled over. He had always been like a koala, clinging and touching, and I certainly didn't mind one bit.

We watched a replay of last season's football grand final but it wasn't even into the second half when his head was on my shoulder and his blinks were getting longer and longer. "Wanna go to bed, baby?" I asked.

"Tired," he said. "Always tired. Wish I wasn't."

"You need to sleep," I said gently. "Your brain is recovering."

He was quiet for a bit. "You call me baby. Or Jussy."

"I do, sorry. It's a habit."

"What'd I call you?"

Such an innocent question, but damn, it hurt my heart a little. "You'd call me Dall. Short for Dallas. Or babe. Not in front of the boys at work; just when it was us."

He hummed sleepily. "Like that."

Me too, baby. Me too. And maybe one day we'll get back to that.

I got him up to use the bathroom and I got him his meds and he was almost asleep when I helped him into bed. He mumbled something that I couldn't understand, and with a deep breath, he was out like a light.

I leaned down and kissed his head, right next to the scar above his ear. "I love you, Jussy," I whispered, knowing he was asleep. I wanted him to know, even on a subconscious level, that he was loved.

Squish quickly joined him, like he always did, curling up at his side and purring loudly, and I left him in charge. I got everything tidied up and went to my room, smiling at the rumpled blankets where Justin had slept. I inhaled the faint scent of him as I settled into sleep. I'd barely dozed off when Justin's voice woke me.

"Dallas?"

I shot up, wondering what was wrong. I got to his room, and he was sitting up in his bed. "Can't sleep," he mumbled, then pulled the covers back in invitation.

I didn't need to be told twice. I slid in between the sheets, and before my head was on the pillow, he was snuggled into my side. I rolled and pulled him against me, his head against my chest, and he mumbled again, but this time I heard him just fine.

"Don't leave me."

Chapter Three

I WOKE up with Justin plastered to me. He was snuggled right in, his heavy cast across my belly, his thigh across mine. Once upon a time it might have been annoying, waking up with a heat-seeking koala wrapped around me, but now I relished it.

My body liked it too.

Needing to pee didn't help, but having him so close after so long . . . my body *definitely* liked it.

He was sound asleep, and I figured it would be best if he didn't wake up with my persistent dick staring right at him. I'd crawled into his bed wearing only my boxers, so there wasn't much hope of hiding it.

I gently lifted his leg off mine. It was his injured leg so I had to be careful, and when I slipped out from under his arm, he stirred but never woke. Once out of bed, I took a second to watch him sleep.

Fucking hell, he was gorgeous.

His injuries reminded me that he was vulnerable, but by God, he was resilient and strong too. And sexy as hell.

My dick agreed, which reminded me to leave before he saw me. I used the bathroom and I tried to think of everything we had to do this morning, listing his appointments in my head, but my problem wasn't going away on its own.

Shower first it is, then.

Jerking off hadn't been something I'd done much of since Justin's accident. I'd either been too tired, too distracted, or too heartsore. But now that he was home and sleeping in the same bed seemed to be something that might happen often, I figured I should probably get used to it.

It didn't take much . . . the hot water, a soap-slicked hand, and memories of Justin and me and the countless nights of frenzied fucking or gentle lovemaking, of being buried inside him, making him come just from having my cock inside him. God, how he loved that . . .

It didn't take much at all.

I finished my shower, feeling a little lightheaded and much looser. I dressed and went to the kitchen and put the kettle on. I was making some toast when Justin came out on his scooter. He looked still half-asleep.

"Morning," I said brightly.

He grumbled and I handed him his coffee. He never was much of a morning person, and seeing this familiar side of him made me smile. "You always so chipper in the morning?"

"Yep. And you're always cranky. Actually, never thought I'd miss seeing you scowl at me first thing in the morning until you did it just now. I've missed it." It was a sure sign he was improving.

He grumbled something else as he sipped his decaf coffee.

I had to bite the inside of my cheek so I didn't grin. "Cast comes off today. That's gotta be a good thing, right?"

He didn't grumble, so that was a yes.

He became a little more human with every sip of coffee and each passing moment. He ate some toast, and by the time he was showered and dressed, he was his usual smiley self. I raced his scooter and his papers down first, then helped Justin down the stairs, and he laughed as I helped him into the ute.

And he was still smiling as we arrived at the hospital, though I was fairly sure he wouldn't be smiling by the time we left. It was going to be a long, gruelling day for him.

He stopped at the entrance of the hospital, looking up from

his scooter to the sign above the door. "Not too keen to come back here," he said.

"Me either," I admitted. "I must have walked through these doors a hundred times in the last month."

"Just promise me one thing," he said very seriously.

"Anything."

"We won't have lunch here. No more hospital food, ever. I don't care if they're giving it away."

I laughed. "Promise."

We made our way to the plaster clinic and went through all the paperwork, and thankfully we didn't have to wait too long. Justin was adamant that I was going with him, so I sat and watched as they cut his cast off. His arm was paler than the rest of him and thinner than his left arm. He had final X-rays done, and he had to wear one of those collar-cuff things, which just kind of kept his hand tucked up to his chest. The bone from his shoulder to his elbow still needed to sit right for another week or so, but at least the collar-cuff wasn't heavy and cumbersome like the full arm cast.

"How does it feel?" I asked as the nurse fitted his hand into the cuff thing.

He smiled at me. "Much better. Can't wait to have a shower and scrub it." He ran his fingers along his forearm. "Why isn't it itchy now? So not fair."

"No doubt the doc will have a whole lot of exercise and physio for it too," I said.

He grimaced. "More homework."

"Well, at least they let you leave. You could still be doing all this from your hospital bed."

"Yeah, no thank you," he said. "I'm done with hospitals forever."

"You *are* done," the doc said, giving him a big smile. "Well, you're done here." She gave him a few tips and pointers about his arm, but I didn't think he was listening. His mind was already out the door.

His physical therapy appointment was with a new out-patient doctor. Doctor Michaels seemed nice enough, though he gave me a questioning look, obviously wondering where I fit into Justin's care. But as soon as Justin transferred himself from his scooter to his seat, he reached over and took my hand. "This is Dallas," Justin said to him. "He'll be sitting in with me." I grinned at Justin—that was a pretty ballsy move for him—and he squeezed my hand in response.

The doc just smiled. "Okay then, let's get started."

The appointment itself was more of an introductory thing. Sure, he had Justin's file and could read all about his injuries, but he was more interested in observing and listening. He had Justin show him his range of motion in his leg, and now that his arm was out of his cast, he showed him what strengthening exercises he could do. Justin's daily routine was mostly all from a sitting or lying perspective because dizziness was a factor with brain injuries, and fatigue, of course.

By the time we were done, Justin's blinks were getting a little longer. It might not have been too noticeable, but I saw it; he'd had enough. And, of course, we had to wait for Doctor Chang— she was busy with patients on the ward. When she came into the waiting room to call us, she took one look at us with Justin's head on my shoulder while he rested his eyes, and she grinned.

"My two favourite customers," she said quietly.

Justin sat up, blearily trying to get his bearings. "Oh, hey."

"You up for this appointment?" she asked him.

"If it means I don't have to come back," he replied. A guy in the waiting room laughed and Doctor Chang rolled her eyes.

"Come on through."

"It's been a busy morning," I said once we were in her office. "First appointment was to get the cast off his arm. Then we met the new physical therapist, so we had to show him where we're at. And now we're here."

She gave me a nod, then turned her attention to Justin. "How're you feeling, Justin?"

"Yeah, I'm good. Just tired 's all."

"Is it good to be home?"

"Yeah," he answered. "I remembered a few things."

"Excellent," she said with a smile. "And you brought your

journal?"

"Oh yeah," he said. He looked at the papers I was holding for him. "Babe, the journal . . ."

Babe.

He called me babe.

"You can talk about what I wrote," Juss said. "In front of Dallas, I mean. I don't mind."

Doctor Chang smiled. "Okay, thank you." She took the journal and turned the pages. "Ah, this is all great, Justin."

"The memories don't come back to me," he added. "No flashback or anything. They're just already there. Like Dallas' ute and the scratch on the fridge, and the old radio." He shrugged. "I just knew it."

She nodded. "That's perfectly normal."

"I just expected the mist to clear but it didn't. Nothing came to me; it was just already there."

She gave him a patient smile. "The mist?"

"Yeah, the mist. In my head. Like it's . . . hazy."

"Like everything's foggy?" I suggested.

Justin nodded. "Yeah. Foggy." He shrugged again. "Misty."

Doctor Chang read something in his journal and looked up, surprised. "Oh, the wing dream?"

Justin laughed and I felt my cheeks heat. "Yes!" he replied. "It was Dallas all along. I knew I'd remember him. Some part of him had to come back to me. I guess it was my mind's way of telling me what he meant to me."

"You have wing tattoos?" she asked. Obviously Justin had just written the word *tattoo.*

"Uh, yeah," I answered, waving my hand across my front. "Two big wings, right across my chest."

"He can show you if you want?" Justin added with a smile.

"No, I can't," I shot back, blushing even harder. *Jesus.* I gave the doc an apologetic smile, but she just chuckled.

"I believe you," she said. "And I'm happy you found the meaning of them."

"Me too," Justin replied. He gave me a shy smile that made my belly flip. "Remembering Dallas was the best thing."

My heart swelled and he smiled at me.

Doctor Chang turned another page and took a moment to read what Justin had written. "You have some points here," she said. "Are these things you wanted to ask about?"

Justin nodded. "Yeah. I keep . . . I know there are things I should be asking. Things I should know about and worry about. I know I should. But I can't seem to get my brain to ask. It's weird. There are things I used to worry about, and I guess I still should, but I don't have the . . . room for it."

"The room for it?" I asked. "In your mind?"

"Well, yeah," he replied. "Like my head is full. Like . . ." He made a pained face, trying to find the best way to describe something. He nodded to Doctor Chang's coffee cup. "Like a cup that's full to the top. There's more to go in, but it's full already."

"Full of mist," I clarified, from what he'd told me before.

"Yeah. Everything is simple now. I can't think too hard, about anything. There's just no room."

"That's quite common," Doctor Chang said. "What you're experiencing is very normal for people who have suffered a TBI. But you want to know about these things." She tapped his journal. "And that tells me your cognitive processing is improving. Three, two, or even one week ago you wouldn't have thought to ask. And you recognise there are some issues you should be more aware of. That's a pretty big step forward."

"I know I should, but I don't know if my head can. Does that make sense?"

"Perfect sense," she replied.

"Is it something I can help with?" I asked, feeling out of the loop. I had no clue what they were talking about.

Doctor Chang replied, "Justin's noted down some things he recognises that should be important."

"Things I should know but don't."

"Such as?"

The doc read from his journal. "Money, work, rent, bills."

"I should know about that stuff, right?" Justin asked. "But I can't seem to get . . . Those are things I worried about before, in Darwin. I should worry about them now, but my head is full."

I squeezed his hand. "Well, I can answer those questions. You have your bank account and your pay from work gets deposited straight into that. We split all the utilities and bills equally between us. You pay me rent, and that goes into my mortgage. I've kept all your mail, like bank statements and all that; it's all unopened on my desk. I wasn't sure you were up for any of that. I'm sorry if that confused you."

"No. I just didn't know. I mean, I couldn't . . . my brain is full," he said. "I just kept thinking I should be worried about this stuff. Like, real-life stuff, but I couldn't seem to grasp it."

"All your bills are direct debited out of your account," I explained. "Same as mine. Phone bill, electricity instalments, that kind of thing. It's all automatic. And I've been taking care of everything else. I don't expect you to be worrying about this stuff. You need to worry about getting better, that's all."

He thought that over for a bit and frowned. "And work? My job is . . . I can't do my job."

I turned to face him better and rubbed his hand in mine. "Your job is secure. You're still getting paid even though you're not working; you're entitled to sick pay. We're waiting on workers' comp to deal with the insurance from the accident. You were driving to a job when you were hit in the van, so it should all be covered. You don't have anything to worry about. That's all being taken care of."

Even though it hadn't come through yet. It was my concern, not his. Jesus, the last thing he needed to be stressing over was money and work.

"I can show you everything when we get home," I added. "Anything you want to know."

"Are you happy with that?" the doc asked. "Is there anything else you'd like to know?"

He grimaced as he tried to think, and it was a sure sign that he was tired. Something the doc recognised as well. She closed his journal and slid it toward him. "Over the next week, I want you to write anything down you think of and we can discuss it in your next visit."

"'Kay," he said quietly. Then he sighed. "How 'm I doin',

doc?"

She smiled. "You're doing great, Justin. I know it might not feel like it but you are making great progress." Then she looked at me. "Dallas, is there anything you'd like to ask?"

"Um, not that I can think of. He's been doing some jigsaw puzzles, and he's better at them than me. He's eating a little more, which is good." I smiled at him. "He'll be happier now that heavy cast on his arm is gone, though. It'll make his life easier, for sure. I think we'll have a good week."

"I think so too," she agreed. "Just get some rest this afternoon, and take it easy for a day or two."

Justin slow blinked but he was smiling. "We had our first date," he said. "Sorry, our second first date."

Doctor Chang grinned. "You did?"

"Yep. Chinese food and footy on the TV," he said, tiredly.

I grinned at him. "It was fun."

"M'heart knows him, but m'head doesn't," Justin said. "Just tryin' to catch up."

"We'll get there, Juss," I murmured.

"Sounds like you have a lot of catching up to do," she said, smiling. She spoke a little bit more about Justin's recovery, but seeing how tired he was, she boiled it right down to basically keep doing what we're doing and she'd see us again next week.

When we finally got back into my ute, he held his journal on his lap and closed his eyes.

"Wanna drive along the beach? Or just wanna go home?" I asked.

"Beach sounds good. Another day," he mumbled.

"Okay. Home it is."

He slept on the drive home, and I felt bad for waking him up when we got there. I opened his car door and gently roused him. He looked at me with bleary eyes and it took him a second to focus. He smiled. "Hey."

"Hey, beautiful," I replied. "We're home."

His grin widened and I was helping him out of the ute and onto his scooter when Sparra came over. "Got your arm out, I see," he said.

Justin glanced down at his arm in the cuff sling. "Yeah."

He always moved and spoke so much slower when he was tired, and Sparra didn't need to be told. He simply gave Juss a pat on the back. "Good to see ya, mate." Then he gave me a quick nod. "Davo wanted to see ya when you got a minute."

"Okay. I'll be right back down."

We got Justin to the bottom of the stairs but there was no way he could get himself up there. He stood up and took hold of the railing.

"Hang on," I urged. "Let me carry you."

"Carry me?"

"Yep." I slung his left arm over my shoulder and slowly picked him up, bridal style. I had to be careful of his head and his leg and his right arm. It was the only way. "Hold on."

Sparra dashed up the stairs and opened my door for me, then grinned as he came back down.

Justin chuckled and put his head on my chest. "Could get used to this."

Yeah, he was shorter than me and smaller, and he wasn't heavy at all. But carrying him up the stairs, kinda on an angle so his foot didn't catch on the railing, wasn't exactly easy. When we were inside, I gently set him down on his feet and righted myself with a groan. "Been a while since I've lifted weights or done cardio."

He smiled sleepily at me. "Was fun."

He hobbled to the couch, using his right leg as much as it would let him, and sat himself down. I got him a bottle of water while he reclined and got himself comfy. "Hey, Dall?"

I smiled at the name I hadn't heard in far too long. "Yeah?"

"Sorry 'bout the journal," he said, his eyes half-closed.

"What are you sorry for?"

"For not askin' you." His eyes drifted closed. "Just got no room for thinkin'."

I flicked the blanket out over him and planted a kiss on his forehead. "Don't be sorry," I whispered, but he was already asleep.

Chapter Four

DAVO WAS busy under an ATV when I came down into the shop. I helped him without being asked, and together we pulled out the transmission. "How's Jusso?" he asked, eventually.

"Good. Tired today. Doing too much knocks him around. He'll be asleep for a bit now. Sparra said you wanted to see me?"

"Yeah, John Simpson called. Wanted to know if we'd still be right to take on his contract. Didn't really know what to tell him. Wanted to say yes, but it's a big job and we're short-staffed."

Shit shit shit. "I know. I'll call him. I'm here for the rest of the week. Juss's got no more appointments. Sorry for dumping all this on you."

"Nah, it's okay. I just didn't want to tell him the wrong thing. I told him we were business as usual and that you'd call him back today."

"Thanks, mate. I'll go call him now."

He scratched the back of his neck, nervous. "And, uh, the order for four-stroke oil didn't go through. Something with the payment. I told them you'd call 'em back today too. We're gonna need that by Friday."

Fuck.

"Yeah, sure. I must've stuffed up the account or something. I'll sort it out, thanks. I'll go do that now. Then do ya need me to help you or Sparra? Or does something else need doing? Just tell me where we're at."

"If you wanna get started on the old Beemer. The driveshaft's had the Richard, and the swing arm on the rear is out. He thought it was a torque reaction." He rolled his eyes. "Anyway, if you could get it started, that'd be good." He cringed. "Ah, boss. Thanks."

He might have had issues with giving his boss orders, but I had no issue in taking them. "Consider it done."

A quick phone call to John Simpson sorted out that spot fire. We needed that contract and I reassured him we'd be on top of it. He said he was sorry to hear about Justin, and I could tell he was genuine, but business was business. Something I understood well.

Then to fix the next spot fire, I logged onto my bank account. Because I wasn't feeling like shit before . . .

I transferred what I could into the trading account and called the oil company to reconfirm the order, and that would have to do for now. I did a quick doublecheck of any outstanding accounts and sent them off a quick reminder to pay. No one owed us a fortune, but every dollar would help right now. I'd probably have to call the bank sooner rather than later and ask about a redraw or refinance. It wasn't something I'd ever wanted to do but maybe I didn't have much choice.

I noticed more notes on my desk with more phone messages, and with a heavy sigh, I sorted through them and made the priority calls and left the others for later.

I wanted to get that road bike up on the stand. Davo had asked specifically, and he'd really pulled through for me these last four weeks and I didn't want to let him down.

But there was another issue, which I'd tried to ignore, that probably couldn't be ignored any longer either.

We were short-staffed, and if I started to let customers down, it would be irreparable to the business. I couldn't ask any more of Davo and Sparra. I'd asked enough of them already. I needed to be the one who did this. It was my business, my responsibility. I had to work harder, faster, better, and now that Juss was home and recovering, I should be able to do just that.

I had three men depending on me. Not just Justin, but Davo and Sparra depended on me too. They needed their jobs, and Justin needed a home and a job to go back to when he was ready. I had to pull it together for them. I couldn't be losing contracts or having loyal customers feel they needed to go somewhere else.

The truth was, when I told Justin that workers' comp was taking care of everything, that wasn't exactly true. They were supposed to be, but of course, these things took time. I didn't need him worrying about that stuff. Stress could set back his recovery, and guilt was the last thing he needed.

So yeah, when I said that Justin being alive was the most important thing and everything else didn't matter, that wasn't exactly true either. Don't get me wrong; him surviving the accident was the most important thing, without question. Having him in my life was everything. But the business and clients and bills and insurance, all that mundane shit, that was kind of important too. Well, it was important now he was out of hospital and real life reared its ugly head.

Maybe Justin thinking about these real-life problems—money, work, bills—made me realise I needed to think about them too.

So with that in mind, I got my arse out onto the floor and put a few hours in fixing an old BMW driveshaft. It was good too, using my hands, doing familiar work. It was good to switch the brain off for a bit.

I'd almost got it done when my phone beeped with a message. Juss had obviously woken up.

Where are you?

I thumbed out a quick reply. *Just downstairs. You okay?*

His reply took a few seconds. *Yeah.*

I wondered what the pause was for. Did he have a headache? Did he pause to consider telling me he wasn't okay but decided against it? *Need me to come up?*

Another pause. *No.*

I sighed, and when I looked across the shop to Davo, I found him looking at me. "I'll just be two minutes."

"No worries," he replied.

I took the stairs two at a time and found Justin getting onto his scooter. "Hey," I said. "Everything okay?"

"Yeah." He gave me a smile that, no matter how busy or distracted I was, would stop me in my tracks. "You busy down there?"

"Yeah, but it's no problem for me to come up. How's your arm?"

His arm was still in the cuff sling and he moved all his fingers. "Good. I need to pee."

I snorted. "Okay. Want me to fix you something to eat? We kinda missed lunch." I should've been more aware; he needed to eat with his meds. I went to the fridge. "Sandwich okay?"

I set about making us both a quick sandwich and put some crackers and grapes into a container for him. I got his pills and a glass of juice, and when he came back out, he downed the pills first with a long drink of juice and ate a cracker.

So no, he wasn't okay. He was in pain and hungry.

"I'm sorry. I lost track of time," I said.

"'S okay," he said. "I just woke up and you weren't here. I asked Squish where you were, but he wouldn't answer me."

I put his sandwich on the table and pulled out the seat next to him. "He can be so rude."

Justin smiled at me and took a bite of his sandwich. "Thanks for this. I should do this for you. Maybe if I set a timer on my phone . . ."

"You were exhausted. If you need to sleep, then sleep."

"It's weird," he said with a shrug. "If there's food there, I eat it. If it's not there, I don't. I don't really get hungry. I just feel sick if I don't eat but my brain doesn't tell me I'm hungry."

I think I remembered one of the docs saying something about that. How his brain might have trouble sending and receiving messages, and how hunger was one of the most common. "Then we can set an alarm on your phone," I said brightly. "If I'm stuck downstairs and you haven't eaten by one o'clock, an alarm will tell you to get yourself something. And your pills."

He frowned. "I hate that you have to do things for me."

"Hey," I whispered, reaching for his hand. "I like doing things for you. And if we have to set an alarm or something, then that's just what we have to do. It's no problem. It's just a tool we use to help us, like your scooter."

He chewed on his bottom lip and it slowly morphed into a smile. "Do you always know what to say?"

God, I could have laughed at that, because most days I had no freaking clue. I finished chewing my sandwich and swallowed it down. "Uh, no. Actually, I don't know what I'm doing. I'm just doing my best, hoping I don't get it wrong."

His smile faded as his gaze met mine. "Don't be worried about getting anything wrong, Dallas. Your best is kinda perfect."

I pulled his hand to my lips and kissed his palm. "I gotta get back downstairs. I'm sorry, I wish I could stay here with you. But I just need a few more hours, then I'll be back."

"'S okay," he said. "I feel better now, but I'm still beat. I'll be having another nap, I think."

"Can I get you anything before I go?"

"Nah, I'm good."

I stood up and took my plate to the sink. God, I wished I didn't have to leave him right now. I looked at the door and sighed.

"Dallas?"

"Yeah?"

Justin got off his scooter and stood up slowly. "There is something you can get me."

"What's that?"

"A hug. I need a hug."

Christ, I could have cried. I threw my arms around him and held him, breathing him in, his scent, his warmth, the feel of him against me. I didn't want to let go. Not now, not ever. "I needed this too," I whispered.

He rubbed my back with his good arm and buried his face in my neck, and for a long, perfect moment, we never moved. All my worries stripped away; everything that plagued me just minutes earlier was gone. This was what mattered. Justin was what mattered most.

"One more thing," he said.

I pulled back so I could see his face. "Sure."

He pointed to his mouth. "Kiss me?"

Smiling, I took hold of his face and watched as he gasped, his eyes fluttering closed. I brought his chin up and caressed his lips with mine, ghosting a kiss before kissing him deeper. I gave him the barest of tongue, the sweetest taste, before pulling away. His eyes were still closed and when he opened them, he looked drunk. It took him an adorable second to focus on me.

"Oh," he breathed.

I laughed. "You 'right to stand by yourself?"

He chuckled and sank his teeth into his bottom lip. His cheeks were pink, his eyes had stars. "Wow."

"Here, let me get your scooter," I said, helping him sit on it. "You okay?"

"Mm," he replied. "Much better."

"Me too," I said. I put my finger under his chin and leaned down to peck his lips again. "I won't be long."

He gave me a lazy smirk as I walked out. I took the stairs with a skip in my step. Davo spotted me. "Is Jusso all right?"

I was certainly happier now than I was when I dashed up the stairs earlier. "Sure. Just a bit of a reality check, that's all."

He cocked his head. "Reality check?"

Yes, reality. Both the business and Justin needed me equally. I needed to do more, be more. "Yep. Now, what else did you need me to do?"

DAVO AND SPARRA left at knock-off time and I stuck around to get as much done as I could. I did some maths before putting in a few stock orders, making sure I had enough in my account this time. I hated that I needed to be so cautious, that I had to count every cent and transfer money between accounts so I could pay bills. It was a stress I just didn't need.

I returned some phone calls, tidied up, and swept the whole shop out. I got everything ready for the morning, locked up, took all the papers from my desk and my laptop, and went upstairs.

Juss was asleep on the couch when I walked in, Squish purring loudly on his lap. The TV was on some animal documentary and I smiled at the thought of Juss putting something on for Squish to watch. The photographs I'd given him at the hospital were on the couch beside him, with his journal and his phone, and the jigsaw on the table was almost complete, so he'd had a busy afternoon.

He stirred when I put my stuff down. "Hey, didn't mean to wake you," I said quietly.

"Just dozing," he replied, sitting up. "What time is it?"

"Almost six."

"Was gonna cook dinner," he said. He sat the recliner up, then lifted Squish off his lap so he could stand. "Got the meat out of the freezer."

"You want to cook?" I asked, surprised.

"Yeah." He frowned. "Is that okay?"

"Absolutely!" I said, grinning.

Happier now, he got on his scooter and went to the cupboard by the stove. "I want to do stuff. Help out, ya know?"

"I have some paperwork to get through, so you cooking dinner would be incredibly helpful, thank you."

He beamed. "Well, I dunno how good it'll be. If it's awful, we might be having toast."

"What are you gonna cook?"

"My nan's spaghetti. I remember how to cook it, so . . ."

"Was always a favourite of mine." He used to cook it often, and I was oddly glad that his nan had passed away before he moved to Darwin. He remembered she was gone, and I couldn't bear the thought of him having to grieve a second time. I squeezed his shoulder on my way to the fridge. "Can I get the chef a drink? Orange and mango mineral water, plain water, juice?"

"Um . . . A mineral water, thanks. Sick of plain water today."

Truth be told, I didn't get much work done. He needed help lifting stuff, but it didn't matter. Helping him reclaim some independence was important. I didn't do any of the cooking part; that was all him. But he couldn't fill the pot and carry it to the stove with one arm whilst on a scooter.

And when I wasn't helping, I was watching. It was good to see him doing things, even mundane things like cooking. Especially mundane, everyday things, even though I had to remind myself this was far from mundane for Justin. The fact he wanted to help out, and even that he thought to help out, was a pretty big deal.

"You keep staring at me," he said. He was now standing by the stove, stirring the pot. The smell in the flat was amazing, and seeing him concentrate and taste, adding a bit of this and a touch of that, and stirring some more just made me so damn happy.

"Because you're kinda great, you know that?"

He made a face and shook his head, as though it was too absurd to be true, but then he shot me a strange look. Startled and confused? He put his hand to his head. "Oh."

"Oh, what?" I said, getting to my feet. If he felt dizzy, should he be about to fall . . .

"I . . . I think I remember something," he mumbled. He frowned again. "Did we . . . ? Did I . . . ? I made this for you before." He looked around the kitchen as though something didn't make sense. "But not here. The kitchen was yellow."

I took a step toward him. "You remember that?"

"Did that happen?"

"Yes! At your old flat. Where you lived at when you moved back to Newcastle from Darwin. The flat was tiny and the kitchen was just one small bank of cupboards with a sink. The walls were yellow."

"I remember," he said. "I had a flashback. Of me cooking. I can't see you but I know I'm cooking for you, and I was nervous but you said it smelled great and then I said . . . something. And you said, 'Because you're kinda great, you know that?' just like you said now." He stared at me, his eyes wide. "Oh my God, I remember that."

I went to him and put my hands on his shoulders, his neck, his jaw, and I pulled him in for a hug. I was surprised by how emotional it made me. But he remembered something else, something to do with me, with us.

"You asked me to your place for dinner. You were so nervous," I told him. "But dinner was amazing. You had an old table with three mismatched chairs and a couch you'd bought second hand. We watched a movie on TV. Um, *Beverly Hills Cop*, I think."

He laughed into my neck, but it was teary. "That's something I'd watch."

I pulled back and slid my hand along his jaw. I stared into those dark brown eyes and thumbed his cheek. "You remembered something."

He nodded, still teary. "Must have been what you said and me cooking the same food. I don't know. But it came back to me."

I rested my forehead to his. "I'm so happy for you."

He closed his eyes. "It's just another random thing, though. Nothing too important."

"Are you kidding, baby? That's huge and very important!"

He sighed and one corner of his mouth lifted. "I like it when you call me baby."

That made me smile. "Anything you remember is important," I said. "Every single thing."

"I wish I could see your face," he said sadly. "In my memory. I can hear your laugh, though. And I know it's you. I can feel it."

I lifted his chin and pecked his lips. "Baby, that's amazing."

He rested his head on my shoulder and looked at the stove. "Shit, I'm burning dinner."

I laughed and we turned everything off and I drained the spaghetti and he plated it up. We sat at the table and he waited for me to take the first taste.

"Oh, this is good," I said with my mouth half-full. "Just like you always make it."

He took a small bite and gave it an approving nod. "It's not bad."

We ate in silence for a few bites, and I paused to take a sip of my drink. I tapped my can to his. "Compliments to the chef."

He was happier, and if that was because he'd cooked dinner or because he remembered something or because he liked my compliment, I wasn't sure. Maybe it was all three.

"Did you say accounts?" he asked, nodding toward where I'd stacked the papers on top of my laptop.

I wasn't gonna tell him about my money worries, but I didn't want to hide this from him. Maybe just not the extent of it. It was a fine line. "Yeah. I just have a few things to get done tonight. I'll need to be working in the shop with the boys this week and not in the office, so if I can keep on top of the paperwork . . ."

"Is that because I'm not there?" he asked. "Do you have to do my job?"

Shit. I withheld the sigh that threatened to escape and put my fork down. "Not exactly. I mean, yes, a little bit. But it's nothing we can't handle until you're ready to come back."

His brow furrowed and I gave him time to think about what I'd said. He ate some more of his pasta but then pushed what was left around his plate with his fork. "Do Davo and Sparra have to do my work too?"

Shit.

I didn't want him to feel bad, but I also wouldn't lie to him. "The three of us are filling in the gaps. When I was at the hospital every day, Davo and Sparra did everything. They really covered my arse. So now we're home, I'm trying to do as much as I can to help them out. We have an important contract coming up, one we do every year, and it's good money. I can't drop the ball on it."

"I don't like letting you down," he whispered.

I reached over and squeezed his arm. "You're not. At all. In any way. You're my priority, first and foremost, Jussy. But my business is important too. Davo and Sparra depend on me for a job and I don't want to let them down. I just need to get the balance right, that's all. So if I have to do some work on the computer while we sit on the couch after dinner, then so be it."

He tried to smile but couldn't quite manage it. "My accident . . ."

When he said nothing else, I did. "Your accident was not your fault. It wasn't anyone's fault. And we'll get through this, I have no doubt. I just want to try and do the right thing by everyone, that's all."

"I want to help. I can do . . ." He frowned again, like he couldn't find the right word. He shrugged. "I don't know what I can do."

"You can get better, and you can rest and recover," I said. "And you can make an awesome spaghetti."

That earned me a small smile, but it didn't last long. "I hate that everything is so hard. I want to do things but I'm tired, and my leg and my arm are stupid, and my head hurts most of the time. And the worst part is that I can't think properly. Like sometimes it's clear, and sometimes it's foggy, sometimes it's like I'm underwater. I hate that I can't remember everything, and I hate that I feel so lost."

"Lost?"

He gave a small nod. "I dunno who I am. I mean, I know I'm Justin, and I know where I come from, and all that shit. But I dunno who I was. The last five years were so important and I've lost that. I dunno who *that* Justin is."

I pulled my chair around so I faced him, and I took his hand. "Baby, I wish I could fix that. I wish I knew how to get everything back. I hate that you feel that way, but I completely understand why you do. I'm sure I'd feel the same if it were me in that van that day."

"I just feel . . . lost. And sad." He shrugged. "I guess today's just a bad day, but I . . ." His chin wobbled and his eyes became glassy. "I dunno."

"Oh, baby," I whispered. "You're allowed to have bad days." To be honest, I was surprised he hadn't had more bad days before now. "Do you want a hug?"

He nodded quickly, and I stood up and helped him to his feet. I pulled him against me and he snuggled in, fitting the side of his head against my neck. I rubbed his back and held him tight, and for the longest moment, we never moved.

"Thank you," he mumbled.

"What are you thanking me for?"

"For everything. For knowing what I need when I don't."

He made no attempt to move and I certainly wasn't going to. "I need your hugs too."

"I mean it. When I'm all fuzzy and . . . not together . . . I can't think of the word. Anyway, when I'm like that, you hug me and it fixes me."

"Well, you're welcome. You can have a hug any time."

He was quiet again for a bit and he leaned heavily against me as though he were falling asleep. "Thank you for staying."

"Staying where?" *In this hug?*

"With me. For not leaving me. You could have, but you didn't."

I pulled back then so he could see the seriousness in my eyes. "Justin, baby. I love you. I've loved you for years. You are loved. And I know that's probably weird for you, but I need you to know this: I'm not leaving you. Not then, not now, not ever."

His face softened and he almost smiled. "It's not weird. Well, maybe a little bit but not really. We've been on like, one date."

I laughed. "Does tonight not count? You cooked me dinner. It could be our second date."

"Nope. I forgot the candles."

I chuckled and pulled him back in for a hug. His left arm went around me and held me just as tight as I held him. He was warm and smelled like home. "Candles make it a date," I said quietly. "Got it."

He was quiet again and heavy against me. "I like hearing you say it," he mumbled. "That you love me. I know you do. You look after me, and you care."

He liked knowing he was loved, and I couldn't blame him. It was an amazing feeling, comforting like a soft bed and warm blankets on a cold night. I knew he loved me too. I *knew* he did. It was just trapped, hidden under the surface. He'd already remembered slivers of me from our life before the accident. He said my wing tattoos felt safe, like home. And he trusted me, and for a guy who was surrounded by strangers, that was a helluva statement.

His heart knew me, even if his head didn't.

And I clung to that with everything I had.

"Tired," he mumbled.

"Let's get you into bed," I said, leaving his arms to get his scooter.

He took his meds, brushed his teeth, and I helped him into bed. He was too tired for anything else tonight, and I reasoned he'd feel better in the morning after a shower. Squish followed him onto the bed and I sat on the edge of the bed beside Juss. He was smiling as he drifted off and I kissed his forehead before I left them to sleep.

I cleaned up after dinner—Justin had never been a tidy cook—then sat at the table and fired up my laptop. I managed to put a dent in my paperwork, paying what bills I could afford and watching my bank overdraft with every invoice, but after a while, I could barely keep my eyes open.

I turned everything off and used the bathroom, then stood in the hall wondering which bed I should sleep in. My head told me to go to my room, but my heart was across the hall in our old bed . . .

I didn't get to make that decision, though. Because Juss started to stir and fuss in his sleep, and as I got to the door, he startled awake, sitting up with a gasp and a cry. "Dallas?"

I went straight to him. "Hey, baby. I'm right here."

He clung to me, pawing at my arm and my hand. "Sleep here. Need you here with me."

"Okay," I whispered. I crawled over him and got under the covers. He was snuggled into my side before my head was even on the pillow. "You okay now?"

He murmured something affirmative and sighed, slipping straight back to sleep. I wrapped him in my arms and inhaled deeply. It was so familiar and lovely, but a little strange. Our relationship was now unusual and complicated, to say the least. I knew everything about him, but he was just beginning to know me. We'd been together for years but were technically dating again, we'd made love hundreds of times, but to him, we'd only kissed a handful of times. Four weeks ago, he had no clue who I was, yet he couldn't sleep without me.

So yeah, it was weird and complicated, but it was kind of wonderful too.

We got a second chance, and not everyone did. I wasn't about to waste that. Sure, I had to juggle work and a business and clients and staff. I never expected this to be easy, and honestly, I reckoned we got out of it easier than those in a lot of the stories I'd read about brain injury.

I just had to count my blessings and take each day as it came.

Was getting to hold Juss while he slept a blessing? Hell fucking yes it was.

I WOKE up when Justin rolled over. He slept soundly. Clearly having the cast off his arm was more comfortable for him. He sure was peaceful.

I got out of bed before him because I was only wearing boxer briefs and I didn't want my morning wood to make things awkward. A shower and a quick wank took care of the wood issue. I got dressed and began making breakfast.

Justin came out on his scooter, scowling, still half-asleep. His grumpy morning face always made me smile. "Coffee?" I asked.

"Hmm."

"Toast?"

"Hmm."

I chuckled as I handed him a piece of toast. "Butter and Vegemite," I said as I went to the fridge for the milk.

He even chewed grumpily. "You're happy this morning?"

"Yep." I grinned at him and put his coffee on the kitchen counter. This was our morning routine now. Same as the day before, and the day before that. It wasn't monotonous to me. It was establishing familiarity for Juss, someone with a brain injury, something he could depend on. "Sleep okay?"

He frowned. "Can only sleep if you're there, apparently."

"I don't mind. I sleep better when I sleep with you too."

He sipped his decaf coffee and his scowl lessened a little. "Need a shower."

"Okay," I said easily. "What are your plans for the day?"

His angry brow returned. "Couch. TV. Jigsaw puzzle. Boring shit. Nap, followed by more boring shit."

"How d'ya feel today? Okay?"

"Better. Not as tired as I thought I'd be."

"Your home-care nurse will be here at nine."

He sighed and drank more coffee, and I began to wonder if there was more to his demeanour than just being his old not-a-morning person. He seemed more sad than grumpy.

I waited for him to get out of the shower, tidying up and wiping everything down. I packed up my laptop and all my papers from last night and was pulling my boots on when he came out. He walked, limping on his injured leg and pushing his scooter, to the couch. He was wearing a pair of shorts and one of my old T-shirts that looked really good on him. He offered half a smile, but it wasn't very happy.

"How does your arm feel out of the cast?" I asked. "Good to finally be able to wet and wash it?"

"Yeah," he said. He opened and closed his fist and wiggled his fingers. He straightened his elbow a bit and turned his palm upward, but not all the way. "Doesn't like to move much, but it's better."

When he was on the couch, I put a bottle of water beside him and planted a kiss on the top of his freshly washed hair. "I'll be downstairs. Call or text me if you need me."

"Hmm" was his only reply.

Yeah, he was definitely sad and cranky today. I left him to it and went downstairs, opening up the shop, trying to get a head start before the boys arrived. Before I knew it, they rolled in and work began. And I swear, just a few minutes later, Justin's nurse, Megan, arrived.

I needed more hours in the day.

I met Megan at the bottom of the stairs. "Just a sec," I said quietly, wiping my hands on my work pants.

"Everything okay?" she asked.

"Yeah, he was just a bit out of sorts this morning. He's never been a morning person, but he seems . . . sad." I didn't want to say depressed because I certainly couldn't diagnose that. "Just wanted to give you a heads up."

"Thanks. I appreciate it."

"Let me know if there's something he needs," I added. "He might be more comfortable telling you? I don't know . . . He said last night he worried that he was a burden, basically. Not working, not contributing, that kind of thing. I told him the only thing he needs to do is get better, but I don't think that helped much."

She patted my arm and smiled. "I'll go check on him."

I watched her go up the stairs and when I looked back into the shop, I saw Sparra watching me. "Everything all right, boss?"

"Yeah, mate. Jusso was a bit down last night and this morning. I just wanted to give the nurse a heads up, that's all."

Sparra frowned. "Is he all right?"

"Yeah. Just part of the process, apparently. He's okay. I'll wait to see what Megan says after she sees him."

"Has to be hard on him. He must feel like a stranger," Sparra said. "Let me know if there's anything I can do."

"I will, thanks," I said, clapping him on the shoulder before we went back to our work. I went back to the bike I'd been working on and tried to keep myself occupied, which wasn't entirely easy with one eye on the back stairs. And I couldn't help but think of something Justin said last night and what Sparra had said earlier.

After an eternity, which was probably closer to thirty minutes, Megan appeared. I left my station and she smiled as I walked over. "How is he?"

She gave a serious nod. "Yeah, he's okay. Like you said, he's feeling pretty low. It's not uncommon. But his arm looks good, his range of motion is good. He's walking more, his meds are all fine."

"He remembered something yesterday," I said. "Like an

actual memory. Everything else has been kind of factual, but this was a memory."

Megan smiled. "He told me that."

"Hey, can I ask you something?" Then I added quickly, "It's about Justin."

"Sure. You can ask; what I can answer is a different story."

"Yeah, that's fine, it's just that . . . He said he was feeling kinda lost and even bored, I guess. Everything feels so strange to him, which is understandable. But what if he came down here into the workshop for an hour or two every day? Maybe just in the mornings, when he's not so tired. Not to work or anything, but just to be . . . included."

Megan smiled. "I think he'd like that."

I know he'd like it. "Yeah, but is he up for that? Is it too soon? I don't want to rush him if he's not ready. And what if he gets hurt?"

"I think he's up for it. But maybe start with a short time first up," she suggested. "It might help him reconnect with who he is. It's very common for someone with amnesia to feel disconnected with who they were before and who they are now."

"He's a mechanic," I said. "One of the best motocross bike mechanics in town."

"Then, sure," she replied. "Let him try. Just remember, he tires easily. Nothing strenuous, nothing heavy or fast. He'll need to readjust to how his brain receives and responds. His reaction times are much slower."

"Yeah, of course."

She said she'd be back tomorrow, though I didn't even wait for her to get halfway to her car before I raced up the stairs and into the flat. Justin was at the table, staring at the jigsaw puzzle. "Hey," I said. "How was your session with Megan?"

He shrugged, then sighed. "Okay."

"How's the puzzle going?" I asked.

"It's shit." He'd almost finished it, but clearly, he wasn't happy with it. "This isn't my idea of fun."

I went and sat beside him. "I know, baby."

He chewed on the inside of his lip, not making eye contact

with me. "I just . . . I know I have a long road ahead of me. But I'm starting to think I'll never be back to who I was."

"What if I suggested something that might help?" I asked. "If you're feeling up to it, that is."

"I don't want to do any more fucking puzzles, Dallas."

I took his hand. "What about a different kind of puzzle? One you love and could probably do with your eyes closed."

His gaze met mine, interest piqued.

"It would mean coming downstairs for a bit. Like maybe an hour or so every morning."

"A puzzle?" he asked with the barest hint of a smile. "Downstairs?"

"Yep." I stood up. "Come on, on your feet."

He smiled now and slowly stood. "Okay . . . ?"

"I'll take your scooter down the stairs," I said, picking it up and running it to the bottom of the stairs. When I got back up to the top, Juss was at the door. "Okay, you ready?"

He nodded and we came down the stairs like we did the other day. Him, slowly, one step at a time, and me, in front and facing him, going down backwards so I could hold him. I helped him onto the scooter, and when we went into the workshop, he was smiling.

"Here's the big fella," Davo said, spotting him, grinning. "Has he got you working already?"

"Not sure," he replied. "Some kind of puzzle."

Davo nodded, knowingly. "Ah, great idea."

"It was Davo's idea," I admitted. "And then Sparra said something earlier about how you being upstairs must make you feel like a stranger, and I realised he was right. You need to be included, down here where you belong. With us. Doing what you love."

Justin's eyes met mine and his smile softened. "Thanks."

"You're welcome. The puzzle, though," I said, waving my hand to the back corner. "Two Kawasaki two-stroke engine blocks that need to be pulled apart and cleaned, moving parts replaced, and all put back together again."

The truth was, this was a menial task. Pain-in-the-arse jobs we'd put off forever, but they could be perfect for Justin. No brain splitting thinking required, just procedural motions. Sparra's jigsaw puzzles had been a great idea, but Davo's real-life motorbike engine puzzle idea was even better.

Justin stared at me, disbelievingly. "You want me to do that?"

"You reckon you're up for it?"

His smile morphed into a grin. "Hell yes." But then he got a little teary. He swallowed hard and took a deep breath. "Thank you."

I stepped in closer and put my arm around him. "You're very welcome."

Chapter Five

DAVO LOWERED the movable workbench and locked the wheels down tight, giving Justin a workstation which was more suitable to his scooter. I carried the first engine over for him but left him to find all his tools and equipment. It was part of the process, after all: getting him back on the team and keeping him busy and productive.

I kept an eye on him, and even with his right arm still in the collar-cuff, he never stopped smiling.

Even when he became tired just before lunch, he really was so much happier.

He found everything he needed: he sometimes walked to it, sometimes scooted over to get whichever tool he needed. But his smile . . .

It was so worth it.

When his blinks began to get longer, I went over. "How're you going with it?"

"Good," he said, looking up at me. He was happy but oh so tired. "Got lots done."

It was true. He was making great progress. "It's almost lunchtime," I said. "And you look beat."

He gave a small nod. "Wish I wasn't tired."

"I know. But the best part is that you can do this again tomorrow."

"Tomorrow?"

"Yeah. Nurse Megan said you should only do a few hours each morning. Just to start with." Okay, so that wasn't entirely true, but a medical professional's opinion held more water than mine. She had suggested just a few hours, but it was really me who didn't want him to overdo it. Plus, I was pretty sure once he got himself onto the couch, he was gonna nap for a good while.

"Okay," he murmured. "I can finish this off tomorrow, right?"

"Sure you can. If you want to."

He smiled again. "I want to."

"Come on, let's get you upstairs." We went to the bottom step but there was no way he was gonna make that climb, not with how tired he was. He stood up off his scooter and held the handrail. "Hey baby," I whispered. "Put your arm around my neck. I'll carry you."

He shot me a humoured look. "Only 'cause you called me baby."

I picked him up bridal style, careful of his leg and arm, and carried him up. I got him inside, and when I lowered his feet to the floor, he kept his arm around my neck. We were incredibly close, our faces barely an inch apart. His eyes went to my mouth, then to my eyes.

I knew that look . . .

"Kiss me," he murmured.

I brought our lips together, but it was he who deepened the kiss. Like someone flipped a switch and he suddenly remembered that kissing was a thing, he tilted his head and opened his mouth for my tongue. I slid my arms around him, pulling our bodies flush, every cell in my body alight.

He groaned and felt heavy in my arms. He was tired, and his kisses were like the sleepy Sunday morning kisses we'd shared so many times. I broke the kiss and he smiled before letting his head fall to my chest.

"Okay, sleeping beauty," I said. "Let's get you onto the couch."

I helped him sit and he reclined his seat, closing his eyes already. "Tired."

I gently brushed my fingers through the hair at his temple. "Go to sleep. I'll put your lunch beside you for when you wake up."

"Hmm," he murmured, but was already out.

I studied his sleeping face; the small scar above his eye, the huge scar down the side of his head. The way his dark lashes fanned out, his stubble, how his lips were wet from our kiss, smiling . . .

God, he was beautiful.

I made him some cheese sandwiches and put them in a Squish-proof container, along with a bottle of water and a banana, and set them beside him. He stirred awake. "Sorry, baby. Didn't mean to wake you. Here's your lunch."

Bleary-eyed and barely awake, he ate half a sandwich and downed half the water and was already snoring softly by the time I put my plate in the sink. Certain now that he'd eaten something, he'd sleep for a while, I went back to work.

"He seemed happier," Sparra said as I walked in.

"So much happier," I replied, though I was sure he and Davo could tell by my smile.

"Is he resting okay now?" Davo asked.

"He's snoring already. So I reckon I've got about three hours before he wakes up and I get a text from him." I checked my watch. "Let's see how much I can get done before then."

Davo laughed, but I did get a lot done. I was also right about getting a text message from Jussy as soon as he woke up.

Thanks for the sandwiches

I grinned at my phone. *You're welcome*

Did you kiss me?

I stared at my phone, wondering what the hell that was about when he sent through another.

Or was I dreaming?

Now I laughed. *You weren't dreaming. You asked me to kiss you*

His reply took a little while. *Was thinking . . . maybe second date tonight?*

I replied immediately. *Yes please*

Second second date. With candles

Yes, I typed out. *Our second second date. What did you want to do?*

More kissing

I barked out a laugh, the sound echoing through the workshop. *Yes please*

There was nothing for a few moments and I wondered if that was the end of it. Then my phone beeped again. *Dallas?*

Yeah?

I think I really like you

I laughed again, and so God help me, I wanted to hug my phone. *I think I really like you too*

I looked up to find Davo smiling at me. He shook his head. "Just like how you were in the old days."

"What old days?"

"When you two first started out. That's how you used to look at your phone all the time."

I rolled my eyes. "Did not."

He snorted. "When he's down here tomorrow, need me to lock you both in your office again? I'll do it. Just say the word."

I smirked. "Nah, thanks. I think we're good."

He nodded, smiling. "Glad to hear. Now can you help me get these bearings out?"

"Yeah, of course." I really liked working with Davo. We'd worked together for a lot of years, since I was nineteen, actually. He was a champion bloke and had become my closest friend—outside Justin, that is. We didn't need to talk when we worked. We just got it done, each knowing what we had to do without saying.

It made time go quicker, and we were twice as productive. It was a good distraction too. I only thought about Justin maybe fifty times instead of a hundred. Yes, it was great to get work done, but I was grateful when knock-off time rolled around.

Same as the day before, when I locked everything up, I took

some paperwork upstairs with me. The TV was on, volume low, but there was no Justin and his scooter was beside the couch. I was just about to call out when I heard the toilet flush and then the water at the bathroom sink.

I put my laptop down on the table just as Justin walked out. Well, it was a limp, but he was still walking. "Hey. I thought I heard the roller door close," he said with a smile.

The fact he heard anything from downstairs was kind of new. His brain registering new and different things was a good sign.

"Hi," I replied. "You look good."

"Oh," he looked down at his clothes. "Um, thanks? I don't know who owns this shirt."

I laughed. "Sorry, I meant you looked good, up and walking around and happy."

He walked over to stand a foot in front of me. "Leg feels pretty good, though I had a decent sleep at lunch. I'm always better after a good sleep. And me and Squish spent the afternoon resting pretty easy."

I noticed then, a little late, that he wasn't wearing his collar-cuff thing. "How's your arm feel?"

"Yeah, all right. That sling thing was pissing me off. I took it off not long ago." He slowly straightened his arm, proving his point that his arm was fine.

"Good, I'm glad," I said. "Must feel good to be on your feet again and to have your arm back."

"Hell yes."

"And the shirt was mine, originally," I said. "But we usually just wear whatever's clean. Our wardrobe merged a long time ago."

He looked down at the Rip Curl shirt. "Thought it was too big for me, but I still like it. Or maybe I like it because it's yours."

That sent a bloom of warmth through my chest. "So what were you thinking we should do for our second, second date?"

"Dunno. It's probably gonna be something boring like dinner and maybe that TV show you mentioned, which I'll probably fall asleep trying to watch." He made a face. "Is that lame? You probably want to do something like going out or—"

"Are you kidding? That sounds perfect to me."

He took a small step closer and took my hand. He seemed suddenly nervous, blinking and licking his lips. "I want to thank you for today."

Oh, baby. "You don't need to thank me. You seemed so sad, like you needed to do something you used to do. You needed to do something familiar and something that reminded you of who you are."

"I did. But I didn't know that was what I needed. I just felt all wrong and useless, but I didn't know how to say that. But you knew what I needed."

"Because I know you, Juss." I gently skimmed my fingers from the hair at his forehead and down to his jaw. "I know the old Justin needed to be working and pulling bikes apart, and fixing them is what you know. It's what you do, what you've always done. The new you isn't much different at all."

"Sometimes I don't think I know who I am," he whispered. "But you do."

"You're still the same, Juss. We just need to help you reconnect with that, that's all."

He sighed. "I don't know where I'd be without you."

I took his face in my hands and kissed his forehead, his cheekbone, his lips. "You're gonna be okay, baby. We got this. You and me."

He leaned into me and his arms went around me, and for a long moment, we just stood there holding each other. Until my dick started to get ideas . . .

Needing to put some space between us, I pulled back. "Okay, so let's make a start on dinner." I went to the fridge and pulled out some minced meat. "How about rissoles and gravy and some mash."

He gave me a lazy smile. "Perfect."

There was something else in his eyes, something warm and kind that glittered with familiarity. It was how he used to look at me. I tried not to read too much into it or to get ahead of myself, but it was hard to ignore the flood of butterflies in my belly.

I began making the rissoles and Justin peeled the potatoes,

and being side by side with him at the kitchen sink felt kind of surreal.

"What are you smiling at?" he asked.

I chuckled and gently nudged him with my shoulder. "Nothing. Just happy."

He grinned at that. "Me too. I'm already looking forward to tomorrow."

That made my heart soar. Giving him the smallest, mundane job had impacted him so much. He was finally beginning to feel like himself again, even if for just a few hours a day. "Me too."

After we'd eaten and cleaned up, we ventured to the couch. And just like always, I sat next to him and he automatically moved closer and snuggled in. But this time, instead of putting the footrests up, we ended up lying down, with my head on the armrest and him at the front as the little spoon. We turned the TV on, but Justin rolled over to face me, careful of his arm and leg.

He was smiling and peaceful and a little dozy. "Hey, Dall, tell me what we did on our first holiday. Where did we go? Did we even go somewhere?"

I trailed my fingers through his hair. "Just for long weekends, usually," I murmured. "I couldn't really leave the shop for long, maybe just a day or two. First time we went away together was just up the coast to Hallidays Point."

"Did we stay on the beach?"

"Yep, but it was freezing cold," I said, smiling at the memory.

"Did we take our bikes?"

"Sure did. We put them in the back of the ute and drove up, but we rode our bikes along the trails in the national park up there."

The corner of his mouth pulled upward. "Sounds like something I'd do."

I chuckled. "It was a great weekend."

"But it was cold? Why'd we go to the beach in winter?"

"It was some winter escape deal you saw in the paper."

"Did we go swimming?"

"We, uh . . . No, we didn't venture out too much. Just to ride our bikes."

He slow blinked and gave a lazy smile. He didn't seem to cotton on to the reason why we didn't venture out too much. Because we basically spent the entire weekend in bed, save two rides on the bike trails. But now, with him lying so close and me thinking back to that weekend, my dick started paying attention.

I shuffled my hips back a little as much as the couch would allow, though he was oblivious to my growing erection.

"Hey, when's your birthday?" he asked.

I grinned. "July thirtieth."

He met my gaze. "Winter. Did we go away for your birthday?"

"Yes. It was your idea. You surprised me with a weekend away."

He chuckled. "That was nice of me."

That made me laugh. "It sure was." I studied his eyes for a long moment. "We can do that again one day. A weekend at the beach or in the country somewhere. When you're feeling up for it."

He sighed. "I just want to get back to work. That sounds weird, probably. But . . ."

"But what?"

"But I know work. You showed me that today. I know how to pull engines apart, like how I know how to get dressed, or how to walk. It's just like you said: it's what I am, it's what I do." His mouth drew downward. "Since the accident, there hasn't been much that I really know. Losing five years of my life has been shit, and there's been so much that I've had to relearn. But I know bikes."

I thumbed his eyebrow. "You sure do. And baby, if you wanna work, then we work. I don't mind one bit. I have some catching up to do."

"And I want to help."

"You will. Tomorrow morning, for a few hours until Megan turns up, you're back on duty."

That earned me my favourite grin again, but his eyes closed

and I thought he might fall asleep. "I like being here, like this, with you."

I stroked his cheek again, taking in every aspect of his beautiful face. "I like it too."

"Tired again," he mumbled.

"We should get you into bed. I'm kind of pinned-in here. Gonna need you to get up first."

He didn't open his eyes when he mumbled, "You make me sleepy. Warm and safe."

I could have kissed him, and I almost did. But he was half-asleep and that would've felt wrong. "C'mon, baby. Time to get up."

He cracked one eye, then the other, and after a bit more rousing, he finally got up. We got ready for bed and I turned everything off with every intention of going back out to the table to do some paperwork while he slept. But I helped him into bed, and he kept a hold of my hand, so I had a choice: I could leave him and get my work finished, or I could crawl into bed with him and relish the feel of him in my arms.

It was never a contest.

And he never stirred with a nightmare, because he clung to me like a magnet and I never let him go. He slept right through until morning when he woke up with a start.

He sat up in bed, scowling his usual grumpy morning glare at me. He rubbed the scar down the side of his head, and his right eye closed before the left and he squinted like he had a headache. Then he yawned and looked around the room, then at me. "Oh."

"Oh, what?" He sounded disappointed when he saw it was me he was in bed with. "You okay?"

"Yeah. Just a stupid dream. Remember that time we went to your Aunt Robyn's seventieth birthday and she made that lime jelly cake with coconut, and it was the grossest shit ever? I dreamed about eating that." He shook his head slowly. "Fucking weird."

I stared at him and sat up because he didn't even realise . . .

"Justin, you just remembered something."

"Yeah, it was—" His eyes went wide, his jaw slack. "Holy shit."

I barked out a laugh. "But you're right. That cake was the grossest shit ever."

He laughed too, disbelieving. "I remember it. A stupid cake, of all things." He screwed his face up and shook his head. "I dreamed it, but now I remember it! You were there! You wore that chequered blue shirt and you were laughing at something . . ."

"Probably the cake," I said. "But oh my God. You remembered something! And you can remember the shirt I wore?"

"Yes! When was that?"

"Uh, like three years ago."

He broke out in a grin. "I remember something. Something with you in it! And remember, you wanted to leave early but your brother got really drunk, so then you wanted to stick around to see him make a tit of himself."

I burst out laughing. "Yes!" I gave him a side-on hug. "Baby, you remembered something!"

He stared at me, his expression full of awe. "And we had to call into the supermarket on the way and get some flowers because your dad asked us to. And your cousin had to drive your brother home because he was so drunk and he spewed in his car, and you laughed for two days. And the next week we had that delivery fuck-up with the spare parts. Remember? They sent us the wrong order. And we tried that new pizza place. And holy fuck, Dallas, I can remember this." He became teary and his chin wobbled. "I remember it. I was there. I can actually remember and what it felt like . . . I can remember that week, or parts of it, at least. What does that mean?"

I rubbed his back. "I don't know, baby. But it's a good thing. Can you think of anything else?"

He squinted a bit, then shook his head. "I dunno. Maybe. Not really. It's just there, snippets and pieces, like it was never gone."

I leaned down and kissed his bare shoulder. "That's so awesome."

He laughed. "We tried that new pizza place and it was too fancy for us. Who the fuck puts rocket and feta on a pizza? But we tried the meat lovers and you reckoned it tasted like goat." He covered his grin with his hand; his eyes became glassy. "Dallas, I remember! I remember you."

Then he took a deep breath and nodded and began to cry.

"Oh, baby. It's okay," I whispered, pulling him down onto the bed so I could hold him properly. "It's okay."

He cried and sobbed into my chest and I held him as tight as I could. "I remember you," he mumbled. "It was all I wanted, to remember you, your face, your smile. I felt like I was letting you down because I couldn't remember . . ."

I rubbed his back and kissed the side of his head. "You could never let me down. I love you, Justin, whether you remember me or not."

He pulled back a little and, taking my hand, put my palm to his chest. "I felt those memories in here." He kept his face down so I couldn't see his eyes. "That connection. I felt it, in my memories. In here." He looked up then. "What we have is real."

I laughed and kinda cried at the same time. I was so freaking happy and relieved and floored. All my emotions were scrambled. "It's real, Juss. It's the realest thing I've ever known."

He sighed and put his head back to my chest. "These wings," he said, putting his hand to my tattoo. "I knew these wings and how they felt like home. But these memories are different, somehow. And there was a yellow Charger. Who drove a yellow Charger?"

"Sparra owned a yellow Charger," I answered. "But that was years before my Aunt's birthday and awful cake."

"It had a black stripe up the side."

"Yes, that's right."

"And you gave me my KTM . . ." He shot back and stared at me. "You gave it to me as a birthday present. Oh my God, you bought that for me! For my thirtieth. I remember! And Becca and the girls came up. Holy shit, I remember . . . Sophie's all big now!"

I laughed. "My God, Juss. Those memories are all over the years."

He was teary again. "They're not in any order. Nothing kinda makes sense, and it's random as hell. Makes my head hurt, not gonna lie."

I put my hand to his forehead. "Do you feel okay?"

He gave me a smile. "No, nothing like that. I feel great. My head's still foggy, but something obviously cleared up. Just feels . . . like the hinges on the memory door could use some WD-40, that's all."

I barked out a laugh. "What about some coffee?"

He smiled. "Suppose. Even decaf."

As much as I wanted to stay in bed with him, I knew we couldn't. "You have an engine to finish today, remember?"

He brightened. "Oh shit, yes." He rolled away from me and sat on the edge of the bed. "You make the coffees. I need to pee."

I watched him get up and limp-walk out to the bathroom across the hall. He would never stop amazing me.

He paused at the door and turned to face me. "I can't believe you bought me the KTM. You never told me that when we talked about it."

"Because I'm not supposed to plant memories. You were so stoked that you finally owned a KTM, I didn't want to tell you in the hospital I bought it for you in case you thought you owed me something. I had to be careful with how I worded things, that's all."

He frowned now. "Yeah, sorry. I'm not blaming you for not telling me. I just can't believe you bought it for me."

I chuckled. "It wasn't brand new when I got it. I couldn't afford brand new."

"I don't care about that," he added quickly. "It's new to me. And now it's new to me again." He snorted. "Anyway, it just means the sooner I can ride it, the better."

I laughed to hide the horror I felt at that thought. "I bought it because it was your dream to own one. But how about we wait for the riding part. I don't think we're there yet." I put my hand to my chest. "Not sure my heart could take it."

He grinned like that was a challenge, then turned back toward the bathroom. "I need to pee."

I chuckled as I got out of bed and pulled on some shorts. I didn't dare hope that we were getting back to how we used to be, but this was us, this was us before the accident—aside from him telling me every time he needed to pee. That was new. And funny. And kind of a very Justin thing to do.

The memory development was amazing. But his emotional connection, his emotional memory, what he felt about me, how he could feel how very real we were . . . well, that was better than any memory to me.

That was everything.

Chapter Six

THE NEXT WEEK was filled with small improvements. Justin could get rid of the collar-cuff-sling thing he hated so much, and he was walking more and more. He still used the scooter, mostly around the workshop, but in the unit he was on his feet. He tried to use a crutch, but it aggravated his arm and he got frustrated with it in about ten seconds and went back to the scooter.

I'd joked with his physiotherapist it was all about the wheels. *If you want to make Justin happy, give the man some wheels.*

He'd been back to the neurologist, and the doc was happy with Justin's health. He'd had a session with Doctor Chang, and she was so happy with his improvements and regained memories she almost cried. Or maybe that was because Justin got all teary when he was telling her and she welled up in sympathy. He'd remembered a few other things during the week. All small, seemingly inconsequential and random things, like a pair of shoes, when we'd gone to the races and he'd won fifty bucks on a horse, and when Squish was a kitten. But every tiny piece of the puzzle made the picture a little clearer.

He'd finished working on the two old engines we'd dubbed his therapy puzzles and had begun helping Sparra with some small jobs. He never pushed himself, though, and he knew his limits because he knew all too well if he went too hard for too long, he'd be absolute cactus the whole next day.

So he put in a few hours every morning and called it quits every day when his nurse arrived. He'd have lunch and a nap on the couch with Squish, and he'd begun cooking dinner before I came upstairs.

He'd even searched a few recipes on his phone, and that was a real sign to me that he was improving. He was using initiative and thinking ahead. After the accident, Justin had been in such a foggy daze, he would just sit and wait, agreeing to whatever I suggested. Now he was reading more and watching more shows on TV that required brainpower.

It was easy to believe things were . . . improving. I didn't want to say 'returning to normal' or 'going back to what they were' because that was never going to happen. The accident had changed him forever. It had changed us forever. But right now, we were in a real good place; Justin was getting better and stronger every day, he was happier, and we'd hold hands and snuggle on the couch, he'd cling to me in his sleep, and we'd kissed a handful of times.

It was just like dating all over again.

And in many ways, it was sweeter the second time around. It wasn't all about sex now, which it had been the first time. We'd fallen hard and fast and couldn't keep our hands off each other back then. Now we were taking things slow and learning about each other.

Sure, I woke up with a hard-on most days, but that was just my body reacting to him being wrapped around me. I was very content with keeping things slow between us. Justin seemed oblivious to my morning wood, and he never seemed curious about sex at all. He wasn't ready, physically, mentally, or emotionally anyway, and being cosied up with him on the couch and kissing and giggling in the ad breaks was all kinds of perfect for me.

If that was all we ever did for the rest of our lives, I'd be a happy, happy man.

On the Friday night, Justin had cooked dinner, and I'd cleaned up while he chatted with his sister, Becca, and the girls on the phone. The weather had turned cool, so he was settled on the couch with a blanket, and I joined him soon after with a bowl of popcorn just as the football was starting.

Justin was staring at the screen but not really looking at it.

"How was Bec?" I asked.

"Oh." He turned to me and smiled. "Yeah, she's good. Busy."

"And the girls?"

"They're great. Loud, to be honest. I dunno how Bec does it."

I chuckled but he seemed distracted. "Everything okay?"

"Yeah . . . just tired."

It was the end of the week, that was true, and he'd been walking more. But I wasn't convinced. "Yeah. Looking forward to the weekend. Did you want to do anything in particular?"

He studied the TV for a long second. "Not really. I dunno."

"Juss, you feel okay?"

"Yeah, of course," he said, affording me a smile that didn't seem to sit right. "Sorry. Tired and over . . . thinking."

Okay so there hadn't been much word confusion lately, until now, and he was out of sorts. I slid the popcorn onto the coffee table and pulled a cushion onto my lap and patted it. "Lie down, baby."

He lay down with his head on my lap, without a word, without any facial expression. Just robotically, the way he was a few weeks ago. I gently ran my fingers through his hair, and not even twenty seconds later, he was asleep. I managed to pull my phone from my pocket without waking him and sent Bec a quick text.

Hey, when you spoke to Juss earlier, was he okay?

Her reply came through half a minute later. *Was okay. Said he'd had a great week but was tired. But then I might have put my foot in something . . . sorry.*

Well, that was never good.

About what?

I asked him if the sex was better the second time around. I meant it as a joke. We'd always talked about that stuff before, Dallas. I'm sorry. He went real quiet. Said he had to go. I'm so sorry.

Fuck, fuck, shit fuck.

It's okay, Bec. He's asleep right now. Will talk to him about it. Give the girls a kiss for me.

Thanks, Dall. Again, I'm really sorry xx

So yes, he was tired. He'd had a really busy week. He'd been productive and he'd made huge strides in his recovery and he was exhausted.

But one mention of sex had knocked him down a peg. Maybe it was my fault for not talking to him about that and asking him if he had any questions. Maybe he'd been trying to figure stuff out in his head and couldn't get the puzzle pieces to fit.

I traced my fingers through his hair and studied his profile. He looked so peaceful. His full lips were parted, his long eyelashes cast perfect shadows, his stubbled jaw, his perfect nose.

There was also the new scar above his eyebrow and the long L-shaped surgical scar along the side of his head. It was hidden by his hair now, though I could see it this close up. I could even see the staple punctures that ran along the outside, making it look like a skin-coloured centipede from a Tim Burton movie.

And yet, he was still beautiful.

I loved him more now than I ever had.

"Hey, baby," I whispered, rousing him gently. "Time for bed."

He cracked one eye and grumbled, but he sat up. It was slow and measured, and I doubted he'd be getting to bed unassisted, so I got to my feet and helped him to his. He all but fell into me, so I helped him to the hall. "Bathroom first?"

It took a second for him to answer. "Yep."

"You okay by yourself, or do you need me to help?"

His brow furrowed but he didn't answer. He just shuffled into the bathroom. So I turned down the bed and waited for him to pee and brush his teeth. I helped him undress and he got into bed wearing just his briefs and I pulled the covers up.

"You stay," he mumbled, his eyes closed.

"Of course," I whispered. "I'll just turn everything off and be straight in."

He was already out of it, so I turned the bedroom light off

and went back out to the living room. It was still early and I wasn't exactly tired, so I tidied up a bit and watched some of the footy. I straightened up the couch, fixing cushions and folding the blanket. Justin's journal was on the coffee table and I left it untouched, but the photos I'd given him weeks ago when he was in hospital were in a pile there as well.

He'd always kept them close by, looking through them periodically. He'd remembered a few of the images and what he'd been doing at the time. But I couldn't help but notice the photos of him and me together were at the top of the pile. The one where we were all dressed up and posing for the camera; the one where we were on the couch, laughing. And the one of us in our bed, his naked torso sweaty and flushed. It was pretty clear what was going on in that photo and he'd picked it straight away. Not that he remembered that particular memory—or any memory of us being intimate, for that matter—but he knew what intimacy looked like. He knew it was us in that photo and that he was bottoming. He even said he was glad that hadn't changed. That he was still the same. He knew all this, but I guess he never put it all together until now. I'd noticed these photos had been looked through more this week. I just assumed he was becoming more familiar with the images and the few memories he'd recovered.

The poor guy had probably been trying to figure out everything on his own. And knowing Justin, he'd probably been stressing over it but didn't want to ask.

We'd definitely have to have a chat tomorrow.

No longer interested in the football game, I turned the TV off, and by the time I'd done my teeth and changed into some sleep shorts, I was grateful for the early night. I slipped in beside Justin, and as soon as my head hit my pillow, he stirred and shuffled over and snuggled into me.

I wrapped an arm around him and kissed his forehead. "Love you, Juss."

I wasn't expecting a response. I thought he was asleep. But his reply came fast and quiet. "Love you, Dall."

My heart came to a screeching halt and I froze, yet his breaths were deep and measured. He was sound asleep. His words had come so fast and so sure, it was like the old Justin. It was something the old Justin and I had said to each other a thousand times. In fact, it was our usual goodnight to each other.

Had something in his sleeping mind answered for him? Without his conscious brain being aware, had some part of his hippocampus relaxed and let a memory slip through? I had no idea. I'd have to ask Doctor Chang during the week.

But right now, I turned into Justin and held him so much tighter.

Love you, Dall.

I fell asleep smiling and I reckon I woke up much the same way.

Chapter Seven

I HAD coffee and toast on the table when Juss came out of the bedroom. He was walking, no scooter, with his hair all messed up and a scowl on his face. His angry-puppy face was so adorable in the morning, and it made me smile.

"Morning," I said, trying not to be too cheerful.

"Hmm," he said as he huffed onto a seat at the table, mindful of his leg. "Morning."

I slid his coffee closer, then his plate of toast. "Sleep okay?"

"Hmm." He sipped his brew and tried a bite of toast. "Yeah."

I smiled behind my coffee cup. I'd always loved his pouty morning face. It was like a puppy learning how to growl. But today I loved it even more. I was still on a high from last night.

He told me he loved me.

So what if he was asleep? His sleeping brain had let a truth trickle out, and I was gonna hold onto that forever.

"What did you want to do this arvo?" I asked. "Supposed to be a nice day out."

He shrugged a shoulder as he sipped his coffee. "Dunno."

"I have some stuff to do downstairs this morning, but I thought maybe we could go and have some fish and chips on the beach for lunch. Sound okay?"

Another bite of toast, another sip of coffee, then the hint of a smile. "Sounds good."

It never took him too long to come to grips with being awake. "I'm gonna go have a quick shower."

"'Kay."

Thirty minutes later, we were both showered, the kitchen was tidied, and I was helping Juss down the stairs. He was getting better and stronger every day. Small steps every day didn't seem like much, but in hindsight, looking back to a week or a fortnight, he really had come far.

He used the scooter in the workshop because the shed itself was huge, with flat concrete floors he could zip around on. He was using his arm more now he'd gotten rid of the collar-cuff. He still couldn't lift anything heavy with it or even hold it out for too long, but he could use it. He had physio exercises for it, and every so often I'd see him rotate his wrist or open and close his fingers.

Always trying to improve.

Such an old-Justin thing to do. Though I really had to stop thinking of him as two different people. There shouldn't be an old and a new Justin. There was just this Justin. My Justin. This was who he was now.

And as soon as I had the roller door up, he made himself busy, cleaning, tidying, sweeping while I ducked into my office. I'd fully caught up on my paperwork, debtors and creditors, orders, and whatnot. We'd completed the Simpson contract and had been paid, which was a relief and took some pressure off. But what I hadn't done was finalise the insurance claim on the van. Or, rather, the insurance company hadn't.

I checked my emails and sighed when there was no reply to my request for an update. I even checked the spam and junk folders. There was nothing. I'd been told that workers' comp and insurance claims could take an eternity, but my case manager was hopeful for a quick turnaround.

Apparently not.

And it wasn't just the van, but the several thousand dollars' worth of tools, equipment, and fit-out in the back of the van that we'd lost as well. None of that was salvageable, and it had been a huge financial loss. After a few weeks of scraping by, things at the shop weren't getting back on track as fast as I'd hoped. And the very last thing I wanted to do was have Justin be worrying over bloody money and having guilt impede his recovery.

Justin's face appeared at the door. "Uh, Dallas? There's a guy pulled up out the front. He's coming in."

The shop was technically closed, and the only people who called past to see us on a weekend were our friends. I followed him out and, sure enough, saw Simmo at the front gate. It was locked, so I went to let him in.

"Long time no see," I said, unlocking the padlock.

"Was just driving through. Thought I'd call in and see how you guys were getting on."

Simmo had worked as a parts rep for years and he used to call in at least once a week. He was a real good bloke and a knock-about kinda guy who loved bikes and motocross as much as us, and over the years, he'd become a mate. He got promoted two years ago to some regional area management role and spent most of his time crunching numbers now instead of riding, but he'd call in every chance he got just for a chat and a laugh.

"We're good," I said, locking the gate behind him. "All things considered. We're doing real good."

He looked over at the workshop and kept his voice low. "How's Justin?"

"He's doing okay. Simmo, I dunno if he'll remember you. He didn't remember Davo or Sparra, so . . ." I gave him a smile. "Let's go find out. He was pushing a broom around last I saw him."

We walked back into the workshop, and sure enough, Justin was on his scooter pushing the broom in front of him. He looked a little too into it, and I kinda got the feeling he might have been watching us chat at the gate and now he was trying to act like he hadn't been. That made me smile.

"Hey, Jusso," I said and waited for him to scoot over. "Do you remember Simmo?"

Justin's gaze went from me to Simmo, then back to me. He shook his head. "No, sorry . . ."

"That's okay," I said brightly. "Justin, this is Luke Simpson. We call him Simmo."

Justin gingerly held out his right hand, and Simmo could obviously see that and thankfully, he shook it gently. "G'day," Juss replied. "Did I . . . ? Did I know you before?"

Simmo glanced at me, then gave a nod. "Yeah, mate."

"Sorry." Justin frowned and gestured loosely to his own head. "I'm missing a few years. Brain got a faulty recalibration."

I chuckled and Simmo laughed. "But you haven't changed much," Simmo said. Then he motioned toward his scooter. "New wheels."

"Yeah, not as fast and four wheels instead of two, but it'll have to do." he replied.

It was then Simmo noticed the scars down Juss' leg. "Holy shit, Jusso."

"Yep," he said, smiling at how Simmo called him that. "Matches the one in my head." He pointed to the scar above his ear.

"Fuck," Simmo breathed, going in for a closer look. "Ouch."

They began talking about scars and surgeries and laughing about stupid shit. It was funny how they were kind of only meeting again now for the first time but still talking like old friends.

Human brains were strange and complex things.

And Simmo was probably the first person to call around to see him as a friend, apart from Davo and Sparra, of course. It was good to see how Justin reacted to meeting someone he guessed he knew before the accident but had no memory of. It didn't seem to upset him at all. He just rolled with it.

I guess this was his new normal.

There was just so much he had to roll with because he didn't have a choice.

And as he took Simmo over to his KTM and showed it to him like he hadn't already seen it, I fell in love with him a little bit more. And Simmo, God bless him, just went with it too. Justin had just given Simmo the rundown on the engine capacity and torque specs, which of course he already knew.

"You've probably seen all this before," Jussy said, a little embarrassed now. "Sorry."

"Nah, mate. Don't apologise," Simmo said. "I'd be excited too if it were mine. And anyway, I could talk about bikes all day long."

Justin smiled. "Same."

"So have they told you when you can ride again?" he asked.

Juss looked to me. "No. Did they tell you, Dallas?"

"No, they haven't said, but if his doctors have any say, it'll be never," I answered with a smile. "But we'll get there."

Justin grinned at me. "Yeah. We will."

"Did you get the insurance sorted from the accident?" Simmo asked.

Shit.

My gaze shot to Justin, something neither of them missed. "Uh, not yet. Still waiting. All the reports were done and in our favour. But you know how insurance and workers' comp are."

Simmo gave me a strained, sorry look. "Yeah, terrible on a good day. Keep on them, though. Squeaky wheel and all that, ya know?"

"Yeah, it's just all red tape and paperwork," I said. "Shouldn't be too much longer."

"Good," he said, then gave Juss a clap on the shoulder. "It's real good to see you up and about. And next time I come through, I wanna see you on that KTM."

Justin smiled and they said their goodbyes, though I knew Justin would have questions for me. I walked Simmo to the gate. "Shit, man," he began. "I'm sorry for bringing the insurance up. I didn't think . . ."

"Nah, it's okay. I just don't want him to stress over it. He has enough to worry about."

"He's doing okay, though, yeah? I mean, he's had more stitches than a baseball."

That made me smile. "He's doing much better, now. Early days were touch and go, but he's made some great progress. He's remembering bits and pieces, which is great."

He shook his head. "Crazy how it can all change so quick, huh?"

"Oh yeah. Every single thing." I snapped my fingers. "Just like that."

He sighed and offered me his hand before he slipped out the gate with promises to see us again soon. I waved him off and walked back up to the workshop, knowing I'd have to face Justin's questions at some point.

But he wasn't sitting on his scooter anymore. He was sitting on his motorbike. I baulked. "Uh, what do you think you're doing?"

"Just wanted to see how it feels," he replied.

I didn't want to know how he got his leg over it. Christ. The idea of him riding a bike again so soon damn near gave me heart failure. I relaxed when I remembered he couldn't start it, at least. He didn't have the key. "How does it feel?"

"Feels good." He held the handlebars and cranked the throttle. "Feels familiar . . . but it's not. I don't remember it, like this bike exactly, but it feels right."

"Well, you look great. How does your leg feel?"

He glanced down at his injured leg, then up at me. "This feels okay. No way I could ride yet, though."

"Not gonna lie, kinda glad to hear that," I admitted. "Not sure my heart could take it just yet." I'd said it with a smile, as a bit of a joke, but it was the truth. If he took any kind of fall off a bike, if he hit his head, even with a helmet . . . I shuddered at the thought.

"But you said I look good," he replied with a cheeky smirk.

"Shut up. You always looked good on a bike and you know it."

He laughed. "I do not. And anyway, I couldn't ride it yet because I don't think I can even get off it without some help."

I snorted and helped him, holding onto him while he manoeuvred his leg. When he was back on his own two feet, he was standing impossibly close and my arm was still around him. He looked up at me. "You could kiss me right now," he whispered.

I didn't need telling twice.

I cupped his jaw and brought his mouth to mine, kissing him, opening his mouth with mine and tasting his tongue. I felt his surprise give way as he melted into me and he kissed me back. I could have stayed right there forever. I could have kissed him like that until we both ran out of air. How easy it would have been to take it one step further, to pull him in close and grind against him, to slip a hand between us and grip him . . .

I pulled away, breaking the kiss far too abruptly and far too soon for my liking. He was dazed, his jaw slack, his eyes heavy-lidded, his lips wet.

"You okay?" I breathed.

"Uhm." He blinked and a slow smile toyed with his lips. "Wow."

I chuckled. "I could say the same." I pecked his lips once more, soft and sweet. "Did you still want to go to the beach for lunch? We can do it another day if you want."

"No, today'd be great."

"Sure? We've had a busy week."

"Yeah, I'm sure." He sighed. "It's weird. And difficult, I guess."

I took his hand. "What is?"

"The need to rest, and not wanting to waste any more time." He shrugged his good shoulder. "I have a lot to catch up on, and don't want to waste a day, but I know I need to take it easy or it puts me on my arse for two days."

"There's a balance, and I think we're doing okay. I'll do whatever you want to do, baby, but the second you've had enough, you need to tell me."

He rolled his eyes. "I don't need to tell you nothing. You know when I'm tired before I do."

I laughed, guilty as charged. "Maybe." I could tell him every sign; the way his right eye blinked slower than his left, or the way his words were slower and a little slurred when he was really tired, the way it took a second for him to answer. All these things had improved so much, lessened with every day, but they were still there when he'd reached his limit. "Come on, then, let's go now. Sooner we go, the sooner we can come back. I wouldn't even mind a nap on the couch this arvo. Then the footy starts at four, then dinner, maybe a movie. I'll even let you pick it if you like."

He smiled and shook his head.

"What?"

"Nothing," he answered.

"Does that sound lame to you? Did you want to do something else? We can do something else if you want."

"God, Dallas, no. That sounds amazing. Lunch at the beach, a nap, footy, dinner, a movie. It's . . . Well, it sounds perfect." His face softened and there was something in his eyes . . . something that looked a lot like happiness. "Yes, I know this is nothing new to you, but it is to me. We like the same things, and you want to spend your day off doing the same things I like to do. I don't wanna do anything fancy; I just wanna hang out, and I'm still getting used to the fact that you want to do that with me. I just . . . it just blows me away, that's all. Like I can't believe it. Like I've woken up in some dream."

I sighed as I smiled and put my hands to his face. "It's no dream, Juss. We got lucky when we found each other. Well, I got lucky the day you walked in here. We never had to pretend to be something we're not. We just . . . we were just right, from day one."

He closed his eyes, and when I thought he might kiss me, he ducked his head and put his arms around me instead. I wrapped him up in a hug and rubbed his back, and he took deep, measured breaths. "Thank you," he murmured. "For everything. I don't know where I'd be if it weren't for you."

"You'd be just fine, Juss. You're stronger than you know." I planted a kiss on the side of his head and pulled back. "I'll just run upstairs and grab everything. Won't be long."

Ten minutes later, we were on our way to Merewether Beach. It was going to be busy. Sure, it was winter, but the sun was out and people would be enjoying the Saturday sunshine. But the access paths were concrete and relatively flat for Justin's scooter and there were a lot of grassed areas at Dixon Park we could sit on. I highly doubted he'd be up for walking on sandy beaches just yet.

I still drove carefully, more aware of having Justin in the ute with me and of how he might react to certain situations in traffic.

I dreaded what memories the sound of screeching tyres or honking horns might bring out, but thankfully it was uneventful.

We ordered fish and chips from the kiosk, then found a parking spot at Dixon Park and I went around to Justin's side of the ute and took his scooter from out of the back. I helped him out, and while he got himself sorted on that, I collected the picnic blanket and pillows. When I locked the ute and joined him on the footpath, he had his eyes closed and was smiling up toward the sun.

Christ, he was beautiful.

"Feel good?" I asked.

"Feels amazing. The sun, the smell of the saltwater. Everything."

After spending weeks in a hospital bed and then the last few weeks seeing nothing but our flat, the work shed, or doctors' offices, I bet it all felt amazing. "Then let's find a spot and you can lie down and enjoy it."

So that's what we did.

We found a secluded spot not far from the ute, overlooking the Pacific Ocean. I laid the blanket out, threw the pillows down, and helped him sit down. We sat and ate our lunch, watching the beach for a bit, watched the pulse of the ocean ebb and flow. We watched people walking dogs, pushing prams, throwing frisbees, jogging . . . The winter sun was just warm enough, the breeze was cool, and it was a perfect reminder to enjoy the little things.

Just to take a minute to breathe.

We lay in the sun with our heads on the pillows and pointed out shapes in the clouds. Then he asked me questions about things he'd missed in the last five years. Things from who the Prime Minister was and which famous people had died, and a bunch of little things that made me realise his mind was getting clearer.

These were questions he wouldn't have thought to ask two weeks ago, but now he was wondering about things outside our lives. And that was a very good sign. I thought he might ask me about sex, and I knew it was something we'd have to discuss, but instead, he asked me something else.

"And what's happening with the insurance with the accident?" he asked. "That guy Simmo asked, and I should have known to ask before now."

I rolled onto my side to face him and tucked the pillow under my neck. "I don't expect you to ask," I replied gently. "Though maybe I should have told you before now so you didn't have to ask. The insurance is taking longer than I thought. They keep saying it's just procedure and how these things take time, but I can't get anyone to return my calls, and when they do, they tell me there's no progress to report."

"Is that normal?"

"Apparently. But still, it's a pain."

He frowned and chewed on his bottom lip. "Are we . . . do we need the money?"

Shit. I couldn't lie to him.

"Things are tight. We're okay for now, but if we don't get it soon, we might have to look at some options."

"Such as?"

"Asking the bank to lessen the loan repayments, getting a redraw, extending credit cards, that kind of thing. But we're not there just yet." I reached over and took his hand. "I didn't tell you because I didn't want you to worry. Doctor Chang said that stress and anxiety can impede your recovery and that's the last thing I want to do."

"But the accident . . ."

"The accident was exactly that. An accident. It wasn't anyone's fault. Certainly not yours, and the insurance company and workers' comp all know that; they've all agreed to that. It's just a matter of the paperwork being signed off on, I'm sure." I skimmed my thumb over his knuckles. "The van, the fit-out, the tools, and your wages and the medical bills will all be covered. It's just a matter of time, that's all."

"I don't want you to have money troubles, Dallas." He was still frowning. "After everything you've done for me."

"Hey, Jussy. It's just paperwork. We'll get it sorted. It's just a matter of juggling things until then."

"I hate that it's a problem though." He chewed on his bottom lip for a long moment. "I could sell my bike."

"You what?"

"My bike."

"No."

"I can't ride it right now," he said, frowning. "I know you bought it for me and I love that you did. But it's the least I could do. It's all I own. If we need the money . . ."

Oh my God, that broke my heart. "No, Juss. No. We don't need to do that."

This was why I hadn't wanted him to know about it. Because he would worry, even if I told him there was nothing to worry about. There was no way I could tell him about having stock orders cancelled because of unpaid accounts.

I needed to change the subject, get his mind off worrying.

"You know what I realised?" I asked. "When you were lying in that hospital bed and you still hadn't opened your eyes, and we didn't know if you ever would at that stage, the boys were manning the workshop taking care of everything for us. It was very clear to me what my priorities were. If it came down to it, if I had to choose, I'd choose you. No matter the cost. No matter the sacrifice. I'd choose you, Juss. And right now, if I had to choose again, it'd still be you. And every day in between, and every day from now till forever."

His eyes became glassy and he gave me a sad smile. "Can I tell you something?"

"Sure."

"When I was in hospital and they talked about sending me home, I was shit scared. I didn't know you, but I knew I could trust you. I could feel it. I just knew. There was something in your eyes that was so honest." He swallowed hard and let out a shaky breath. "So I had to choose: go home with you or find my own place. I chose you, and if I had to choose again today, I'd choose you. You are my home, Dall."

"Oh, baby." I kissed his knuckles. "Thank you."

"Five years ago, or whenever we met, I chose you the first time." His dark brown eyes shone in the sun. "And I choose you again. This second time . . . well, second time for you, first time for me, really." He laughed nervously; a blush crept over his cheeks. "So does this make us boyfriends? Even though we live together and have been together for five years. And I can't seem to sleep without you. But maybe we should make it official?"

I grinned while my heart banged around in my chest. "Uh, yeah. Yes, definitely. I mean, I'd really like that."

He laughed. "Me too. I'd choose you again a third time too, just so you know."

I leaned over and kissed him, which wasn't easy considering I was grinning like an idiot. "You just made me so freaking happy."

He covered his eyes with his hand and laughed again. When he peeked through his fingers, his eyes were like glittered bronze. "You really want to be my boyfriend?"

I scrambled to my knees and sat back on my haunches and let out a happy sigh. "More than anything in the world."

Justin sat up slowly, careful of both his leg and his arm. "You just made me really freaking happy too." He looked out at the ocean, smiling. "Boyfriends, huh. Kinda feels weird. I always wanted a boyfriend. Someone just to hang out with. Someone who gets me. And now I have that. Except I've had it all along. Sort of." Then he let out a bit of a chuckle. "I mean, it's new and exciting but familiar and comfortable, so I guess I get the best of both worlds."

I cupped his face and pressed my lips to his. "I remember every single thing, Juss. And it's new and exciting but familiar and comfortable for me too."

He slow blinked, still smiling, but he'd had enough. "How about we get going home?" I suggested. "I have a nap in my future."

Justin snorted. "Me too."

I jumped to my feet and took his left hand, pulling him to his feet. I waited a moment for his head to catch up. "You okay? Not too dizzy?"

He slow blinked again. "Nah. 'M okay."

We got everything packed up and back to the ute just fine, but he was asleep in the car before we got halfway home.

Chapter Eight

THE MORNING VENTURE had taken its toll and as soon as I got him upstairs, he made it to the couch and put his feet up on the recliner and fell straight back to sleep. I pulled the blanket over him and turned the TV on, volume low for background noise while I got some housework done.

Later on, I'd thrown a bunch of meat and veg into the slow cooker hoping for some kind of Irish stew, and when I walked past the couch, Juss was awake.

He was squinting and frowning.

"Hey," I whispered. "You feel okay?"

He paused for a long moment, then gave a slight shake of his head. "Headache."

I fetched him some pills and a glass of water, then closed the blinds. I found the remote for the TV and went into settings and turned the brightness way down. "Is that better?"

He sagged back against the sofa and closed his eyes. "Hm."

Squish recognised Justin's bat-signal and trotted over to curl up with him. I gave Squish a scratch for thanks and pressed a kiss to Juss' forehead. "If you need anything, just ask," I whispered.

I cleaned the bathroom, changed the bedsheets, and remade the bed, trying to be as quiet as I could. About an hour later, he had his eyes open but was staring absently at the TV. I sat beside him and watched the screen for a bit. Turning the brightness down actually made a lot of difference and it was less straining to look at. It was on some billiards highlights that he wasn't really watching. "How're you feeling?"

"'M okay," he said slowly.

His hand was between us, so I traced patterns on his palm with my finger. "Can I get you anything?"

He blinked. "Nah." Then after a long while, he added, "Just sit with me."

His speech was a little slower than it had been the last few days, and I was reminded that his recovery was two steps forward, one step back. Just like Doctor Chang had said it would be.

"I'll sit with you anytime," I whispered, and his fingers curled into mine.

"Headache was bad," he mumbled.

"But it's okay now?"

He gave a small nod. "Better."

Better, but still there, obviously. And even if the pain had been dulled, the residual effects weren't lessened. The spaced-out fogginess remained.

Squish stretched out and Juss rubbed his belly with his other hand, and he looked up at me and smiled. "I like this."

"Like what? Being all cosy on the couch with the cat?"

He slow blinked again, and he smiled at me. "Yeah. With my boyfriend. I haven't forgotten that."

I grinned, then leant over and kissed him. "I haven't forgotten either." I snuggled in a bit closer and his head fell against my shoulder, our fingers still entwined. It had grown overcast outside, so it really was a perfect way to spend a cold and blustery afternoon; cosied up on the couch, Squish purring between us, the footy about to start, and dinner cooking away in the kitchen.

"Did you say the Bulldogs were playing?"

"Yep. Be prepared to watch the best team in the NRL."

He chuckled. "The Knights aren't playing."

The game began and I got us some snacks and a bottle of water each, and he enjoyed the game but he seemed a little distracted. The Bulldogs ended up winning, though even I wasn't sure how, and I served up our stew, which we ate on the couch.

He was speaking better and his blinks were fine, so I believed him when he said his head was feeling okay, though he seemed to have something on his mind. He'd look at me, then at the TV, and he chewed more on his bottom lip than he did of his dinner.

"Is there something you wanted to talk about?" I asked, trying to be casual.

He smiled. "That's not fair."

"What's not fair?"

"That you know me. You can tell these things because you know me."

I laughed. "Sorry."

He ate some more dinner and I gave him time to get his thoughts in order. "I've been thinking," he began. "Well, trying to anyway. And I know I probably should have asked before now."

"You can ask me anything," I tried.

"Then Becca said something the other night . . ."

Oh shit. Here we go. The sex talk.

But I couldn't let him be the one to struggle to bring this up. That most certainly wasn't fair. "She told me. She was worried that she'd said something to upset you. Juss, I want you to know, there is no pressure for anything physical between us."

He made a face and studied his bowl of stew for a bit. "I know we kinda talked about it before. You said I still bottomed so that was one thing that hadn't changed."

I snorted and put my bowl onto the coffee table. "Ah, yeah."

"And the photo . . . of us. Of me. It's pretty obvious what you're doing to me . . ."

"I wasn't going to put that photo in but Bec thought it might show you that you and I were a couple," I said. "Sorry if it upset you."

"No, not upset. I like the photo," he replied, blushing and smiling all shy-like. "But . . ."

Oh. "But what?"

His lip drew downward. "I haven't thought about it. Sex, that is. I haven't thought about it, not once. I haven't wanted it," he said eventually. "And I don't know why."

"Because your body isn't ready yet," I offered. "Your brain needs time."

"Maybe," he mumbled. "Do you think . . . do you think something broke? In my brain?"

I scooted over and took his hand. "Baby, no. You'll want it when you're ready. And I don't care when that is. Tomorrow, or ten years, or never. Sex isn't the reason I love you."

He sighed and leaned against the back of the sofa, holding my hand and looking at me all gooey. It did crazy things to my heart. "You make it easy, you know," he whispered.

"Make what easy?"

"To fall in love with you."

I stared.

My heart stopped.

My mouth fell open. "What?"

He laughed and ducked his head. "Don't make me say it again."

I was so fucking giddy I almost vibrated off the couch. I grabbed his face and planted a kiss on his mouth. "I love you, Juss. Always have, always will."

His eyes unfocused, just for a second. "Whoa," he whispered. "I think I just had a flashback." He blinked a few times. "You've said that before."

I grinned. "I've said it a hundred times."

"No, you were wearing a black hoodie and we were outside. At the beach." His eyes grew wide. "I remember that. Oh my God, Dallas, I remember that."

Black hoodie . . . at the beach . . . "Yes, at Hallidays Point. Our weekend away."

Then his eyes glimmered with something else and his cheeks grew red. "Oh. I think I remember something else . . ." He put his hand to his forehead. "Oh yeah. There was a couch and a blue bed . . ."

Oh God . . . I'd bent him over that couch and fucked him until he came. He'd begged me to do it. He'd leaned himself over the back of the couch and undid his pants, offering me his arse. He'd writhed with need, and he'd begged me. Was he remembering that?

The blush on his cheeks told me yes.

And that big blue bed . . . we barely left it all weekend.

"Yeah," I said, my voice rough. "There was. You remember it?"

He nodded and let out a ragged breath. "Fuck. Parts of it, I think. God, we uh . . . I mean, you . . ."

I chuckled and tried to take a calming breath. "Uh, yeah."

He sat back, and from the slightly bewildered and embarrassed look on his face, I could tell he was reliving his new memories. And they were memories that included me, which made me ridiculously happy.

"You got new memories," I said, lifting his hand to kiss his palm.

But then he put his fingers to my chin, he thumbed my beard, savouring the texture and tugging on it a little, his eyes taking in all the details. "I remember. I remember what we did and how you made me feel." He swallowed hard. "It's not just the visual, it's the emotion that goes with it. That makes it real, and I can feel what I felt back then, how you made me feel. That's *my* memories, not photos, not what someone says happened. Me, mine." He was breathing hard; his chest rose and fell with each beat of my own. "You."

"Me? Me what?"

"You made me feel that way. You. Christ, Dallas. I remember what we did."

I took his hand and held it in both of mine. "I remember too. The beauty of it, the love."

He nodded, but then he licked his lips and shook his head. "I don't know what it means." He swallowed hard again. "No, I know what it means. I mean, I know what we did and I know how it made me feel. I remember wanting it so bad I thought I was going to combust."

I laughed. "Same."

"But I don't know what that means for me now."

"What do you mean, baby?"

"I haven't thought about sex in . . . well, since the accident. I mean, yeah, I know we used to have sex, and I get that. But I haven't thought about actually doing it. I haven't wanted to. Not once."

I lifted his hand and kissed his knuckles this time. "That's okay, baby."

"Is it?"

"Sure it is. It'll happen when you're ready. Maybe it's your brain's way of making sure you're ready first." I took a deep breath. "Baby, you had a shit time in Darwin. And before that, here in Newcastle. Guys treated you like shit, expecting a quick fuck and nothing else, and all you wanted was someone to love you. When we first got together, you were adamant that you wanted trust and respect, and rightly so. It's not any different this time around. When your body and your heart, and your mind, are all ready, you'll know."

His gaze flickered between mine and he opened his mouth to say something, but then he closed it again. He shook his head. "How can you just say that?"

"Say what?"

"Be so understanding!"

"Because I love you. I'm not going to rush you and risk ruining what we have just to get off. I told you before, you mean more to me than just sex."

Juss' eyebrows furrowed and he sank back in his seat. "I don't get it. I keep expecting you to get pissed off or frustrated, but you never do. It's like you're too perfect or something."

I snorted out a laugh. "Hardly. I'm far from it. But Juss, I know what we had, and I know it's worth it. You're worth it, what we had, and what we have right now, is worth it."

He gave me a sad smile. "There you go being all perfect again."

"I'm not perfect. I'm just looking after you, like I know you would if it had been me in that van that day. You would've moved heaven and earth for me. I know you would have."

He got a little teary. After a little while, he said, "I guess I just don't know . . ."

"Don't know what, baby?"

"How you love me when I don't know who I am. I feel half put together with missing pieces, yet you still love me, and I don't know how I can love you when I don't know who I'm supposed to be or who you fell in love with. And what if that guy isn't who I am?"

"Oh, Juss. I love the real you." I put my hand to his chest. "The guy who laughs at blooper videos, and the guy who was scared to death to put his heart on the line but did it anyway. The guy who rescued a little black kitten and fed him every three or four hours for weeks. The guy who stood up to shitty men because he demanded better; the guy who worked his arse off to be better than anyone else to prove that a gay man could do it. That's who you are."

A solitary tear escaped his eye. "You can stop being perfect now."

"I'm not perfect," I said again, wiping his cheek. "I'm far from it. I just love you, that's all."

He gave a teary laugh and leaned in to kiss me. But then, without breaking the kiss, he slid closer on the couch and deepened the kiss. I couldn't hide my surprise when he climbed into my lap and kissed me so thoroughly it made my eyes roll back in my head. I didn't want him to force himself to *try*, but damnit it felt so good...

And then he rubbed himself against me and I had to put my hands on his hips to stop him. I held him off me and broke the kiss, his forehead pressed to mine. "Stop," I breathed. "I'm not *that* perfect."

He almost smirked. "Oh, sorry."

I shifted in my seat and gently pushed him off my lap. Then I had to readjust myself, my now-aching dick protesting his absence. I grimaced. "Don't be sorry. It's just . . . my dick doesn't understand."

He stared at me, then burst out laughing. He covered his mouth with his hand. "I'm sorry. That's not funny."

"Then why are you laughing?" I asked. I couldn't help but smile. It was so good to see him laugh.

He let his hand drop and he stared at me; his whole face lit up with a grin. "I dunno, I just . . . you're turned on, by me. It's just." He put his hand to his forehead, flustered. "I wasn't expecting that. It's weird. I guess, I'm sorry. I just didn't think of that. See? I don't think about that. I haven't thought about it since . . . since the accident. I'm sorry."

His smile was long gone and in its place was confusion and conflict. I took his hand and let out a breath that hopefully was a show of patience. "Hey, don't apologise. It'll happen when you're ready."

His gaze darted between my eyes. "What if it doesn't? What if it never happens?"

"Then it doesn't."

"Would you miss it?" he asked, his gaze imploring. "Do you miss it already? God, you do. You said your dick doesn't understand."

"Justin, baby, listen." I turned on the couch to face him more squarely and I held his hand in both of mine. "In the last four years we had a lot of sex. Like, a lot. We were very . . . physical, and before your accident I would have said that, yes, sex was important. But I know different now. It's not important. Not anymore. What's important is that you're alive, for one thing. Because you almost weren't. And secondly, that you're healthy and happy. Sex is just one aspect, and it's not compulsory. If we could never have sex again, for some medical reason, I'd still love you. I'd still be with you. What kind of arsehole would I be if I broke up with you because we couldn't have sex?"

He sighed and put his head on my shoulder, then sidled in a little closer, and when I put my arm around him, he sighed again. "I want to. I mean, I want to have sex again. I want to want it. I want to do that, with you."

I rubbed his back. "When you're ready, baby. There's no rush."

"Maybe now I know it's something I *can* think about, I'll start thinking about it."

I chuckled and kissed the side of his head. "Maybe. Don't stress about it, Juss. If it happens, it happens."

"I like kissing you though," he murmured. "A lot. I like it a lot."

"I like it too."

"Even though your dick doesn't understand?"

I snorted. "My dick will get over it."

He sat up and looked at me. "This is a totally normal conversation to be having, right?"

I laughed. "One hundred per cent."

He looked at me for a long moment. "Thank you. For not getting mad or making me feel bad. I'm trying to find myself and find my feet. It's confusing and it's not fair, to either of us, but you're really great, Dallas. I honestly don't know where I'd be without you."

I could tell by his voice and by how slow he spoke that he was getting tired. I gently booped him on the nose with my finger. "You're really great too, Juss. And I don't know where I'd be without you either."

He smiled and blushed, looking down at his lap. "So, uh, so we used to have a lot of sex?"

I laughed again. Most days, for the all the years we've been together. I didn't say that though. "Uh, yeah."

"I remember that couch and the blue bed," he whispered. He shook his head and licked his lips. "Was it like that all the time?"

I nodded. "Pretty much."

He chuckled and chewed on his bottom lip. Lord, help me, he had no idea how seductive that was . . . Then he took out his phone. "What are you doing?" I asked.

"I'm gonna put a reminder," he said. "Every hour, think about sex. If I need to retrain my brain, I should start tonight."

I barked out a laugh. "You always were dedicated."

He slumped against the back of the couch, smiling but tired. He threaded his fingers with mine. "Thank you."

"You're very welcome." I stood up, and still holding his hand, I helped him to his feet. "Let's get you to bed."

He fell into me, very deliberately, pressing his front to mine.

He slipped his arms around me and snuggled his head into my neck. "Hug first."

I would never say no to that. I hugged him tight and relished his warmth. Holding him in my arms was soul-fixing. It felt good to comfort him and protect him, and it felt amazing to have that in return.

"Wish I wasn't always tired," he mumbled.

I pulled back and cupped his face. "I know you probably don't see it, but you're getting better every day. Two weeks ago you would've been in bed hours ago." I kissed him softly. "Every day is a step forward, baby. We don't need to run. Just a step a day, that's all."

Justin put his hand to my face and pulled me down for another kiss before putting his forehead to my chin. "I don't know what I ever did four years ago to deserve you, but I'm so thankful for you."

"I know you are. But thank you for telling me." I took his arm. "Come on. Let's go to bed."

While he used the bathroom, I turned everything off and locked up, and after brushing my teeth, I slid into bed beside him. As always, he melded himself into me and I welcomed the embrace.

I wasn't exactly tired, but I wasn't missing this. Not for anything. But sure enough, with his weight and his heat and that contented, peaceful feeling, I was soon drifting off.

Juss stirred a bit during the night but he stayed asleep, and he clung to me more than usual. I assumed it was all the talk about sex and his uncertainty surrounding his lack of desire for it. He was confused as to why he hadn't even thought of it, let alone wanted it. I was fairly certain it would come back to him when he was ready.

I meant what I'd said to him earlier. Sex wasn't compulsory for me. It wasn't a critical component of a relationship to me. I loved the man, not his body. Well, my heart loved the man. My dick, on the other hand, loved his body.

I woke up to find myself spooning him, though he was awake. He wiggled against me for a moment, then stopped before he peeled himself away from me and sat up, taking most of the blankets with him. "Jesus," he mumbled.

I opened my eyes to find him staring at . . . well, at my dick.

"Fucking hell, Dallas," he said. "Your dick is huge. Should I . . . I dunno, should I get it its own pillow?"

I snorted and scrubbed my hands over my face. "Good morning."

"It's huge." He was still staring at my dick. "I mean, it explains a lot, like why I spent four years with a Bulldogs supporter."

I barked out a laugh and readjusted my very-hard cock. I was only wearing briefs—probably not a great idea, but I'd woken up every day before him, so it had never been an issue before. "Sorry," I croaked. "I'm normally up by now."

"You are," he said, nodding toward my dick.

I wasn't sure what to say to that. He was still staring at it. Was he uncomfortable? "I'll go have a shower," I said, sitting up. "Wanna make some coffee?"

He didn't answer, and when I looked at his face, he was staring at the blankets now pooled at my hips. "I want to watch."

Watch? What the . . . ?

"Watch me do what? Shower?"

"No. Well, sure, yeah, that too. Probably. But I mean . . . I want to watch . . ." He swallowed hard. "God, I can't believe I'm going to say this. I want to watch you get yourself off."

Christ.

"You want me to jerk off? Now?"

He nodded woodenly and met my eyes. "Yeah." He licked his lips and let out a shaky breath.

Fucking hell. He was dead serious. Could I jerk off in front of him? We'd certainly done more than that before, and my dick was most definitely keen. "Um." I cleared my throat and gave myself a squeeze. "Just like this?"

He propped the pillows up against the headboard behind me, then moved to the end of the bed on his side. Okay then, we were doing this. I shuffled up and leaned against the pillows, my legs spread. My briefs were barely restraining my cock and I pulled it free. I didn't need to be too comfortable; this was going to be over in seconds.

Justin's mouth was open, his eyes fixated and dark. He was breathing hard, and his gaze felt like hands on my body.

I fisted the base of my cock and stroked, sliding up to the tip and smearing the precome that was leaking from the slit. As soon as I twisted my palm over the head, a stab of bliss hit me, so I did it again, and again, and my balls drew up tight. I worked my hand up and down the shaft and it was too much. There was no going back, I was too far gone.

"Fuck, Juss. I'm gonna come so quick."

He was almost panting, and he nodded. "Do it. I want to see it."

Oh God.

My orgasm burned hot and fast, trailing a line of fire from the base of my spine, deep in my balls. It scorched hot and heavenly and spilled onto my belly. I groaned through my release, writhing with the pleasure of it.

"Fuck," Juss whispered.

I could barely open my eyes, and I laughed through my post-orgasmic haze. "You liked that?"

"That was hot as hell," he said, giving his dick a squeeze, and he groaned.

"Did you want to do the same?" I asked, nodding to the bulge in his boxers.

He looked down at his crotch and then at me. "Um, no, I'm good, thanks. I mean, I don't need . . . that. I just wanted to see you. And it was sexy. Christ. But I'm not . . ."

"You don't need to do anything until you're ready," I said. "But I probably should have a shower."

He nodded quickly, and his unease and awkwardness made me a little sad. I figured the best thing for me to do was clean up and get rid of the evidence currently drying on my belly. A quick shower later, I followed my nose to the kitchen. Justin had made coffee and toast, and he offered me a full cup.

"Thanks," I said, taking it from him.

Keeping his gaze averted, he slid the plate with toast over. "I'll just . . . I'm gonna take a shower too. I won't be long."

Before I could swallow my mouthful of coffee, he was gone. Goddammit. I didn't want things to be awkward between us. This was why he wasn't ready for sex. Sure, his body had liked what he'd watched, but his mind wasn't ready for the next step. I sighed and finished my breakfast before cleaning up, and it wasn't long until Justin reappeared freshly showered and dressed. He was wearing grey tracksuit pants and a hoodie, and he was holding a pair of socks and headed straight for the couch. "We still going shopping?" he asked. He pulled his left sock on easily enough, but his right was always a bit trickier, and I wasn't sure if it just took a little longer than necessary or if he was avoiding looking at me.

I sat at the other end of the couch and pulled my sneakers on. "You sure you're up for the supermarket?" It had been my idea but he was excited to go. It'd been weeks since he'd really been anywhere, and when I'd mentioned needing to grab a few groceries, he was keen to come along.

He shot me a quick look and gave a tight smile before reaching for his sneakers. "Oh yeah, for sure. I want to. Pretty lame when the supermarket is my social outing."

"It's not lame. This way you get to choose which ice cream flavour we get."

He got his left shoe on okay, but he struggled a bit with his right. I knelt in front of him and helped slide his heel into his sneaker and quickly tied his laces. It certainly wasn't the first time I'd helped him with shoes or getting dressed, but he seemed a little pissed that I was helping him now. Or maybe it was because I was on the floor between his knees . . .

I got to my feet and helped him stand, and he smiled and mumbled his thanks, but he was definitely uncomfortable. And, like he knew I was about to bring it up, he gave me a smile. "We ready to go? If we leave it too late, I'll need a nap in the soup aisle."

Okay then, he clearly wasn't ready to talk about it. And who knew, maybe he just needed some time to get his head around it and to process his newfound sexual awareness. So we threw his scooter in the back of the ute and headed to the local Coles. It was good to see him smile as we went around each section. He chose the fruit and veggies while I grabbed the bread, but then we took our time going up and down each aisle.

Most of it was mundane stuff and food and packaging he was very familiar with, but there were a few things he had to look at twice. Things that were new in the last five years, some things he had no recollection of eating, a lot of changed packaging, and even the layout of the supermarket had changed. There were so many small changes that I hadn't even considered until he'd commented.

I put a packet of our favourite taco kits in the trolley. "Have I eaten that before?" he asked. "Do I like that kind of pasta? Where've the eggs gone? They sell clothes here now?"

But I appreciated his questions. It was proof to me that he was getting better, that his mind was clearing, and his cognitive recognition was improving.

"Oh my God, Snickers ice creams are a thing now?" he asked, staring at the freezer.

I just laughed and threw a pack in the trolley, then we headed for the checkout and made our way home. The trip itself didn't take us long and it wasn't overly strenuous, but it was a great test for Justin. And sure enough, by the time we got home, he was tired.

I carted all the bags up the stairs and he put things away, but he was fighting every long blink and shaking his head trying to stay awake. "Hey, why don't you go get on the couch and find us something to watch. I'll finish up here and—"

"I'm fine," he replied sharply.

Which was basically Exhibit A of him not being fine.

"Okay," I said, trying to smooth it over. I left the bag of dry goods for him and began putting Squish's food in the bottom of the pantry.

"I can help you with the damn groceries, Dallas," he snapped. "I'm not completely useless."

I slid the last can of cat food in, stood, and faced him, startled at his outburst. "I know you're not, Juss. You're far from useless."

"Well, I couldn't get my shoe on earlier, so that was pretty fucking useless."

"Your shoe?" I was lost for a moment. "You couldn't get your shoe on because you had surgery on your shattered leg and your arm was broken in two places."

"You don't need to remind me!"

"That's not useless, Justin. That's—"

"That's what? My reality? Because apparently there's a lot of things I can't do."

"Juss," I tried.

"You know what? Forget it. Put the . . ." He looked at the unpacked groceries. "You put them away."

He stormed off, limping as he walked to the bedroom, and slammed the door behind him. I stood there, stunned. What the fuck was that about? His struggle to find the right word was a clear sign he was tired, and maybe going to the supermarket had been too much. Though I was certain it was the sex-incident this morning that had him so off-kilter.

His mind was obviously working overtime trying to figure shit out, and he was tired, and yeah, the doctors had said to expect mood swings. I knew this wasn't about me. This was about Justin and his recovery, both physical and mental.

But fucking hell . . . It hurt me too.

Not knowing what else to do, I put the groceries away. He clearly needed some space and some sleep, so I left him to it and went downstairs. I checked my emails and wasn't surprised to find the insurance or workers' comp people hadn't replied. Not that I expected them to on a Sunday, but I was fast losing patience and it added to my frustration and stress levels.

I resisted throwing my laptop across my office. Barely.

I stood in my office at a loss of what to do next. Every pressure, every worry, was bearing down on me, and I wasn't sure how much more I could take. I wanted to punch something, to vent the anger, the blame.

I wanted to blame something for this whole fucking mess,

but there was nothing, no one. It wasn't anyone's fault. It was just what life threw at me. *Here, Dallas, have some more fucking shit. You can handle it.*

Well, life. Guess what? I'm beginning to think I can't.

If I had a limit, I was pretty sure I'd found it.

Justin yelling at me was the cherry on top of a whole mountain of clusterfuck. And him yelling wasn't his fault either. He couldn't help it.

I hated that it was going to come down to money. Maybe Justin was right about selling his bike. Not that I'd sell *his* bike, but I could sell mine, or my ute. I'd just have to buy something cheaper to get us from A to B. He still had doctor appointments we needed to get to, and he wasn't ready to be on the back of a bike.

I had a rough idea what the market value would be for a ute like mine, and it would get us out of trouble for a little while.

Christ.

It really was something I was going to have to think about this week. If I didn't get some money coming in soon, selling some stuff might be my only option.

I couldn't bear to think about it anymore. I needed to do something with my hands to get my mind off my freaking money troubles, so I rifled through the cleaning cupboard and found a half-used, long-forgotten bottle of window cleaner and a roll of paper towel. I cleaned every window I could reach, then found the old ladder from the storeroom for the windows I couldn't. I doubted some of those windows had ever been cleaned.

It felt good to scrub the shit out of them; using physical strength was great for venting frustration. Using mindless elbow grease was a much-needed distraction. I lost track of time and was working up a sweat scrubbing the last window when I thought I heard something . . .

Then I heard it again.

"Dallas!"

I was down that ladder and sprinting up the back stairs as fast as I could. I burst inside the flat. "Justin?"

He replied with a sob and I raced into the bedroom. He was

sitting up in bed with tears streaming down his face. "You were gone," he cried, his chest heaving. "You left me."

I sat on the edge of the bed beside him and pulled him against me, my heart hammering, trying to catch my breath. "I'm here, baby. I was just downstairs. I'll never leave you, I promise."

"I can't do this without you. I thought you'd left me, and I had a nightmare and you weren't here."

I rubbed his back to soothe him. "Oh, baby. I'll never leave you."

"I'm sorry," he mumbled. He pulled away and looked at me, his eyes so full of sadness. "For what I said. I'm sorry. I don't know why I was horrible to you."

"It's okay. You were tired."

"It's not okay. I'm sorry."

I wiped his tears and pushed his hair back. "Baby, I forgive you."

Which of course set off another wave of tears. "I want to be normal for you," he sobbed. "I want to be what you need, but I don't know if I can."

"Juss, you are normal," I replied, not really knowing what normal was anyway. "You're perfect, just the way you are. You don't need to try to be anything."

He searched my eyes; his bottom lip trembled. "I want to have sex with you, but I don't know if I can."

Wait, what?

My mind spun from my own troubles, but there it was. The truth about what he was so stressed about.

"Juss, you don't have to worry about that."

"I want to. And this morning in bed, you wanted it too. What you did was so hot. And my body wanted it, but my brain couldn't . . . not yet. I don't know why."

"Because you're not ready, that's why. And baby, that's okay."

"You're not mad?"

"Mad? Why would I be mad?"

"You wanted me to . . . do what you did." He got all teary again. "In bed."

"No, baby. I just asked if you wanted to, that's all. I didn't mean you had to or that I wanted you to. I just . . ." I sighed. "I'm sorry if I made you feel that way. That wasn't my intention."

"I don't want to disappoint you. I want to be with you. I want to make you happy," he said, scrubbing at his face.

"You do make me happy," I whispered. "You could never disappoint me."

He gave me the most adorable puppy dog eyes. "I was horrible to you."

I smiled and cupped his face. "You weren't horrible. Juss, you couldn't be horrible if you tried." I kissed his forehead. "We had a little fight, that's all. Just a misunderstanding. You were tired, and anyway, I like putting the groceries away."

That earned me a small, brief smile. "I'm sorry."

"I know you are." I studied him for a second. "You had a nightmare?"

He frowned and gave a small nod. "Because you weren't here. I called out to you but you didn't answer and I called out again, but . . ." He swallowed hard. "I remembered the look on your face before I walked out and I thought, fuck, I'd really done it this time. I thought you'd left me, and I wouldn't have blamed you. I can't do this without you."

I crawled over his legs and lay down in the middle of the bed and pulled him in for a proper hug. I could hold him better this way. "I was just downstairs, cleaning. I lost track of time, I'm sorry you were scared."

He sighed, and with his head on my chest, I held him tighter. "You're a bit hot and sweaty."

I snorted. "Sorry."

"No, I like it." He very slowly rubbed his face along my chest. "You smell good."

I sighed, and for a few unspoken minutes, we just lay there while I rubbed his back. "Feel better now?" I asked.

"Yeah. I meant what I said, though. I can't do this without you."

I kissed the top of his head. "Just as well you don't have to."

"Dallas," he whispered. "I want to . . . start doing things with you. Physical things. Sexual things. Because my body is, well, my body says yes."

"But your mind says no."

"My brain is messed up."

I chuckled. "No it's not, Juss. Your brain is recovering. It'll happen when you're ready. Just be patient."

"How long will it take?"

"I don't know. How about you talk about it with Doctor Chang this week? She knows so much more than me."

He sighed and lifted his head up off my chest so he could see my face. "I'm sorry about this morning. I feel bad."

"You don't have to feel bad," I murmured. I trailed my fingers through the hair at his temple. "Just talk to me next time, okay? About anything. You can ask me anything you want to know."

"Can I ask you something now?"

"Sure."

"Can you kiss me?" He was so genuinely nervous, it was cute. Like I'd ever say no to that. "I just want to feel close to you and I really like kissing. Is that too much to ask?"

I leaned in and captured his mouth with mine and rolled us onto our sides. I had to be careful of his body: his arm, his leg, his head. But if I cradled him, held him close, and wrapped him up in my arms, it was almost impossible to hurt him.

He melted into me and opened his mouth, deepening the kiss. Our bodies aligned and he slid his arm around my back, but we never pushed to take it any further. That's not what this was. This wasn't about me pushing to see how far he'd let me go or for him to see how far he wanted to go. This was purely a reconnect, an act of intimacy, of tenderness, between two men in love.

He did love me; I knew he did. He'd said before I made it too easy for him to love me, and I took that as a declaration.

This was about Justin feeling some kind of normalcy. There had been so much taken from him, so much disconnection. If kissing made him feel in control or if he was taking back something that was stolen from him—or even if he did it because it made him feel good—then I would kiss him all day long.

Or I'd kiss him until my stomach growled so loud it made him laugh.

"Is that lunchtime?" he asked, smiling against my lips.

"Yeah, probably later than that, actually."

He frowned. "I kinda messed up our whole day, didn't I?"

"Not at all."

"You have gorgeous eyes," he murmured, his gaze darting back and forth. He put his hand to my face. "And I feel like I know your eyes. They're familiar, like we've lain like this hundreds of times."

That made me smile. "Well, I never counted."

"I know your eyes," he whispered again. "I always liked them, didn't I?"

I kissed him, soft and warm. "Yes you did."

"They're a grey-hazel that I've never seen anywhere else. And it's not even the colour, but it's what's in them, what's behind them." His gaze intensified as he studied me. "They tell me all the things you don't say."

Why was that both scary and heartening? "What's that?"

"Honesty, and the truth. You see me, and you love me."

"I do."

"I know. And I'm so grateful for you."

"I never was much good at hiding anything from you."

My stomach growled again and he smiled. "Including when you need food. We should feed you."

So we went to the kitchen and made sandwiches and we stood leaning against the kitchen counter as we ate. I hadn't realised just how hungry I was until I had food in front of me. I shoved half my sandwich into my mouth and Justin laughed at me as I struggled to chew it. "What?" I managed to ask around the food, trying to not laugh.

He smiled at me for a long moment, his sandwich in his hand. "I love you."

I was so stunned I almost couldn't swallow.

He took a small bite, smiling as he chewed. "It's true, I do. I think some part of me knows I always have. But when I woke up and you weren't here, I realised I don't just need you. I realised that I love you. My heart never forgot you, Dallas. I just thought you should know."

I threw my arms around him in a fierce hug. "Oh my God, Juss."

He laughed, then mumbled into my chest, "You're crushing my sandwich."

I laughed and let him go, planting a kiss on his lips, his cheek, his temple. "I love you too."

Chapter Nine

Doctor Chang welcomed us into her office. "How are you both?" she asked. "Justin, you look great!"

He sat in one of the two seats opposite her desk; I took the other. "Oh, thanks."

"No scooter today?"

"No, it's in the ute but I thought I'd walk. I'll need a nap when I get home, but it's nice not to need it all the time."

She smiled. "And how's your week been? Have you had any other memories or other breakthroughs?"

"Memories, yes. Flashes of some, full memories of others."

"That's great! Were they happy memories?"

He glanced at me and blushed. "Well, yeah. Intimate ones."

"Oh." Her smile twisted, amused. "And how did that make you feel?"

"Um." He barked out a laugh and reached for my hand. "Loved. It made me feel loved. But more than that, I remember how I felt. The memory wasn't . . . empty, like a photo of things I didn't remember. I was there, I remember being there, what we did, how it felt." He put his free hand to his heart. "I remember it."

"The correlation between memory and emotion is very strong," Doctor Chang said. "Experiencing something firsthand

and remembering it help provide a connection between memory and self, who you are."

Justin nodded. "I've had other memories, but this one was . . . I mean, they all mean something, but this one meant the most."

"Because of the emotional connection." Doctor Chang smiled proudly at Justin, then turned her attention to me. "And Dallas, how was your week?"

I squeezed Juss' hand. "We had some ups and downs. More ups than downs, but we ended on a high."

"What were the lows?"

"I was an idiot," Juss answered.

I laughed. "No you weren't. He wasn't," I told Doctor Chang. "He was tired and overwhelmed and a bit scared about what everything meant. It was totally understandable, and we talked about it until he felt better."

She frowned. "Scared? Justin, what were you scared about?"

He gave me another look and his grip on my hand was bone-crunching. "Sex. I hadn't thought about sex, not really. Or, not even once. Since the accident. And I mean, how could I not think about it?" He made a face. "Being reminded that sex was even a thing that I did was like being told I used to speak another language before the accident, only I couldn't remember it. All awareness of it was gone. I mean I knew it was a thing, but I hadn't thought about actually doing it."

"Loss of libido is not uncommon," the doc said gently.

"It's not that I don't want to have sex. Now that I've remembered it, it's just . . . I do want to. I think. God, I dunno." Justin met my eyes. "And Dallas was really good about it. I mean, Dallas is good about everything. But he was patient and told me not to worry about it until I was ready and there was no rush. But then I worried that there was something wrong with me." He looked back to the doc then. "Is there? Something wrong with me?"

"Not at all, Justin," she replied. "It's very common."

"I want to try," he admitted. "And my body is like an RC 390 but my brain is the handbrake, ya know?" He made a face. "Sorry, an RC 390 is fast."

She smiled at that. "You think something's holding you back?"

"You mean my broken brain?"

"Your brain's not broken, Juss," I offered.

"So why is my brain being stupid? Why do I freak out at the thought of it?"

That was something I couldn't answer. I looked to the doctor. She smiled gently and said, "Our minds put up warnings when it senses danger. It's a defence mechanism."

"Danger?" Justin asked.

"Fear," she replied. "Are you afraid of something?"

Justin's eyes flashed and his grip on my hand pulsed. She'd hit the nail right on the head, and Justin looked panicked. God, was this something he wanted to discuss in private? I didn't want him to be uncomfortable.

"Do you want me to wait outside?" I asked.

"No," he shot back quickly, pulling my hand to his body as if to keep me close. "Please stay."

"Okay," I murmured, nodding.

He swallowed hard and took a second before he looked back at Doctor Chang. "I guess, yeah. And I don't know why."

"You don't know why, what?" she asked patiently.

"I don't know why I'm scared. I shouldn't be. I've done it before."

"What are you scared of?" I asked.

Justin seemed stuck, unable to answer, so Doctor Chang did. "After a traumatic experience, where someone has experienced significant levels of pain, it's not uncommon for that person to reject any scenario where they may experience any kind of pain again."

What? Pain? Oh God . . .

"Justin," I breathed. "I would never hurt you."

His eyes darted to mine, full of fear and honesty. "I know. It's why it doesn't make sense."

"It does make sense," Doctor Chang said. "And it's completely justified. What you went through was a significant ordeal, where you spent many weeks in all kinds of pain. And you still have pain, yes?"

He nodded. "My leg. My arm doesn't hurt much unless I wrench it or overuse it."

"And your head?"

He slow blinked as though even the mention of his headaches made his head hurt. "My head hurts most days. The meds help."

"Is the severity of the pain getting less?" she asked.

"I think so," he replied. "I mean, yeah. I guess."

She talked him through some techniques and recognition signals and basically suggested that if it was something he really wanted to do, he use the small steps system. Proceed slowly and stop when it became too much, and of course, to practise patience and be open with how we both felt.

But Justin had done the right thing by admitting his fear and it was the first step, she said, and she was happy that we were talking about it. A lot of couples didn't and she said it showed how much we cared for each other. "There's a very strong bond between you," she said as our meeting finished.

"I love him," Justin said, his cheeks a rich pink. He glanced to me and laughed, his fingers laced with mine. "I always did, I think. Even when he was sitting by my bed in hospital and I wasn't sure who he was, I never wanted him to leave. His visits were the highlight of every day, and when I had to leave the hospital and go home, I wanted to go with him. I can't tell you why, apart from the fact he made me feel safe, but I honestly think my heart knew."

I would have kissed him if we weren't in a doctor's office. "I love you too, Juss. Always have, always will."

Juss smiled all shy-like and he breathed out a laugh. "Always have, always will," he repeated.

For a brief moment, I think we both forgot we were sitting across from Doctor Chang. When I looked over, she was smiling at us, her whole face soft. "You two just kill me."

Justin promised to keep up his physio and to write any new developments in his journal and, of course, not to overdo anything, and with another promise to see her again next week, we were on our way.

Halfway home and Justin still hadn't said anything. "You okay?" I asked.

He turned and gave me a tired smile. "Yeah. Feel good, actually. Better now we've talked to her."

"I'm glad. I feel better too. Relieved, I think."

"Yeah." He nodded. "You know how she told me to go slow, with sex, and see what I'm comfortable with?"

"Yeah? What about it?"

"What do you think she meant by go slow?"

"Oh, well . . . I think she meant we should start by making out, and as you get more comfortable, progress from there, but just a step at a time, that kind of thing."

He smirked. "Well, I think we should try that."

"You do?"

"Yep. It's technically a doctor's order."

I laughed. "True. It was."

He grinned. "Making out. In bed. This afternoon."

"Is that right?"

"Or on the couch. I can't decide."

I laughed again. "Less pressure on the couch," I suggested, thinking the idea of making out in our bed might be too much, that it may lead to sex.

He stared at me. "I can remember what we did on that couch on our weekend away, remember? At Hallidays? There was a leather couch and I can remember what you did to me on it." Then his bottom lip drew down. "I also remember what we did in the bed . . . God, is there anywhere we haven't had sex?"

I snorted. "Um . . ."

"The bathroom?"

I made a face.

"God. The kitchen?"

I made another face.

"Christ. The dining table? You know what? Don't answer that. Did we have sex everywhere?"

"Pretty much."

He sighed. "Well, maybe we should start with the couch."

I took his hand and brought it up to my lips, kissing his knuckles. "I'm sure we'll figure it out."

"Have you gotta work today?"

"Yeah."

"Shame."

I groaned. "You're cruel."

He laughed. "I'm sorry. I shouldn't tease." Then he turned serious. "Honestly though, I don't know if I can go through with it . . . Dallas, I'm sorry."

"Don't stress, and don't overthink it." I shrugged. "And anyway, you being a flirt and a tease is just like the old you, so I don't mind one bit."

"Yeah, but saying stuff is one thing. Going through with it is something else. God—"

"Hey," I said, kissing his knuckles again. "If you want to say something, then say it. I don't want you to censor yourself. I'm not gonna pressure you into sex because you say something flirty."

He sighed and sagged into his seat. "Thank you. It's weird. I have these moments where I feel completely normal, like nothing's different and there was no accident. As if my brain is playing some stupid before-and-after game. And I'll want to say something or do something, but then reality kicks in and I freeze because I don't know if it's something I'd do or say."

"Just be you, Juss," I said. "Whatever feels right."

I didn't want to say anything, but his recognition of these changes was huge. That he could recognise what was before and after, and adapt to suit, was a pretty big deal. Even though it confused him a little, his brain was changing gears and his thoughts were faster and clearer.

I pulled the ute around near the back stairs and Juss made his way up to the flat. If he worked at all today would depend on how he felt this afternoon. His doctor appointments always drained him. I followed him up and he plonked himself onto the sofa while I grabbed him a bottle of water and some crackers and grapes. I set them on the seat next to him and he pressed the button to activate the recliner. I settled the blanket over him and he gave me a tired smile.

"Thanks, babe," he murmured.

Babe? That term of endearment got me right in the heart and he was so cute, I just couldn't help it. I put my knee on the edge of the couch and leaned over him, kissing him. He responded immediately by deepening the kiss and I let him feel part of my weight on his body. When he put a hand on my waist and he moaned, it almost did me in. But I stopped and pulled back. "Get some sleep, baby," I murmured.

He made some disgruntled groan-sigh noise and I smiled as I stood up. His eyes drew down to my crotch where I was very aware of my arousal. He clearly liked what he saw and he licked his lips.

It almost buckled my knees, but I let out a laugh instead, trying to get a hold of myself. *Small steps, Dallas.*

"I'll just be downstairs," I said, waiting until I was out of view before I readjusted myself.

"Now who's the tease?" he mumbled as I got to the door.

I laughed as I bounded down the stairs and was still smiling when Sparra and Davo saw me. "Good day, I take it," Davo said, grinning at me.

"Yeah, not bad."

"Good to hear," he said. "Now get to work; we got two bikes to do this arvo."

I laughed and clapped his shoulder. "Sure thing, boss."

Sparra laughed and the three of us hooked in and worked our backsides off to get it all done with time to spare. I got some admin stuff done in the few minutes the boys were finishing up, checked my bank account and saw one client's late payments had come through, which meant I could pay wages without having to dip into my credit card, and maybe put off selling my ute for another week. It felt like a game of financial chess that I wasn't fit to play. I confirmed some more bookings for next week, thank God, and checked my emails for anything from the insurance company about the accident.

Still nothing.

Then I heard Davo and Sparra talking to someone, and a familiar voice and laugh filtered through the door. It was Justin. A few seconds later, he appeared in my office doorway, smiling. "Hey."

"Hey," I replied. "You get bored up there?"

"So bored." He walked in and parked his arse on my desk beside my chair. "Dinner's in the oven. I made shepherd's pie."

"Oh wow, thanks."

Davo cleared his throat at the door. "You, uh, you want me to lock you both in here again?"

I laughed. "Nah, I think we're good, thanks."

Justin was smiling too. "Actually, I wouldn't mind if you did."

Davo burst out laughing. "See you fellas tomorrow. I'll lock the gate behind us."

"Thanks, mate."

Sparra waved us off, leaving us alone. I closed my laptop and looked up where Juss still leaned against my desk. I put my hand on his thigh. "How're you feeling?"

"Pretty good. I slept for a while. Must have been tired."

"You want to help me close up?"

He smiled. "Yep."

So we made sure the gate was locked, then pulled the roller doors down, locking everything as we went. I helped Juss up the stairs, not that he needed it. He really was getting so much better. I doubted he'd be running up the stairs two at a time soon, if ever again, but at least each step wasn't a mountain.

Dinner was amazing, and he showed me what he'd added to his journal while we ate. Afterwards, I cleaned up the kitchen and told him to go get comfy and choose something for us to watch on TV. And when I was done and turned the lights off, he wasn't using the recliner part of the couch, but he was lying lengthways on the sofa. He had a cushion shoved under his head and was pointing the remote at the TV.

"I can tell you something that hasn't changed in five years," he said. "There is nothing to watch on TV."

He settled for some nature documentary and tossed the

remote. "You comfortable there?" I asked. He looked comfy in his trackies and hoodie. "Where am I supposed to sit?"

"No sitting," he murmured, patting the couch in front of him. "Lie here with me."

"Oh."

"I was thinking you could kiss me again, like you did this afternoon."

"We've kissed before."

"But not with your body on top of mine." He shuffled around a bit so he was on his back and not on his side so much.

Oh Christ. "You want me to lie on top of you?"

"Yeah. You know, the doctor said we should."

I laughed. "She did."

"You'll just need to watch my leg," he said. His right leg was bent at the knee and pressed against the back of the couch, which, yes, kept it out of the way, but it meant if I lay on him, I'd be between his legs.

Hell yes . . .

"I'll be careful," I whispered. "And you can tell me to stop at any time. If I hurt you, like if I accidently bump your leg or your arm, tell me."

"I will." He held out his hand to me.

So, very carefully, I put a knee on the couch and gently lowered myself on top of him. I was between his legs, holding my weight on my arms, but my hips were aligned with his. There was no way he couldn't feel my semi-hard dick. "How's that feel?"

He nodded quickly. "Really good."

I ghosted my lips over his, slow and tender, and he lifted his head to chase my mouth. It made me smile. "Small steps, baby."

"Shut up and kiss me."

I barked out a laugh because that was such a Justin thing to say. But I gave him what he wanted. I kissed him hard, opening his lips with mine, tasting his tongue and sucking it into my mouth.

He groaned and rolled his hips, then he gasped.

I stopped and pulled back. "You okay?"

He nodded, breathless. His cheeks were flushed and his pupils were blown. "Yeah. That was hot."

I kissed him again, slower this time, less urgent. He slid his hand under my shirt and up my back and it took every ounce of self-control not to lift his leg up, buck my hips, and drive into him.

I shuddered with restraint and he smiled into our kiss. "You like that?" he asked.

I put my hand to the side of his face, thumbing his hair back. "I like everything we're doing right now."

"Me too. This feels . . . right."

That earned him another kiss, then another, and we settled into a lazy make-out session. There was no hurried groping, no hurtling toward getting each other off. It was languid and dreamy. I could feel his erection against mine, but we simply revelled in the closeness, the intimacy.

I didn't even want to come. I just wanted to ride out this incredible high for as long as possible. And when the kissing ran its course, we simply held each other and traded soft touches and smiles until he was dozing off.

"We should get you to bed," I whispered.

"You too," he mumbled, his eyes still closed.

"Of course."

He was clingy; even when we brushed our teeth, he wanted to be touching me, and when we climbed into bed, he nestled right in against me. He rested his head on my shoulder, his warm breath on my neck. He'd always been my very own cuddly koala in the way he clung to me, and I pulled him even closer. I kissed the side of his head. "I love you, Juss."

"Love you too," he mumbled.

I smiled into the darkness and held him just that little bit tighter.

Chapter Ten

"Christ, you have a really big dick."

I opened my eyes and barked out a laugh. Justin was sitting up in bed, the blankets pooled at his hips, and he was staring at the bulge in my briefs. "Good morning," I replied, my voice croaking. "Sleep okay?"

"Mm, guess."

"What time is it?"

"Dunno."

I rolled over and checked my phone. "Six thirty."

He was still looking at my dick.

"Juss, you okay?"

His eyes darted to mine. "Yeah. I'm fine."

But he wasn't. This seemed more than his usual not-a-morning-person thing. His brain was overthinking again.

I pulled the blanket up to cover my crotch. "Want me to make eggs on toast for brekky?"

His gaze darted to mine again, and he seemed to snap out of his own head. "Um. Yeah. I think. I dunno. Whatever you think."

I reached over and rubbed his back. "Everything okay, Juss? If you'd rather I slept in some shorts or trackies, I can. It's no problem."

"No, I just . . ." He swallowed hard. "I like it. I'm just not . . ."

"Not what?"

"I'm not sure what I'm supposed to do?"

"About what? My dick? You're not supposed to do anything."

"Not yours . . . I mean, yours is . . ." He let out a breath. "Yours is fucking hot. But mine . . ."

"Yours? Juss, what's wrong? Is something wrong?"

"No." He scrubbed his hands over his face. "I, um, I had a dream that we were . . ." He cringed. "I woke up with a hard-on, and I dunno . . . what the hell do I do with it? I mean, I know what I can do with it. Ugh God, this is embarrassing."

I almost laughed with relief but managed to offer a smile instead. "Baby, you can do whatever you want. If you want to ignore it, then ignore it. If you want to jerk off, then do that. There's no judgement here."

"Really?"

"Yeah, really. Believe me, I've jerked off in the shower a lot since I started sleeping in here with you these last few weeks."

"You have?"

"Sure. Like I told you before, my head and my heart understand what's going on, but my dick didn't get the memo."

He almost smiled, but that line between his eyebrows was back. He studied the doona for a bit. "I'll just go have a shower," he said, then stopped. "Not to . . . jerk off. Just to shower. God, that's not what I meant."

I chuckled. "It's fine, baby. I'll go make a start on breakfast."

I rolled out of bed and filled the kettle before switching it on, then pulled the eggs out of the fridge when Justin walked out of the bathroom. He was still wearing his boxers; his hair was still a mess from sleep. He looked both worried and determined.

"Juss, what is it? Is something wrong with the shower?"

"Not the shower, no." He put his hand over his eyes, and with a frustrated groan, he sagged and then gripped his dick. "It won't go away. I thought maybe you'd like to help me . . ."

Hell fucking yes, I would.

After sliding the eggs onto the kitchen bench, I took his hand and led him to the couch. Once he sat in the middle seat, I pressed the button for the recliner to come up and gently lifted his right leg so it was resting on the recliner, his left foot still on the floor.

I knelt between his legs. "Comfy?"

He nodded.

"Tell me if you need me to stop, at any time, and I'll stop."

He nodded again, but his eyes were darker, his lips were parted.

God, he was so sexy.

I palmed his dick first, and yeah, he was rock hard. He pushed his hips up at the touch, desperate for friction. "I need . . ."

I pulled the front of his boxers down and freed his cock. It thwacked against his belly, red and swollen, leaking precome. It looked painfully hard. I gripped his shaft and he groaned.

"Feel okay?" I asked.

He nodded again. "Need to come, Dallas."

I leaned in and licked his shaft from base to tip and he hissed, but he raised his hips again, desperate. So I sucked him into my mouth and tongued the head before taking him in as far as I could. I sucked him good and hard until he arched, and his cock pulsed and shot his load into my mouth.

He tasted familiar and wonderful, and I drank, sucking and licking him clean. He writhed with the pleasure of it, then sagged when it was over. I was pretty sure his muscles, particularly in his leg, weren't used to that kind of strain.

"How are you feeling now?"

He replied with a snort and a laugh.

"Okay, smiley. That's gonna wear off in a minute." I got to my feet and gently pulled him to his. "Let's get you into a hot shower."

He let me lead him to the bathroom, let me undress him, reminding me almost of the early days after his accident. There were no thought processes, just blind obedience. But this time it was a little different; he was just blissed out. I turned the water on and held his arm. "You okay?"

He nodded. "Yeah. I feel . . . really good."

"I'm glad. Okay, water's hot enough. Hop in."

"You too," he replied, taking my hand. "You can shower with me."

"Um . . ." I hesitated.

"I could fall," he said.

I met his gaze, trying to see if he was joking or not.

"Don't want me to fall, do you?" he added with the hint of a smirk.

"The shower's not real big."

"Then we better stand close," he said. He stepped into the shower and held his hand out. "You're getting water on the floor."

I rolled my eyes and slid my pants down before following him into the shower. There wasn't much room at all, so I pressed my back against the tiles. He stood with his head under the spray, letting the hot water course over his neck and shoulders for a long moment before he handed me the soap. "Do my back?" he asked, throwing me a dirty smirk as he turned his back to me.

I soaped him up, good and proper. His back, his shoulders, his arms, his arse. Fuck, his arse was beautiful.

When he turned around, his eyes went straight to my now very erect cock. He licked his lips. "Fuck, Dallas." He took the soap from me and washed my chest, my stomach. But then he ditched the soap and took my hand, wrapping my fingers around my dick and he helped pump me a few times. "I want to watch you come."

And the combination of last night and all that making out, waking up with a hard-on, then giving him head on the couch and being naked with him in the shower had me close to the edge in no time.

No, he wasn't ready to be the one who jerked me off, let alone suck me—not that he could in a shower anyway, not with his leg —but this was a big step for him. And knowing he was taking this step for me . . .

I tweaked my nipple as I stroked myself, then reached down to my balls. "Oh, fuck," I mumbled. The hot water, the steam, Justin standing there, watching me like he wanted to devour me.

I came so hard the room spun, and without any warning,

Justin kissed me. His hands were in my hair, his tongue was in my mouth, and a wave of aftershocks barrelled through me as my come spilled between us.

"That was so fucking hot," he breathed. Then he traced a finger along the wing of my tattoo. "God, I love this ink, I love your body." He put his forehead to my collarbone and fell into a hug. "Love you too."

I was still in some post-orgasmic haze, but I managed to wrap my arms around him. "I love you, Juss. And I wish we could stay here forever but the water's gonna run cold soon."

He grumbled but we got out and dried off. "Need to use the bathroom," he said awkwardly, not meeting my gaze.

"Okay, I'll go start breakfast." I left him to it, quickly getting dressed before making coffee and cracking some eggs into a pan, all the while hoping his sudden downturn in mood as we dried off wasn't regret.

He took his time in the bathroom and getting dressed, so I was putting the toast on our plates on the table when he came back out. "Oh, hey," I began. "I made you scrambled—"

He cut my words off with a fierce hug. He slotted perfectly against me, holding me tight with his face pressed into my neck. "Oh!" I was stunned, to say the least. "You okay?"

He nodded against me. "I am now." He sighed but never made a move to let go. "Thank you, for not freaking out. For giving me what I needed when I didn't even know what I needed."

"You're welcome, baby. Was what we did okay? I thought you might have regretted what we did. Or that you weren't ready. It wasn't too much?"

"No, it was perfect." He pulled back. "I was a bit freaked out when I first woke up. I was so turned on, and that was really the first time I've felt like that since my accident. It wouldn't quit and I didn't know what to do. I wasn't ready to jerk off, I don't know why. But I thought you'd know what to do. And holy shit, did you ever."

I laughed at that. "I'm glad you're feeling better. And believe me, it was my absolute pleasure to help you with that problem."

He blushed. "It's so weird to talk about this stuff."

I kissed him softly, then pulled out his seat. "Sit down and have some brekky. We need to get downstairs. We've got a busy day at work today."

He smiled as he sat. "God, I'm starving. Thank you!"

I HUNG up the phone after taking another booking for next week, and Davo came into my office and sat down. "Jusso's helping Sparra with the full service on the Honda."

"Good. How's he going?" I'd been stuck in my office most of the morning and hadn't been on the workshop floor at all.

"He's handling it just fine. There's a change in him today," Davo said. "I dunno what, exactly, but he's almost like his old self. He's still moving slow with his leg and all, but his thinking is much clearer."

"Yeah. This morning . . . his brain told him he was actually hungry. That's a good sign." I shrugged. There was no way I was telling him anything else that went on this morning. "It's a real good sign. But we're still taking it one day at a time."

"Well, it's good to see. He was laughing out there before, so something's going right." He eyed me for a long second. "And by your smile, I reckon you agree."

I tried not to smile and failed. "Yeah, something's going right. We were so lucky. It could have been so much worse."

"He's getting better every day."

"He is."

"Good," Davo said with a grin. "He's been slacking off for too long."

I chuckled. "Did you come in here for any particular reason."

He nodded. "Yeah. To tell you it's lunchtime and pizza sounds good."

I laughed at him. "Yeah, righteo. Message received and understood."

Pizza ordered—and paid for on my credit card—I was just

tidying up my desk when the phone rang again. "Muller's Mechanics, Dallas speaking."

"Uh, hello, Dallas," a man replied. He sounded older. "It's Jimmy Litchfield. We met at the hospital. I came in to see the young man, Justin, and you said I should call in a few weeks."

"Mr Litchfield. Yes, I remember you. I was there with Justin that day."

"How is he? Is he getting on okay? I worry about him."

"He's getting by okay, Mr Litchfield," I said. "Did you want to call in one day? I'm sure Justin'd like that."

"I sure would, if that'd be no trouble. Please, call me Jimmy."

"Just gimme one sec." I put the call on hold and went out in search of Juss. He was on his scooter, taking a spring off a suspension rig while Sparra was next to him unfastening an engine cap off the same bike. "Hey, Juss?" He looked up at me. "Do you remember the old guy, Jimmy Litchfield? He came to see you at the hospital."

Juss squinted one eye. "Uh, yeah. The truck driver, right?"

"Yeah." I held up the phone. "He wants to know if he can call around sometime and see how you're getting on. Is that okay with you?"

Justin shrugged. "Sure. I guess."

I let Jimmy know it was all fine, that mornings were best, and he said he'd see us soon. The pizza arrived and we made real short work of that, and I didn't really give the phone call another thought until dinner time when Justin brought it up.

"What do you think the truck driver wants?" he asked.

"Honestly, I think he needs to know you're okay. I think he feels a lot of guilt, and knowing you're okay helps him with that."

Justin nodded slowly and pushed his salad around his plate. He hadn't slept for long this afternoon and I could see he was tired by his delayed speech and slow blinks. Clearly he had a lot on his mind. "He must be a nice guy."

"He seemed it," I replied. "When he came to the hospital, he was very upset. I thought he was genuine."

He nodded. "Says a lot that some stranger wants to visit but my own mother hasn't even called me."

I put my fork down and covered his hand with mine. "Oh, Juss. I'm sorry. Have you been thinking about her?"

He gave a slight shrug. "Mm. Bit hard not to. I mean, I didn't for a while when my brain was all foggy, but then I realised that she hasn't even called, so now I . . ." He sighed. "Now I know how she really feels, I guess."

I squeezed his hand. "Baby, I'm sorry. I'm sorry she's a horrible person. You deserve better."

"Did she call at all when I was in hospital?"

I shook my head. "No."

He frowned. "Becca said she told her and that her reaction was about as good as expected. She didn't say what was said, exactly, so I guess it was awful."

"Baby, she hasn't really been a part of your life since you came back to Newcastle. Not in the last five years. She certainly doesn't like me."

"Have you met her?"

I nodded. "Yeah. We went and saw her. You'd been back from Darwin for about six months and you hadn't seen her in two and a half years. We thought we'd see if she'd changed her attitude."

Something flashed in his eyes. "Was she mean to you?"

"Not directly. She was mean to you and disgusted that I wasn't a woman. She said some pretty horrible things."

His nostrils flared. His eyebrows knitted. "She never called me when I was in Darwin either. She hasn't really spoken to me since she found out I was gay. I dunno why I ever thought that'd change."

"Because you're a decent human being who never loses hope. And she's a terrible person and an even worse mother."

His gaze darted to mine and he smiled. "True. Still sucks, though."

"It does. I'm not denying that. My relationship with my family isn't much better. But we know what we're worth, and we know we deserve better." I put his hand to my face and kissed his palm. "We choose our own family, Juss."

"I'm so glad I found you," he whispered. "Twice."

I chuckled at that. "And I'm glad for the second chance."

And right on cue, Squish decided to yell at us from his bowl. "Yes, Squish. We're glad for you too," I said. "And for the record, there are biscuits in that bowl. You're not starving."

Justin laughed. "You know this . . ." He gestured between us and then to the cat. "This was all I ever wanted."

"The family we choose, right?"

He laughed again but got teary as he nodded. "Yeah."

"Oh, baby," I said, sliding my chair over and pulling him in for a hug. "I didn't mean to upset you."

He leaned his head against my neck and let out a shaky breath. "Dunno why I'm upset. Tired, I guess."

"You're allowed to feel whatever you feel. Why don't you go lie down? I'll clean this up."

He looked at his plate like he hadn't noticed it before, then shook his head like the fog was back. "I'm sorry I'm kinda useless tonight."

"You're not useless, baby."

He pouted. "I wanted to make out some more tonight."

I chuckled. "I'm sure we can arrange something."

He gave me a lazy smile, but he got up from the table and limped to the couch. I cleaned up and he was asleep when I joined him. I commandeered the remote control and surfed through the channels for a few moments before his sleeping mind registered my presence. He curled into me, his head on my chest, and my arm went around his shoulder. I kissed the top of his head.

I hated that his mother's rejection had been playing on his mind. It brought out my protective side, which wasn't too pretty. But I'd be damned if I'd let that hateful bitch hurt him all over again. What she'd said to him, and how she'd said it, the last time he'd seen her had devastated him.

For all the memories he'd lost, I was glad he couldn't remember that.

And now, after all he'd been through, watching him deal with crippling pain, I couldn't bear the thought of anyone hurting him again. Instinctively, I tightened my hold and rubbed his arm, causing him to stir.

He lifted his head, his eyes half-closed, and he began to kiss me, clumsy and sleepy, but he shifted and climbed up to lie on top of me. He kissed me deep and I let him lead, setting whatever pace he needed.

It was slow and lovely, no pressure for anything else. Just kissing, tasting, and touching. He put his hands to my face, caressing and mapping out my features with his thumbs, as though he was committing every angle to memory.

He drew the kiss to a close and nuzzled into my neck. I half expected him to kiss me there, but he inhaled deeply and began to snore. And Squish chose that very moment to plant himself between us and the arm of the couch, and all I could do was laugh.

***

JUST ON SMOKO-TIME the next day, an old car pulled into the drive and Mr and Mrs Litchfield got out. Mrs Litchfield was holding a Tupperware container and Jimmy nervously flattened his shirt before they walked into the workshop.

I took a few long strides to meet them at the roller door opening and held out my hand. "Morning."

Jimmy shook my hand. "And what a good one it is," he said. "Thanks for agreeing to see me. I wasn't sure if it'd be too soon."

"Not at all," I replied. Then I turned around and called out, "Jusso? You got some visitors."

The workshop was kinda dark compared to the bright sunlight of outside, so it wasn't real easy to see. But Justin appeared on his scooter, wiping his hands on an oily rag. He was curious and trying to see their faces in the bright light. "Oh, hello," he said when he figured out who it was. "Hang on, let me lose the wheels."

He got up off his scooter and walked the last few steps to stand beside me. He shoved the rag into his back pocket and held out his hand, nodding to his arm. "I can shake your hand this time."

Jimmy shook his hand gently, smiled, and gave a nod.

"Jimmy, and my wife, Nancy," he said. "You've come a long way since I last saw you. Up on your feet now."

"Yeah, mostly," Juss answered. "Still use the wheels to get around sometimes, especially down here in the workshop. It's much easier on my leg. Faster too."

Jimmy nodded again and wrung his hands. The poor guy was so nervous. "How about we go sit in the breakroom," I suggested.

"I made some biscuits," Nancy said. "Jam drops. Fresh this morning."

"Then a cup of tea sounds great," I added. "Come on through."

They sat at the old table in the breakroom while I made four cups of tea. Davo and Sparra came in and grabbed a cuppa and Nancy was quick to stand and offer them a biscuit. Davo was about to decline, but when Sparra grabbed two, saying his mum used to make jam drops like this, she just about beamed and Davo gave a polite nod and took a jam drop. It clearly made her happy, and Jimmy gave her a fond look. "We've been wondering how you've been getting on," he said.

"I'm getting better every day," Juss said. "I've got physio exercises and stuff that helps, but honestly, getting back to work has helped the most."

I smiled at that. "It has made a huge difference."

"I remember how to do everything," he furthered. "I can't remember much from the last five years, but I can still pull a two-stroke engine apart, clean it up, and put it back together in no time."

Jimmy smiled at that. "It must be a comfort."

Justin nodded. "It is."

Jimmy sipped his tea. "But your memory didn't come back?"

Juss gave a shake of his head. "Nah. Some things, but not much. I remembered Dallas, though. Just snippets of us." He smiled at me. "So it's not all bad news."

Jimmy got a little misty-eyed. "I'm glad to hear that." He cleared his throat. "I gotta say, I've been better since seein' you at the hospital. And I'm real grateful you don't mind us calling in today. It helps," he said, turning his cup of tea. "To know you're getting better."

"It helps me too," Justin said. "I told Dallas after you came to see me in the hospital that it helped putting a face to the accident." Jimmy's eyes widened, and Justin was quick to clarify. "Not in a bad way. In a good way. It wasn't some scary, unknown thing anymore. I can't remember the accident at all, and there was so much unknown always hanging over me. But now I know it was just that. It was an accident. And the guy driving the truck wasn't some bad guy who didn't give a shit. He was a nice guy who never meant to hurt me. And I dunno why, but that really helped."

Jimmy was teary now, and he nodded. "I get it, son. I know exactly what you mean." He smiled at his wife. "It helped me knowing you were both nice young fellas too. You showed me a kindness when you didn't have to."

Nancy nodded. "It means a lot to both of us." She pulled her handbag onto her lap and pulled out a folded piece of cardboard. She handed it to Justin. "I hope you don't mind, but my granddaughter drew this for you. We babysit her some days when her mum works, and she knew that her poppy was sad about the accident and she wanted to help."

He opened the card, as it turned out, to see a crayon drawing. There was one couple, a man and a woman at the top of the page, and a second couple, two men, down at the bottom. There was a truck in between the two couples. The man at the top had a very big frown, and one of the men at the bottom had a broken leg and a broken arm, if the yellow squiggles were what I thought they were. It was very clearly done by a little kid.

There were also love hearts and shining sun and clouds in the top corner, and . . . "Is that a fish?" I asked.

"She just got a goldfish. She wanted to include it." Nancy nodded, giving me a sad smile. "She just turned five and she wanted to do something to help."

"It's amazing," Justin said. "What's her name?"

"Bethany."

"Please tell Bethany I said thank you. And it did make me feel better.”

Jimmy was teary again. “She drew me one too. It’s no secret that I haven’t coped too well since the accident. I’ve told all my family what happened and how you two boys were so nice to me.”

My God, these two were just the sweetest. “How many kids do you have?” I asked.

“Five children and twelve grandchildren,” Nancy said. “Each one’s a blessing.”

To my surprise, though maybe it shouldn’t have been, Justin got a little teary. “You’re real lucky to have such a big, happy family.”

“You don’t?” she asked him.

“I’ve got Dallas,” he said with a smile in my direction. “And I have a sister and two nieces, who are just the cutest. They live in Sydney. My mother doesn’t like my—” He made a face. “—choices.”

Nancy reached over and took his hand. “It was never a choice for you, sweetheart.”

I almost snorted my tea out my nose. “Oh, we know that. But thank you.”

“Don’t mind Nancy,” Jimmy said fondly. “We’ve got a gay granddaughter, and my Nance protects her brood. Like a mother hen, she is. We don’t care what walk of life the kids are, as long as they have manners and eat all their dinner.” He gave a hard nod. “Oh, and I don’t mind too much if they bring their old Pops some Turkish Delight every once in a while.”

Justin and I both chuckled again, and Jimmy told us a story of being on the road a lot when his own kids were little and how he was real sorry about that, and how he was trying to make up for that with his grandkids. Then he asked Justin all about his recovery and how he was coping with it all. He and Nancy were such a genuine couple, we could have stayed chatting the whole day. I’d completely lost track of time when Davo knocked on the door.

He held out the office cordless phone. “Sorry, boss. But it’s a call you need to take.”

I frowned because I hadn't even heard the phone, and it wasn't like Davo not to either take the booking or take a message. I stood up. "Won't be long," I said, making my excuses as I left the room.

Davo handed me the phone. "Compo lady," he whispered.

"Oh shit, thank you." I clapped him on the arm as I went into my office and closed the door. My heart was in my throat, so much depended on this. "Dallas Muller speaking."

"Hi, Dallas, it's Angela Jarrett. Sorry I didn't get back to you sooner." I listened as she went through all the red tape and jargon I couldn't really follow. "Anyway, it's good news," she said. "It's been determined there was no vicarious liability by you or your employee."

Vicarious liability?

"What does that mean?"

"That you weren't at fault."

"Yeah, I'm aware of that."

"The van your employee was driving was in good working order, all safety precautions were made. Any and all modifications made to the storage area of the van were legal and did not contribute to the personal injury of your employee."

I was also aware of that. "So what does that mean? What do we do now?"

"The findings are in your favour. First of all, you'll be fully compensated for the van and the loss of income pertaining to the van and all the tools. I don't have a date for the recompense as yet."

I sagged with relief. It took me a second before I could speak. "And what about Justin?"

She paused. "I can't discuss his personal claim—"

"Yeah, but as his employer, what does this mean?"

"His wage compensation payment, or his personal injury benefit payments, will be ninety-five per cent of his income for thirteen weeks, then eighty-five per cent for the following fourteen weeks after that. You'll receive all backpay in full. He'll be reassessed after six months, which is standard." She paused. "I can tell you all his medical costs will be covered."

God, I could have cried. I actually had to try to swallow a few times before I could manage actual words. I squeezed my eyes closed and shook off my tears. "That's good news."

"It is. I'll be in touch when I have some dates of payment for you, but I'll send through an email confirming everything I have so far today and snail mail as well."

"Thank you. For everything."

She said goodbye and clicked off the call, and I just had to sit at my desk for a bit. I hadn't realised the weight I'd carried on my shoulders until it was gone. I felt so relieved, so fucking relieved, I couldn't even describe it.

All that worry, all that stress about money was over. I let out an almighty sigh just as I saw Justin by the door. Oh shit. I'd forgotten Jimmy and Nancy were here!

I met them all at the door just as they were leaving. "Sorry about that," I said.

"Oh, don't worry. I know you're busy," Jimmy said.

I didn't know what they'd talked about in my absence, but the three of them looked happy, though I could tell Juss was tired. We walked them out and waved them off, and Jimmy told us not to be strangers as he got into the car.

"Everything okay with that phone call?" Juss asked me.

"Couldn't have been better. It was the workers' compensation case manager. It's all been approved, for the van and your wages and all the medical bills."

Justin shot me a look. "For real? All of it?"

"For real, baby." I grinned at him. "Such a relief, right?"

He nodded. "You were really worried about it, weren't you?"

"Yeah. I was. But it's over now." I pulled him in for a hug just as Jimmy and Nancy drove out of the yard. They waved and we waved back, with Justin still pressed into my side. "Sorry for leaving you alone with them," I said.

"Oh no. It's fine. I really like them."

"Me too. They're a nice old couple."

"I'm glad. Because they invited us around for a barbeque next weekend. I said we'd go."

Chapter Eleven

I WAS SURPRISED, to say the least, that Juss agreed to a barbeque at Jimmy and Nancy's place. Having them call around to see how Justin was getting on was one thing, but going to their place was something else.

But this was something Justin decided he needed to do. It made him happy. And, the most important part, this was him making a decision and wanting to see it through. And being sociable and getting out of the house.

So who was I to disagree with that?

After Jimmy and Nancy left, Justin went upstairs and crashed out for a few hours and I read over the compensation claim information Angela had sent me. The van could be replaced, along with the thousands of dollars' worth of tools that had been in it. Ninety-five per cent of Juss' wage was covered, and one hundred per cent of the medical bills.

Yes, the relief I felt was immense but so was the gratitude. And with that in mind, after doing a little maths, I called Davo and Sparra into my office.

"What's up, boss?" Sparra asked.

"Take a seat, guys."

They both shot each other a nervous look as they sat.

"It's not bad," I said, easing their worries. "It's the opposite, actually. Justin's accident hit us pretty hard in a lot of ways and

I'd be a shit boss if I didn't use that as an opportunity to implement a few things that would make your jobs easier and safer. So, I want you guys to have a think and put forward some ideas."

Davo cast me a cautious look. "Like what?"

"Well, I'm certain we could go through our toolkits and upgrade a few pieces, sure. Like new pressure kits and battery testers. That'll make all our jobs easier. But I was also thinking we could use some hydraulic hoists. I know we've been using old-school bike stands for years, but we should upgrade. They're safer and better for our backs. And that'll mean new shop seats as well."

"The fancy ones?" Sparra asked. "We can have scooter races with Jusso from one end of the workshop to the other."

I chuckled at that, and even Davo smiled. But then he shook his head. "Dallas," he whispered, "you don't need to do that."

"Yes I do. I should have done it years ago."

"Those hoists cost a fortune."

"We got the approval for workers' comp and insurance," I said. "Finally. And I should use the money to make everyone's job safer."

"Are we getting a new van?" Sparra asked.

"It's been approved, yeah." I let out a sigh. "But I'll be honest with ya's, I dunno how I feel about having someone on the road again. I know it was Justin's idea, it was his baby, and it was a good business decision, but the thought of another accident . . ." I shuddered. "I don't know if it's worth it."

"You'd worry about whoever went out now," Davo said quietly. And that was very true. I really would.

"Maybe Jusso will want to get back out there. Like you said, it was his idea to begin with. It was his job." Sparra shrugged. "Not sayin' I want him back out there either. I'm just saying it should be his choice. When he's right to drive again." His eyes met mine. "Will he ever be right to drive again?"

"Not for a while," I answered. "He'd have medical tests to get through and his neuro doctors would have to sign off on it. I think. We haven't really got that far yet. Definitely not for six months, I'd reckon."

Davo frowned. "But will he ever *want* to drive again? That's probably a better question. He can't remember the accident, but on some level, he'd have to be scared to get back behind the wheel, yeah? I know I would be."

That was a really good point. "He's been okay when we've been in the ute before," I said. "I think I was more worried about hearing some screeching tyres or something that might trigger something for him, but he seemed oblivious to it. Like getting into cars was no big deal at all. But you're right, Davo. Whether he'll ever be up for driving again is a really good question."

"HEY," I said, walking into the flat. Justin hadn't come back downstairs, so I was surprised to see him lying on the couch with a blanket and Squish. The TV was on but the volume was on real low, not that he was watching it anyway. "Everything okay?"

"Yeah," he said. "Just got a bit of a headache, that's all. Thought I'd take it easy."

I sat beside him and put the back of my hand to his forehead. He wasn't running a temp, thank God. "Sure you're okay?"

He gave a tired smile. "I put a frozen lasagne in the oven, but I didn't know what you'd want to have with it. I'm not real hungry."

I lifted his chin, ever so slightly, and looked into his eyes. "On a scale of one to ten, how bad is your headache?"

He slow blinked and tried to smile. "'Bout a six."

"A six? Your six would be my nine, Juss, because you know what an actual nine or ten feels like," I whispered. "Baby, you should have messaged me. I would've come up."

"I'm okay. Just taking it easy."

"Did you take your pills?"

He nodded and took my hand, threading our fingers. "Yeah. At three."

Shit. And his pain was still a six. In hindsight, I should have checked on him when he didn't come back down. "I got busy and lost track of time. I should have come up. I'm sorry."

"'S okay, Dall. It's not too bad. I just didn't want to overdo it, that's all."

Which was a good thing, I allowed. And a good sign that he recognised the need to rest. "Can I get you anything? A juice or a cup of tea?"

He smiled. "A cuddle. Always makes me feel better."

"I can do that."

"A proper lie-down cuddle," he added. "And you can rub circles on my back and put your fingers through my hair."

Chuckling, I shuffled down a bit and lay beside him on my side, boots still on and all. But he quickly pressed himself into my chest, one arm under his head, the other drawing lazy patterns on his back. "That better?" I whispered.

"So much better."

We lay like that for a few minutes and I stroked his back and his head like he asked. His face became peaceful, his breathing even. I could watch him sleep forever. I hated that he lived with such awful headaches, though.

And I could finally lie with him without the dark cloud of money hanging over me. I didn't realise just how much it had overshadowed me. Like I could breathe deep and exhale properly for the first time in weeks.

The oven timer went off and I groaned. "Oh man, I'm sorry," I whispered, extracting my arm from under his head. I planted a kiss on the scar above his ear and went to rescue the lasagne. I served up mine with some salad and cut Juss a small piece of the lasagne as well. He said he didn't want to eat, but maybe he could have a few bites, especially if he'd had pain meds.

He begrudgingly sat up and held Squish away from the food, and I fed Juss small bites of dinner in between forkfuls of my own. When I was done and satisfied he'd eaten enough, we lay back down on the couch with Juss as the little spoon, and he fought sleep long enough to take his meds, then go to bed.

I tidied up and watched the rest of the Friday night footy, but the movie after that was crap so I showered and went to bed. Justin was sound asleep—his pain meds would knock him out pretty hard—but as soon as I was in the bed beside him, he stirred and somehow sensed that I was close and snuggled right into me and went straight back to a deep sleep.

All he'd ever wanted was to feel loved. To be held, to be protected and safe; everything that had been lacking in his life, everything his mother never gave him. So, even though he was out like a light, I held him a little tighter. "I love you, Justin Keith." I planted a soft kiss to his forehead and closed my eyes. "Always have, always will."

A SEX DREAM woke me up. An amazing dream where I was on top of Justin, inside him. He was rocking his hips and I drove into him with his upswing. God, it was so good, I didn't want it to ever end. But it flitted away like dreams sometimes do and it took a second for reality to kick in.

A reality of being on our sides, pressed up against Justin's back, and . . . oh, sweet mother of God, he was rocking his hips.

"Morning," he rasped. "Didn't think you'd ever wake up."

"Fuck, sorry," I said, trying to get my mind in gear.

He put a hand on my hip. "Don't move."

Of course, I froze and it gave me a split second to take stock of my body and where exactly my dick was for it to feel that good. My erection was pressed between his legs, between his arse cheeks, behind his balls . . . Oh God.

"Feels good," he murmured.

"Oh fuck." My hips curled without my permission, seeking more . . . of everything that felt so good.

I kissed the back of his neck, his shoulder, and tried to get my hips under control. I wanted to thrust so bad. But then, just like in my dream, he rolled his hips, pulling on my cock. It hadn't been a dream. It was Justin getting off on my cock.

Was that his arm moving? Was he jerking off?

Oh, fucking hell, he was.

"Fuck, you feel so good," I ground out.

"God, Dallas." He flexed his hips, rolling and rocking on my erection between his legs.

It was almost too much to bear. "I'll come if you keep doing that."

He groaned and did it harder.

Fuck.

I began to thrust gently in time with his tempo, and after only a few more thrusts, I gripped his hip and he cried out. At first I thought I'd hurt him, but he went rigid against me and convulsed as he came.

His arse cheeks clenched around my shaft and I followed his lead, spilling hot come between his legs, behind his balls.

"Oh God, Justin," I growled, and he arched back, relaxing into my arms. He was spent and breathing hard.

We were both rattled with aftershocks, and I held him tight. I didn't pull back. I wanted to be as close to him as I possibly could. "That was crazy," he said with a gravelly laugh. "I woke up like that. You were hard and sliding your cock against me for a while. It felt so good, so thank you."

"I was dreaming," I replied, chuckling. I kissed his shoulder again. "I was having this hot sex dream and I woke up to find out it wasn't a dream at all."

"Well, the bed's a mess. I'm a mess." He wiggled his arse a little and I pulled my sensitive dick away. "We need to shower and change the sheets."

I was reluctant to let go of him. "How's your head feeling?"

"'S okay. It'll be better when you wash me in the shower, then feed me breakfast."

I laughed. He was obviously feeling better, and he wasn't even his usual morning-grumpy self. I kissed the back of his head. "Your wish, my command."

WORK WAS steady for the next few days and Justin's headaches subsided enough for him to work again. He really was happier when he was busy, getting his hands dirty and being productive.

There really wasn't that much difference between the old Justin and the new Justin. He was never happier than when he was working on a bike. He was still on light duties and always worked paired with someone, and he still needed a rest around lunchtime. Though he was coming back downstairs mid-afternoon to resume his work.

The improvements every day were small, but in hindsight, I could see him come so far.

He was happier, and I was certainly a lot less stressed now I knew the insurance and compensation money were all approved. It wasn't in the bank yet, and I was still swapping money around to pay for stuff, but knowing it was coming was a helluva relief. Davo and Sparra were happier too; morale was high because I included them in deciding which work improvements we should prioritise. I really did value all they did for me and their opinions, but I wanted to give them something else as a token of my appreciation.

So, given it was Friday and I had to go to the bank, I told them all I'd bring back an early lunch. At the bank, I had them increase my business credit card limit an extra ten grand. Not something I'd ever wanted to do, but now I knew the insurance and compo money were coming, it would take the pressure off.

Afterward, I swung past Charlestown Square shopping centre and picked up a whole stack of Japanese dumplings plus a surprise something for the breakroom.

When I got back to the workshop, I carried the bag with my surprise in it through to the breakroom along with the takeout containers. "Lunch is here."

Tools down, the three of them followed me in. I opened the dumplings and grabbed some forks and pointed to each container. "Beef, chicken, pork."

"Whatcha got there?" Juss asked, nodding to the big bag behind me.

"A little surprise and a thank you," I said. I lifted the box out of the bag and set it on the counter. "I thought it was about time we did away with the instant coffee and got some real stuff."

It was just one of those pod machines that everyone had these days and something I'd heard the boys talking about. I pulled out a few packets of the pods to go with it, even some decaf ones for Juss.

"Oh, hell yes," Sparra crowed, his mouth half full of dumpling. "We're drinking the fancy shit now."

"And that's not all," I said, suddenly nervous. I pulled two envelopes out of my back pocket and handed one to Davo and one to Sparra. "From me to you both. As thanks, for everything."

Davo opened his and took out the piece of paper. It was a bank cheque for a thousand bucks. His eyes shot to mine. "Dallas . . ."

Sparra opened his with less finesse and pulled out the cheque. "What is it?" He read it and shot a confused glance to Davo, then me. "Is that for me?"

"Money was tight for a while, not gonna lie. But now the insurance has all been approved, I can breathe again. I wanted to thank you both. For everything you guys did while Juss and me couldn't be here. You really stepped up and got us through a really hard time."

"What is it?" Juss asked. Sparra showed him the cheque and Juss looked at me with a soft smile. "You did that for them?"

I nodded. "I was gonna book the four of us in for the MotoGP on Phillip Island, or maybe the motocross championship finals on the Sunshine Coast. I couldn't decide, but then I thought the cash might be better. Sparra, I know you've been eyeing off a new pair of riding boots and a set of Pirelli's. And Davo, I know you and Lauren wanted to fix up the back patio at your place." I shrugged. "Or whatever you want to spend it on, I dunno. It's your money."

"I wouldn't have said no to a trip to the Grand Prix," Davo said with a smile. "But this is . . . I didn't expect this. Not sure what to say, actually."

"Same," Sparra said. "Thanks, Dallas. And Jusso. You paid us for all the overtime. We didn't expect nothing extra."

"I know," I replied. "I wanted to do it."

"And a coffee machine!" Davo said. "You weren't messing around."

I rolled my eyes. "Yeah, and you guys are gonna have to show me how to use it."

Juss pulled out the seat next to him at the table and patted it. I sat, and we ate all the dumplings and talked and laughed. It felt so good to give them something back. Not that the money was an amount of their worth, but just a small thanks to let them know what they did to help me out didn't go unnoticed.

As we talked and ate, Juss kept his hand on my thigh, and when Davo and Sparra decided to get the coffee machine up and running, Juss leaned over and kissed the tip of my shoulder. "You're a really good guy, you know that?" he whispered.

"I wanted to say thanks, that's all."

Juss looked at me with such love. "I'm pretty sure that's another reason why I overlooked the fact you're a Bulldogs supporter," he said with a wink.

I laughed, and Davo and Sparra argued about the coffee machine and whether it needed a cycle of water through it first, and Sparra was adding water to it while Davo was reading the instruction booklet. They bickered like old hens, and Juss laughed as he slipped his hand in mine. He put his tired head on my shoulder and I could feel him vibrate every time he chuckled.

A few minutes and a full comedy routine later, we had our first taste of coffee, and I had to admit, it was so much better. Davo and Sparra both thanked me for lunch and went back to their workstations, and Juss sat up and stretched his back.

"You okay?" I asked.

"Yeah. Just tired. I might head upstairs for a bit."

"Okay. I'll help you."

"Nah, it's okay. I can manage."

"I was really just using that as an excuse to check your arse out on the way up the stairs, and maybe steal a proper kiss when we get inside."

He laughed. "Well, that's okay then. I'll allow that."

We walked out of the breakroom just as Sparra was reaching for the old stereo. "Hell yes. Some classic Chisel!" he crowed just before he turned the volume up.

"When the War Is Over" was playing. God, I loved this song.

Juss and I had danced to this song when we first got together. I turned to Justin, smiling, wondering if he might remember this song as ours, only to see him stop.

Frozen.

His face blank but somehow horrified.

Then his right eye closed, then his left. Both squinted shut and he put his hand to the right side of his head, to his scar, and he swayed.

And then he screamed.

Chapter Twelve

"Justin!" I grabbed hold of his arm. "Justin, are you okay?"

His right eye squinted shut and he fell into me. "I remember . . ."

Holding Justin, I glanced at Davo. "Call an ambulance."

"No, no ambulance. No hospital," Justin said, putting his hand out. "I'm okay. My head . . . God, I remember."

Sparra appeared with a chair from the breakroom and I lowered Justin into it. I knelt in front of him. He was pale and sweating, and his right eye being closed was scaring the shit out of me. It hadn't been like that for weeks. "Juss, you don't look too good."

He put his hand to his head; his right eye was still squinted closed. "I don't feel too good."

Davo upended an old ice cream container, spilling old bolts and washers onto the floor. He handed it to me and I put it on Juss' lap. "How bad is the pain? From one to ten."

He shook his head. "Dallas, I remember. Driving the van. This song. 'When the War Is Over.' It came on the radio. It's our song, Dall. I remember. The light was green. It was just getting to Jimmy Barnes' part of the song."

He was panting and still so pale. But his eye. His eye squinting like that scared me the most.

"I can hear the brakes and horns. And it's pissing rain. I

turned to see out my window, Dallas, and the truck is right there. The grille is right there."

He put his hand up to his right, as though he could touch the truck in his memory.

"Then there was glass and metal. My head. God, the pain, I can feel the pain. It's bad. Then the darkness." He sobbed. "That awful nothingness in my dreams. That's all that's left. Just darkness and pain."

"Oh, Juss," I whispered, my hands to his face.

He began to cry and curl in on himself. "Oh my God, I remember it. Our song was playing, and the truck didn't stop. It hurts so bad, Dall. I can feel how much it hurt."

His right eye didn't seem to want to open at all, and I worried that he was having some kind of stroke. "Juss, I need you to look at me. Can you open your mouth for me? Show me your teeth?"

Tears spilled down his cheeks. "What the fuck for?"

Stunned for a second, I laughed with relief. His brain and mouth were working just fine. "I was just worried about . . . your right eye's closed. I was just checking for a stroke."

He was still far too pale and sweating, but his breathing was better at least. He put his hand to his head. "Christ, my head just hurts. Like when I first woke up in hospital. Like the truck just hit me, all over again."

"Is the pain too much, Juss?" I asked, looking up at him. "I can call an ambulance—"

"No." He squinted and put the heel of his hand against his scar. "Just need pills and sleep. No hospital. I don't want to go back to hospital, Dall. Please. Please. I can't go back."

"Okay, okay," I said, trying to calm him. The last thing he needed right now, was to be more upset. "We'll get you to bed. But Juss, if it gets worse, you have to tell me."

He nodded, but I could tell the exhaustion was kicking in.

"I'm gonna pick you up and carry you upstairs, okay?"

He nodded again, and the fact he didn't even want to try to do it on his own told me all I needed to know. I carried him up the stairs and put him straight on the bed. I pulled off his boots, got his pills, which he also took without argument.

"That song, Dall," he whispered. "'S our song."

My heart hurt, good and bad. "Yeah, baby. It's our song." I kissed his forehead. "Go to sleep."

"When the War Is Over." Appropriate for a whole other lot of reasons now. When would this war be over? Would it ever end for him?

I was beginning to think it wouldn't.

I watched his beautiful face as he slept, his parted lips, his closed eyelids, and took out my phone.

"I GAVE him his heavy-duty pills. He's sleeping."

"Okay, that's good," Doctor Chang said. I'd called her office and told her what had happened. The whole flashback had freaked me out just as much as it had Justin. "Memory flashbacks can trigger the memory of physical pain," she said. Then she spoke for a bit on psychosomatic something or other and it was comforting to hear her say what Justin experienced was okay. It wasn't uncommon or unusual, and what I did was right, and having him resting right now was the best thing for him.

Having that reassurance was a godsend. "Thank you."

"You have an appointment on Tuesday, so I'll see you both then," she said. "But if his headaches get any worse, or if he experiences more dizziness or nausea, fever or anything like that, take him to outpatients and call me."

"I will. Thank you."

I clicked off the call and sat on the edge of the bed. He was out like a light, so I went back downstairs to let Davo and Sparra know he was okay. Davo was working on a bike and Sparra was cleaning down his station. They both stopped what they were doing and came over, and I noticed the radio was off.

"How is he?" Sparra asked.

"He's okay. He's sleeping right now. I spoke to the doc. She said it wasn't unheard of to experience the pain associated with a memory, especially in amnesia patients." I shrugged. "Which is good. If she was concerned, I'd have him back at the ER."

Davo clapped my arm. "He'll be all right."

"Kinda scary, though," Sparra added. "That a song could trigger a memory. I didn't know, otherwise I wouldn't have turned it up."

"You weren't to know. None of us were. Hell, not even Justin knew until he heard it. Some memory wire in his brain tripped, and it was like the truck hitting him all over again."

Davo studied me for a bit. "I would suggest taking you out tonight and getting shitfaced, but I know you won't leave him."

I smiled at that. "Maybe next weekend the four of us can go out and grab a pub feed and watch the footy. We won't be drinking, though, but getting out might be a good idea."

"Deal." Davo looked back to his workstation. "We can finish up here if you wanna go back upstairs."

I scrubbed my hand over my face. "How about the three of us hook in and get everything done so we can all clock out early?"

"Done!" Sparra said quickly, and that's what we did. Davo finished up on the bike he was working on, and by the time the customer came to collect it, me and Sparra had the whole place cleaned and ready to be locked up.

I pulled the roller door shut and both the guys thanked me for lunch, the coffee machine, and their bonus cheques. It felt like that all happened a week ago.

"See ya's Monday, bright and early," I said.

"Call us if you need anything over the weekend," Sparra said, and Davo nodded.

God, I loved these blokes. "Will do."

I locked the gate behind them and raced up the stairs. Justin was still sound asleep, now with Squish keeping guard, so I left them to it and made a start on dinner. I was torn between wanting home-cooked comfort food and not being arsed to do anything but call for a pizza, but it was cold outside and I wanted comfort. I threw a bunch of stuff into a casserole dish to make up some kind of goulash stew and set it in the oven, had a steaming hot shower, and changed into some trackies, socks, and a hoodie.

I poked my head into the bedroom and found Justin awake. He was lying on his side, stroking Squish. "Hey," I whispered.

He smiled. "Hey."

"How're you feeling?"

"Okay. The drugs work."

I chuckled and sat beside him. Both of his eyes were open, though heavy-lidded. "I'm glad."

"I woke up and you weren't here, but I could hear you so it was okay."

I rubbed his hip. "I'm never far away, baby."

"I know." He closed his eyes for a bit. "Sorry about before. In the shop."

"Don't apologise. You have nothing to be sorry about."

"It just hit me," he said. "The memory. The song. The pain." *The truck . . .*

"It must have been scary as hell."

"Yeah."

"I spoke to Doctor Chang. I called her to ask if we should come to the hospital and she said no, just to keep an eye on you. She said what you experienced wasn't uncommon. But if you get dizzy or more headaches, she wants to see us."

He gave a bit of a nod, and his right eye was back to normal: a sign the worst of the pain was gone. "I hate it, ya know," he murmured. "I hate that you have to look after me, that I have these problems. I feel like an invalid."

"Hey." I took his hand and waited for him to make eye contact. "Juss, I love looking after you. It's not a problem. It's just what we need to do right now. It won't always be this way. And even if it was, I'd still do it. Together forever, remember?"

He smiled. "No, I don't. Amnesia, remember?"

I chuckled and leaned down for a kiss. "Dinner's in the oven. I made some kind of pasta stew. I thought we could bring the doona out to the couch and have a bowl of comfort food and watch the footy. Just take it real easy."

He sat up slowly and gave me a nudge. "You don't have to do that for me. I know I'm kinda fuzzy on those painkillers, but I feel okay."

I sighed, my heart suddenly heavy. "I know, Juss. But I think tonight I need to do it for me."

His gaze shot to mine. "Oh."

"I'm just feeling a bit raw this arvo," I admitted. "I dunno why. Just want a quiet night holed up under the doona with you, that's all." I tried not to cry but my eyes burned with tears and in the end, I just let them fall. I didn't want to hide this from him.

"Dall?"

"I'm okay," I said, wiping my cheek. "I'm just... I dunno. Relieved about the money, like a huge weight is off me. And I was worried about you this afternoon. I guess I reached a limit."

Juss frowned. "I'm sorry."

"You don't have to apologise," I replied, giving him a smile despite my tears. "But Juss, sometimes I'm not as strong as I need to be."

"I know I lean on you for everything. But you don't need to be strong all the time."

"I want you to lean on me, to need me. I like being that for you. I like being the protector and the provider. But I dunno, I've been so stressed and worried. I just feel a bit low right now and I need to be with you tonight. Just us and nothing else."

He nodded and squeezed my hand. "I'm sorry I didn't think of you. Anything you want, Dall."

"I want to block the world out and I want to know you're okay, that's all."

He leaned over and kissed the side of my head. "Then let's do that."

Juss picked up Squish and I pulled the doona and pillows off the bed and we made ourselves a nest on the couch. It was raining outside now, and with only the light in the kitchen on, it felt cosy and warm inside our little cocoon. We ate bowls of stew and watched the Friday night footy with the volume down low, and for the first time in our relationship, I was the little spoon.

I lay with my back to Juss' front, and he either had his arm around me or his hand stroking my hair. It felt so damn nice to be taken care of, just this once. I'd always assumed the role of protector. Even as a teenager, I was always looking out for the kids who couldn't defend themselves. I was always taller and bigger—I was already six foot at fifteen years old—and sure, even the arsehole kids at my high school knew I was gay and they only tried to back me into a corner once. I put three of them on their arses and the fourth ran away.

I was always the protector, the defender, the one who would wrap my arms around them and tell them it was all gonna be okay. But tonight it was me who needed it, and I couldn't even say why.

Maybe it was a combined meltdown of the last month, all the stress and worry, the relief of the workers' comp being approved, and then the uncertainty of Juss' episode today. But I just needed . . . reassurance.

After trying to hold it all together for so long, I felt like I was barely holding on.

"You okay?" Juss asked. He stroked my hair, then gently scratched my beard.

I shuffled onto my back, though there wasn't much room. "I am now," I murmured. "I feel better."

He had his head propped up on his arm as he studied my eyes and ran his thumb along my bottom lip before cupping my face. "I'm sorry I didn't think of what you need."

"Juss," I began.

"No, please, hear me out. Everything since my accident has been about me. Every minute of every day, and to be honest, I haven't been able to think of anyone else. I mean, I think of you, of course. But when I was still all foggy, I couldn't think of anything. Then it was just all about my recovery, my body, my brain. Managing pain and physio and trying to get my brain to think normally. And you . . ." He thumbed my cheek. "You were just always this *mountain* of strength, and throughout this whole thing, you never took a backward step. God, Dallas, even when I didn't remember you, you still showed up every day. You never gave up; you never doubted our love." He got a little teary. "And I never stopped to think that you might need . . . something. Anything."

"Juss, I just felt a bit down, that's all."

"But that's my point. You know all my moods, you know

how I'm feeling, and I don't even have to say a word. You just know. And I want to be like that for you."

"But you are. I said I needed a night where we could block out the world and you did that for me."

He made a face as though he didn't really agree. "I just want you to know I'm going to try harder. I want to be for you what you are for me."

I touched the side of his face. "And what's that?"

"Everything. Dallas, you're everything to me."

That made my heart full and my tummy swoop. "And you're everything to me as well."

He tapped his finger to the tip of my nose. "And you giving Davo and Sparra that money today was really great," he whispered. "I don't think I realised how stressed you were about the money."

"I didn't want you to worry." I scanned his face. "But I was, yeah. And now we don't have to worry. I mean, I'm not gonna go crazy. I just wanted to show Davo and Sparra how much I appreciate them."

"Just proves what kind of guy you are. And how I'm so lucky to be with you."

I leaned up and kissed him. "I love you, Justin."

"And I love you, so much." He kissed me this time, allowing his body to fall onto mine. I let him set the pace he was comfortable with and there was more urgency this time. More passion, more desire, and he could no doubt feel my body react. I could certainly feel his. He pulled his lips from mine. "Do you think we could go to bed. This lounge isn't great for my leg and the drugs are wearing off and I really want to keep making out."

I chuckled. "Bed sounds great."

"I just can't decide if I want a shower before or after orgasms."

I burst out laughing and put my hand to his face. "Shower. Then you can go straight to sleep while you're all blissed out."

"You really do know me so well."

I peeled myself out from underneath him and carefully helped him to his feet. I let him get his equilibrium before helping him into the shower. "You know, I could do this by myself," he said.

"Oh, I know you could."

He smirked. "You just like to be thorough."

I chuckled. "And you like me being thorough."

"I really do."

He washed himself and I stayed right there in case the steam and hot water made him dizzy, and I handed him a towel when he shut the water off. His erection was still half-hard, though his blinks were a little slow. He was getting tired. "We better get you to bed."

"Yes, you better." He looked at his PJs but didn't put them on. "I want to sleep naked with you. I want to be close to you all night."

"Sounds good to me." God, it sounded like heaven to me.

We got into bed and I stripped down to nothing and slid in beside him. He was all warm and he smelt clean and delicious. "I'm sleepy, Dallas," he murmured.

"I know, baby."

"So you better do the orgasms quick."

I snorted out a laugh. "Is that right?"

"Yeah. I know I'm supposed to take care of you tonight, but I can't do . . . I can't kneel or bend or do stuff like that."

That was all the permission I needed to get. I rolled on top of him and took our cocks into my hand. "I'll always take care of you, baby," I whispered, sliding our shafts together. "Just like this."

"Holy shit." Justin squinted his eyes shut.

I froze, thinking I'd hurt him. "You okay?"

"Don't stop. Please. Christ. Don't stop." He hooked his left leg up, his knee to my ribs. He opened his eyes as though his own leg had surprised him. "Dallas . . ."

"I know, baby," I whispered. Because I did know. I knew exactly what he meant, what he felt, what he couldn't put into words.

I knew, because I felt it too.

I slid our cocks in my fist, holding my weight off him the best

I could. But I was between his legs, and with his left leg hitched up in this position, I could have so easily been inside him. He nodded like he thought the same, then his eyes rolled back and he drove his cock up and spilled his orgasm between us.

The sight of him, the smell of our desire, the feel of his pulsing cock, and I followed over the edge with him.

Justin put his hand to my neck and brought me down for a kiss and the full weight of my body on his, and we kissed until our passion simmered into sleepy nudges. Justin was almost asleep, but he kept his arms around me.

"I need to get us cleaned up," I murmured.

"Mmm." He dropped his arms to his side. "Hurry."

I unstuck our bellies, making him chuckle, though his eyes stayed closed. I cleaned us both up, and as soon as I was back in bed with him, he clung to me like he always did. "Love you, Juss," I whispered with a kiss to his forehead. "Always have."

He mumbled sleepily. "Always will."

Chapter Thirteen

JUSTIN

Dallas wasn't sure we should attend the barbeque lunch at Jimmy and Nancy's place because of my little episode with the memory pain the day before, but I felt good.

In some way, I felt better because I could remember it.

It was scary and the pain that hit me along with the flashback was nauseatingly real. But I could remember it. I could remember how and why my whole life changed, and that was, in some fucked-up way, reassuring.

But now, I could see the memory in my mind and there was no pain with it anymore.

I woke up pressed against Dallas and his enormous dick was squashed against my arse cheek. It felt so good, that familiar buzz in my belly, that drawing-down feeling in my balls.

My body was starting to like the idea of doing more with Dallas, and my mind was too. I knew it would happen; it was only a matter of time. The night before, when he was between my legs and holding my cock against his, it was so much like making love, and for a fleeting second, I'd wanted it.

Not quite yet.

But soon.

"Juss, you okay? You zoned out there for a minute."

"Yeah, sorry. Was just thinking . . ."

"About?"

"I dunno, stuff."

"Pleasant stuff, I take it. Because you were smiling."

"Yeah, okay, I was thinking about you."

Dallas' whole face lit up when he smiled. "Really?"

"Yeah, of course." Man, to see him smile like that . . . "I think about you all the time."

"Good thoughts, I hope."

He looked at me in a way that made my heart feel too big for my chest. "Always. There's bits and pieces in my head that I don't know if are real memories or parts of dreams. I can't remember anything I dreamed of in the last five years either. But I see snippets that I think are real."

"Such as?"

"You yelling on the phone to a dodgy supplier for fucking up an order. You laughing at something Sparra said. You walking out of the bathroom naked. You making me coffee in the morning." I shrugged. "But it's not really what I see. It's what I feel. When you put your arm around me, or if you take my hand while we were watching TV. I just feel so happy, right here." I tapped my breastbone. "And I dunno if I'm remembering something that happened or something I dreamed, because I'm pretty sure I'd feel the same. Real hand-holding or dream hand-holding, it'd all feel the same to me."

"You'd be happy if you dreamed that I held your hand?"

"Sure I would."

"Does it feel real?"

"Yeah. And the clothes you're wearing seem real. Like actual T-shirts we own, and I'm sure if it were all in my dreams, you wouldn't be wearing any clothes."

He laughed at that but then met my eyes. "Sounds like you're remembering a lot more than you realise."

"Yeah, maybe. Nothing concrete. Nothing like yesterday when I remembered the accident."

"Did you want to talk about it?"

I shrugged again. "Not really. There's not much to say. I was going to a job at Glendale, it was pissing down rain, and our song came on the radio."

"I never realised it was *our* song," he said.

"It's our song, unofficially. I guess. I remember thinking as I was singing along that we didn't really have a song, but if we did, that would be it. But I can't remember why I thought it was our song."

He smiled thoughtfully. "We danced to it at the Lion's Arms pub. We'd been together about a month."

"We danced at the Lion's Arms? Together?" That pub wasn't exactly gay-central.

"We did. We were drunk."

"Obviously."

He laughed. "You were drinking Bundy."

I made a face. "God, I hate that stuff. I haven't drunk that in . . . well, I don't know how long it's been. Literally, I have no clue."

He chuckled again with kindness in his eyes. "You haven't touched it again since that night. But yeah, we danced to that song. And if I can remember correctly, we sang along pretty badly."

It was those things I missed the most. The memories of the little moments, things that seem insignificant or silly but the parts that make everything so real. "I wish I could remember that."

He lifted my hand to his lips and kissed my palm. "I know you do, baby." Still holding my hand, he met my eyes. "Are you sure you still want to go?"

I nodded. "I said we would, and I'd like to." Then it occurred to me that maybe he didn't want to go to Jimmy and Nancy's place for a barbeque lunch, and he had to take me because I had no other way to get there. "Dallas, if you don't want to come . . ."

"No, it's not that I don't want to, it's just that I worry you might overdo it. Or it might get too much. I dunno. We haven't really gone anywhere, apart from the supermarket and to the doctor's offices. Especially after yesterday. Remembering the accident . . ."

"Dall, I'm okay. I feel pretty good. And I know better than to overdo it. We won't stay long. I'll be falling asleep at their table if we stay too long."

"Okay, if you're sure."

"I'm sure."

And I really didn't know why I was so sure. But I wanted to go. I really liked old Jimmy and Nancy. They were sweet and kind, and I hadn't had a lot of that in my life. It felt rude to turn down their invitation, and if it became weird, Dallas and I would just leave.

But it wasn't weird . . . Well, not in a bad way. When we arrived, we weren't the only ones there. Jimmy and Nancy's house was an old but cute little white house with a small porch with flowerpots hanging from the beam, an old concrete path, and immaculate grass and gardens. As soon as we walked through the door, we were bombarded with the smell of good food and the sound of chatter and laughter.

"Come in, come in," Nancy said, ushering us down a short hall through a kitchen and family room to the back door. "Everyone's out the back. Go on through." Then she hollered at the door. "Jimmy? Look who's here."

The backyard was a fair size with tidy lawns and gardens, a small shed to the side, kids playing soccer, and a circle of a dozen people all sitting around on camping chairs. Jimmy put his drink on the table and welcomed us. "Boys, come on out and let me introduce you."

He went around the chairs with names I had no hope of remembering, but there were smiles and nods and warm welcomes. Jimmy and Nancy's kids were all older than us, and I realised some of the younger folk closer to our age sitting around were Jimmy's grandkids. "We're just neighbours," one guy said about himself and the woman sitting next to him.

"And we're just ring-ins," another guy said. "Grew up a few doors down and still come back for Nancy's caramel tart."

Everyone laughed and someone else mentioned some other food as their conversation broke away, and Jimmy looked up at me. "No wheels today?" he asked, motioning toward my leg.

"My scooter? It's in the ute," I replied. "Leg's feeling okay today. Not sure how long that'll last though."

"Here," Jimmy said, pulling up a seat. "Take a load off."

I sat and Dallas found a chair beside me, and Jimmy offered us a drink. "Oh, we can't drink," I explained. "Dallas is driving and I can't drink alcohol anymore."

Jimmy stopped. "I've been on the wagon for thirty years. All I got here is lemonade, ginger beer, or water." He picked up the can he'd put on the table. "I fancy a lemonade, but now Nancy's got me on that sugar-free stuff."

"So you don't get diabetes, Dad," one guy said.

Jimmy smiled and rolled his eyes. "Yeah, yeah."

We took our ginger beers and Nancy called out for Jimmy to check the meat, and when he went off to the barbeque, the guy sitting next to me turned out to be Jimmy's son. "Dad hoped you'd show up today," he said. "He told us he and Mum called around to see how you were getting on."

"Ah yeah." I wasn't sure what else to say. Clearly they knew all about us and all about the accident, no doubt. "I didn't know it was a family thing."

"Ah, no," he said, smiling just like his dad. "Mum and Dad have been having these lunches every month or two for as long as I can remember. Anyone who's anyone comes along. Old friends, current neighbours, and even the old neighbours who moved away but we can't get rid of." The caramel-tart guy raised his beer to that, making us smile.

Apparently Jimmy and Nancy had lived in this house for fifty years and Jimmy grew all kinds of veggies in the back gardens and they'd swap goods with other houses in the street. For a few zucchinis, capsicums, and tomatoes, they'd get fresh eggs from Beverly, dried salamis from old Cranky Franky. "And Dad's new favourite neighbours, Ensar and Nida. Ensar makes the real Turkish Delight. The real, traditional stuff."

Jimmy turned around at the barbeque and whisper-shouted, "And don't you say anything about it to your mother."

A woman laughed. "She knows where your stash is, Dad."

I laughed at that, then someone else asked if Ensar and Nida were coming today, but no, their son had some soccer thing on. And so it went on. It was like something out of a family TV show, where everyone was nice and genuine and just really good people.

People played some musical chairs as they all chatted with everyone else, and a woman ended up sitting next to me. She introduced herself again. "Kathy, Mum and Dad's youngest." Apparently, it was her daughter Bethany who had drawn the picture with the fish. Kathy pointed out a little blonde girl with the other kids.

"You've got a great crew here," Dallas said, nodding toward where the kids were now playing a game of chase while the adults laughed.

"We weren't supposed to bring anything, were we?" I asked. "Your mum told me not to bring anything, but I feel bad."

Kathy shook her head. "Oh no. She does the lot. Always has. Spends all week cooking. If not for us, for the women's auxiliary or the Rotary Club. She'd be offended if you brought something. And Dad's in charge of the barbie. He just does what Mum tells him, basically." She winked.

"Oh, okay," I said with a laugh. "Yeah, your mum brought some biscuits around the other day when they called in. They were delicious."

Kathy's smile saddened a little. "Dad was devastated about the accident. He was so upset that someone got hurt."

I noticed that other chatter had died off. They were listening now, curious to hear about the crash, I guess. Jimmy had taken a tray of meat inside the house, so now was the best time to broach the subject. "Yeah, he came to see me at the hospital," I said.

Dallas put his hand on my arm and he smiled at Kathy. "Your dad was quite nervous that day, but he seemed genuine. I wasn't sure what to expect, but he was very nice."

Kathy gave a nod and smiled sadly at me. "He said you were in a bad way."

"Yeah. I got busted up pretty bad."

Everyone was watching me and listening now, and Jimmy came back out and took his seat. He gave me a nod to continue.

"I have two metal plates in my leg," I said, looking down at my right leg. "My arm was broken here and here." I pointed to my forearm and below my shoulder. "And I have this," I said, turning a little and lifting my hair so they could see the huge scar down my head. "How many staples was it, Dall?"

"In his leg and head, sixty-two staples and nineteen stitches," he answered, smiling at me. "A fractured skull, fractured orbital socket, and a subdural haematoma."

I nodded. "And I lost five years' worth of memories," I added. "Five years of my life were just gone."

Dallas took my hand. "When he woke up, he thought he was twenty-five and living in Darwin."

Kathy looked horrified. "You had no memory of Dallas?"

I shook my head. "Nope."

"That was the worst part for me," Jimmy said. "The hardest part. I couldn't imagine waking up one day and not knowing who my Nance is."

The girl next to Jimmy patted his leg. "It's all right, Pop."

I hadn't meant for the mood to sour so much, but she had asked me about the accident. I wasn't going to lie about it.

"Do you remember anything now?" Kathy asked.

"Some things, but mostly not." I smiled at Dallas. "I have bits and pieces, but not much."

"God, that must have been hard," someone said.

I nodded and tried to lighten the mood. "I didn't even know where home was, but apparently I lived with this really good-looking guy who came to visit me at the hospital every day," I said, smiling at Dallas. "And there was a cat who was very happy to see me when I walked through the door."

They laughed, thankfully. And Jimmy raised his lemonade. "To the power of love. And to life. Thank you, Justin. And Dallas, for coming along today. It means a lot to me. I know we met in terrible circumstances, and I'm sorry for that. But you both showed me a great kindness in your forgiveness. Our door is always open to you, and you'll always have a seat at our table."

Oh wow. I wasn't expecting that, and I wasn't expecting to be so moved by his words. Dallas' hand squeezed mine just as another couple walked in through the side gate. The guy, about forty years old, was carrying an Esky and a camping chair, and as they said hello to everyone and a few jokes were made at the:r lateness, it was a welcome relief to have the attention off me.

Kathy gave me a sad smile. "Dad didn't mean to upset you. He's just a big ol' softy. He says mushy stuff all the time."

"No, it's okay. I just . . . I don't really have . . ." I cleared my throat. I couldn't finish that.

She seemed to understand because she nodded to the guy who had just arrived. "That's Steve. Dad found him at a truck stop when he was sixteen. Homeless, in trouble. Dad brought him home, sorted him out, and got him back into school," she said. "It's just what my parents do. They're good people."

I swallowed hard. "I can see that."

Just then, a line of younger kids came out of the house, each carrying a dish, plates, trays of meat, and different vegetable dishes, sauces, breads, and put them on the table. It was like a production line. "Lunch is served!" Nancy said, following the last kid out.

Everyone grabbed a plate and helped themselves. Dallas got mine for me, and before anyone began to eat, Jimmy stood with Nancy at the table. He put his arm around her, raised his lemonade, and said, "A full house is a full heart. And as always, compliments to the beautiful chef."

Everyone thanked Nancy and she waved her hand like it was nonsense, but it was pretty obvious she was proud to feed people. We all ate—the food was amazing—and talked quietly and laughed. The winter gods had blessed us with sun and warmth, and it was just a really lovely day.

Some of the guys asked us about the shop and Dallas was in his element talking about bikes and mechanical things, and yes, the caramel tart was amazing. But as much as I wanted to stay longer, my eyelids were beginning to betray me.

"I better get you home," Dallas said gently.

I nodded. "Yeah."

"Want me to get your scooter for you?"

"Nah. I'll be okay."

We said our goodbyes, and everyone said they'd see us 'next time' and it was funny because I was one hundred per cent sure there would be a next time. I really liked these people. Dallas helped me to my feet and held me while my head caught up. My leg didn't like the grass too much—it was too spongey—so Dallas took my arm and helped me walk to the concrete path.

"I'll walk you out," Jimmy said.

I thanked Nancy again for the food and Dallas helped me up the small step and inside. Jimmy held the door for me as we made it out the front of the house, and he walked at my pace to the ute. "Thanks again for coming," he said.

"Thanks for inviting us," Dallas replied. "It's been lovely."

"Sorry we can't stay," I said, knowing my words were slow. I hated that my brain did this when I was tired. "It's nap time for me."

Jimmy nodded and put his hand to my arm. "You need to look after yourself, son."

"Can I ask you something?" I asked.

"Sure."

"My compensation claim from the accident," I began. "Does that hurt you?"

"Hurt me?"

"Yeah. The money. I don't want you to lose money. Or your home. I don't want that."

"Ah," he said, finally clueing into what I meant. "No, it's all insurance. Don't you worry about that, Justin. My insurance company is dealing with all that, not me. I pay my insurance premiums and it was all deemed an accident so it was all covered."

I sighed. "Good. I was worried."

Dallas rubbed my back. "You don't need to worry about that, baby."

"Yes, I do."

Jimmy's smile faded. "Did you get your insurance sorted?"

"Yeah," Dallas said. "We just heard this week. The van's covered, and all medical bills."

Jimmy put his hand to his forehead. "Oh, thank heavens. You had me worried there for a second."

I smiled at him. The truth was, I still wasn't much good at thinking about money. I knew I should be, but it was all a bit too much. Another reason to be thankful for Dallas. He took care of me. He took care of everything. But my brain was starting to get fuzzy and my eyelids wouldn't stay open. "I'm tired."

Jimmy opened the ute door and Dallas helped me into my seat. "You don't be a stranger now," Jimmy said.

As we drove away, I sighed contentedly. I held my hand out for Dallas to hold, which he did. "I like them," I mumbled. "Good people."

"They are."

I closed my eyes, and the next thing I knew, we were home.

Dallas helped me up the stairs and he put me on the couch and took my boots off and I fell straight back to sleep. When I woke up, he was sitting with my feet in his lap flicking through rolled-up catalogues.

"Hey, handsome," I mumbled.

"Hey," he replied, smiling. "How you feeling?"

I thought about that for a second, took stock of my leg, my arm, my head. "I feel good." I held out my hand. "Help me sit up." He pulled me up to sitting, and I shook off any lingering remnants of sleep. "I need to pee."

He laughed and helped me to my feet, and when I came out of the bathroom, he was looking through the fridge. "Did you want something to drink?" he asked, collecting two bottled waters.

I leaned against the kitchen bench. "I just want to cuddle, if that's okay."

He grinned and stepped in front of me. "Always."

I opened my arms and he stepped into them. "How are you feeling today?" I asked.

He smiled against my neck. "I feel great today. Thank you for asking."

I chuckled but tightened my hold on him. "I love you, Dallas. You take care of me, and I dunno where I'd be if I didn't have you. I don't think I say thank you enough."

He gave me a squeeze and rubbed my back. "You don't have to thank me."

I pulled back so I could see his handsome face and those grey eyes that owned me. "Yes I do. I should thank you every day."

He kissed me sweetly. "You're welcome, baby."

"Today was a good day. Yesterday wasn't great, but today was. I really enjoyed us having lunch with Jimmy and his family. It felt good to be included in that."

Dallas smiled warmly. "It did. I wasn't sure what to expect, but they're very sweet."

"I want to see them again. If they ask."

He chuckled. "Okay. But I'm pretty sure your invitation is ongoing."

I sighed contentedly. "I know I can only take it one day at a time, and it's baby steps, according to Doctor Chang. But today was a good day and we should talk about the good days too. From now on, we should talk about the good things."

"We should," Dallas murmured. He studied my eyes, fixed my hair, and smiled. "You sound like you're talking about the future. And that's a real good thing, Juss."

The future, yes. Something I hadn't thought about much at all. "I've spent all this time trying to put my mind back together. Maybe I need to stop concentrating on the pieces that are missing," I admitted. "And start focusing on the pieces that I have."

Dallas' smile was breathtaking. "You talk about putting the pieces of you back together, but Juss, you're also putting the pieces of me back together as well."

"The pieces of you?"

He nodded. "My heart broke into a million pieces the day of the accident. I thought I'd lost you. Then you woke up and didn't know who I was, and it broke all over again. But then you remembered my tattoos. You remembered me, and it meant so much. And every day since, you're getting better and stronger, and you look at me now like you used to look at me, and piece by piece, you're putting me back together."

I put my hands to his face. "All the pieces of you are perfect, Dallas."

He smiled and kissed my lips, my cheek, my eyebrow but he didn't speak.

"You said it sounded like I was starting to think of the future," I whispered. "And I guess I am. I didn't for a long time, but now . . . Now I can think of it. And I want a future with you. I can't think of my future without you in it."

Dallas pulled me against him, holding me tight, our bodies fitting together perfectly. I was safe in his arms, as he was in mine. "And just like that, Juss, you put another piece of me back together."

PIECES OF

MISSING PIECES SERIES
BOOK THREE

Chapter One

JUSTIN

I was up before Dallas, which was unusual, drinking my decaf coffee and staring out the kitchen window. He was normally awake before me, but a headache somewhere around five in the morning had me up searching for my pills. Headaches were nothing new; sometimes I'd catch myself thinking life was returning to normal, but then the constant pain inside my head reminded me otherwise.

I was so used to headaches now I barely registered them. That continuous ache was sometimes dull, sometimes sharp, but always there. Except for this morning when it woke me up.

I was never too cheerful in the morning, but today I was feeling particularly sorry for myself. Not even watching Dallas sleep improved my mood. If anything, it made me feel even shittier. He was so good to me. He was, without doubt, too good for me as well.

But for some stupid reason, he loved me. He loved me before the accident, and that didn't change anything for him. If anything, he reckoned it made him realise he loved me more now. It had been a lesson in taking things for granted, he'd said. I could see it in his eyes just how much he loved me. Those hazel-grey eyes couldn't hide a thing, and I found myself recognising his moods in them.

Losing myself in them.

Dallas had said that we fell in love hard and fast the first time, and it was much the same for me the second time. He was caring, attentive, thoughtful, funny . . . everything I ever wanted in a boyfriend. He was also tall, strong, and handsome. How on earth I'd ever scored him once was a mystery to me. The fact he'd stuck around for a second time was just crazy.

But stuck around he had.

I hated to think where I'd be without him. If I'd decided not to go home with him when we'd left the hospital—not that I had anywhere else to go—well, they would have found me some-where, apparently. But my heart said to go with him, and now I knew why.

Because my heart knew him.

My heart loved him.

And on days when I felt like shit—not just physically, but emotionally as well—I just felt . . . useless.

Like a kid who needed babysitting. Who couldn't walk up or down stairs without supervision, who couldn't even have a shower in the house by himself. And being at work was like my first day as a sixteen-year-old apprentice. I knew it was all for my safety or whatever, but that just pissed me off. I wasn't a kid. I wasn't incompetent. I knew how to do this stuff. And some days my brain was slow as hell; but some days my mind was fine and it was my body that betrayed me.

I hated being like this.

I hated being so dependent on other people. I hated that Dallas had to look after me like I was a toddler and how Sparra had to babysit me at work. I hated that I was aware of just how much I couldn't do, of how much I used to do and now couldn't.

We'd spent a few hours on Saturday at Jimmy and Nancy's house, and I was so wiped out, it put my arse on the couch for all of Sunday. I napped on and off all damn day. I tried to do a few things around the flat with Dallas but was no good at anything.

He'd simply kissed me with a smile and told me to rest while he pottered about getting everything done while I parked up in front of the damn TV like a simpleton.

I couldn't help but wonder how long he'd put up with it.

How long would it take until he realised he could have any guy he wanted who didn't have a brain injury? That didn't have a fucked-up leg and who didn't speak slow?

I heard the bedroom door open and didn't even have to turn around. The sound of his feet got closer, then his huge warm hand slid up my back. "Hey," he murmured. "I woke up alone."

I sighed, now feeling even shittier than before. "Sorry. Headache woke me up and I didn't want to disturb you."

"Oh, you feel okay?" he asked, concerned. "Want me to get your pills?"

I turned then and offered a small smile. "I already took one, thanks."

He put his fingers to my chin and inspected my eyes. "Baby, what's wrong?"

I shrugged. "I feel . . ." I couldn't find the right word. And it wasn't aphasia. There were just too many words to choose from: awful, like shit, bad, low, worthless, horrible, useless . . . "Sad."

Frowning, Dallas took my empty coffee cup from me, put it on the sink, and pulled me into his arms. Into those huge, strong, and warm arms, holding me against his chest where I was safe and protected and completely enclosed. I could feel my worries dissipate, and the tension left my shoulders as I melted into him.

It was such a relief and so comforting, I could have cried.

I was stupid to think for one second that I could live without him. Well, not that I thought *I* could, but I had wondered why he didn't leave me. *I wouldn't survive this without him.*

He rubbed my back and took deep, calming breaths which I somehow unknowingly mimicked, making myself feel a little better.

"I'm sorry," I mumbled.

"You don't have to be sorry," he replied. His voice rumbled smoothly in his chest against my ear. He never moved to let go of me or even pull away. "Did you feel sad for any reason? Or just because."

"Just because." I sighed since that felt like such an easy way out. I needed to talk about this. I owed him that. "I just feel . . . I hate being useless and I hate how my brain doesn't work sometimes. I hate that you have to look after me, and I hate that I can't do everything. I just woke up feeling pretty low today."

He rubbed my back some more and kissed the side of my head. "I get that," he said, still hugging me. "And you're allowed to feel those things. I can tell you that you're not useless, but I don't want to make what you feel invalid. Because if you feel it, then it's real and we need to work on why you feel like that." He pulled back then and cupped my face. "But baby, you're the strongest guy I know. You're determined and capable, and you've accomplished more in the last two months than you realise. I know you must be frustrated with everything, and I don't blame you. But if you could just see how far you've come."

I frowned, because I certainly didn't feel like that.

"You're allowed to feel useless and frustrated. And angry and sad," Dallas added. "Thank you for telling me."

I sighed again, sagging against the kitchen counter. "I would be so lost without you," I mumbled.

He kissed my forehead and pressed me up against the cupboard and wrapped his strong arms around me again, squishing my face into his chest. "I'd be lost without you too," he replied. But then one arm was gone from around me as he reached over to the kettle and flicked it on. "I'd be lost without coffee too."

That made me smile, despite my mood. "You drink decaf now." Another change he'd made for me.

"Just because it's a bit different now doesn't mean I still don't need it," he replied. I was certain that was aimed at me and not all about coffee. Because I was a bit different now and he still needed me . . .

Then he shuffled me over so he could keep one arm around me while he reached for the cups. "You can let go of me," I suggested.

"Nope. I can do both. I can make two coffees and give good hugs."

I managed a chuckle. *How had he managed to make me laugh?* "Yes, you can."

He turned his head. "Ugh. The milk's in the fridge. Black coffee it is."

I pushed him away with a laugh. "Get the milk."

He quickly grabbed the milk and came straight back to his spot, which was pressed tight against me, pushing me against the cupboard with one arm around me. I gladly hugged him back, using the magic of his hugs to fix me for as long as I could.

"Coffees are done." He sipped his. "Now, shall I try for toast?"

I chuckled again. "Depends where the bread is."

He leaned and stretched. "Got it."

But the margarine was in the fridge so he had to let go of me, which gave me a chance to sip my fresh coffee. He made breakfast and we shared triangles of Vegemite toast, and by the time we'd showered and dressed for work, I was feeling better.

I should have stayed in bed and hugged him there rather than getting up and wallowing by myself. Dallas knew how to fix me, and I was stupid to pretend otherwise.

He stopped me at the door. "You sure you're feeling up to work today?" Dallas asked. "How's your headache?"

"It's okay. And yeah, I need to work today."

He grinned. "Good. Because I need you to work today. You're part of the team, Juss, and I need all hands on deck this morning."

And there he went, telling me how not useless I was without even trying. I was part of the team. He needed me. No matter how small a job I did, he needed me to do it. I gave him a nod and even managed a smile. "Okay."

With that beautiful smile, he led the way downstairs. He had me open the front roller door and unlock the front gates; then he wanted me to check the stock levels and see if anything needed to be reordered.

I knew what he was doing.

He was making me not useless.

Sneaky bastard.

By the time Davo and Sparra arrived, I was actually feeling pretty good about myself. They were both keen to use the new coffee machine, so that gave us some time to talk about our weekends until we were interrupted by our first clients of the day.

Sparra and I went to work on an old Yamaha while Davo serviced an ATV, and Dallas did some time in his office until another client dropped off a KTM. "Hey, Juss, I need you with me for this," he said.

It was gonna be a pretty big job. The rider had stacked it on the trails, and there was damage to the front forks, suspension, steering shaft, handlebars, and the front tyre would need replacing. The rider, the teen nephew of the owner, was okay, thankfully. But they'd learned an expensive lesson about going downhill on a loose surface using front brakes. Such a rookie mistake on an awesome bike.

And for a few hours, Dallas had me doing everything I could physically do. He let me take lead and he helped me when I needed it. He was proving a point—that I wasn't useless—and when we'd taken the front brake hose line clamp off and we were on opposite sides of the bike, I watched as he ratcheted a bolt undone, concentration and sweat on his brow. He caught me smiling at him. "What?" he asked quietly.

"I love you," I replied. I hadn't meant to say those words, not in the workshop, not so blasé. Davo and Sparra hadn't heard a thing, not that I cared. But holy shit, this man . . .

His smile became a grin, the ratchet in his hand forgotten. He seemed a little lost for words.

"I know what you're doing," I added. "Giving me jobs I can do, making me feel not useless."

He chuckled and put the tool down. "Just proving a point. Did it work?"

"Maybe."

"It totally worked."

I laughed but met his eyes. "You do these little things for me, to help me, without having to say a thing. Everything you do for me, you do because you love me, and it's like the saying 'actions speak louder than words.' I never really knew what that meant. But now I do."

His eyes softened. "Juss . . ."

"It's an amazing feeling knowing you're loved, so I wanted you to know too. I've said it before, but I wanted to say it again. I need you to know, Dall."

He walked around my side of the bike, took my face in his hands, and kissed me. It was all soft lips and scruffy beard and far too brief. He pulled back and put his forehead to mine. "I know you love me, Juss. But you can tell me as many times as you want."

"I love you," I whispered this time, and he closed his eyes and smiled as though he could just bathe in those words.

The shop phone rang right then, interrupting us, and Dallas stepped back and took the call. "Muller Mechanics."

Sparra came over, looking concerned. "You okay, Jusso?"

I smiled at him. "Yeah."

"Oh, I just looked over when I heard the phone and saw Dallas holding your face . . ." He smiled. "You two bein' all lovey-dovey again, huh?"

I snorted and watched Dallas as he stood with the phone to his ear. "He's kinda wonderful, isn't he?"

Sparra put his hand to his heart and squinted at me. "Personally, not my type. Great bloke, but I prefer 'em a whole lot prettier. And, well, female."

I laughed at that and Dallas turned to look at me, his face serious. "Justin's right here. I'll put him on." He held the phone out to me. "It's Angela from the workers' comp place."

Needing to sit for a bit to give my leg a break, I took the call in the breakroom. "Justin Keith speaking."

Angela replied, talking a mile a minute, and it took my brain a second to change gears. Apparently, she had filed all the appropriate paperwork and ticked every box that needed ticking, all the medical reports and doctors' findings had supported the claim, and the matter had been resolved.

"What does that mean?" I asked. "I don't . . . I can't follow, sorry. Dallas said the medical costs were covered. And the van."

"Yes, that's correct. But this is a separate matter. This is your personal claim, Justin. We talked about this a few weeks ago."

The truth was, I couldn't really remember. I knew the claims were going on, but I couldn't seem to get my brain to think about money or process what any of this meant. "Uh, my memory isn't too good, sorry. That time was blurry for me." And even now, my words were coming slower. I'd had a busy morning and I hadn't slept much and I'd woken up strung out, and it was starting to catch up with me. "I'm tired, sorry. My brain doesn't work right when I'm tired."

"That's okay, Justin. I won't keep you. I just wanted to let you know that the claim is now resolved and a payment figure has been awarded in your favour."

"Okay, that's good."

"Would you like to know how much it is, Mr Keith?"

"Uh, I probably should, shouldn't I?"

She was quiet for a moment. "The amount awarded to you, Mr Keith, is three hundred and eighty thousand dollars."

As she spoke some more about getting the paperwork and signing off on everything, my mind began to turn in circles. That was a lot of money and I knew it was, but I couldn't quite get a grasp on it, and then Megan drove into the yard and it was all a bit too much.

"Are you still there, Mr Keith?"

"Yeah, but my homecare nurse is here. I have to go. Did you need to speak to Dallas again?"

She said yes, we'd need to organise a time for an appointment to sign off on everything, so I got to my feet and found Dallas speaking to Megan near the stairs to the flat.

"Hey, Dall. Angela needs to speak to you," I said, passing him the phone.

"Everything okay?" he whispered, holding the phone to his chest.

"Yeah 's fine. Just tired is all. Might need a nap after my torture session with Megan though."

Megan laughed but studied me. "You look tired, Justin. Your boss isn't working you too hard, is he?"

I looked at Dallas. "Nah. He's kinda dreamy though, isn't he?"

Dallas laughed and went back to the phone call, and Megan held out a walking cane. "I brought a present for you, Justin."

I stared at the cane. It was black and looked perfectly fine as far as canes went, but I didn't want it. "No thanks."

She smiled. "You'll like it better than the scooter."

Well, no, I wouldn't. "It doesn't have wheels. I like the scooter 'cause I can go fast."

She laughed and rolled her eyes and followed me up the stairs. There was something I really wanted to ask her, and I'd kept reminding myself all weekend to ask her when I saw her on Monday . . .

Oh, that's right.

I took a seat at the dining table and waited for Megan to do the same. "Can I ask you something?"

"Of course you can," Megan replied.

"Well, I've been thinking about it a lot. And with my leg and m'arm, and m'head too, I guess, being what they are." I shrugged. "But I was wondering what'd be the best position for me and Dallas to have sex?"

Chapter Two

DALLAS

I was pretty sure Justin would be sleeping after his homecare appointment. He'd been getting tired before Megan arrived, and I worried a little that I'd given him too much work to do this morning. He hadn't slept well and he'd been all out of sorts, but there was no way I was letting him believe for one second that he was useless.

Useless.

That fucking word.

The last thing in the world he was, was useless.

When Megan was finished, I met her at the bottom of the stairs. "How is he?"

"He's fine," she replied with a smile. "He was just about asleep on the couch before we finished, so I'd say he's gonna sleep for a while. I left the walking cane hanging over the back of a dining chair. If it's missing, ask him where he's thrown it to."

That made me smile. "Sure. Uh, he was kinda depressed this morning. I dunno if that's the right word, but he was real down on himself."

"He mentioned it. Said you were very good at making him feel better without him realising."

"He saw straight through me."

She smiled but gave me a serious look. "He's recognising his moods and that's a good thing. He can tell when he's not in a good headspace and he knows to ask for help. Mood swings and depression are very common, and in all honesty, he's been more stable than most I've worked with. Just keep an eye on him, and if these episodes become more frequent or more severe, notify his primary doctor and we'll look at some options." She put a hand on my arm. "But he's doing great. He's kept up his physio exercises and he's getting his strength back. I think you can expect some frustration in the coming weeks by what he wants to do versus what his mobility allows, but as long as he doesn't overdo it, I think he'll be fine."

I nodded. "Yeah, of course."

She smiled and went on her way, and I went back to work on the KTM. I picked up the ratchet I'd been using and smiled when I remembered the reason I'd put it down. Juss had told me he loved me. Unprompted, unnecessary, and yet completely believable. He'd just looked at me—like he used to look at me, before the accident—and said those three words that made my heart soar.

I didn't care that I'd kissed him at work, where the guys or customers could see. I didn't give one single fuck anymore. If I wanted to touch him, kiss him, tell him I loved him, I would. I would never waste an opportunity ever again.

"Oh my gawd," Sparra droned. "Jusso had the same look on his face earlier. That *I'm so in love* look." He grinned. "In case you didn't know, Dallas, that guy's giddy as hell over you. Again."

Davo smiled beside him. "Not again. Still. He never stopped. His brain just needed some time to catch up, that's all."

I couldn't help it. I was grinning at both of them. "Ah, yeah. He's . . . he's . . ."

"If you say he's kinda dreamy, I get to knock off early," Sparra said. "That's the rules."

I snorted. "What?"

"That's what Jusso said about you this morning. *He's so dreamy*," Sparra added, imitating Justin's voice. "Asked me if I agreed. Now, boss, I reckon you're a lot of things, but dreamy ain't one of 'em."

I laughed at that but couldn't help but ask. "Did he really say that?"

They rolled their eyes in sync, and Sparra laughed. "Thank God it's lunchtime," Davo said, walking into the breakroom. Sparra followed him and I put the ratchet back down and went in too. "Did you guys watch the footy last night?" Davo asked.

"Nope," Sparra said proudly. "I had a date."

Davo and I stopped and stared. "A date?"

Sparra grinned. "Yep. Wasn't gonna say anything. But this is the third weekend in a row I've seen her, so maybe it might be something."

Sparra told us all about Carissa, how they'd met, and how he'd asked her out for dinner, and it was really good to sit and listen to him. He was excited about the prospect of a girlfriend, though he was trying not to read too much into it just yet. They were seeing each other again on Wednesday night. That sounded pretty promising to me. He showed us a selfie of them on his phone, and she looked sweet and he looked happy.

I loved hearing about someone else's life for a while, as weird as that sounded. I'd been so absorbed in our lives, I'd lost touch of where they were up to.

"You might get to meet her this weekend," Sparra said. Then he gave me an uncertain look. "If we're still gonna meet up at the pub for lunch and the footy?"

Oh, I'd forgotten about that.

And you know what? Sitting around talking shit and having a laugh for a few hours sounded exactly like what I needed. "Absolutely. Not sure how long we'll be there for. We went out for a few hours on Saturday and it knocked Juss around a bit. He was pretty wiped yesterday. So I'll see what he says, if he thinks he's up for it. But I'm not gonna lie, it sounds damn good to me."

Then I remembered something else. "Oh, that reminds me. Justin and I have some appointments tomorrow: one at nine, then another one at ten. We shouldn't be too long. Doctor's appointment first, then we just need to sign some papers or something and we'll be straight back. We've only got two jobs in tomorrow and I was gonna spend most of the day in the office anyway."

Talk turned to work and what else we had booked in this week, and then we each went back to the bikes we were working on. I got busy and lost track of time and by three o'clock, I still hadn't heard anything from Juss, so I went upstairs to check on him.

The couch was vacant, though the TV was still going. The walking cane still hung over the chair. "Juss?"

"In here."

I followed the sound. The bathroom was empty, and I found him sitting on the edge of my side of the bed with a confused look on his face.

I walked in. "Everything okay?"

He met my eyes. "Oh yeah. I'm just looking for something. I think."

That didn't sound good. "Anything I can help you with?" He made a face, and was that a blush? I sat beside him on the bed. "Juss, what is it?"

He swallowed hard, suddenly nervous. "Oh God, I don't know how to say this . . ."

"Say what?"

"Well, I've been thinking. A lot. About . . . Ugh, about sex." He glanced at me, then looked back at his hands. "And I asked Megan today about stuff and she mentioned a few things that I haven't even thought about. And I should have. It was stupid of me not to. I mean, I trust you, and you didn't bring it up either. Not that we've really talked about it."

"Juss, baby. What are you talking about?"

He reached over and opened the top drawer of the bedside table. "I found lube," he said, his cheeks red. "But no condoms. I can't find them anywhere. I assumed we used them, because I've never not used them. Did we just run out? Or did you throw them out? I looked in the bathroom and in our wardrobe. Because if we're working on maybe having sex one day, we should have them."

Oh Christ.

Was he ready for this? Was I ready?

I took his hand. "Juss, we haven't used condoms for a long time."

He stared at me. Like, stared.

"We did, in the beginning, of course," I added. "But we agreed to be monogamous and faithful, and baby, I haven't even looked at another guy. Not once, not ever. So we got tested and we stopped using them."

"We . . ."

I nodded. "Yes. We used to have sex without condoms."

"That means . . ." He blushed, hard, his eyes wide. Then he whispered, "You'd come inside me."

Fuck.

My blood got a whole lot warmer. I nodded.

He licked his lips and swallowed hard, and it took a moment for him to look at me. "That's really fucking hot."

I barked out a laugh. "Uh, yeah. Every time."

He let out a long breath. "Damn."

"And you know what?" I said. "You're right. I should have brought this up with you before now. It was kind of irresponsible of me not to. But I didn't want to talk about sex in case you felt I was pressuring you. The last thing you need is for me to keep talking about it. But we should absolutely go and be tested again."

"No, we don't have to," he said, shaking his head.

"Yeah, we should. This is all new to you. Everything is new, so you should absolutely know, without any doubt, that we're being safe."

"I do trust you," he whispered.

"I know, baby. But for our own peace of mind." I kissed his knuckles. "If we get to do everything over again for a second-first time, then we should do *everything*."

Justin chuckled and put his free hand to his forehead. "Okay."

"We can go tomorrow. The clinic is super quick, from memory. Or we could ask Doctor Chang in the morning and get a pathology request form."

He made a face. "Clinic's fine."

"We have an appointment to sign off on the workers' comp papers after we see Doctor Chang," I said. "We can go after that, if you're not too tired."

Juss nodded and gave me a smile. "I can't believe I was worried to talk to you about this."

"You don't need to worry. You can ask me anything."

"I can't believe we . . . go bareback." The blush flared on his cheeks. "Was it . . . I mean, is it . . . ?"

"The hottest sex ever? Yes. Is it the most beautiful kind of lovemaking?" I nodded. "Yeah. Well, it was for us. I never felt closer to you than I did when we did that."

He let out a shaky breath and met my eyes. "I want our first time—I mean, our second-first time—when we have sex, I want it to be like that."

I kissed him. "When you're ready, Juss. I'll make it so good for you."

Chapter Three

Justin came back downstairs with me, but he mostly stuck to light duties. He helped me finish off the KTM but then unhurriedly tidied up for Davo and Sparra. He seemed content to go slow, just at his pace, and I was more than happy to encourage that.

It was . . . peaceful.

When the guys left, we locked up and Juss finished sweeping out while I sorted out some bookings and which parts we needed to order in. Finishing before me, he leaned against the doorframe to my office. "Hey."

I smiled up at him. "Hey. You done?"

He gave a nod. "What did you want for dinner?"

"There's minced beef in the fridge."

"It's gotten cold out," he murmured. "So maybe something . . . like meatloaf and mashed potato."

"That sounds great."

"I wasn't gonna make it. I was suggesting it."

I barked out a laugh. "Is that right?"

He smiled. "I guess I could help."

I shut down my laptop and stood up, and when I walked to him, he didn't move. I expected him to step out of the doorway or move so I could walk through, but he didn't. He looked up at me with something in his eyes I hadn't seen in a long time.

Fire.

He leaned his back against the jamb, his eyes on mine, and he waited . . .

It was an invitation I had no intention of refusing.

I pressed against him and captured his mouth with mine. He responded in kind, kissing me with equal passion. He pulled me closer, our bodies aligned that perfect way they always did. He was turned on, hard already, and feeling his erection pressing against me made me groan into the kiss.

He slid his hand down over my arse, and that was . . . new. I mean, not for the old Justin. He'd done that a million times, but this new Justin hadn't really been inclined to explore too much.

And then he squeezed.

I broke the kiss with a laugh. "Hello there," I said, pulling his bottom lip between mine. We needed to cool it a little.

"I think we should go upstairs," he whispered.

Or we could not cool it at all.

I hit the lights, locked the door, and took Justin's hand. He could have easily walked up those stairs, but we got to the bottom and he slung his arm over my shoulder. "Carry me."

Grinning, I picked him up bridal style and carried him up. He never took his eyes off my face, the heat of his gaze burning into me. Once inside, I gently put his feet to the floor next to the couch. But he didn't pull his arm away. Instead, he trailed his hand along my neck and down my chest where he fisted my work shirt and pulled me toward him.

I walked him backwards until his arse hit the back of the sofa, and with a hand to my jaw, he pulled me in for a hard kiss.

He was so into it. Like a switch had flipped in his head, like some part of his brain had woken up.

This was just like the old Justin.

Justin, before the accident, was all about sex. He loved it. He was horny all the time, wanted me to suck and fuck him almost every damn day. I wasn't kidding when I told him we had a lot of sex. But I also wasn't kidding when I told him I'd wait until he was ready.

He'd been pushing boundaries in the last week or so, but this was . . . this was quite a step. And it was freaking hot.

My dick was definitely into it, and the hardness of Juss' erection felt divine.

I kissed him deep, tangling our tongues and sucking on his bottom lip, while grinding my hips into his. I was trying to be mindful of his leg, but the way he gripped me and grinded, I assumed his leg was feeling okay.

I slipped my hand between us and palmed his erection. "Tell me what you want, Juss," I murmured against his mouth.

"I want . . . I want your mouth . . . on me. Right here."

Oh, hell yes.

I dropped to my knees, sliding down his body, my eyes locked on his. I undid the button and fly of his work pants and let them hang open, off his hips. I nudged his cock with my nose and inhaled the scent of him before I pulled his briefs down and freed my prize.

He was leaning against the back of the couch, his legs spread comfortably with me between his feet. The last thing I wanted him to do was strain his leg or his arm . . . I wanted him to feel nothing but pleasure.

I licked the underside of his shaft, from his balls to the tip, and he groaned, frustrated, and he shook his head. He clearly didn't want me to tease him or drag this out, so I licked the head and tasted his slit before taking him into my mouth.

"Oh, fuck yes," he said.

I worked him over, swirled my tongue, sucked on the head, and pumped his base. He began to thrust his hips. This was what he wanted. This was what he needed.

I took him all the way in and looked up at him. He was staring down at me, his eyes dark, his lips open. He put his fingers through my hair. Then he touched my face and he drew his thumb along the side of my mouth, feeling how my lips surrounded his cock.

So I swallowed around him, and it pushed him over the edge. He cried out and his body flexed tight as he came down my throat.

He tasted like heaven.

When he was done, I got to my feet to make sure he was okay. "How're you feeling?"

He replied by laughing and taking my shirt and pulling me in for a hug. A few aftershocks tremored through him but he just chuckled. "Fucking hell."

I kissed his forehead, his eyelid, his nose, but when I went to take a step back, he had hold of my shirt and didn't let go. His eyes took a second to focus. "Your turn."

"Juss, you don't have to."

"I want to," he replied firmly. "Please, can I?"

Fucking hell. As if he'd ever have to beg. I looked around to where might be the best spot—he certainly couldn't kneel on the floor—but Juss took my arm and pulled me toward the coffee table. He sat on it, his right leg out straight, and grinned up at me.

"This is a good height," he said.

I laughed and he tugged me closer. Fuck. He pulled open my work pants, rough and eager, and then delicately took out my cock like he was about to defuse a bomb.

"Oh fuck," he breathed. "It's so beautiful." He studied every detail, every angle, and I had to remind myself that this was new to him. He was probably committing everything to memory. He lifted it and gave me a long stroke. "It's huge, Dallas. Like a porn star."

I scoffed and was about to reply when he flattened his tongue and sucked on the head of my dick.

Oh fuck.

"I've thought about this," he murmured between licking and sucking. "A lot."

"Have you?" I was panting, not sure what else to say. I was so hard, it was almost painful.

"Since you told me we don't use condoms." He looked up at me as he sucked me like a lollipop. "I've been imagining how it feels."

Christ, I was gonna come so fast.

He explored with his hands, touching, feeling, pumping, sliding with his tongue . . .

"Baby, I'm gonna come."

He smiled as he took me into his mouth, deep and wet heat. I gripped the back of his head and he groaned, and that was all it took. I filled his mouth and he hummed between swallows.

Fuck.

He released me and I swayed, my blood was buzzing, my bones were like jelly, and he held my hips. "You okay there?"

I put my hands under his arms and lifted him to his feet so I could hold him. Or so he could hold me. I wasn't sure which. I just needed the contact.

I needed him.

"You okay, babe?" he whispered.

I nodded into his neck. "So very okay."

He chuckled. "Just so you know, I asked Megan which positions we could try that won't hurt my leg."

I snorted and pulled back. "You did?"

"Yeah, I think she almost died."

I laughed and kissed him softly. "We'll figure it out, baby."

He sighed and met my eyes. "I don't think I'm scared anymore. I don't even know why I was. I just couldn't bear the thought of pain or being vulnerable, I dunno why. I know you won't hurt me."

"I wouldn't."

"I used to love sex."

I smiled. The truth was, he loved it *a lot*. "You did."

"And I think about how gentle you are and how kind you are and how you know what I need," he whispered. "And I began to imagine what that would be like in bed. What you'd be like, how you'd treat me, and what you'd do to me. And my body was like, 'hell yes,' and my brain was like, 'okay, even I agree to that.'"

I laughed. "Glad they agreed."

"They haven't agreed on much since the accident," he replied dryly. "But they agree on this. Mostly my body, not gonna lie. But Dallas, I want it. I want you. I've had enough pain in the last few months to last me a lifetime. I want to feel good. I want to know what pleasure is. And I know you'll show me."

"I will."

"Just promise me something . . ."

I cupped his face. "Anything."

"Please don't be mad if I freak out or need you to stop."

"Oh, baby. I would never be mad."

"Because your dick is huge."

I snorted out a laugh. "It's not really."

"Did it . . . did we ever have any . . . fitting issues?"

I laughed at that. "Ah, no." I traced his eyebrow with my thumb, down his jaw, and across his bottom lip. "Baby, you loved it. You'd beg for it. You wanted it for hours."

His nostrils flared and he swallowed hard. "Oh."

I kissed him softly and whispered against his lips. "I will make it so good for you, you'll never want it to end."

His dick twitched against mine. "Uh, maybe we can have toast for dinner. I think we need to go to bed," he said. Then he made a face. "I'm not ready for a sex marathon, but I'm sure you can make me come again. Maybe twice."

I kissed him deeper, giving him some tongue, and his dick pulsed again between us. "Toast for dinner it is."

<hr>

WE BOTH SLEPT like the dead. I'd wrung two more orgasms out of him like he'd asked, but maybe the last one had been too much. His body couldn't handle that kind of muscle-expenditure, being so tense and taut, and as much as I'd tried to relax him, orgasms were a strain on a tired body.

But I'd had him lie on the bed, face down, his legs spread. I'd massaged and rubbed him down, sensually and intimately. Then with a little bit of lube, I'd rubbed his hole and fingered him, working him into a frenzy before I rolled him over and sucked him.

Then I'd knelt between his thighs and jerked off, spilling my come onto his belly. He was too tired to shower, so I cleaned him up and finally crawled into bed beside him. He wrapped himself around me and I held him just as tight.

"When we get the test results back," he'd mumbled. "I'll be so ready."

We fell asleep and I don't think either of us moved all night.

I was up before him and had the scrambled eggs on toast and coffees made as he came out of the bedroom. "Perfect timing," I said.

He scowled, which was completely normal for Justin first thing, but he was limping more than usual.

"You okay?" I asked.

"Sore."

"Oh, baby. I'm sorry," I said, helping him to his seat.

He sipped his coffee first. "Nah, 's okay. It's a good sore. Well, not *good*. Physio sore is a bad sore. Overdoing it sore is a bad sore. Sore from too much sex is good sore." He shrugged. "You know what I mean."

I couldn't help but smile a little. "I do. What I think was, coming three times last night was probably one time too many."

He picked up his fork. "Speak for yourself."

I snorted. "Okay, well, last night it was fine. Today, not so much."

"I'll be okay after a hot shower." He ate some breakfast and nodded. "This is good. Thank you. One day I'll cook you breakfast."

I stabbed some egg with my fork. "Juss, you've never been a morning person. Ever."

He made a face that was almost a smile. "Mornings'd be all right . . . if they started around lunchtime."

I laughed. "Good to know some things never change, though, right?"

He conceded a nod, then sipped his coffee. "You know, this decaf stuff just isn't great. Do you reckon I could have some real coffee one day?"

"We can ask Doctor Chang."

"We see her first, right?"

"Sure do. Nine o'clock." I checked the time on the

microwave. It was six forty now. Plenty of time. "But today's gonna be pretty busy, Juss. We've got Doctor Chang first, then the meeting with Angela to sign off on all the van and the medical costs, and if you still wanted, go to the clinic after that. But we can see how you're feeling, and if it's too much, we can go to the clinic another day."

Juss bit into some toast. "I'll be fine."

"We can bring the scooter or the walking cane today."

He shot me a not-pleased look. "No thanks. I can walk to a few appointments. And anyway, pretty sure I'll be planted on the couch for the rest of the day. I was gonna spend the afternoon watching porn."

I almost choked on my eggs, and one of Justin's rare morning smiles formed behind his coffee cup. "I'm assuming Pornhub is still a thing? I haven't checked," he said.

After I'd collected myself and managed a mouthful of coffee, I gave a nod. "Ah, yeah."

"You know," he added, "for a long time, I didn't think about sex at all. Now I know it's a thing, I think about it a lot."

My dick was particularly interested in this conversation. It was pressing awkwardly in my briefs and I had to shift in my seat. "That's a good sign, right?"

"I think so." He pushed his empty plate away and smiled at me. "Now, about that hot shower."

Fucking hell. "If I join you in there, we'll be late."

He stood up, and sure enough, his boxers were tented at the front. He made no attempt to hide it. In fact, he stood there and smiled when I couldn't take my eyes off it. "Pretty sure the doc said I wasn't to shower alone."

I laughed out a groan. This was the old Justin. This was the bossy, playful Justin that I'd missed like crazy.

He turned and made his way to the bathroom. I dumped all the plates in the sink and was naked before I got to the bathroom door. He laughed as I joined him in the shower, though he wasn't laughing for long.

I made short work of him, and me, then quickly ran the soap over both of us. He was still in an orgasm haze when I shut the water off and handed him a towel. "Did we get any work done?" he asked as he dried himself. "Before, I mean. When we first got together. Did we ever have days when we couldn't be stuffed going to work and just spent the day in bed? Because I feel like that's something I would have done with you."

I chuckled. "Not really. There were days we were late to open the shop and some weekends when we never bothered with clothes. But we never missed work, no."

He sighed. "Did we ever have sex on your work desk?"

I laughed at that. "Nope."

"The table in the lunch-break room?"

I grimaced. "Ew, no."

He smiled. "Yeah, I agree. But your desk . . ."

I tied my towel off around my waist. "We're not doing that."

He towel-dried his hair and grinned at me. "What about on the bike hoist? I reckon I could lie on that and press the button till I was the perfect height for you to . . . you know, give me a grease and oil change."

I laughed, like really laughed, but shook my head. "No. We didn't do that." I nodded to the door. "Come on. We need to get dressed."

We opened the shop up and got everything ready for Davo and Sparra, and we left not long after they'd arrived. Juss was still in a good mood and it easily rubbed off on me. Seeing him happy and positive filled me with a real sense of hope.

Doctor Chang seemed to pick up on it too. "How is my favourite patient?" she asked, smiling as we walked in. "You look happy, Justin."

"Yeah, I'm pretty good today." He told her about his shit day the other day, and how hearing the song "When The War Is Over" had brought back the memory of the accident because it was playing on the radio when the truck had hit him, and the pain that went with it.

Doctor Chang explained to him what she'd said to me over the phone and how, while it might have felt frightening and overwhelming, it wasn't uncommon. But Justin could only shrug.

"I kinda felt okay afterward. Not about the pain, but remembering the accident," he said. "It's probably weird, but I like that I can remember it. The unknown was always the scariest part. There was so much unknown. Still is, of the last five years, I guess. But I prefer to remember it, even if it's not a happy memory."

"That's not weird at all, Justin," Doctor Chang replied.

Then he told her about the good days he'd had this week and how he'd been out to lunch and what he'd been doing at work. He still needed to rest every day, but that was getting less frequent over time, and he could do more things and his mind was clearer. No, he hadn't remembered anything else this week, but he told her how he wanted to focus more on the now, not a past he couldn't really remember.

She smiled like a proud mum. "And Dallas," she pressed. "Seems like a positive week?"

"Yeah," I agreed. "There's been some changes. Good changes," I said to Justin with a squeeze of his hand. I looked back to the doc. "The other night, Justin was talking about the future, and that was . . . that was amazing. Just a few weeks ago, he couldn't think far enough ahead to know if he wanted lunch; now he's making plans, so it's a huge step forward. His mind fog seems to be really clearing now."

Doctor Chang nodded, and she spoke about cognitive improvements and recognising milestones and achievements, remediation and compensation. But no, she couldn't recommend he drink proper coffee because of how caffeine reacted with a TBI, but yes, exploring sexual intercourse was fine, and no, it was still too early to tell if he'd recover any more memories.

"So, Justin," she said. "I want to see you next week, and the week after that you're scheduled for a follow-up MRI and CT scans. Then if everything is as it should be and moving forward, we might see how you feel about follow-up appointments every two weeks instead of every week."

"Oh. If you think I'm ready for that."

"I do. I think you're ready to move onto the next phase of your recovery," she said. "These next scans will be the three-month mark. Then fortnightly appointments will take us up to the six-month mark. That's a big milestone. Then you'll move to monthly appointments until your next scans at the one-year mark." She smiled. "So we might still only be taking things one step at a time, but you're making some pretty big strides, Justin."

He looked to me and smiled before he squeezed my hand. "Sounds good to me."

We left Doctor Chang's office and Justin was still smiling. He was a little tired but he wasn't falling asleep on me like he used to when we left these appointments. "How you feeling, baby?" I asked as we drove out of the car park.

"I feel good. Bit pissed off that I can't have caffeine."

"One day." I chuckled.

"And I'm thinking maybe that stupid cane might not have been such a terrible idea."

"Is your leg sore?"

"Nah, it's just draining. I don't wanna trip over because I can't lift my feet. Don't tell Megan I said that."

I chuckled. "Doctor Chang seems happy with your progress."

He smiled. "I really like her, but I won't be sad to see her every second week instead."

I reached over and took his hand. "Me too, baby."

"Do you think we could get a coffee after this next meeting? I mean, just a shitty decaf one."

I laughed. "Sure, we can."

A short time later, we arrived for our meeting with Angela, and thankfully we didn't have to wait long. After some small talk, we sat in her office as she began to go through the files in front of her, and she explained to me, the way lawyers do, the itemised accounts for the van and the tools and then the hours and wages for Justin. It was everything she'd already told me and it was fair, so I was more than happy to sign off on it.

I couldn't sign it quick enough.

Next was Justin's lump-sum compensation. I knew he'd be entitled to something, and his medical costs were now covered. Angela explained things to Justin, though I had to wonder how much he was taking in. He was doing a fair amount of nodding and smiling, but it was more out of courtesy than agreeing. I followed along, and again, she reassured us it was all procedure and, in her opinion, very fair.

"Not many others are so lucky. Though each case is assessed on its merits, yours is quite deserving," she said. "The funds will take some time to land in your account, because it's quite a substantial sum. But once this is lodged, it should be straight forward. No long wait like last time."

Justin nodded. "And we pay the medical bills with this, right?"

She shook her head. "No, this is separate. All the hospital bills are taken care of. This is your money." She glanced at me before smiling back at Juss. "To spend however you see fit. The sum of three hundred and eighty thousand is compensation for your accident."

Juss shrugged. "Oh, okay."

Three hundred and eighty thousand . . .

"I'm sorry, what?" I asked. "Three hundred and eighty thousand . . . dollars?"

Angela looked at me. "Yes. Did he not tell you?"

I shook my head, and Justin shrugged again. "I was going to," he said. "But then I had my appointment with my nurse, then I fell asleep, and then we talked about sex and I haven't been able to think about much else, sorry."

My mind was spinning, but not enough to realise he just talked about sex in front of Angela. She was blushing and somewhat horrified, and I couldn't help but laugh. "Sorry," I said to her. "We got sidetracked yesterday. I'm just a little stunned. That is quite a chunk of money."

Angela nodded. "I was happy with the result. The doctors agreed there was a significant change to the quality of life and that there will be long-term effects for Justin, so it was awarded accordingly." She handed Justin the pen. "Are you ready to sign off on it?"

"I just want it all to be over," Juss said. "Actually, what I want is my memories back and to be able to drink coffee again. And to have a leg and a brain that work properly would be good, but I'll settle for this to be over so we can have some kind of normal again."

Angela smiled. "That sounds good."

Justin signed, though his signature wasn't great, and he smiled at me when he put the pen down. Angela talked for a bit more, handed us our copies of files, and told us she'd be in touch once the payments came through.

We walked back to my ute, slower for Justin's pace. He was getting tired now. But as soon as we were in, I burst out laughing. "You didn't tell me how much they said you were getting."

He just smiled and shrugged. "I forgot, sorry."

I shook my head, still disbelieving. "Juss, this sets you up."

He stared at me. "Me? Sets me up for what?"

"For life. For whatever you want."

He didn't smile. In fact, he stared out the windscreen and frowned. "What I want is my life back. What I want is for this to never have happened. I want to remember everything, and I want my head not to hurt. That's what I want. No amount of money can do that."

Shit.

"Oh, Juss, I'm sorry. That's not what I meant. Sorry, it's just a bit of a shock, that's all. I know the money doesn't make up for anything. That's not what I meant."

"I know." He sighed. "I don't mean to sound pissy. But I don't want the money. And that's not fair because you've been stressed about money, but I haven't even thought about it all this time. I try to, and you've shown me my bank statements, but . . ." He shrugged. "I dunno. I guess I'll need to start."

I reached over and took his hand. "Baby, don't worry about it. We can have the bank set up a separate account for it that only you can access." Not that anyone could access his everyday account either, but I wanted him to know I wasn't including myself in this. "Just let it sit there earning you some interest until you're ready to look at it."

He met my eyes and managed a small smile and a nod. "Sounds good."

"You don't need to worry about it until you want to. Not anyone else."

"Thank you," he sighed. "It's just a bit overwhelming, I guess. But you always know what to do."

"Not always."

"To me you do. You're like some pillar of strength. When I don't know what to do, I know you'll help me."

His words got me right in the heart. I lifted his hand to my lips and kissed his knuckles. "Because I love you, Justin Keith. Always have . . ."

He smiled, tired and cute as hell. "Always will."

Chapter Four

WHEN WE GOT to the health clinic, I asked Justin twice if he was still okay to go inside or if he wanted to leave it for another day, but he was adamant. He was tired, physically, but also mentally—a doctor appointment followed directly by a legal appointment was enough for anyone.

But Justin was determined.

He wanted to get this done.

And it didn't take long. The whole process was quick and easy.

"Do they really just send the results to your phone these days?" he asked as we were done and finally heading home. "The same day?"

"Yep. Some tests take longer, and if anything's positive, they usually ask you to make an appointment. But with the rapid testing, if you get the all-clear, it's just a text later that day."

"Jesus. It used to take two weeks."

I chuckled. "Some still do, but a lot's changed in five years."

He leaned his head on the headrest, looked at me, and smiled. I was pretty sure I'd be carrying him up the stairs. He could barely keep his eyes open. "The guy swabbed my dick," he mumbled.

I laughed. "Yep." It was a full sexual health check. Swabs and bloods.

"You went before me, so I asked him if he'd ever seen a dick as big as yours."

I shot him a look. "You didn't."

He grinned sleepily. "Did. But he didn't answer me. Did smile though."

"Oh God."

He chuckled. "Tell me, what was my reaction when I saw your dick the first time?"

Jesus H Christ. So apparently when I said he could ask me anything, my dick would be a constant topic of conversation . . .

"Uh, well," I began. "You were . . . happy."

"Bet I was."

"You wanted it a lot."

His eyes were dreamy, tired; his smile was smug. "Bet I did."

I chuckled at the memory. "Actually, after the first time we had sex, we were in bed, up to about round three, I think it was, and you said my dick was better than when you got a Transformer truck for your birthday when you were six."

He laughed, a deep rumbling sound. "Oh my God. Optimus Prime. Loved that truck."

The sound of his genuine belly laugh made me laugh too. "You said it was just like a normal toy truck, then in bed it transformed, and *bam!* Optimus Prime."

Juss laughed again, but his eyes were closed. "Optimus Prime dick," he mumbled. Then he chuckled some more, even as he slept.

God, I'd forgotten about that whole Transformer conversation. When we first got together and he shoved his hands down my pants, he was like a kid in a candy store. And when we'd first fallen into bed together, he'd been insatiable.

I'd taken for granted all those memories. I never recalled them, never relished them, never thought for one moment I wouldn't miss them should they be taken away.

And there was Justin, who would give anything to have any of his memories back.

It was a sobering realisation.

I GOT some drive-thru lunch for all of us, pulled the ute into the workshop, and drove around the back near the stairs. Justin was sound asleep in the passenger seat. "Hey, Jussy. We're home."

He stirred when I opened his door, and when I leaned in to undo his seatbelt, he opened his eyes slowly and smiled. "Hey, you," he whispered.

"Hey, handsome," I said, giving him a quick kiss. "We gotta get you up these stairs. Then you can sleep."

He groaned and carefully lifted his right leg to set his feet on the ground. Sparra walked out, grinning. "How's the man of the moment?"

"The what?" I asked.

"Newspaper guy was here earlier. Wants an interview," he replied. "Said he'd call back tomorrow."

"An interview?" Juss asked. "Me? What for?"

Sparra shrugged. "The crash was pretty big news. He wanted a follow-up."

I resisted snarling, but Justin just snorted. "Must be hard up for news," he mumbled as he made his way to the stairs. "Love to stay and chat, mate, but fuck, I'm tired."

Sparra burst out laughing and clapped me on the shoulder. "You heard the man. Get him upstairs."

I followed Justin up, one step behind him in case he lost his balance, and grinned the whole way. That was such a Justin thing to say . . .

He sagged onto the couch and pressed the button to bring his legs up and recline, and by the time I pulled the blanket over him and kissed his forehead, he was already asleep.

I left his Squish-the-cat-proof lunch beside him and carried the rest back downstairs. Davo and Sparra were grateful for the chicken and chips, and we talked about the jobs they were working on, and inevitably they asked me if we got all the paperwork sorted out that I'd mentioned to them the day before.

"Yeah. I need to decide if we'll replace the van or maybe opt for something else," I said. "I don't know how I feel about anyone going out again." I shrugged. "I just don't know if any financial gain is worth the risk."

"Have you spoken to Jusso about it?" Davo asked.

I shook my head. "Not yet. He's had enough on his plate, and he can't even think about driving again for another three and a half months. And that's just driving. Not working on his own or going out on his own." I shrugged. "We'll see."

"If he wants to?" Sparra asked.

I sighed. "Then he can."

Davo gave a wry smile. "Yeah. And every time he drives out, you can stay here with your head between your knees in the brace position until he gets back."

I conceded a nod. "Probably." I threw my rubbish into the bin. "Did the newspaper really send someone around?"

"Yep," Davo replied. "He seemed nice enough. Didn't ask for details or nothin'. Like he didn't try and get the scoop on what Jusso's been like." He smiled. "Probably didn't fancy getting his nose broken."

I chuckled. "Smart."

"Said he'd be back tomorrow."

"Then we'll see how he fancies getting his nose broken tomorrow."

They laughed and tossed their rubbish in the bin before getting back to work. I stuck it out in the office for as long as I could stand it before I went out into the shop to help get some real work done. Well, real work that I enjoyed, anyway.

Juss came down around four, just as the boys were getting ready to leave. They chatted for a bit, then he helped me clean up and close everything down. I locked the front gate, and when I walked back into the shop, Juss was staring at his phone.

"Everything okay?"

"Still haven't heard," he said. "About the results. What if it's bad news? What if there was some medical thing from the accident, like if they gave me bad blood. Dall, I don't think I could deal with that right now."

Oh Christ. I hadn't even thought of that.

"Baby, they screen blood for all that stuff."

"It happens. I googled it."

Well, he was googling stuff now, which meant he was thinking about different things, which was a good sign. But this . . . this wasn't good. I wrapped my arms around him. "Juss, it'll be okay."

He mumbled against my chest, "What if I had some crazy affair and got some awful STI and I can't remember him because of the accident but we found out about him from the police and he's plotting some horrible—"

I pulled back. "Justin, what did you google?"

He frowned, his face so sad. "It was something from Florida. There was a crazy lady who lost all of her memory and the police found out who she was and that she'd had an affair for years, and she fed her lover to the alligators so her husband wouldn't find out." He looked up at me, mystified. "I clicked on a link. The internet's a scary place. I mean, it has porn, which is good. But then there is some weird shit out there."

I burst out laughing and went back to hugging him. "Baby, you didn't have any affair and neither did I. There's no one else in this world but us. I promise."

He sighed. "There was a link about a guy in England who had some kind of stroke and he lost his memory, but when he woke up, he spoke French and had a different name, who turned out to be some guy that died in 1882. I don't know if he had an STI."

I snorted. "Juss, baby, it's okay." I kissed his forehead and made him look me in the eye. "But if you want to click on some crazy links, how about we do it together so you don't get freaked out."

He nodded just as my phone beeped with a message. It was the clinic, so I opened it. The rapid testing results were negative. I showed him my phone. "See? Too easy. The rest of the results will take a week."

Then his phone beeped, and he nervously handed it to me. "You read it."

I opened the message, and sure enough, the rapid test results were negative. I faced the screen to him and grinned. "Negative."

He almost sagged. "Well, that's . . . a relief."

I realised two things right then. Firstly, that'd he'd been legitimately worried over these test results and I'd downplayed his stress. And secondly, that he didn't deal with stress too well. At all.

The Juss before the accident was kinda laid back and didn't really stress too much over anything. But now he did, and I should have realised it would have affected him differently. I gave him another hug and kissed the side of his head. "You feel a bit better now, baby? I'm sorry if I didn't seem worried enough."

He nodded. "I feel better. We have another week to wait for the others, but this was the big one, right?"

"Sure. It was just the rapid test, what they pricked your finger for. They'll run a full diagnostic with the blood they drew out of your arm, and that'll take a week. But this rapid testing is pretty good." I gave him a soft kiss. "But baby, even if we got different results just now or next week, I'll still love you. Promise."

He squeezed me and nodded against my chest. "Same, Dallas. I'll still love you too." He sighed. "I just worried, and my brain was stuck on it, sorry."

"Hey, don't apologise." I pulled back and gave him a smile. "How about I make us that meatloaf for dinner?"

"Sounds great."

We finished locking up and went upstairs. Justin stayed with me in the kitchen while I made the meatloaf, so I put him to work peeling potatoes for the mash. "So," he said, "because we had unprotected blowjobs already, that means we can keep having them until we get the swab results, right?"

I stopped combining the meat mixture so I could stare at him. "Juss."

He shrugged. "I mean, if we're gonna need treatment anyway . . ."

I snorted. "Not sure that's how it works."

"But we could."

"Or we could wait. Because I should have thought of this before and not pressured you into sex without talking about testing."

He frowned. "You didn't pressure me."

"Sorry, wrong word." I stood behind him and, keeping my messy hands out, gave him a kiss on the cheek. "I still should have offered you some options."

"You did the opposite of pressure me." He put the last peeled potato on the chopping board. "And what options do you mean? Like more blowjobs?"

I chuckled. "We'll see."

"That's a yes."

It wasn't a yes, but I doubted how much I'd be able to argue with him over this. Over anything, to be honest. "How did your porn watching go this afternoon?"

He stopped and stared at me. "My porn watching . . . Oh, shit. I forgot. I was gonna spend hours catching up on Pornhub."

I chuckled. "You have a week of no sex where you can watch all the porn you want."

He gave me a cheeky smile. "Or we could watch it together. Because you did say something about options."

I laughed at that. "I kinda walked right into that, didn't I?"

He grinned victoriously, so I went back to making my meatloaf. "Dallas?" he murmured.

I turned to find him right behind me. He crooked his finger in a *come-here* motion so I leaned in closer to him thinking he wanted to whisper something in my ear, but he surprised me with a kiss to the cheek.

He didn't say anything. Just a kiss to my cheek, and it was somehow the sweetest thing ever. It made my heart bloom with love, and my stomach did that swooping free fall. I turned back to the meatloaf with the dopiest grin, and I'm pretty sure I went to bed much the same way.

I'D TOLD Justin about how the newspaper guy said he'd be back, but to be honest, I didn't expect him to turn up at smoko time the next day. As we got busy with work, I kinda forgot about it. But sure enough, when Davo was mastering his barista skills at the new coffee machine, Justin was helping me with a Yamaha and Sparra walked out holding a tray of Arnott's biscuits. He nodded toward the front of the workshop. "Return visitor."

A young guy had parked his car out on the street and was walking in with another guy sporting a fancy camera around his neck. They certainly didn't look like a couple of guys who rode bikes, and they weren't here to sell me anything. "Can I help you?" I asked, wiping my hands on a rag as I went to meet them.

"Samuel Cormie," the guy without the camera said, holding out his hand. "*Newcastle Times*." The other guy didn't speak.

"Ah, right," I said, shaking his hand. His hand was cold and limp, and I didn't care too much that I smeared some grease on him. "You called in yesterday."

He grinned at me, all university shine and preppy attitude. "Yeah, I was hoping to have a chat with a Mr Justin Keith if he's in today."

I normally didn't dislike anyone straight up, but knowing he was here to question Juss for shits and giggles didn't sit well with me. And as much as I wanted to tell this kid to piss right off, it wasn't my place. It was Justin's decision.

"He is. Come on through."

When he saw us, Justin got off his scooter and walked over. I didn't even get a chance to introduce them because Mr Smarmy beat me to it. He shook Juss' hand with a little too much enthusiasm. "Samuel Cormie, *Newcastle Times*."

As soon as his hand was free, Juss wiped it on his work pants like he had to get rid of the gross feeling. It made me smile. "Justin Keith."

"I covered the accident when it happened," Cormie said. "And I was hoping I could ask you some follow-up questions on your recovery. I'm sure our readers would love to know how you're getting on."

"Uh, sure." Justin shrugged. "I guess. Not much to tell." He looked back to his scooter. "I'll just grab my wheels."

He limped back to his scooter and I went with him. "Sure you want to do this?"

"Yeah."

"Want me to stick around?"

"Nah, I got this."

"Okay, but if he asks anything about the money or compo, just say you can't speak about it."

Juss gave a nod and I left them to it, but not before giving Mr Sleazebag a look of fair warning. They walked—well, Juss scooted —out to the end of the workshop where the sun was coming through. I walked into the breakroom where I could stand and still see Justin, and Davo was chuckling.

"So you didn't like the bloke?" he asked with a laugh. He nodded to my coffee mug, which was filled with a fresh brew.

"Thanks. And no, not much." I kept an eye out the door at where I could see Justin talking. "Do you reckon I should've stayed with him?"

"He'll be fine," Sparra said. "Let him do this."

I resisted sighing and sipped my coffee instead. I watched Juss talk for a bit. He nodded and smiled, but he kept looking my way every so often. I wanted to go to him, to see if he was okay, but Sparra was right. Juss needed to do this, to do something on his own. And by the time I'd rage-dunked several bikkies into my coffee, Mr Douche gave me a wave and hollered goodbye—I didn't care that he could see me watching the whole time—and he and his silent cameraman walked back out to their car.

Davo made Juss a decaf and had it ready for him by the time he scooted to the breakroom.

"How was it?" I asked. There was no point in trying to deny my concern. "Was he rude? Pushy?"

"Overprotective?" Davo asked with a grin.

I gave him the bird and he laughed as he walked back to the bike he was working on.

"Nah, he was okay," Juss said. "Just asked me a bunch of stuff. About my memory, of course. Apparently amnesia is inter-esting. And my leg and my recovery in general. Shit like that."

"We saw your photoshoot," Sparra joked.

"I told him to get the shop sign in the photo," Juss said. "Fig-ured a promo shot couldn't hurt."

That made me smile. "As long as he wasn't a dick to you."

Sparra pushed my arm. "Dallas here watched him like a blue heeler from the shadows. Thought he was gonna start growlin' there for a minute."

I rolled my eyes. "I just didn't want him asking anything he had no right knowing."

Sparra just laughed. "Jusso, when you're done on break, I could use a hand. Got a fuel line to replace. And Dallas ate all the Kingston biscuits."

"I did not," I shot back. "I had three."

"Sure thing," Juss replied with a laugh.

I handed him the tray of biscuits, knowing damn well he loved the plain milk bikkies and no one else would dare touch them. "You okay?"

He dunked his first biscuit. "Yeah. I know you were worried about me."

"I couldn't help it. I tried not to be."

Juss gave a smile as he dunked another biscuit and shoved it in his mouth before it could break off. "He was actually nice. He did ask about how the accident affected me financially though. I told him the accident affected everything. He didn't push me for any info."

I rubbed his arm. "Good."

He sipped his coffee. "I'm sorry I fell asleep last night."

"Don't apologise."

"I had plans. I wanted to do—" He glanced to the door to double-check no one was there. "—some things."

I chuckled. "We're supposed to wait a week."

Justin rolled his eyes. "I'm not gonna forget to watch it today. I have a whole lotta porn to catch up on. Then, by the time you finish work this arvo, I'll have had all the inspiration I need. You should probably be ready."

I barked out a laugh. "Gee, thanks. I won't be thinking about that all day or anything."

He smiled like the cat who got the cream . . . or the cat who would get the cream later . . . Jesus. "We better get back to work."

Juss finished at lunchtime, and over the hours that followed, I tried really hard not to think about whether he was actually watching porn . . . whether or not he was jerking off to it, or maybe touching himself in other places . . .

He didn't come back down before closing time, which was a bit odd—recently he'd been coming back down to see Davo and Sparra before they left and to help me clean up—so, wondering if everything was okay, I locked everything up when the guys left and raced upstairs.

There he was, lying lengthways on the couch, propped up with pillows. He was watching something on his phone, which he pointed in my direction when I walked in. "There's a lot to catch up on. Did you know cartoon porn was a thing?"

I began to laugh as I walked over to him. I picked up Squish from Juss' side and gently put him on the floor, then very carefully lowered myself onto Juss' body. I kissed him with smiling lips. "I didn't know cartoon porn was a thing, no."

"Wanna watch it with me? There are human cartoons or animal cartoon porn. Like humans but they're animals, like horses and dogs. It's kinda weird, kinda hot. I don't wanna judge anyone," he said. I laughed as I kissed down his neck and he tilted his head, giving me more room. "Oh, I like that."

I could feel his erection, so I pulled back to look in his eyes. "Did you jerk off to it?"

His nostrils flared and his pupils blew out. "No. I wanted to wait for you."

I crushed my mouth to his and he grunted as our tongues touched. He shifted his hips and moved his good leg so I could settle between his thighs. Our cocks were aligned, our mouths fused . . . It was glorious.

We kissed, hot and heavy, grinding and rolling our hips, feeling every nerve ending flood with desire. Juss broke the kiss, panting, his lips swollen. "You better not be playing me right now, Dall. If you tell me we should wait a week, I'll . . ."

I grinned. "You'll what?"

He growled and gnashed his teeth, nipping at my chin. "I'll . . . jerk off and finger myself and you'll only be allowed to watch."

Shock at his words and a blast of desire coursed through me. I had to push down the urge to come. "Is that so?"

"Dallas, I've just watched porn for three hours. I'm aching in a really good way and I need you to finish me."

Fuck.

I extracted myself from him, getting to my feet. A look of hurt and confusion crossed his face until I held out my hand. "Get up, and get your arse on the bed."

He grinned, and I helped him stand and followed him to our room. He stripped out of his clothes, revealing his very hard cock. Mine jerked in my briefs, dying to be free, dying for more touch, heat, and slick friction.

He sat on the bed at first, then lay down, but I pulled off my shirt and shook my head. "Roll over."

I got him comfortable with pillows under his hips to keep the pressure off his leg, and he raised his arse and stretched out like a cat. This was the old Justin. This was the pre-accident Justin who wanted to be fucked for hours, who begged for it and got pissy when he didn't get it.

"The fuck you waiting for?"

I chuckled, because that was him to a T. "Just enjoying the view," I replied. I pulled off my boots and took off my pants, finally joining him on the bed. I knelt between his spread legs and kneaded his arse cheeks. "How does your leg feel?"

I thought for a second he was going to spit some barb at me about taking too much time, but this was a serious question. His body, his injuries, and his recovery were a priority. "Feels good."

I ran my hand up the back of his thigh and he instinctively raised his hips. "Keep still, baby. Let me do the work."

He growled at that, but he stopped moving.

I ran my hands up his back and kissed one arse cheek, then the top of his crack.

"Dallas. I'm not kidding. Stop playing. I don't know how long I can lie like this."

Okay, I didn't really think of that. "Sorry, baby. Just trying to make it feel good." I spread his arse and licked my thumb before running it over his hole.

"Holy shit, yes," he hissed.

I reached over and took the lube from the bedside and poured some to slide down his crack. He let out a long breath, and I massaged his now-slick skin. I pressed a fingertip inside him and out again, making him moan.

"Dallas," he whispered hoarsely. "More."

So I gave him more. I pushed my finger in further, sliding it in and out, and he gripped the pillow above his head. "More."

I moved my finger in circles, stretching him a little, then added a second finger. Just two fingertips and he groaned with pleasure. I pushed them in deeper, slowly in and out. I brushed his prostate and he lifted his hips.

My cock was rock hard and leaking precome. So close to his hole, so close to where I wanted to be. But not today. Not yet.

I swiped his prostate again and I leaned my weight on his arse, as though it was my cock inside him, and I thrust my fingers in.

He bucked underneath me, crying out as he came. I thrust my fingers in a few more times, milking him as his orgasm took hold, but I needed my hand. I pulled out and gripped my own shaft, a few quick pumps, and I came so hard, shooting come onto his back.

Fucking hell. It was so intense, the room spun.

I collapsed on top of him, trying to be careful with his body, but too spent to move. My cock slid between his arse cheeks and he rolled his hips. "Just a bit lower," he whispered. "You could slide into me."

And I'd been going to ask him if he was okay. Clearly he was fine.

He rolled his hips again. "Just a little bit, Dallas. Please."

Christ almighty. I never could handle his begging. But I needed to prove to him what we had was more than physical. We needed to wait, and I had to be the strong one.

"Next time, baby."

He growled in frustration but he didn't push me. I wasn't sure I could have stopped myself if he did . . .

We lay like that for a few moments, catching our breath and enjoying the feeling of being close and naked. The full-body contact was bliss. But we were a mess, so I rolled off him and pulled him into my arms.

I kissed his forehead. "You feel okay?"

"Hmm." He was sleepy. "Yeah. Sorry for asking you to . . ."

I tightened my hold. "Don't apologise. I wanted to."

"You said next time."

I laughed and tucked him into my side, holding him tight. "You caught that, huh?"

"Sure did." He snuggled into me. "I wouldn't have minded. We got those rapid results back. And they were fine."

That was true. But still . . .

He shot back to look me in the eyes. There was hurt in his, and confusion. "Do you regret what we just did? Did you not want to do anything until—"

I cupped his face. "No, baby. Never. It was amazing and beautiful."

He sighed. "Good. 'Cause I'm not sorry. I have jizz smeared on my back, on my front, on the bed covers, on the pillows, and I'm not even remotely fucking sorry."

I laughed and pulled him against me, ending with a sigh. "I don't regret it, Juss. We were tested regularly before the accident. These tests were just to ease our minds, that's all. And like I said, the full results won't change how I feel about you. Not one thing."

He settled his head against my chest and was quiet for a long moment. "Did we do that before? I mean, me asking for you to . . . be inside me or something. Because it felt . . . familiar. I didn't remember anything, there was no flashbacks, but it felt . . . I dunno. Like my body knew what it wanted."

I gave him a squeeze. "Yeah, we did. A lot. You loved it when we'd stay like that."

"I came fast. I was thinking about it."

I chuckled. "Watching porn for a few hours had you kind of worked up."

"I'm gonna do it again tomorrow, just so you know. There's a lot of videos to get through."

I laughed again and was reminded that we were a sticky mess.

"Shower time. Then you can heat up leftovers for dinner and I'll remake the bed and put these in the wash."

I helped Juss off the bed and we showered together. Then he went to sort out dinner, and I stripped the bedding and set it going in the washing machine and remade the bed with clean linen. When I went back out to the kitchen, I noticed Juss' limp was more pronounced as he took the plates to the table.

"You okay? Is your leg sore?"

"Yeah, a bit. Just time for my pills, that's all." He managed a smile. "I feel good. Great, even. A little achy in all the right places, but in a good way."

That was true. It was time for his night-time pain pills, but still . . . "You'll tell me if something hurts or gets worse though, yeah?"

He rolled his eyes as he sat down. "Yes, I promise. I am achy and tired, because I've been freshly had. But I won't object if you want to have me again."

I chuckled as I ate my first mouthful of leftover meatloaf and mash. "Your body won't be thanking me tomorrow. You might be sorer in the morning."

He made a *maybe* face but shrugged. "On the bright side, we found a position that works."

Chapter Five

Two days later, all the insurance money had hit my account. I paid off all the credit cards and put a chunk on the overdraft, feeling like things were finally—finally—starting to be okay. It was one thing knowing the money troubles would be over soon, but it was a whole other thing to know it was *actually* over.

The bank account was looking pretty fat, Juss was more himself, and life was looking pretty damn good.

Until Davo came into work and handed me a folded copy of the *Times*. "Jusso's interview is on page three. There's a photo of the crash. Not sure if you want him to see it."

My stomach dropped. "Thanks, mate."

Davo gave a hard nod and went out and made a point of having a chat with Sparra and Juss, probably so I could have a quick look and decide how best to prepare Justin. He'd seen some insurance photos as part of the van claim, but nothing too graphic.

I turned to page three, my heart in my throat. There were two photos: one of Justin just a few days ago, and one of the mangled van. The photo of him was on his right side, getting a good look at the scar down his head. I remember Juss saying he wanted to get the name of the shop in it, and it was . . . but the photographer knew what he was doing. The picture emphasised his scar more than anything else.

The photo of the van was one the paper had run after the accident. The van was barely separated from the truck, the door was missing from where they'd obviously had to cut him out. It was . . . crumpled, smashed, barely recognisable. There was debris all over the wet road, glass, pieces of metal. It looked like a war zone.

God, it made me feel sick.

Then I read the article.

Memories Erased

Justin Keith's life changed forever on that rainy morning almost four months ago when the van he was driving was hit by a truck. Taken to John Hunter Hospital, he was rushed into surgery for a serious head injury, multiple broken bones and fractures to his skull.

Not that he remembered any of it.

Because a few days later when he woke up, Justin thought he was five years younger and still living in Darwin. He'd lost the last five years of his life. He had no memory of his job, his home, and no memory of the four-year relationship with his partner.

Justin was diagnosed with retrograde amnesia, a condition which affects memory. But it's more than that, Justin says.

"I didn't just lose the memories. I lost all the emotional connections from the last five years as well. I lost who I was and where I fit in. Where I belonged."

A motorbike mechanic by trade, Justin says getting back to work was paramount to his recovery. "I couldn't tell you who the Prime Minister is or who won the last five footy premierships or even where I lived. But I could pull a bike engine apart and put it back together again, no worries. I know bikes, and doing work that I knew by heart really helped remind me who I was."

Justin says he's limited by what he can do. "I can only do a few hours in the mornings, then it gets too much. My brain can't do what it used to, and my leg and arm don't work like they should. And I still have a lot of doctor appointments, and headaches are a constant part of my life now."

He's recovered a few memories, but only pieces. "Amnesia isn't like the movies. It's awful. I remember a few things, like flashes or random stuff. I feel robbed. My leg and arm will heal, but I've lost those memories, probably forever."

It hasn't been easy on his relationships. "I've been real lucky to have such good people in my life who've stuck by me." His smile brightens. "And I got to fall in love for the first time. Again. I don't remember the first time."

Traumatic brain injury is a leading cause of disability in Australia, with links to violence, homelessness and suicide. In fact, many people who suffer serious TBI end up in care homes or in long-term care, and there have been links to other cognitive degeneration in later years.

Investigations into the crash concluded it was an accident, and the matter was settled for an undisclosed amount.

"Nothing is like it was. Everything is different. But I'm alive and I have plans for the future, so maybe I'm one of the lucky ones."

I SWALLOWED hard as I considered what Justin had said. None of it was a surprise to me—I knew all of that—though I did smile at the falling in love again comment . . . But I had to wonder if the comment about the undisclosed amount was just a general wrap-up or if that smarmy reporter knew. At any rate, I'm glad no figure was noted.

Now I just had to break it to Justin. It wasn't like I could shield him from this, or even if I should. I was just weary of the fallout, how he would react, and if it might upset him and set him back a day or two.

I could hear the boys talking in the breakroom, laughing about the coffee machine or something. I picked up the newspaper and went in. Justin grinned when he saw me and pointed to my now-full coffee mug. He was playing barista today, apparently, which probably explained the laughter.

I held up the newspaper. "Your interview."

"Oh." His smile wavered and his eyes met mine. "Is it okay? Is something wrong?"

"No. There's just a photo of the van, after the crash, if you're ready to see it."

He stared at me for a long second, his eyes full of determination; then he gave a nod. "I'm ready."

He took the newspaper and sat at the table, and when he looked up, Davo had dragged Sparra out, leaving just me. I sat down beside him and waited.

Justin looked at the photo of the van. He shook his head like he couldn't believe it and chewed his bottom lip. I slid my hand over his and squeezed, just to let him know I was there. I wasn't going anywhere.

He nodded to let me know he was okay.

We didn't need to speak. We just knew.

"Wow," he whispered, staring at the photograph. "Was that what the van looked like? I don't remember it at all. Not before the accident, certainly not like that . . ." He let out a low breath. "Jesus."

"You okay?"

He nodded again, giving me a small smile. "Yeah. Not surprising I got messed up though, is it?"

I didn't want to say he was lucky, because telling him that, after all his injuries and memory loss, would be just insulting. "It could have been so much worse, Juss. We could have lost you that day."

Then he squeezed my hand and studied me for a second. "Are you okay? Seeing this picture?"

Him asking me that made me smile, but I looked at the photograph again. "I'm okay, baby. Just thankful I still have you."

He leaned over and gave me a soft kiss, then went back to the newspaper. "This photo's okay," he said, pointing to the picture of him. He smiled proudly. "Got the shop name in it."

It also got the huge scar that snaked down the side of his head, but I didn't say that. "He's cute."

He smiled again, then began to read the article. He didn't read too fast now, so I just held his hand, giving him all the time he needed.

He nodded when he was done and pushed the newspaper away. "Did it read okay?" he asked. "Did I sound okay? I know sometimes I don't talk great."

"Hey, baby, you were perfect," I replied, turning to face him and holding his hand in both of mine. "You sounded great, and you talk just fine. Don't worry about what anyone else thinks. You're doing better than the docs ever thought possible, so give yourself some credit, baby."

He made a face but conceded a smile. "You have to say that."

I snorted. "I don't *have* to say anything. I said it because it's true." I traced a line on his palm. "And you said you got to fall in love again."

His eyes met mine. "Because I did."

"I love you too, Juss."

"Well, I better get some work done," he said. He tried to smile but it didn't quite sit right.

"You sure you're okay?" I asked. "If you're mad or upset about the article or the photo, you can tell me."

He frowned. "I don't know how I feel about it," he admitted. And that was a good start. Last time he bottled stuff up, it messed with him for days. His brain couldn't handle the overthinking right now.

"That's okay, Juss. That's good. Take your time, think some more on it, and see how you feel," I suggested. "We can talk about it later."

He nodded, relieved. His smile was more genuine this time. "Thanks."

I stood and pulled him to his feet. He drank half his now-warm coffee and tipped the rest down the sink. I drank mine and followed him out to the workshop. Juss headed straight for Sparra—he was helping him with a Honda—and Davo gave me a nod to come over.

"How is he?" he asked.

"He's okay. Still not sure. He needs some time to think about it. But thanks for giving me the heads up about it first."

"No worries," he said.

We went about our work as per normal. It was busy: customers, the usual bookings, phone calls, suppliers. And when we stopped for smoko, Justin said he might, if it was all right with me, call it a day.

"Headache's not getting much better," he said.

"Yeah, of course," I replied. "Go on up and rest. I'll order some lunch in for everyone today and bring it up later."

He gave a nod and took the stairs one at a time, and I knew the newspaper article was playing on his mind.

"Is he okay?" Sparra asked. "He's been quiet this morning."

"Yeah. He'll be okay." I sighed. "But I feel like calling that fucking newspaper reporter dickhead and telling him to add this part of Justin's amnesia to his story. That some little interview piece for ratings will fuck Juss up for a day. How seeing that photograph would mess with the way his brain's wired. Stress and bullshit do a real number on him now."

"Yeah," Davo agreed. "He looked kinda spaced."

I nodded, and it got the better of me. "I might just go up and check on him." I got to the breakroom door. "Save me a Kingston."

I took the stairs two at a time and opened the door as quiet as I could. He wasn't on the couch, so I stuck my head around the bathroom door, but it was empty too. That left the bedroom. I peeked inside, and there he was in bed lying on his side, his boots on the floor, the covers pulled up, and Squish curled up at his stomach. Juss was stroking Squish's neck, his eyes almost closed.

"Hey, baby," I whispered as I came in. I sat beside him and put my hand on his arm. "You okay?"

"Just feel . . . awful."

I stroked his hair, feeling his forehead as I did. He didn't feel hot. "Can I get you your pills?"

"Nah. Just need some sleep. Tired. Headache. Same old."

I frowned, hating that this was his new normal. "Okay, I'll leave you to rest. I just wanted to make sure you were okay."

He slow blinked. "Didn't mean to make you worry."

I leaned down and kissed his temple. "I will always worry." I noticed his phone on the bedside. "Call me if you need anything."

His eyes closed and he hummed. "'Kay."

I gave Squish a pat too, and he purred louder. "Look after him, Squish. You're in charge."

The corner of Juss' mouth lifted, just a touch. And with another brush of Juss' hair, I left them both to sleep.

Work got busy for the next few hours, but I did remember to order some pizzas for lunch, for which Davo and Sparra were very grateful. I took some upstairs for Juss, not sure if he'd even be awake, but he was. He was on the couch now, changed out of his work gear and wearing trackies and a hoodie, though he was mostly hidden under a blanket. The TV wasn't on, but he was looking at something on his phone, and Squish, as always, was purring beside him.

"Pizza delivery," I said, putting the box next to him. "How are you feeling?"

He put his phone down. "Okay. Better. Drugs kicked in."

"Good." I knew his meds made him drowsy and spacey, but it had to be better than searing pain. I grabbed us a bottle of water each from the fridge and slid his next to the pizza box. I helped myself to a slice and sat at the other end of the couch. "Can I see you at least eat a piece?"

Justin rolled his eyes and let his head fall back onto the headrest, but he didn't say anything.

"What?" I asked with a smile. "You want to tell me to piss off?"

His gaze went to mine.

"You're allowed to be pissed off or frustrated with me," I added. "I know I'm pushy."

Juss sighed. "I don't mean it."

"I know." I took another bite of the pizza, chewed, and swallowed. "But those pills make you nauseous if you don't eat."

He sighed again, with more bite this time. "I'm not a kid."

"No, you're not."

He scowled at the wall for a bit, but his grumpy face softened. "Thank you for bringing me food."

I smiled at him. "You're welcome."

Now he pouted. "And thank you for checking up on me."

I stood up and, leaning down, kissed his forehead. "Any time. I'll leave you to rest."

"You don't have to go. I didn't mean to make you feel unwelcome."

"No, it's fine. I better get back down there and steal a piece of the Supreme before Davo eats it all." The truth was, I reckoned Juss would eat a piece or two of pizza and sleep hard for a few more hours yet. He was still tired. And I had work that needed doing. "Make sure Squish doesn't steal any pizza."

Juss managed half a smile before I got to the door, but I wasn't wrong in my prediction. He ate and slept a while longer, though he did come back down to the shop for a bit before closing time. He still wore his track pants and hoodie, but he found the broom and put it to work, keeping busy though mostly keeping to himself.

At knock-off time, Davo pulled the roller door down, the sound giving a metallic rumbling finality to the week. Thank God it was the weekend. "Hey, you still wanna grab a drink at the Arms tomorrow? It's all right if you wanna leave it."

"What's that?" Juss asked, overhearing.

Had I asked him this? I was going to, then we'd just got sidetracked. "Wanna meet the boys at the pub tomorrow? We can grab a feed and watch the footy. We don't have to stay long."

Juss, still holding the broom, looked from me to Davo and Sparra, then back to me. "Sure. Sounds good."

He was still a bit off. His expression was flat and his eyes didn't shine when he smiled. The boys probably thought it was just the meds, if they noticed it at all, but I knew him.

He had something on his mind, something was bothering him and weighing him down. I was certain it was that damn photograph, and I was so grateful it was closing time on a Friday so me and him could just chill out on the couch and talk.

"See ya's tomorrow at four," I said, waving Davo and Sparra off.

"It's your shout, remember?" Sparra called back with a grin.

I laughed. "I haven't forgotten." I locked the gate behind them and went back into the workshop, ready to close everything down. "Thank God it's the weekend."

Juss walked right up to me and into a hug. I held him warm and tight, rubbed his back, and kissed his head. "You ready to go upstairs?" I murmured.

He nodded. "Yeah."

I closed my office door, and when I went to shut the break-room door, I noticed the damn newspaper. I picked it up and aimed it for the bin, but Juss stopped me. "No, keep it."

"You sure?"

He nodded again. "I dunno what for. Just don't want to throw it out."

I frowned but wasn't about to argue. "Okay then, let's go home."

That made him smile. "Sounds good."

I turned everything off and made sure everything was locked, and we went upstairs. Justin went to the kitchen and leaned against the counter, his arms folded. Then he went through the fridge, not finding what he wanted, then he put the kettle on, and then he cleared off the table before he straightened up the couch cushions.

"Baby, what's wrong?"

He stopped and leaned against the back of the couch and folded his arms again. Then he shoved his hands in the pockets of his hoodie, and when that wasn't right, he folded his arms again. I went to him and unpeeled his arm away and held his hand.

"Was it the photograph?"

He looked away and squinted. "Not really. A bit, but . . ."

I put my hand to his cheek and gently turned him so he'd look at me. "Then what is it?"

"What he said, at the end."

I tried to remember . . . "The undisclosed amount of money?"

He shook his head. "No. The part about the brain injuries." When it was clear I couldn't remember, he frowned. "The part where he said that people like me end up in a home."

Wait, what? "Juss, I don't . . ."

He went to the table where I'd put the newspaper and found the article. "Here. 'Traumatic brain injury is a leading cause of disability in Australia, with links to violence, homelessness, and suicide. In fact, many people who suffer serious TBI end up in care homes or in long-term care, and there have been links to other cognitive degeneration in later years.'" He looked at me. "Did you not read that part?"

"I did, but I . . ." I shook my head, flustered. "I didn't apply it to you. I just read it as statistics for the article. I . . . I should have taken more notice. Sorry."

He stared, bewildered and stunned. "How does it not apply to me? Dallas, how does that not apply to me?"

"Because it doesn't. I dunno! I would never let you get put into a care home. Jesus, Justin. Never."

"But you can't say that. Because you don't know."

"I do know that." I went to him and cupped his face. "I wouldn't."

He chewed on his bottom lip. "I know. It's just . . ." He sighed. "This afternoon, since I read that article, I've been reading up on the long-term effects of TBI. What it will mean for me when I'm fifty, sixty. It's not good, Dallas. I'll be more prone to dementia or stroke. My brain is . . . damaged."

I lifted his chin so he'd look into my eyes. "You listen to me. Your brain is part of you, who you are. I love *all* of you. And I promise you, Justin, I will love you at fifty and sixty, seventy, or one hundred, God willing. There are no guarantees what will happen between now and then. Hell, something could happen to me next week."

"Dallas . . ."

"No. Justin, no. There are no guarantees. And it doesn't matter to me if you have some long-term effects. It won't ever change how I feel about you. If things got worse or bad and I couldn't look after you like you needed, I'd hire someone to help me. But I wouldn't send you away."

"Didn't you hear what I said?"

"What?"

"Dementia, Dallas," he said with tears in his eyes. "Dementia! What if I can't remember you again? You can't go through that again. I saw how much it hurt you, how the light left your eyes when I didn't know who you were. Knowing that might happen again just kills me. It fucking kills me."

Oh no, no, no . . .

"Baby, we'll get through it. If and when that ever happens, we'll deal with it. But we can't worry about that now. If we have thirty years before we need to start dealing with that shit, then let's make the most out of those thirty years. Let's not waste a minute worrying about something that might not ever happen."

"I don't want to get dementia," he said, letting his tears fall. "I don't want to lose my memories again. I've lost enough. I've lost—" He couldn't speak for crying.

I pulled him into my arms and let him cry. He needed to cry for everything he'd lost, for everything that had been taken from him. To grieve for what was gone and in fear of what his future might hold. When he'd caught his breath, I kissed the side of his head. "Sweetheart, who knows what medical advancements they'll have in twenty or thirty years. You don't have to worry about it now, my love. And even if it is something we need to deal with, we'll deal with it together." I held him a little tighter and rubbed his back. "I'm sorry I didn't pick up on that part of the newspaper article."

He pulled back a little, his face still downcast, his eyes red and puffy. "I just started to think of the future, ya know? I hadn't thought about anything past the next few minutes in so long, like

I'd forgotten the future was even a thing. Then you mentioned it the other day. You said it sounded like I was starting to think of the future, and I was. And now I find out that my future's been taken away too." His bottom lip trembled. "It's not fair."

"I know it's not. It isn't fair, and it shouldn't have happened to you. I hate that it happened to you. But I promise we'll work it out. Whatever life throws at us, we'll tackle it together."

He nestled his head against my chest. "I couldn't do this without you."

"And I couldn't do it without you, Juss. So we're even."

"Yes, you could. You'd cope all right. Me, on the other hand . . . I wouldn't have a home or a job. I couldn't get anywhere or do anything. I can't even go to the supermarket without needing a nap afterwards."

"Baby, you don't ever have to worry about being without me, okay?"

He didn't reply.

"Hey," I said. "You wanna know what real love is?"

"What's that?" he mumbled into my chest.

"Real love is hard. And sometimes it hurts. Sometimes we need to change what was our normal course and take a different path. Sometimes everything we knew becomes something different, and we need to adapt. There might be medical appointments and we might have to change the way we shop for groceries or if we go out for lunch. But that's just what we do because that's what love is. It's not all roses and sunshine. It's laundry and dishes, bills and mortgages, and wet towels on the floor, or changing the cat litter. We adapt and we roll with it. So all these changes that we've had to deal with because of the accident, I don't mind one bit, Juss. Because when I fell in love with you, it was forever. In health and in sickness, or however that goes."

He chuckled, just for a half a second, then sniffled into my shirt.

"And you wanna know what else love is?" I went on. "It's amazing and wonderful. It gives me strength and hope, and it makes me realise there's more to my life than just me. Falling in love with you, Juss, was the single best thing to ever happen to me. Ever. I was feeling kinda lost until you came into my life."

He pulled back and lifted his head to look at me. "You were?"

I nodded. "Yep. Work kept me busy for a long time, but I'd meet guys who were just not right for me. They were either all about fitness or money or partying, and I wasn't interested. Then you came along, perfect in every way for me." Then I gave him a wink. "Except the fact you were a Knights supporter. But I forgive you for that."

He finally smiled. Finally.

"What I'm trying to say, Juss, is that love has its ups and downs. But you and me, we got this. We found each other years ago, and when the universe tried to pull us apart with the accident, we found each other again."

He got a little teary again, but he still smiled. "I love you so much," he whispered.

I kissed him softly. "I know."

Chapter Six

Juss was adamant about going out to the pub with the guys. After our talk about the possibility of him getting dementia when he was older, we'd had dinner and spent the night snuggled up on the couch with Juss as the little spoon. I'd watched the footy, but Juss rolled over and faced me, snuggled into my chest for most of the game. He dozed on and off, but clearly, his day of anguish had taken its toll.

We'd gone to bed after that and he'd slept right through, so he'd woken up feeling better. I mean, he was still his usual grouchy-morning self, but he was feeling less insecure about his future.

Which was why he was adamant we go out with the guys. He wanted to enjoy all that he could now. Like I'd said last night, we should make the most of every minute of every day, and going out and being sociable, even for a little while, gave him a real sense of normalcy. So after breakfast and showers, we went downstairs to get some odds and ends done in the office, and overall it was a productive morning, without overdoing it. Juss even wanted to go back upstairs and rest for a bit before we went so he wouldn't be too tired.

"Because it's what we do now," he said with a fond smile and a roll of his eyes.

I grinned at him using my words against me. "It sure is."

So while he dozed off for a bit, I got some laundry done and cleaned the bathroom, doing all that boring housework stuff that needed doing. I didn't mind doing it all now because I had every intention of coming home when we left the pub and spending the entire night as the big spoon on the couch again.

I wanted to do that every night for the rest of my life.

Just me and Juss, forever.

I refused to believe that he'd end up with dementia or some other degenerative disease. Okay, so maybe not *refused to believe*. Because I did believe that shit was possible. But I refused to live in fear of it. I didn't want it to rob us of *now*, with worry and fear. I didn't want him stressing over something that was possibly decades away.

This whole thing had taught me to appreciate every second of *now*.

I thought he might have a change of heart as we were getting ready to go, but if anything, he was more excited. He even put on a pair of jeans for the first time since his accident. I had to help him get his foot through the leg hole, but he smiled when he got them done up. "Feel fancy," he said as he buttoned up his shirt. "Been a while since I wore anything but trackies and work pants."

I looked at his reflection. "You look great."

He smiled back at me. "So do you. I've seen photos of you all dressed up, but I've never seen you . . . I mean, I don't remember it."

Jeans and a button-down shirt were hardly dressed up, but I guess to him it was when the only outfits he could remember were tracksuits and dirty work clothes. "My jeans are feeling a little tight, not gonna lie."

I turned to check out my backside in the mirror and was reminded of all the running I hadn't done in the last three months. Justin looked down at my legs and raked his eyes up my body. "Yeah, no. I reckon you fill them out just right."

I laughed and gave him a quick kiss before I pulled on my boots, helped Juss with his, and grabbed our coats. I took the cane, which lived behind the front door, and Juss sighed but didn't say anything. Squish was curled up on Juss' blanket on the couch, so we left him in charge and made our way to the pub.

It was a quick drive, though when we got there, the car park was almost full and the walk to the pub was uneven. I handed him the walking cane, and he took it with a roll of his eyes. "I hate this," he grumbled.

"You'd hate tripping or injuring your leg even more," I replied. He took a few steps with it. "Does it hurt your arm to use it?"

"Nah. It's okay. If I was sitting on the ground, I wouldn't like to have to use my arm to get up, like to take all my weight, but like this it isn't too bad." He actually walked pretty good with the cane. He wasn't gonna win any gold medals in a speed-walking contest, but that was okay with me.

I held the door for him and he gave me a cute smile as he walked in. "Thank you," he said.

"You're welcome," I whispered back. I followed him, and once we were in the main bar area, he stopped.

"Do you know where they are?"

It occurred to me then that he had no memory of this place. He'd been here many times, but he'd lost all that. "There's a bar out the back with tables and seats and a huge screen for the footy."

"Ah." He turned to the end of the bar area but didn't move.

"This way," I said, leading the way. It was busy. Not overcrowded but enough that people edged out of Justin's way when they saw him with the cane to give him room to walk through.

Sure enough, Davo and Lauren and Sparra and his new girlfriend were seated at a round table with two spare seats. Davo gave us a wave when he saw us. "Hey," he said. "Was wondering where you two were."

"We're not even late," I said.

"Footy's about to start."

In about an hour, but whatever. "Then I better get to the bar," I said, grinning. I said hello to Lauren and smiled at the new face. "Hi."

Sparra stood up. He'd obviously put an effort into his appearance, and he even looked a little nervous. "Dallas, this is Carissa. And Justin. Carissa, my girlfriend." He just about beamed at the word.

Carissa was short and curvy, with pastel pink hair and a stud in her nose. She had huge blue eyes and a killer smile. She stood and shook our hands. "Nice to meet you. Tony talks about you all the time."

"Nice to meet you too," I replied.

"Tony?" Justin asked. "Oh, Sparra's real name. I forgot, sorry. What the hell kind of name is Tony?"

They all laughed, and I pulled out the seat next to Sparra for Juss and he sat down, hanging the cane handle over the edge of the table. "Okay, it's my shout. What are we having?"

I took their orders and made my way to the bar, ordering for everyone. It was probably long overdue that I shouted these guys a few drinks. I tucked some menus under my arm and carried the tray of drinks back to the table. I got two Carlton Zeros for me and Juss. It was non-alcoholic but it looked and tasted like a beer, and I hoped it made Juss feel like he wasn't missing out.

He took the bottle and shot me a look before reading the label. He gave it a sceptical once over, then took a sip. "I haven't had beer in . . . well, I can't remember having a beer in five years, and this actually tastes pretty good."

Sparra clinked his bottle to Juss' and said, "Cheers, mate. And it's good to have you here."

I sat between Juss and Davo and we chatted about the menus, and once everyone had decided, I went to the bistro counter and ordered and paid for that too.

"You don't have to do that," Davo said. He'd come with me to the service counter to collect the cutlery and condiments.

"I know. I want to. As thanks for what you and Sparra have done, but also as a bit of a celebration. This is Juss' first time going out somewhere for a meal. Like to a restaurant type thing and to watch the footy. He usually falls asleep on the couch watching with me at home."

"I wasn't sure if you'd be here, given he didn't have a real good day yesterday."

"Yeah, he's okay. He's just no good if he bottles stuff up. His brain trips a circuit if he gets stressed. But we talked it out and he slept it off."

"Good." Then Davo nudged me. "Have you ever seen Sparra scrubbed up like that? He's on his best behaviour. Showered and shaved and everything."

I chuckled. "Ah, bless him. She seems nice."

"He's a goner already," Davo said. "Smitten kitten."

I snorted. "How's Lauren? Keeping you in line, no doubt."

"She's great. She's, uh . . ." He looked around, still holding a bunch of forks. "She's pregnant. Six weeks. Don't tell anyone. I'm not supposed to tell anyone."

Holy shit. "Oh my God, Davo," I tried to whisper. "That is such good news. The best news."

He nodded, his smile proud. "Yeah, we're pretty happy."

I could see that. Man, that was just the kind of news we needed. Something wonderful to look forward to. "I'm really happy for you. And if you need any time off for appointments or whatever it is—" I waved a wad of serviettes. "—they do. You just say the word."

He looked back over to the table, where Lauren was watching us. She sipped her lemonade, and with a smile, she shook her head. She knew he was telling me. I laughed and gave him a nudge. "You're in trouble now."

Davo hadn't stopped smiling yet. "Always."

We went back to our table and we finished our meals just before the footy started. "I better get some more drinks," I said. "Juss, you want another or something else?"

"Yeah, I'll have another one of these," he said, draining the last of his bottle. He was all smiles and laughter, no alcohol required. He was just happy to be out and socialising with his friends. And it didn't help that Carissa was also a Knights supporter.

My God, it made me happy to see him smiling like that.

And we watched the footy, and we laughed like we hadn't in months. But it was loud and busy, and I could see Juss was getting tired. The noise had to be killing his head. I squeezed his thigh. "You ready to go?"

He gave me a nod. "Need to pee first." He looked around. "Where's the loo?"

I gave him his cane. "It's just through those double doors on your left." There was a small step into the bathrooms . . . "You know, I can show you."

"I got him," Sparra said. "Need to go shake a leg anyway."

They walked off and I watched, of course. "He'll be fine," Davo said.

"Can't help it," I admitted. If he fell or got dizzy . . .

"He looks good, Dallas," Lauren said. "Dave's been keeping me up to date with how he's going. Bit scary there for a while, huh?"

"Frightening," I agreed. "But he's getting better every day."

"And his memory?" she asked, hopeful.

I shook my head. "Not much, snippets here and there. Nothing new this week. He can't remember this place at all."

She frowned. "I can't even imagine."

"To be honest, neither can I. I dunno what I'd do if it were me in his shoes," I admitted.

"You'd be right where he is, only it'd be him looking after you," Davo said. "No questions asked."

I almost smiled. "Probably. You should have seen his face when I told him I'm a Bulldog supporter. He was horrified."

They were still laughing when Sparra and Juss came back. Juss didn't sit down, so I stood. "You ready?"

He nodded and slow blinked. But he gave them a smiley wave. "I gotta tap out," he said. He smiled to Carissa and Lauren. "Nice to meet you. And I'll see you boys at work."

After a round of goodbyes, we made our way back out through the bar. Juss was leaning on the cane more, evidence of his tiredness. "Wanna stay here and I'll bring the ute closer?"

"Nah," he said, still smiling. We made our way through the car park, real slow and steady, until we reached the ute. I opened his door for him and helped him get in, then got into my seat and helped him do up his seatbelt. "Had a real good day, Dall."

I leaned over the console and gave him a quick kiss. "Me too, baby."

He was asleep before we got out of the car park, and when we got home, he was too drowsy to climb the stairs. "I'll carry you," I said, helping him out of the car.

"Mm," he said, clinging to my neck. "This way."

"Okay, hold on," I said, then put my hands on his arse and hoisted him up onto my hips, like a front-ways piggyback. "You gotta hold on, baby."

He used his left arm to hold the back of my neck, but his right arm wasn't much good, and his left leg went around me, but I had to be careful of his right leg. It wasn't exactly easy, but step by step, I got him up the stairs and through the door. Except when I went to put his feet on the floor, he snuggled his face into my neck, hung on tighter, and refused to get down.

I thought about setting his arse on the kitchen counter, because it was closer, and then the couch, but it was too low. So I walked him into our room and gently lowered him onto the bed. He pulled me down with him and I had to be careful not to land on his leg or bump his head.

He was all smiles, his eyes closed, and he hooked his left leg around me and locked me on top of him. I was going to say something or kiss him or laugh, but he was already asleep.

JUSS WAS PRETTY WIPED for most of Sunday. I did a groceries run in the morning and we took a drive in the afternoon to the beach to soak up some rays. He took his scooter because the pathways at the beach were long-and-wide smooth concrete.

Justin opted for shorts because his legs were paler than pale, and spring was coming to Newcastle so the sun was warm, but I threw in a hoodie because the breeze off the Pacific still had some bite.

He didn't care if people saw the scars on his leg. The fact he used a mobility scooter and had a huge scar down the side of his head kept them staring enough. But he was still in a good mood from yesterday.

"What have we got on this week?" he asked.

We were lying on a blanket on the grass before the sand, staring up at the bluest sky, holding hands. "Just a workday tomorrow, but Tuesday we have your physio appointment and then your session with Doctor Chang. We have to be there by eight. We can go out for breakfast before if you want, have some fancy eggs benny. Or after."

"Sounds good."

"Rest of the week is pretty normal. You got that scan next week though."

He smiled at me before he turned back to the sky. "I hate that MRI machine. And they inject me with that stuff."

"Just think, you've got this next scan appointment, then you've only gotta go in every two weeks instead."

"Thank God."

"And no more scans for another three months." It was hard to believe it had been three months already . . .

He was quiet for a bit. "They say six months is about the cut-off," he said. "For memories to come back. If they haven't come back by then, chances are they're not coming back."

I squeezed his hand. "I wish I knew what to say, Juss. I know you want them back, and I hate that they were taken away. But we get to make new ones."

"Like this? Lying here, holding hands, and staring at the sky?"

"Yep."

"Is this like date number six or something? I think I've lost count."

"We can go back to one if you want. Dinner, candles, a movie."

He chuckled. "No. No more back-to-square-one bullshit. We can go with date number six, right?"

"Hell yes, we can." I laughed. "We can do that tonight if you want. I bought steak for dinner. I'll let you pick the movie."

"Something funny."

"*Deadpool*."

"Dead-what?"

I laughed. "Oh, baby. You are in for a treat."

WE ARRIVED at Justin's physio appointment on Tuesday morning with his cane in hand. He wasn't a fan of it, but it was easier to use and he was far more mobile now. This would also be his last weekly physio appointment, moving into the fortnightly slots with his other appointments. His MRI scheduled for next week meant no physio and Juss wasn't mad about missing it. He did all his exercises regularly, and physically, he was doing great.

Doctor Chang was her usual happy self, pleased with all of Justin's progress. He'd had no new memories this week, and she reassured us that that didn't mean Justin wouldn't recover any memories ever again. His focus was improving and his cognitive connections were too. Overall, he was improving every day. He told her about the newspaper article and how the insurance was a relief. Then he mentioned what he'd read online about the likelihood of getting dementia, and with a reassuring smile, Doctor Chang had discussed medical research and reassured him with facts and statistics.

He was relieved; I could tell by the set of his shoulders. When we sat at the café and ordered our brunch, I gave his hand a squeeze. "Feeling better now?"

He smiled but rolled his eyes. "Yes, but it's still not fair that you know everything I'm thinking just by looking at me."

I laughed. "Wanna know what else I know?"

"What's that?"

"That it's been a week. We should be getting our full clinic test results back today or tomorrow."

His smile widened and his left eyebrow shot up. "Now that *is* good news. Well, if we get a green light, it's good news. If they tell me I need more tests and I need to wait longer, then that will be bad news, and . . ." His eyes shot to mine, panicked. "Dall, what if they tell me—"

I squeezed his hand firmly. "Then we do whatever they tell us to do, and if we have to wait, we wait." I gave him a nudge. "Not that we've exactly abstained anyway. And the rapid testing is usually the only tests a lot of people do. We were just being extra cautious."

He hummed as he sipped his decaf, then cleared his throat and shifted in his seat. "Do you think the mail will have been delivered by now?"

I chuckled and checked my watch. "Yep."

Juss looked around for the waitress. "Where the hell is our food?"

I laughed, and admittedly, we ate our meals pretty quick. I managed not to speed on the way home, though my mind was now on one thing . . .

We were only a block from the shop when my phone rang. The call from work came through my Bluetooth. "Hello?" I answered.

"Hey, Dall." It was Davo. "How far away are you?"

"Just around the corner. Why?"

"Someone's here to see Jusso. Pretty sure he's not gonna like it."

I frowned and Juss looked at me, worried. *What the fuck?* "Davo, we're just pulling in." I ended the call and turned into the shop, driving around the back. There was an old silver car in the customer parking, but I didn't recognise it.

I pulled up around the back and helped Juss out of the ute. Davo met us at the roller door. "I'm sorry," he said. "I didn't know what to say. She's in the breakroom and wouldn't leave until you got back."

She . . .

We went inside, Juss using his cane and me close by his side. And sure enough, like a bad, bad dream, sat the one person who could topple everything. With her emotionless eyes and forced smile, the bitch didn't even stand up.

Juss froze. "Mum?"

Chapter Seven

"WHAT ARE YOU DOING HERE?" Juss asked warily. He was barely in the doorway, a safe distance from his mother. Janet had short dark-brown greying hair, hard eyes, and her lips were pressed into a constant thin line. She wore some hideous grey tracksuit pants and white sneakers that looked plastic. Her sweater was pink, and also hideous, but the look on her face . . . her contempt made her fake smile a sneer.

"Thought I'd come and see you. Rebecca told me about the accident." She looked him up and down, giving the walking cane a once over. "You seem okay now."

I bristled, and maybe I growled because both Juss and his mother looked at me. I was too angry to speak.

"I see you're still . . . ," she said, waving her hand to the both of us, her fake smile tight and uneasy.

"Still gay, still together," I bit out. "Shall we just go with whichever one you hate the most?"

She sneered, but Juss put his hand on my arm. "I got this."

She shot me a satisfied smirk, and I wanted to pull her off that chair and throw her the fuck out of my shop.

Juss limped in and pulled out a chair. He gently lowered himself into it and kept his cane between his legs. I stood in the doorway with my arms crossed, and Justin smiled up at me before patting the chair next to him. "Sit with me, Dall."

Janet's smirk died, and at least *that* made me smile. Juss turned back to his mother. "I'm still not sure what you're doing here," he said. "The accident was three months ago."

"Becca said you needed time to recover," she said, as if that was a justifiable excuse.

"I almost died," he said, turning his head and pointing to his scar. "It's called traumatic brain injury. I was in hospital for weeks and you never even called."

"I know we didn't leave on very good terms last time," she began.

"Justin doesn't remember the last time we saw you," I explained. "But I do. I remember the names you called him, the names you called me. I remember how you told us we were going to hell and how disgusting we are. He doesn't remember." I poked my finger into my chest. "But I fucking do."

Juss frowned at me. "You said she didn't say nice things. Is that what she said?"

I shook my head. "I didn't want to upset you. And I'm sorry, Juss."

She pursed her lips and sniffed. "I was angry. And I didn't say it like that."

I stared at her, stunned that she'd deny it.

"I remember when you told me those things when I came out, and again before I moved to Darwin," Juss said. "So if Dallas says that's what you said another time, then I believe him."

She cleared her throat and spoke like she didn't care about what Justin had just said. "Well, I was hoping we could get past that."

I realised then what she was doing here. Or, more to the point, *why* she was here.

"Jesus fucking Christ," I said, disgusted. "I want you to leave."

She shot me an affronted look. "I'm allowed to speak to my son."

I ignored her and turned to Justin. "Juss, she wants your money."

"My what?" he asked quietly.

"Your money. She read the newspaper article that said there was an undisclosed sum of money from the insurance. That's why she's here."

Juss stared at me, his eyes wide with shock and sadness. He was already tired, and now this was gonna send him into a spin. I could see it in his eyes.

He turned to her and the bitch didn't even try to dispute it. "I just thought we could chat, Jussy."

I fucking bristled again. "Don't even fucking start, and get the fuck out of my shop."

"You can't make me leave. I'm allowed to talk to my son."

"You didn't want to speak to him in the last five years or the two years before that. Or before that. Or when he was lying in a hospital bed, close to dying. Where were you for any of his surgeries or physiotherapy or his weekly medical appointments?" My hands were clenched into fists. I wanted to say this was my shop and if I was so inclined to drag her out by her ear, I fucking would. But I didn't say that. Instead, I said, "So what makes you think he wants to speak to you now?"

Janet glared at me, then that sneer was back. "So you've got your grubby hands on it. You took control of his money, didn't you?"

"Absolutely not," I said, trying to keep my cool. "Justin has full control of all his finances."

"Stop fighting," Juss whispered.

That stopped me cold, and I looked him over. He was pale and his eyelids were heavy. "Sorry, Juss," I mumbled, taking his arm. "You need to lie down. And to take some meds. I'm sorry, baby. Let's get you upstairs."

"Jussy," Janet began, but not out of concern. God, this woman was the worst.

"The money is for me," Juss said quietly. "To pay for a nursing home or a care place in twenty years when the brain damage gets worse, so Dallas doesn't have to look after me anymore."

I stared at him; my heart dropped to my feet. "What? Justin, no. I told you that won't happen. Doctor Chang said this morning—"

"But what if it does? There's a chance it will." He shrugged and looked so damn sad. Then he turned back to his mother, his speech slow. "I have trouble with my brain and will have medical . . . things for the rest of my life."

She paused a long moment, thinking. "So there is money . . ."

"I need to go," Juss whispered, turning to me.

"And I need to talk to you," she snapped back.

I glared at her. "You need to leave."

She shot to her feet and thumped her fist on the table. "Justin, you owe me! I raised you, you cost me—"

I stood as well and yelled over the top of her. "How dare you!"

She flinched but then raised her finger at me. "I'll have a lawyer—"

Justin got to his feet. "Get out!"

She stared, and I did too. I'd never heard Justin yell. Ever.

"I said get out," he repeated, louder this time. "Get out, get out, get out!" He screamed at her, and she took a step back. "Get out!" Justin threw his walking cane at her like a javelin. It missed her head and clanged against the wall behind her, but the message he gave was a direct hit.

Flustered and shaken, she clutched at her handbag and stammered threats of calling the cops as she scurried out the door. She was still yelling obscenities as she walked to her car, as Davo and Sparra stood, staring, open-mouthed.

But Juss . . . he was pale and sweating as he put his hand to his head and swayed on his feet. I caught him before he fell and swept him up in my arms. "I'll get you upstairs, baby."

There was no resistance in him, no reaction, no . . . anything.

I carried him up the stairs and, inside, took him straight to bed. I pulled his shoes off and drew the doona over him, and his only reaction was to put the heel of his hand to the side of his head.

Fuck his mother to hell.

I ran and got his meds and had to help him sit up to sip the water to wash the tablets down. Just like those first days in hospital, he was listless, docile. He fell back onto the mattress, rolled onto his side, curled in on himself, and slowly closed his eyes.

"Sleep, baby," I whispered, tucking the doona in around him and kissing his head. Those meds would knock him out for a while, but I still stayed there for a few minutes watching the even rise and fall of his chest. Squish jumped up on the bed and padded over to his favourite human and snuggled into Juss' side.

Then I remembered Justin's mother and wondered if she'd left yet. I hoped she hadn't, so I could go vent my rage at her. Leaving Juss asleep, I went back down to the shop to find her, unfortunately, gone.

Davo and Sparra came straight over. "Is he okay?" Sparra asked. "Saw you carryin' him upstairs. He didn't look too good."

I shook my head. I had too many emotions coursing through me right then to speak.

"What the fuck was her problem?" Davo said. "Soon as she got here, she walked in all high and mighty, asking for Jusso. I told her you weren't here, and she didn't believe me at first. I said you were both at some medical appointment but I didn't think you'd be too far away, so she just sat in the breakroom and refused to leave. Said she'd wait."

I clawed my hands, imagining them around her throat. "Ever wanted to snap someone's fucking neck?" I asked.

They both stared.

"That fucking piece of shit," I sneered. "She wants the money. She demanded he pay her, said he owes her for raising him."

"Oh, fuck that," Davo said, shaking his head.

"I wanna kick the shit out of something," I admitted, still so fucking cranky. "Juss lost his shit. He went off his head, threw his cane at her."

"We heard," Sparra said.

I shook my head. "He can't handle that kind of stress. He just fucking zoned out after, like he was those first days after the accident. I reckon the pain in his head's at a ten right now."

"Did he take his pills?" Davo asked.

I nodded, finally taking in a deep breath and calmed down a notch. "He'll be out for a while. But it's not good."

Sparra patted my shoulder. "You feeling all right?"

I nodded, then shook my head. "Dunno how I feel. Like I wanna strangle his mother. She read the newspaper article. about him getting some money. Which he thinks he needs to put aside for twenty years' time when his brain damage gets worse and he needs to go into a nursing home."

"What?" Davo asked.

I shook my head and waved my hand. "Nothing. He read some medical research piece about people who have a brain injury and what happens to them later in life. He's been stressed about that. And then she turns up. Of all people, on all the days. The piece-of-shit mother who disowned him and called him . . . horrible things."

"Well, fuck her," Davo said. "I hope she comes back. She won't get near him next time, I promise ya."

Sparra made a face. "Well, she won't be coming back for a few days. Not in that car."

"Why not?" Davo asked.

"She's gonna have two flat tyres in the next twelve or so hours." He shrugged. "She'll be fine getting home, but when she goes out to get in her car tomorrow morning, she'll have a little surprise. She really should check her valve stems more often."

Davo's mouth fell open. "You didn't? When she started yellin' and you disappeared? That's where you went?"

He sighed. "Of course not."

Of course, yes.

I should have reprimanded him, but all I could do was laugh. A stressed, relieved, teary laugh.

Sparra grinned. "And they were perfectly inflated when she left here. and there were no embedded nails or punctures. They'll just slowly go down over the next day or so. She can't say shit."

I let out a sigh and scrubbed a hand over my face. "I still can't believe the hide of that woman."

"She was ranting about calling the cops when she left," Davo said. "Do you reckon she will?"

I shrugged. "And tell them what?"

"That Jusso threw his cane at her."

"It didn't hit her, as much as I wish it did," I replied. "But I hope she does call the cops. They'll love to hear how she kicked him out, called him a bunch of names, and the only time she made any effort to see him was to demand money. After he's had an accident that fucked up his entire life." God, it just made me so fucking angry. "I hope she does. I'd love to see her one more time."

"God, then you *would* end up in jail," Davo said.

"And you wouldn't be able to see Jusso," Sparra added. "So, no homicide, thanks."

I sighed again, long and loud. "Yeah, I better just go up and check on him," I said. "Then I'll come straight back down. We've got three jobs in today, right?"

Davo gave me a nod. "Just do what you can do, mate. Don't stress, we'll get it done."

Of course, just then the phone rang and Davo took the cordless out of his pocket. It was another booking for later in the week, and he walked off toward the office with the phone to his ear. Sparra gave me a kind, sympathetic smile. "Go and check on him," he said.

I didn't need telling twice. I took the stairs two at a time and went inside. Juss and Squish hadn't moved at all. Though Squish opened one eye at my arrival, Justin never even stirred. His breathing was deep and even, and I didn't dare wake him. He needed to sleep, to give his brain some recovery time.

I set a bottle of water on his bedside and went back to work. I checked on him again every hour, but he slept. He'd changed positions, rolled over and upset the cat, but he never woke.

By four o'clock we'd signed off on all three jobs, and Justin still hadn't woken up. I was doing my best not to worry, but that was going about as well as could be expected.

"We've got two Suzukis in tomorrow and an ATV, first thing," I said as we were finishing up. "I don't reckon Justin will be working, but I should be."

Davo gave me a nod. "Just go, Dall. We'll lock up."

"You sure?"

Sparra nodded. "We're done here anyway. See ya in the mornin'. Tell Jusso I hope he's feeling better."

"I will. Thanks, guys."

I heard the roller door going down as I climbed the stairs, more thankful for those two guys with each step. And I'd tell them that tomorrow. But I just needed Juss to be okay first. He was still in bed, though his eyes were open.

He was on his side facing the middle of the bed, so I lay down beside him, with my head on the pillow. "Hey," I whispered.

He slow blinked, expressionless. It took him a long moment to speak and when he did, his voice was quiet and slow. "Tired."

"It's okay, baby. You can sleep."

He sighed and closed his eyes and, just like that, was back in the land of nod. He'd had a shit day, stressed to the max, a blinding headache, and the pills he took usually put him on his arse, so I didn't mind. If he needed to sleep, then I wouldn't argue.

At least he'd been awake momentarily, and he'd spoken. That was good enough for me.

But then he slept all night through and he didn't cling to me like he usually did. He just stayed on his side, curled up, sound asleep. And in the morning, I could barely rouse him. He was sluggish and cranky like he was every morning, but it just didn't feel right. If he needed to rest all day, I wouldn't mind, but something wasn't right.

I got him out of bed and helped him to the couch and he just curled up there instead. I made him his decaf coffee and a piece of toast, knelt in front of him.

"Take a bite for me?" I asked. "I made coffee, but did you want a juice instead?"

He didn't reply, just closed his eyes. So I put the blanket over him and left his breakfast in front of him on the coffee table and went for a quick shower. When I came back out, he hadn't moved. But his eyes were half-open, though he stared into space.

I knelt in front of him again. "Juss, can you look at me?"

His eye movement was slow, but he did look at me. All that

stared back at me was a familiar blankness. His right eyelid drooped a little.

My stomach felt queasy. A cold shiver ran down my scalp and all the way down my spine.

This wasn't good. Something was wrong. Sure, in the past if he'd had a big day, it took him a day to recover, but this felt . . . like something else. Something much worse.

Like all Justin's progress, his recovery, every step forward he'd taken was gone.

"Juss, can you open your mouth for me? Show me your teeth," I said, trying to remember what to ask to check for a stroke. "Juss?"

Nothing. He was just blank.

I didn't know what to do. I wasn't trained to deal with this or to know how to react. So I called the only person who I knew would be able to help. It was early, I knew I'd only get a message bank, but they'd get back to me as soon as possible.

"Uh, yeah, hi, Doctor Chang, it's Dallas Muller. Boyfriend of Justin Keith. Something's wrong with him, and I don't know what to do. If you could call me . . ."

Then it occurred to me, mid-sentence, like I was an idiot. *What the fuck are you doing, Dallas? Get him to hospital.*

"You know what? I'm gonna call him an ambulance. We'll be at John Hunter."

I ended the call, and sitting on my haunches in front of him, I called 000. I explained that he'd had a brain injury three months ago and he'd had a stress meltdown yesterday and he'd been sleeping, but now he was mostly awake but unresponsive.

Even as I said all this, Justin simply stared into space. Like my Juss was gone all over again.

I fought tears as I spoke, giving directions and explaining that we lived above the mechanic's workshop. Leaving Juss, I raced downstairs and unlocked the front gate while I stayed on the line until I heard the sound of sirens. I ended the call and waved the ambulance in.

"He's upstairs," I said before the guy was all the way out of his seat.

They both followed me up, and Juss hadn't moved a muscle. He didn't even blink when two strangers stood in front of him. The guy knelt and asked him questions, but Juss didn't reply.

That's when the panic really started to kick in.

They asked me information about his injuries, his operations, and I tried to tell them everything. I explained that he'd been doing so well, getting back to work, and how his doctor wanted to move his appointments to fortnights instead of weekly. But then how his mother turned up yesterday and caused a scene and how he couldn't cope with stress anymore.

"He zoned out on me after she left, and his head hurt. He took his pills and went to sleep. I thought he'd wake up okay today," I told them, going to the cabinet above the fridge where we kept his meds. I took the bottle and handed it to the medic. "I thought he just needed some sleep. He said his head hurt and he put his hand to his scar. Christ, what if he's had another bleed? I should have got him to hospital yesterday."

"It's okay. We'll get him there now," the second paramedic said, her voice calm. They discussed a few things between themselves; then they mentioned the stairs.

"I can carry him down," I said. "I've done it before." I just needed him to get to hospital. I needed them to get him there now.

Maybe they were about to argue but I went to Juss and scooped him up, blanket and all. "Come on, baby. We need to get you downstairs."

I had to shuffle him a bit to get a good centre of gravity but gave the paramedic a nod before carrying him down. They hurried to get the gurney and we had him loaded into the back of the ambulance just as Davo pulled into the yard.

Fuck.

He pulled up and got out, wide-eyed. "What the hell happened?"

"It's just precautionary," the paramedic said before I could answer.

"He didn't get any better," I said. "I'll call you when I know something. If you could . . ."

"Yeah, mate, don't worry about the shop. We got it. You just go with him."

I nodded and climbed into the back of the ambulance where the other paramedic was tending to Juss. The guy shut the door, and I was holding it together okay until they flicked the sirens on. Then shit started to get really fucking real.

When we arrived at the A&E, everything was a blur. So much happened, so many people, so many questions, so fast my head spun. Until they wheeled Juss away and I was sat in a chair and told to wait. Then everything stopped.

The silence, the isolation. It was dizzying.

It was déjà vu, all over again. These white walls, the foul smell of disinfectant and sickness, the way no one made eye contact. I hated it. I hated being here; I hated that he was here again; I hated that he was going through this again.

I hated that his mother had turned up uninvited, and I hated that maybe me yelling at her stressed him out more than her yelling. That maybe I'd done this to him . . .

I should have known better.

I should have protected him and never raised my voice at her. I should have put him first instead of my temper.

As soon as Doctor Chang walked in, as soon as I saw her familiar face etched with concern and sadness, I burst into tears.

Chapter Eight

Doctor Chang sat beside me and put her arm around my shoulder. "He's had scans and blood tests," she said. "And there's nothing abnormal. There's no bleed or clot, no swelling, no new shadows. No abscess or infection. There's no change to his previous scans."

I wiped my face. "That's good, right?"

She nodded. "Yes. But . . ."

"But what?"

"There is reduced thickness in the right prefrontal cortex and left superior temporal gyrus, some enlarged amygdala volumes, and reduced caudate volumes."

"What does that mean?" I shook my head. She'd lost me after *reduced thickness.*

"Extreme stress."

"Oh God." I felt like I was gonna puke.

"Tell me what happened."

I tried to think . . . *Start at the beginning, Dallas.*

"We left your office and went out for a late breakfast. He was fine. Happy, even. He was tired; he gets tired if we go out. But he was happy. He was keen to get home. We were waiting on formal test results from the sex health clinic and he wanted to go home because the mailman would have been . . ." God, that seems like a lifetime ago. "But his mother turned up. Last time he remembers seeing her was before he moved to Darwin. She told him he was disgusting and how being gay was the worst thing he could have done to her." I took a shaky breath. "She told both of us that when we went to see her like four years ago, but Juss doesn't remember that. Probably just as well."

"So she just turned up?"

I nodded. "She read the interview in the *Times*."

She nodded slowly. "The money."

I put my hand to my forehead. "She's a horrible person. She demanded money, and I yelled at her. She yelled back at me, and I yelled some more. Then Juss yelled." I met her eyes and shook my head. "Doc, I've never heard him yell. Not ever. Not in all the years I've known him. I mean, he'd yell at the footy but never at a person. But he yelled at her and he threw his walking cane at her, and then he just shut down. He went all floppy and I carried him upstairs. I thought he just needed to sleep, ya know? When he gets too tired, he's wiped out, so I thought he just needed sleep. He said his head hurt. I got his pills for him. Just his normal ones, nothing different. He only took what he normally takes. He crashed out for hours, and I thought he needed it. He woke up a bit when I went to bed, mumbled a few words, that kind of thing. And I just thought he'd be okay this morning. But God, he couldn't even speak." Fresh tears welled in my eyes. "Christ, Doc, what did I do wrong?"

"Nothing," she said. "The yelling wasn't ideal."

"I asked her to leave and she refused. I should have picked her up and tossed her on her arse." I swallowed back more tears and anger and guilt. "I defended him. But I should have protected him. I should have *made* her leave."

"You're not responsible for her behaviour."

No, but I'm responsible for mine. And I'm responsible for him.

There was no point in saying that. We both knew it. Instead, I said, "How is he?" Then something horrifying occurred to me. "Oh God. Will he have lost his memory again?"

She shook her head. "It's not *im*possible, but it's not likely. The hippocampus in the scans wasn't changed."

"Oh, thank God," I breathed. Not for me . . . but Juss wouldn't cope with more memory loss.

"He'll be here overnight, at least," she continued. "They've given him something to make him sleep, to get his brain activity back to normal. And something to get his blood pressure down. Doctor Anderson's looking after him so he's in the best care. He'll fill you in on the details."

"Can I see him? I need to see him."

"I asked the nurse to come get you once he's settled."

"Thank you."

She gave me a small smile. "I assumed you'd want to see him."

I nodded, so relieved. My breath caught and it was difficult to swallow. "I was so scared."

She patted my knee. "You did the right thing. Bringing him here was the right thing to do."

"He was like those first few days after the accident. Like a zombie. Catatonic."

"Stress affects everyone differently. For someone without a brain injury, like you or me, there're many cognitive functions that allow us to cope. But for people with a brain injury, their cognitive pathways have almost certainly been disrupted and there's an overload, like a roadblock that leads to a traffic jam. The way Justin's brain processes and deals with stressful situations is very different now. Moving forward, we'll have to identify the triggers and warning signs so we can eliminate risks."

I nodded. Believe me, this was never gonna happen again. "He's gonna be pissed that his recovery took a hit. He was so happy that things were going good. I kept thinking we'd been so lucky . . ."

"You still have been," Doctor Chang said. "Even after this, he's still luckier than a lot of others."

I sighed. "I know. Sorry."

She gave me a smile. "I better go finish my rounds. Can't have other patients getting jealous," she joked. "I'll see you both again before Justin's discharged. I'd say the nurse won't be long. She knows you're here."

"Thank you."

I sighed once she'd gone and thumbed out a quick message to Davo.

Justin's okay. He's staying tonight at least. Haven't seen him yet. I'll be back at the shop when they kick me out at lunchtime.

I checked my watch. Lunchtime was soon anyway. I just hoped they let me see him before then . . .

And just a few minutes later, a familiar nurse, Rasida, came out to find me. "Hello, stranger. Thought we said no returns."

I stood up and tried to smile for her.

"Come on through. You've got about forty minutes before we close the ward."

We began to walk down all-too-familiar corridors. "Is he asleep?"

"Yep. He needs to be right now, so that's a good thing. We're monitoring him, though."

She stopped at a doorway and nodded to the bed inside.

This again: the cold rooms, darkened and much too quiet.

It would never get easier. And it would rip my heart to pieces every time.

Justin, in a hospital bed.

Please let him be okay.

It was such an odd sensation. I couldn't get my feet to work and I wanted to run to him at the same time. Needing to see him but afraid of what I might find.

But there he was. There were no bandages this time, though he was hooked up to the IV, and he had his monitor pads on his head and down his shirt. His face wasn't swollen and no bones were broken, but he looked so small. So fragile.

I pulled the uncomfortable plastic chair over to the bedside and took his hand. "Hey, baby," I whispered, fighting tears. "I'm here."

This was all so familiar, like a reoccurring nightmare. We'd been here before; we'd travelled this horrible road.

Yet it was different this time.

This wasn't just going back to square one and starting over. This was a different game. The rules had changed, and what had become our new normal would now be different again. But I didn't care. If we had to go back to square one every three or four months, I would.

I held his hand in both of mine. "The doc said you need to sleep," I whispered. "You just do what you need to do, and I'll be here when you wake up."

The first of my tears fell, and then another and another. I held the back of his hand to my cheek and cried.

GOING BACK into the workshop without Juss was strange. I'd picked up some lunch for the guys, and both Davo and Sparra stopped what they were doing when I got out of the taxi.

Davo took one look at me and his face fell. "Oh fuck."

"They said he should be okay," I said.

Davo nodded at me. "But what about you? You look like hell."

I refused to fucking cry. I shook my head and breathed in deep. "I brought us some lunch. Sorry for dropping everything onto you guys again."

Sparra clapped my shoulder. "'S all good, mate. Come on, let's eat and you can tell us how he is."

Well, I tried to eat something but didn't really have the stomach for it, and there wasn't a great deal I could tell them. Stress from his mother turning up, stress from the yelling and fighting, had basically shut his brain down. He was still asleep when I left, and Doctor Anderson, the head neurosurgeon, said his scans were okay, but we wouldn't know how long he'd be like that until he woke up.

"He was like a zombie this morning," I said, pushing my mostly uneaten lunch away.

"From stress?" Davo asked.

I nodded. "Yep. His other doc said Juss' brain is a bit like a roadmap and stress puts up roadblocks everywhere, and messages can't get through. He just . . . short-circuited."

"So no more stress," Sparra said with a hard nod.

"No, no more stress."

"When can he come home?" Davo asked.

"Hopefully tomorrow. We have to see how he is when he wakes up first. If he still can't speak or hear commands, then I don't know . . ."

Davo's eyes went wide. "Can't speak?"

"Yeah. It wasn't good."

He frowned. "Fucking hell."

I took a deep breath. "I've got about two and a half hours before they'll let me back in to see him, and I need to keep busy. So tell me what needs doing, and I'll do it."

Two and a half hours of working my arse off was exactly what I needed, and having another set of hands to help was exactly what Davo and Sparra needed. Between the three of us we got almost all of it done, and I felt better about leaving for the afternoon knowing I'd helped out some.

I'd still be lost without those two guys, Davo especially. And knowing he'd be needing time away at some point with his new baby on the way made me more determined to do the right thing by him.

I needed to do something to make the shop run more efficiently in the times I couldn't be there. I just needed to put it away for the minute and concentrate on Juss, and once he was home and on the mend, I could start putting together a plan to make all our lives easier.

JUSS WAS STILL ASLEEP when I got back to the hospital, though the nurse said he'd been stirring. I took my seat beside his bed and took his hand. "Hey, baby," I whispered. "I'm here."

He was utterly motionless, except for the slow and steady rise and fall of his chest. After a few minutes, his fingers flinched in mine and his eyelids fluttered before he startled awake. His eyes opened and he stared at the ceiling for a long moment before he slowly turned his head to look at me.

His face was without expression; his eyes held no emotion.

He stared at me like he had when he first woke up after his accident and didn't remember who I was.

He stared at me like I was a stranger, all over again.

No.

No, no no no no.

Please God, no.

My heart squeezed to the point of pain, and fear sent ice through my veins.

This wasn't happening. Not again. He wouldn't survive going through this again, and I wasn't sure I would either.

"Juss? You're okay. You're in the hospital," I whispered, my voice cracking.

He stared, then he slow blinked, his gaze blank and distant. My whole chest burned and ached, and I fought tears.

Then something clicked in his brain, I could see it in his eyes. His gaze locked onto mine and the corner of his lip picked up. "Dallas," he breathed.

And the weight of relief crushed me. I sagged, put his hand to my cheek, and sobbed.

Chapter Nine

THE DOCTORS DID their thing with Juss and I stood aside to get out of their way. He was okay, and that was all that mattered to me. He remembered me, and he spoke. He even smiled.

He was still totally wiped and slow blinked a lot, but he was going to be okay.

Even still, he was definitely staying in overnight and they'd be back to see how he was in the morning, and then it was just me and him again.

I went back to my side of his bed and pulled the seat over. "Hey, you," I murmured.

"Hey." He smiled, exhausted.

"How do you feel? Can I get you anything? Water?"

He lifted his hand as though it weighed a tonne. "You can hold my hand."

I was quick to take it, threading our fingers. I kissed his knuckles, his palm. "You scared me, baby. I was so worried."

"Sorry. Didn't mean to."

"I know. I'm just glad you're okay."

"So tired."

"You gotta stay here tonight," I said, frowning. As much as I hated it, if the docs said he needed to be here, then he needed to be here. "I'm sure they'll look after you just fine."

He slow blinked. "Stay for as long as you can."

That made me smile. "Baby, I wouldn't be anywhere else."

He dozed some more, and I sat there watching the rise and fall of his chest, watching the lines on the machines and listening to all the beeps, like it was some kind of orchestra. Time dragged, but at least it gave me some time to do some research on my phone.

I needed to get my shit together at the shop. I couldn't do everything. I couldn't be there all the time. And sure, the money stranglehold was lessened with the insurance approval, but if I wasn't careful, I'd find myself right back in trouble.

I needed to work smarter, not harder. And I had a good idea of where to start, too.

"You're cute when you're thinking," Juss whispered.

I looked up to find him, obviously, awake. I put my phone down. "Hey. Sorry, I was just reading . . . How are you feeling?"

"'Kay. Thirsty."

I held a cup of water to his lips and he took a few sips before sagging back onto the mattress. "Thanks."

"How's your headache?"

"'S okay. Wish I was at home."

"Me too. Tomorrow, hopefully."

"Yeah."

"I'm supposed to work tomorrow," he mumbled.

"It's okay, Juss. I know the boss."

He smiled again, though his eyes closed. He lifted his hand again even though he was almost asleep. "Hold, please."

This time I took his hand in both of mine and held onto it until they made me leave at dinner time.

THE NEXT MORNING, Juss was sitting up in the hospital bed. He was picking at food on his breakfast tray and his whole face lit up when he saw me. "Oh, hey."

"Good morning," I said, putting a bag on my seat. I leaned in and gave him a kiss. "You're looking much brighter today."

"Feel better. Still not great, and I reckon I'll need to be the king of naps today, but I do feel better."

"The king of naps," I repeated. "I like that."

He pushed his table tray away. "The food here is still bad."

I pulled his favourite brand of decaf iced coffee out of the bag. "Thought you might want one of these."

His smile turned into something sweet and gushy. "Oh my God. Dall . . ."

I handed it over with a kiss to his cheek. "Anything for my king of naps."

Doctor Anderson came by mid-morning, and after going over his file and having a bit of a chat with us, he declared Justin a free man. His recovery from yesterday to today might seem remarkable, like he was almost back to normal, but the doc reassured us that wasn't the case.

We just had to promise to take it easy for a week, and absolutely no stress. Justin readily agreed, not just to get parole from hospital, but because he genuinely had no intention of getting off the couch.

He was beat.

This whole ordeal had knocked him on his arse and was a stark reminder that we needed to take his health seriously. Because we learned the hard and fast way that it could all go very bad, very quickly.

We were still waiting for the final discharge papers when Doctor Chang stuck her head in. "Someone's looking better today." Then she looked at me. "Actually, make that two someones looking a lot better than they were yesterday."

"Morning," I said with a smile.

She walked into where Juss was sitting on the bed, dressed and ready to go home. "I have some good news for you, Justin."

"I never have to come back?" he asked, hopeful.

She chuckled. "You don't need to have your scheduled scans next week like we talked about, because you had them all yesterday."

"Does he still have to come in for an appointment then?" I asked.

"Yep. You both can't get away from me that easily," she said with a wink. "I know we talked about moving to fortnightly appointments, but we might need to hold off on that for another week or so. We can start focusing on some coping techniques for stress."

"Doctor Anderson already did that," Juss said.

"Yep, and we'll be going over it again," she said brightly. He wasn't getting out of it, obviously.

"I know how to start," Juss said. "Never see my mother again. That's it. Step one and only."

Doctor Chang frowned, but I agreed with Juss. "She's not welcome at our place ever again."

"Well," she said. "At least we know where to start."

I went to Juss and rubbed his back, kissing the side of his head. "If and when you ever decide to see her again, it'll be on your terms. Not hers, okay?"

He nodded and looked up at me, giving me a small smile. "I'm so tired, babe."

I pulled him against me and held him, which was kind of awkward since he was sitting on the bed. But he didn't mind, because he sighed and relaxed in my arms. "We'll be home soon," I whispered, rubbing his back.

Doctor Chang studied Juss for a moment and mouthed, "I think he's asleep." Smiling, she pointed to the door. "See you next week."

I didn't dare move, even long after she'd gone because, yeah, Juss had fallen asleep against me. He was kind of side-on but his neck was well supported, so I left him right where he was. He woke up when the nurse brought his discharge papers, and he didn't even argue about the wheelchair he had to use to leave. That's how exhausted he was.

He slept on the way home and barely stirred when I woke him up to get him out of the ute. I helped him up the stairs and he walked himself straight back to bed. He was out like a light, so I put everything he might need on his bedside table and went downstairs.

Of course, Davo and Sparra had stopped what they were doing. "How is he?" Davo asked.

"He's okay. Tired as hell, probably will be for a while. I doubt he'll be down here working this week, but we'll see."

"Fair enough," Sparra said.

I ran my hands through my hair and sighed. "You two got a second? I wanna run something past ya's before I start making phone calls."

Davo nodded. "I could always have a coffee."

With three fresh brews, we sat at the breakroom table and they waited for me to start talking. "It's been a shit few months, and I know my time has been split between here and everything else. That's not fair on you guys, and I just want you to know that I really do appreciate it." They were both about to argue or say something to downplay my thanks. I put my hand up. "I mean it. And anyway, I've been thinking of something I could do to make things run easier and smoother for you two. And for the business, but mostly for you two. I think yesterday proved to me that I can't always be here. Juss' health has to be a priority. I mean, this place and you guys are a priority too. So I can't do all this on my own. I can't manage this and you guys and Juss and emergencies and whatnot. So I was thinking I needed help."

"What kind of help, Dallas?" Davo asked.

"I don't want to hire another mechanic. I love our little team and I don't want to replace Justin because his station will be his until he's ready to come back to it. And I don't want to spend every minute of every day in the office because that's not what I love doing. I wanna be working on bikes. It's what we do, right?"

Sparra nodded. "Yep."

"So I was thinking I might hire an office manager. Someone to take care of the phones, the bookings, the orders, the . . . everything that I've been slacking on, basically. Everything that Davo's pretty much been doing in my absence. So," I said, looking right at him. "Davo, first choice is yours. If you want to be the office manager here, the job's yours."

He shot me a stunned look. "Like, in your office and not out there working on bikes and stuff?"

"Well, yeah."

He made a face. "Um, well, thanks for the offer, and I don't mind helping out when you need it, but Dallas, I wanna be working on bikes too. It's what we do, right?"

Sparra put his hands up in surrender. "Jesus, don't look at me next. I don't want it."

I sighed with relief. "Oh, thank fuck," I said with a laugh. "I mean, I had to offer it to ya, but damn, I'd be well and truly screwed trying to replace either of you guys on the floor."

Davo smiled. "So you're gonna put someone on the phones? Can't say I'm sad about that."

"Yeah, I know. Me either. I should've done it years ago. When I first started, I just did it all. Then you guys came along and helped out on the floor so I could do more stuff in the office, and that was great, but it was never my strong point. It's just not me. I love my business, and I certainly don't want to lose it, so I should start running it like . . . well, a business."

I sipped my coffee, ignoring the lack of sleep from last night. "That'll let you guys do your jobs with no interruptions, and it will let me do mine. I can be on the floor when I need to be, or I can go to doctor appointments without worrying that you guys are left with everything. And all things going well, it means we can book in more jobs because we're not stopping every five minutes to answer phones and take bookings or chase parts or orders."

"Sounds good," Davo said. "But Dallas, you know we don't mind, right?"

"I know, but I do. I put too much on you both. Oh," I added. "I've got the rep for those hoists coming by next week."

Sparra clapped his hands together and grinned. "We gonna be fancy!"

I laughed and let out a long breath. "Well, enough of the bullshit. I'm gonna go call an employment place and get the ball rolling then I can help both of you on the bikes."

"HEY, BEAUTIFUL," I said, kissing Juss' forehead. He was on the couch when I finally called it a day and went upstairs. He was dozy and had slept on and off all day, but he smiled.

"Hey."

I slumped onto the couch beside him and put my head on his lap. I looked up at him. "I was thinking omelettes for dinner."

His fingers found my hair and he was still smiling at me. "Sounds good."

Well, I wasn't sure about good. But they were quick and easy and required minimal effort to eat with no loud crunching or heavy chewing for Juss.

"But I could just lie here for a bit first," I said. "And you could keep running your fingers through my hair."

He chuckled. "I could." He put one hand to work on my hair but his other hand sat on my chest, and I took that hand in mine, holding it tight. There was some surfing championship on the TV, the volume and brightness were low, but it was relaxing to watch. "This is nice," he whispered.

"Being here with you like this is the best."

He hummed and played with my hair for a bit. "How was work?" His question was slow, so he was still tired, but he wasn't nodding off.

"Yeah, we got it all done," I said. "I'm gonna hire someone for the office, Juss. Someone to answer the phones and organise the booking sheets and do some paperwork and ordering for me. That way I can get more work done in the shop."

His hand stilled in my hair. "Is that because of me?"

"Not at all, baby. It's long overdue, and having to stop halfway through a job to take a phone call is a pain for everyone. I want you and me and Davo and Sparra to be able to get our work done. Especially if you and I are away, then poor Davo is trying to do too much."

Juss nodded and took some time to think about all that. "Sorry I can't do more."

"Don't be sorry, Juss. It is what it is. You need to rest first, then you can worry about that. You'll be back to work soon enough. Oh," I said, remembering just now. "I've got a guy coming next week to see which hoist systems we want. That's kinda exciting, and also long overdue. I should have done that years ago. And we'll get those roller chairs that go with them, and Sparra already wants to race you on your scooter. From one end of the shop to the other."

Juss eventually smiled. "I'll beat him."

I snorted as I got up. "You will." I kissed the side of his head on my way to the kitchen, and ten minutes later, we were eating ham, cheese, and capsicum omelettes. And ten minutes after dinner, Juss was ready for bed again.

Even though it was kind of early, I really hadn't slept much the night before, so I got ready for bed with him. We settled in under the covers and Juss automatically found his spot, snuggled into me. "My wing tattoo pillow," he mumbled.

I wrapped him up tight, his familiar body, his familiar warmth was like a balm. "God, I missed you last night. Squish missed you too."

"Don't ever want to go back to hospital," he murmured.

"I know, baby."

"Was so scared."

"Me too."

"Don't want to be like that again." Maybe it was easier for him to admit these things in the dark.

I rubbed his back. "I promise I'll protect you, baby. I won't let it get to that ever again."

He nodded against my chest and sighed as he relaxed into a deep sleep. I revelled in the fact he was in my arms again, safe and well, where I wanted to keep him forever.

Chapter Ten

JUSS DIDN'T COME DOWNSTAIRS the next two days. He was still wiped, but mostly happy, and spent his time dozing on the couch or in bed. On day three, he came down for a little while in the morning to see the boys. He tidied up a few things here and there, but it was mostly just to be social, to have a laugh, and to feel the warmth of the sun on his skin. He made dinner that night and did some laundry, so he was definitely feeling better.

He was still clingy, though, not that I minded that part. But as soon as he saw me, he needed touch: a hug, a kiss, cuddling on the couch. He'd admitted that his setback had scared him, and I believed him.

He didn't complain about being bored, about being cooped up inside, about not being able to work. I think what scared him most was how close he'd come to going that one step too far, one step from not being able to return.

He was truly listening to his body, not pushing to get back to his new normal, but rather letting his mind and body tell him when he was ready.

On Friday, Juss stayed downstairs with us for a little bit longer, though it was probably just out of curiosity. I was expecting three people to come in for an interview before lunch. The employment agency had done the hard work and narrowed down a prospective employee, but I would get to meet and decide who I thought would be the best fit.

The first girl was young and probably had potential but couldn't even get through the interview without checking her phone. The second was a guy who Davo and I had caught checking out Justin, and when he realised he'd been caught, he just grinned and mumbled something about a snack.

He was obviously a hard fucking no.

I went through with the interview with him, though I'd already made up my mind. It didn't help the fact that Davo stood where I could see him through the doorway of my office, laughing his damn head off.

When he'd gone, Davo, still grinning, said, "Your face. The whole interview. Oh my God, so funny."

"What was funny?" Juss asked.

"That guy thought you were a snack," Davo said, laughing again. "Thought Dallas was gonna kill him."

Justin looked confused and horrified. "A snack?"

"Something to eat," Sparra explained. "It's a new thing the kids say these days."

It took him a second, but he nodded. "Oh."

I grumbled. "He didn't even try to hide it." I pointed to my chest. "Justin's *my* snack. And anyway, he didn't know jack shit about bikes or nothing—"

I stopped talking because Davo was laughing so hard he was gonna bust something. He grabbed his side. "Ow, fuck. A stitch."

Served him right.

Juss was smiling at me. "I'm your snack, am I?"

I was pouting, and I didn't care. "Yes."

That, of course, set Davo off laughing again, though he still had to hold his side. Didn't stop him. "Oh God, jealous Dallas is my favourite."

Fucker.

Justin came into my office, around to my chair, and leaned his arse against my desk. It was good to see him smile. "Jealous Dallas is my favourite too."

I looked up at him and couldn't help but laugh, shaking my

403

head at myself. "Sorry. You're not *my* snack. I shouldn't have said that."

He met my gaze. "Yes I am."

I laughed and pulled out my wallet, giving Juss my credit card. "Speaking of snacks. Can you please put in a lunch order from the takeaway shop down the road and have it delivered? Get the fellas what they want." I looked out the door. "Dunno why I'm feeding Davo."

Davo just laughed from around the corner. "I take it back. Lunch-buying Dallas is my favourite."

Juss took the card and leaned down and gave me a smiley kiss. He limped out of my office and went and sat in the breakroom, and I heard him and Sparra discussing lunch. I thought Sparra might do the ordering over the phone, but no, Juss did it. He was tired and I knew, after lunch, he'd be sleeping for a while.

Davo appeared at my door, trying to look serious. "Someone here to see you, boss."

It was my next, and final, interview, and I was beginning to lose hope. But in walked a woman with short black hair, maybe in her 40s, and she had an easy smile. She held out her hand for me to shake and nodded to where Juss' bike stood in the corner. "Nice. Is that a 2016 or '17?"

She knew bikes.

"Ah, 2016. You like KTMs?"

"My two sons ride," she said. "And my husband, but mostly the boys. Spent a lot of weekends at racetracks when they were growing up."

I grinned at her. "Come into my office," I said, but I already knew.

Her name was Toni and she was a straight-shooter, no-nonsense woman who knew her way around accounting programs and stocktakes like she knew which KTM she was looking at by just a glance.

I liked her, and she was a perfect fit for us.

She had no problem dealing with four guys. She lived with three: her husband and two grown sons. She knew how to catalogue and order parts. She'd worked the last six years at an auto-supply shop but left when the business sold. She had no problem whatsoever with the fact that two out of the four guys working here were gay and that we were actually a couple. She just wouldn't pick sides if we had a fight, because her usual advice that the guy was always wrong wouldn't do us much good.

I had to make it official with the employment agency, but I was certain we'd found our newest team member.

And if I'd felt any apprehension at all, it was gone. Now I just felt . . . relieved.

Toni left and lunch arrived, and the mood around the lunch table was relaxed and happy. Though Juss was smiling as he ate, he could barely keep his eyes open. "I think I'm done," he said slowly, pushing his half-eaten burger away. "It's nap o'clock for me."

I helped him up the stairs, and again, he went to bed and not to the sofa. He was so tired, and with some warm food in his belly, he fell straight to sleep.

I put his boots by the bed, and when I slid his phone onto the bedside table, it vibrated so I naturally looked at the screen.

He'd had five missed calls and three missed messages.

I didn't know the number or look who the messages were from or what they said. I didn't want to intrude on his privacy like that. If he'd missed a medical call, they'd call me, so it wasn't urgent. And if Becca couldn't get through to him, she'd call me as well.

The only person I could think of, and the reason he hadn't answered the calls or taken the messages, would be his mother.

So help me God, if that woman . . .

Then I remembered that my temper had contributed to Juss' stress overload so I took a deep breath and counted to ten. I had to get a handle on that shit from now on.

I left Squish in charge of sleeping supervision and went back downstairs. We had to hook in and get our jobs finished, but the last customer left at knock-off time and we finished the week on a good note. I helped the customer load the bike onto his trailer while Davo and Sparra finished up in the shop. When I came back in, Juss was there helping them.

He looked like he'd just woken up, which meant he must have slept for about four hours. "Hey," I said.

He shoved his hands into his hoodie pockets and smiled. "Hey. Just wanted to see the fellas before they left. Let 'em know I'll be back to work on Monday."

"You feel up to that?" I asked.

He gave a nod. "If I take it easy this weekend, yeah. Just small stuff, though. And if it's too much, I'll just tap out."

I grinned at him. "Sounds great. And you'll be fine. I know it." He had always been determined, but he also seemed to have a newfound respect for his limitations.

"It helps that the boss loves me and we live right upstairs," he added.

"Yes, he does."

"Hey, Jusso," Davo called out as he wheeled the toolbox into the storage room. "Gimme a hand with this."

So while they busied themselves with packing up, I went to finalise a bit more paperwork. I was filling in the weekly EPA report when Davo and Sparra called it a day, and Juss came into my office. He parked himself in his usual spot—his arse against my desk. "Just gotta get this motor oil disposal written up, then I'm all done."

"That's okay, take your time, I'll just wait right here." He was quiet for a bit while I entered in some numbers. "Will you miss this? The paperwork? The office?"

I snorted. "God, no."

"This office could use a pot plant," he said randomly.

"Uh, I guess it could." I looked around the office. It was functional but drab. It was also dusty as hell. "I might give myself one job this weekend, and that's to clean the shit out of here before Toni starts."

"Yeah, it could do with some organising. Some trays and maybe some new pens and stuff. I don't know what office people like."

I chuckled, because this was proof that Juss was feeling much better. He was having proper connective thoughts instead of the zombie he had been since his stay in hospital earlier this week.

"Oh, what's this?" he said, reaching for a pile of mail that still sat in my in-tray. Something else I was going to attack this weekend. "This one's for me." He flipped through the envelopes. "And one for you."

Oh, shit. "They came the other day. I was going to bring them upstairs, sorry. I got busy. Um, I think they might be those test results we were waiting on."

His gaze shot to mine. "The blood tests?"

"Yep. I forgot about them, to be honest. We got a little sidetracked, didn't we?"

He hummed and studied the envelope, turning it over in his hand. Then he held it out to me. "Can you read it for me? I don't think I could handle bad news right now. If something's wrong, just say, 'Oh goodie, more dick swabbing,' and I'll understand."

Chuckling, I took the envelope. "I can read it for you." I undid the envelope and unfolded the paper. It was the lab results, and after a quick scan down the list, I handed it back. "No more dick swabbing."

And yeah, I was relieved. Not for the prospect of sex, but because he wasn't joking when he said he couldn't handle bad news right now.

"Oh, thank God," he said, reading over it. "Now do yours."

I undid mine and read over it. "No more dick swabbing for me either."

Juss grinned. "I can swab it for you if you want."

I laughed and handed him my lab results so he could see. "And just so you know, baby. This doesn't mean we have to rush into anything. It just means we can, when you're ready."

He looked up from the letter and leaned down for a kiss. "I know. But thank you for saying it."

I finished up the last of the report and shut the computer down, and making sure everything was locked up, we went upstairs. Juss suggested lamb and salad for dinner, which sounded bloody good to me, and it would take all of fifteen minutes to make. He put together the salad and I grilled the meat, and when we sat down to eat, his phone buzzed on the table.

He looked at the number and let it ring out. "Not gonna answer it?" I asked.

"No. It's my mother. Should have got a new number years ago."

"Would you like me to talk to her? I can ask her to stop calling you. Or I can just block her number for you."

He chewed a mouthful of salad, frowning as he swallowed. "I don't want it to trigger another episode."

"Oh, baby," I said, rubbing his arm. "Let's just block her number and then you don't have to deal with her at all."

He pushed his dinner around with his fork. "I just want her out of my life. She doesn't love me. She doesn't even like me. If I did give her money, it wouldn't be enough. If I gave her everything and she knew it was all gone, she'd take it and wouldn't speak to me again."

God, I hated that she hurt him so much.

"So, we'll take screenshots of her messages and of how many times she's tried to call, then we'll block her. If she becomes a problem, we let the police handle it, okay? You don't have to worry about her, if that's what you want."

He sighed and nodded. "Sounds good."

"Baby, don't stress over anything. Anything you need me to handle, I will take care of for you. If you need to talk about something to get it off your mind, talk away. Or write it down for Doctor Chang if you don't want to talk to me about it."

His gaze shot to mine. "I don't want secrets from you."

"I know. But sometimes you might want to talk to someone else. And that's okay. Or talk to Sparra. I'm sure he wouldn't mind. Or Becca. It doesn't have to be me, just talk to someone. Don't bottle anything up."

He sipped his mineral water and gave me a smile. "Okay." He ate a slice of meat. "So can we talk about the snack comment today? And jealous Dallas. Because I've never met jealous Dallas before, and I have to admit, I liked him."

I laughed. "I told you before I wasn't perfect. Jealousy is something I need to work on."

He smiled, very pleased with himself. "I've never had anyone be jealous over me before. It's kinda hot. Not sure I'm overly fond of the caveman, chest-beating thing, but hearing you say I'm yours was . . . good."

"Okay, well, first up, that guy was out of line. He came for a job interview and made inappropriate comments about another employee. Another employee who just happened to be my boyfriend, no less. He didn't know that, but that's not the point."

"True."

"And Davo just happened to be there and reckoned the look on my face was funny. But the guy totally checked you out and called you a snack. He was lucky I didn't throw him out, and it was probably just as well Davo was laughing so much or I might have."

Juss seemed to find something very amusing. "I do like jealous Dallas. Have you ever thrown someone out over me before? At a bar or a club?"

"No. Thankfully. I guess I never had to. There might have been a time or two where I had to put my arm around you to prove a point." *Or stick my tongue down your throat.* "But no one ever dared call you a snack to my face."

He chuckled at that. "Probably because you're huge and your 'he's *my* snack' face is pretty scary." Then he sighed happily. "Well, I don't find it scary. I rather like it."

"Just not the chest-thumping caveman kind."

"Right. Although, if you wanted to throw me over your shoulder and take me back to your cave, I wouldn't put up a fight. Like, at all."

That made me laugh. "I'll keep that in mind."

Juss got up from his seat and sat on my lap. I had to pull my chair out a bit so he could fit, but he just sat right down and put his arm around my shoulder, his forehead pressed to mine. "No one's ever stood up for me or got all protective of me. I like it."

I kissed him. "I will always look out for you. Even if sometimes I go overboard and yell, like I yelled at your mother. I'm sorry I did that. It stressed you out, but she wanted to hurt you and I just saw red. I should have reacted better."

Justin scratched my beard with his thumb. "I'm glad you did. And it wasn't just you yelling that stressed me out. Her coming here and demanding money, telling me I owe her . . ." He shook his head. "She stressed me out. Not you."

"But I didn't help, and I'm sorry."

He lifted my chin up and planted a soft kiss on my lips. "I forgive you. I don't forgive her."

And then, because the devil heard her name, Juss' phone rang again. He groaned at the number. "Want me to block her?" I asked.

He nodded, so I ended the call and took some screenshots of her numerous attempts to contact him, then the text messages, which were all variations of *the least you could do is answer my calls* and *how dare you*, and then, with great satisfaction, I blocked her number.

"Done."

He smiled ruefully. "Thank you. I didn't know how to do it and didn't want to press her name and accidentally dial her instead."

I put my arms around him and buried my face against his arm. It was never easy to make cutting off a family member official, and even though he'd wanted to do it, it still had to sting. "I'm sorry, baby."

"Don't be. I'm not."

I looked up at him. "Not even a little?"

He shook his head. "This is her doing, not mine. She disowned me first. Now I'm just returning the favour. And anyway, remember how you said we choose our own family?"

I nodded.

"Well, I've chosen mine." He kissed me soundly. Then he picked up my fork and stabbed some meat and brought it to my lips. "Open wide."

I laughed and he shoved the fork in my mouth. "You're gonna feed me?" I asked.

"For all the times you helped me, now it's your turn."

He continued to feed me until my plate was empty and he even had some more of his own. It was fun and cute, we laughed a lot, and it had been far too long since we'd done anything fun and cute. The fact that he punctuated every forkful with a kiss made it even better.

He put the fork down and turned his full attention to me. "You know," he said with a kiss. "I slept a lot today, so I'm not too tired."

I chuckled because I was pretty sure I knew where he was going with this. "Is that so?"

He kissed me again, a little softer, more playful. "And we did get those test results back."

I hummed, not too sure if he was up for anything rigorous. "You're supposed to be on bed rest."

He smiled. "So take me to bed."

Chapter Eleven

I CERTAINLY WASN'T GOING to say no. I wanted Juss to feel good to replace the pain he lived with, even just for a while. He'd been getting better over the last three days, but he still wasn't anywhere near back to good.

"Are you sure?"

He nodded quickly. "I trust you."

Given he was still sitting on my lap, I picked him up as I stood, making him laugh. I carried him to our room and laid him on the bed, then climbed up his body and gently laid my weight on him.

His smile and the way he chewed on his bottom lip told me he was fine, but I had to be careful of his injuries. He spread his legs, slowly moving his right leg, and I froze. "Juss."

He held my gaze. "I want this."

God, the fierceness in his eyes was so familiar, but still so new. "We'll just take small steps, baby. We don't need to go too far. I just want to make you feel good."

He flexed his hips, grinding our erections together. "I already feel good, Dall. I want you to make me come."

I kissed him. "That I can do." I went to kiss him again, but he stopped me. I worried that I'd hurt him. "What is it?"

"We need to be naked first. Both of us. Right now."

I laughed, because that was such a Justin thing to say. I would never tire of seeing snippets of the real him.

But I obeyed and undressed him first, then myself, and crawled back under the covers with him. I moved on top of him again and he was quick to pull me in for a kiss, and we soon found a rhythm. Our cocks slid against each other and Juss rolled his hips. I grinded in an ebb and flow of desire and love.

He bent his left leg, giving me more room and making himself open for me. I could so easily push into him from this position, and he knew it. He dug his fingernails and I had to stop myself from thrusting into him. I pulled back with a laugh and sat back on my haunches.

"You remember how to push my buttons just fine," I said. Then I took in the sight before me. His legs were spread, his cock hard, his lips kiss-swollen. I went forward, pressing my palm into the mattress to keep my weight off him, my cock aching for touch. "You are so fucking hot right now."

He groaned and tried to pull me back down on him. "Dall, I need something . . . I don't know what I can handle, but I need it."

"I know what you need, baby," I murmured. "And I know exactly how you like it."

He whined and I took that as my cue. His body couldn't handle being so strung out right now.

I kissed him one more time before kissing down his body, his jaw, his neck, his collarbone, his nipples. He groaned when I sucked his nipple in between my teeth, just like he always did.

Some things never changed.

I moved down to his cock, licked up the shaft. He was leaking precome so I swiped it with my finger and rubbed it against his arsehole.

He rocked his hips. "Oh God."

I grinned as I took him into my mouth. I sucked him as I pushed a finger into him, and he welcomed it. I pumped his cock in my fist and worked more precome out of him, using it as lube to push a second finger inside him.

Juss groaned out as I stretched him and sucked him. "Dallas, I'm gonna—"

He came, his back arching and he cried out. I swallowed his orgasm and he was racked with tremors. I pulled my fingers out and worked my own cock, so close already . . . Slick with precome, I fucked my fist, spilling my seed on his belly.

I collapsed at his side, careful of his leg, and pulled the blankets up. I wrapped my arms around him, making him the little spoon, and I kissed the back of his neck. "You feel okay?"

He chuckled. "I feel so good right now. I'm a mess, but I don't care. I don't want to move."

"Good," I whispered, kissing his neck, his shoulder. "I never want to let you go."

His sigh was almost a moan. "I can feel your cock," he whispered. I was pressed right against him, my half-hard dick was against his arse. He writhed a little, trying to get me aligned. He brought his injured leg up slowly and pushed his arse back. "You could just . . ."

"Juss," I breathed.

"Just the tip, just a little bit. Let me feel it."

Fuck.

Of course, my half-hard dick twitched at the idea, and my body moved without any conscious thought. I could have pushed into him so easily. I wanted to be buried inside him, and he wanted it as well . . .

I shifted my hips, getting a better angle, and pushed upward, into.

Just the tip, just a little . . . was never going to be enough.

I pushed my softening dick against his hole; he was still slick and ready.

"Please, Dall."

I never could bear to hear him beg.

I slid into him and he cried out, pushing his arse back and arching his back, just like he always used to. Tight and hot, he took me.

My body knew his body. My cock knew and it glided right

into home. We were joined. We were as one. Like we'd done a thousand times, but brand new.

I held his back to my front as I pushed inside, feeling his breaths, his heart. He felt so, so good.

"Oh God," he whispered. "Fuck, Dallas, just stay right there."

"Am I hurting you?" I asked, kissing the back of his neck. I ran my hands up his sides and down again, gripping his hips.

"No, God no," he said, his voice tight.

I knew that sound. I knew that tremor. Fucking hell, he was going to come again.

"Dallas," he murmured, gripping the blankets before us.

I rolled my hips, thrusting. "I know, baby."

"Oh God."

And just like that, he came again.

I think he was stunned, shocked that his body was able to do that. The truth was, I'd made him come like that a hundred times.

He loved my cock in his arse. He *loved* it. I didn't need to be fully hard or fucking him. Just having me inside him was enough to get him off.

I pulled out slowly and he whined, but I carefully rolled him over so I could hold him properly. "You feel okay?"

"I feel . . . amazing."

I snorted. "You are amazing."

"Your dick is amazing."

I laughed at that.

"You were inside me, after you finished, and you got me off," he added.

I kissed the side of his head. "I know what you like, baby."

He went to move and had to unpeel our skin. "Uh, we're stuck."

I laughed. "Shower time." I got out of bed and helped him to his feet. "How do you feel?"

"I feel good. Tired, but that's nothing new."

"How about a hot shower, toasted sandwiches for dinner, and we hit the couch for whatever's left of the footy?"

"Sounds good."

After a quick scrub clean, Juss made toasted ham and cheese sandwiches, I stripped and remade the bed, and we caught the last twenty minutes of footy. Well, I did. Juss was asleep about ten seconds in.

———

JUSTIN DID IMPROVE over the weekend. He took it easy, never pushing himself, and every day since his most recent hospital stay, he got stronger. By Monday, he was feeling pretty good. He'd spoken to his sister a few times about their mother, and Becca was totally cool with Juss' decision to cut their mother from his life. Actually, Bec was one more snide comment from cutting her out too. It wasn't as though their mother was a huge part in their lives anyway, but Bec was sick of the toxicity as well.

It had been a long time coming and helped Juss feel better about the whole thing. He adored Bec and she him, and even though she lived two hours away, her support was an important part of his overall recovery.

Not just his recovery from his stress-induced meltdown, but his recovery overall.

And so was work. After a week off, he was itching to get his hands dirty. Monday morning he came out wearing his work overalls and boots, grinning. "Hey, boss."

I chuckled into my coffee, because Juss never smiled in the morning. "Keen to get back to work?" He was only going to do a few hours, just to see how he felt.

"Keen as mustard."

I snorted and handed him his coffee. "Toast?"

"Let me make it for you," he said, sipping his coffee, then threw some bread into the toaster.

He really was in a good mood. "Thanks, baby."

He came in for a long hug while the toast cooked. "It's gonna be a good week."

"I think so too," I said. God, I hoped so. "The guys won't recognise the office." I'd spent most of the weekend cleaning and clearing shit out. Juss helped but mostly just sat on the desk and supervised.

"And Toni starts on Wednesday?" he asked as he buttered the toast.

"Yep."

He slathered on some Vegemite and handed me a piece. "And the hoist rep is coming today?"

"Yep."

He grinned. "It's gonna be a good week."

My God, it did ridiculously crazy things to my heart to see him so happy. "In case I haven't told you enough lately, I love you."

He laughed as he ate. "You have, but you can keep telling me. Love you too." He sipped his coffee, still smiling. "And because I'm feeling good, and if things stay good, you get to dick me properly."

I almost choked on my coffee. I coughed and spluttered and he patted me on the back, that cheeky grin in full effect. "The doc said a week, and you promised."

"I promised?" I didn't recall a promise.

"Yesterday, when I had your dick in my mouth, you said you couldn't wait to fuck me. I said, 'Promise?' And you said, 'Promise.'"

My mouth fell open. Okay, I think I remembered that conversation, but God help me, I would have said anything when he was teasing me with his tongue. "You can't use anything I said under duress. That's not fair."

He laughed. "You promised, Dall."

I pinched his chin and drew him in for another kiss. "You don't play fair."

He smiled as he finished his toast. "It's gonna be such a good week."

THE SALES REP with the hoists was a guy named Connor. He was a decent sort of bloke, a bit confident, but he knew his stuff.

He brought with him two types of hoist, one standard model and one higher-end. He showed us all the bells and whistles and explained work safety and ergonomics and all that salesman spiel.

"If you've got a bike we could demonstrate with . . ." he said.

The two client bikes we had in store were both on stands, one without a tyre and one without its handlebars. Not that I would have been comfortable using a client's bike anyway.

"What about mine?" Justin said, nodding to his bike in the corner. "I'll bring it over."

Mine was behind Juss' bike but he was already off his scooter and walking to get it. I went to help him, but Sparra took my arm. "He's got it," he whispered.

I knew I had to let Justin do things on his own, but what if it fell on him?

Juss kicked the stand up and wheeled his bike over, trying not to grin too wide. "Be careful with her," he said to Connor. "I'm gonna ride her again one day, aren't I, Dall?"

Everyone turned to me. He was going to ride again one day. But not just yet. "Yep. One day. Might be a while before we tackle any motocross tracks though."

Connor showed us how to get the bike onto the hoist, secure it, demonstrating all its features. He noticed Juss get back on his scooter and fix his right leg onto the footrest, but Connor never missed a beat. It was obvious Juss had a leg injury, so he showed us how to use the hoist sitting on the smaller stools on wheels, standing up, or for Juss' height on his scooter.

Then, of course, when I was talking deals and dollars with Connor, Juss and Sparra raced each other from one end of the shop to the other. Sparra was on the wheelie-stool and Juss was on his scooter and, of course, Juss won, so there was a bit of yelling and laughing, and both Connor and I stopped to watch them.

To see Juss laughing and so full of life, after being near-catatonic a week ago, made me happier than words could say.

Then it was Davo's turn to race Juss, but his scooter was faster than a little stool. Not to mention that Juss had it down to an art.

"Seem like a fun bunch," Connor said.

"Anything with wheels, I swear," I replied.

"The guy with the mobility scooter," he began. "Leg injury?"

Amongst other things. "Yep."

"Motorbike?"

"Nah. The van he was driving got hit by a truck."

"Holy hell," he whispered. Then the penny dropped. "Oh shit, was that a few months back? I remember that. It was on the news. They weren't expecting him to survive. And that's him?"

"Yep."

"Wow, he was lucky." Then he cringed. "Not that getting hit by a truck is lucky . . ."

"We were all lucky that day," I answered. "Lucky he survived, that is."

We watched on as Juss laughed at something Davo said, and my heart flooded with warmth. *We came so close to losing him.*

I signed off on two new hoists, feeling pretty good about upgrading shop equipment for the guys. When we came out of my office, they had Juss' bike off the hoist and Justin was sitting on it.

"Looks like he misses not being able to ride," Connor said to me, and after a bit of small talk and promises to be in touch real soon, Davo and Sparra helped him load the demo hoists back into his truck, and he left.

Juss was grinning as he sat on his bike, and it was hard not to smile back at him. "I'm telling ya," he said. "One day."

I nodded. "One day." Then what Connor had said and seeing Juss smile like that gave me an idea. "Can you put your foot on the footpeg okay?"

He lifted his right leg and bent it so he could put his foot up. "Yeah. But if I had to stop in a hurry and put my leg down . . ."

"Hold on," I said. I ducked into my office and came back out holding up the key.

"Dallas, I . . ." He shook his head.

"You're not going to. I am. You just gotta hold onto me."

"You're gonna double me?"

"Just out through the shop, around the backyard, and back in. We're not going out on the street."

There was a moment of hesitation before his grin widened. "Hell. Yes."

I grabbed our helmets and put mine on, then handed Juss his. "If it's uncomfortable . . ."

He gently fitted the helmet over his scar, and when he had it on, he grinned so hard, his cheeks barely fit in the helmet. I swung my leg over the tank and handlebars, stood astride, kicked up the stand, and took control of the weight of the bike.

Juss put his hands on my hips, then around my waist. "I like this," he said.

I put the key in the ignition and turned her over. The bike spluttered a bit and kicked to life, and Davo and Sparra raced into the shop. Davo sagged when he saw it was me. "You scared the shit outta me! Thought it was Jusso," he yelled over the sound of the engine.

I tapped the gears down into first and released the clutch, nice and easy. We rolled forward and puttered out past Davo and Sparra —who were grinning madly—through the front roller door into the yard, then around the back near my ute, and through the rear roller door. I made the loop a second time before driving back into the workshop and coming to a stop and turning the engine off.

Sparra helped Juss off the bike, and I took my helmet off, waiting to see Juss' face.

I don't know how he got his helmet off with the way he was grinning. "That was so awesome! Thank you!"

"Oh God, you've created a monster," Sparra said. "He's gonna wanna do it all the time now. And then it'll be on his own. And then it'll be on a motocross track."

Juss was on too much of a high to care. "No, no. Not yet. But that . . . being on a bike again." He met my eyes and nodded. "That's who I am."

Oh, Juss.

Davo clapped him on the shoulder. "How do you feel? Vibrations didn't rattle anything loose?"

"Nah. Feel good."

He was still grinning when he called it a day before lunch. I went upstairs with him and he was just buzzing. He went to the kitchen and leaned against the kitchen bench. "Dall, that was so good. I know it was for like, half a minute. But being on a bike, the sound of it, the smell of the exhaust. The way it feels, that exhilaration. I remember that. Even when I was a kid and things were shit at home, having a bike was what kept me sane. I'd work on it, ride it, tune it. Being on a bike is . . . me."

I kissed him with smiling lips. "I should have thought about doing it sooner."

"I dunno if I was ready before now. I might have freaked out, and for a second I was scared when you first mentioned it. Because what if I came off and got hurt again. But I trust you, and then I wanted to do it." He shook his head like he couldn't believe it. "And Dall, it was . . . It was good to be reminded of who I am. It's not like getting a memory back, not really. More of a confirmation or reassurance that I'm still me."

I wrapped my arms around him and gave him the biggest hug. "I'm so happy for you, Juss. Seeing you smile like that means the world to me."

He sighed. "I told you it was going to be a good week."

I held him for a bit longer, just because I could. "Want me to make you a sandwich?"

He pulled back and looked up at me. His eyes were bright and clear. Happy. "Nah, I got it. You better get back downstairs. You've got a parts delivery coming this arvo, and Sparra wasn't done with that engine rebuild."

"Maybe if someone wasn't racing him on his scooter," I joked.

"I beat him too. And Davo."

I kissed him with smiling lips. "I know. I watched."

"I'll be down later, before knock-off time. I need a nap, and I can't decide if Squish and I are gonna watch some TV or if I'll watch some porn."

I snorted. "Okay then. Well, I'll let you decide." I got to the door and turned back to face him. "But if you wanted to wait until tonight, maybe we could both watch it?"

His smile became something else and he readjusted himself. "Today's the best day ever."

"Well, you certainly look a lot better than the last time I saw you," Doctor Chang said, clearly surprised to see Justin in such good shape.

"I feel so much better," Juss said. "Honestly."

Doctor Chang studied him for a second. "When I saw you last week, you weren't feeling too great."

"No, I wasn't," he replied. "And I didn't leave the hospital too great either. I was pretty much wiped out for three days, literally couldn't get off the couch, but I got better every day. I rested, drank a lot of water, ate well, slept a lot." He squeezed my hand and gave me a smile before turning back to the doc. "Not gonna lie, it scared the hell outta me. Scared Dall, too."

She gave a nod and a small smile aimed at me. "I know. I saw him. I don't know which one of you looked worse."

"Yeah, it wasn't much fun," I said.

Juss' hold on my hand tightened. "That's why I don't want to ever go through that again. I don't want to put myself through it, because it sucked, but . . . God, when I woke up in hospital and saw his face, he looked wrecked. I can't do that to him again."

"I'm glad to hear that," she said. "Did you want to talk about what you felt during the episode or what you experienced?"

He shrugged. "I felt . . . stuck. Like before, after the accident, with the mist, it kind of swirled and moved. But this was thick and heavy, almost like being underwater. I could see and hear but I couldn't get anything to make sense. I couldn't speak. I just couldn't do anything. There was no room in my head because it was so full of fog."

He'd used that analogy before, with the mist and fog. "But it cleared away pretty quick this time."

Doctor Chang nodded. "It's not uncommon that patients

recover quickly from something such as this. It's more of a stumble than a full reset to square one. But we don't want to be making a habit out of it, or the recovery times may start to lag."

"I don't want to go through it again," Juss said again. "Whatever I have to do."

She smiled and went through a list of procedures. How to recognise triggers and how to reduce the harm factor. And how to cope with stress and anxiety, and how to relieve the pressure of an attack.

Juss nodded keenly at everything she said and suggested. "Okay. I can do that. And Dall will help notice any changes that I can't see."

"For sure," I agreed. "And I'll not wait next time."

"Good, because, Justin, I'm writing you a referral for a therapist. She's brilliant and—"

"A therapist?" he asked.

"Yes." Her gaze was unwavering. "We need to treat your mental health as we do your physical health. Not only in dealing with recognising stress triggers, but also with dealing with the accident. This is a long-term health treatment, and one I recommend to all my patients."

I squeezed his hand. "We can do that."

"So you mentioned your mother is one trigger," Doctor Chang said, writing something down.

"Yeah. We blocked her number so she can't call me anymore," Justin said. "It really helps just knowing I did that."

"Less anxiety hanging over you," Doctor Chang said. "Every time the phone rings because you know it can't be her."

"Exactly."

"Good. Okay, so in the event of a stressful situation, what are some things you enjoy that could help relax you?"

"Sex," Justin replied. "Please say sex."

Doctor Chang's eyes went wide and I snorted out a laugh. "Juss."

"No, babe, I'm serious. If she tells me it's a coping mechanism, then it's technically doctor's orders, and then we can have sex all the time."

I laughed again and put my hand to my forehead. "Sorry, Doc."

She chuckled too. "Don't apologise. Justin, you had some anxiety before from just the idea of sex. I take it you've been working on that?"

"Uh, yeah," he replied. "The small-steps approach worked well. Very well, actually. So if you could, you know, say it has medicinal purposes . . ."

She smiled at that. "A doctor's recommendation?"

He didn't hesitate. "Yes, please."

"As long as it doesn't elevate stress or pain levels—"

"Oh, it doesn't," he said, cutting her off. "And I do feel very relaxed afterward."

"Oh God." I wanted the floor to open up and swallow me. "Juss, baby."

Doctor Chang fought a smile. "Sex can increase the body's production of oxytocin which releases endorphins."

Juss nodded. "Yes, it can."

"And that has been proven to reduce stress," she added. *Jesus, she was going along with this.* "But Justin, you should know that having a partner isn't required for sexual release. You don't technically require Dallas' assistance."

"Well, that's true," Juss replied. He let go of my hand and put both his hands out as though he was about to explain the size of a fish. "But he has a dick—"

I pulled his hand down, mortified. "Oh my God, you're not finishing that."

Doctor Chang burst out laughing and blushed a dark pink. "Well," she said. "I won't call it doctor's orders, but a . . . recommendation." Then she grew serious. "And only if it's consensual between both of you. If Dallas isn't comfortable, Justin, masturbation is fine."

"Oh, it's consensual," Juss replied cheerfully. "Isn't it, Dall?"

I sighed and shook my head with a laugh. "In case you were wondering, Doc, this whole conversation is a *very* Justin kind of conversation."

He smiled at me. "I feel good. I feel like me, like I can say the things I want to say. I wondered for a while who I was, and I wondered what version of me Dallas fell in love with. And now I know."

"The real you," I answered.

He nodded. "Yep." He sat back in his seat and sighed, looking right at Doctor Chang. "There is going to be so much sex tonight."

She smiled at us and closed his file. Our time was up. "I want to see you again next week. I know I said we could move to fortnightly appointments, but after last week, I'd just like to make sure we follow-up properly."

Justin looked to me. "She wants an update on the sex."

She put up her hands. "No, I don't. Unless there's an issue we need to discuss, or if you have anything you'd like to talk about. But no details," she said, putting her hands out like Justin had done with the size thing. "And no bragging, cripes."

That made Justin laugh, and it made me blush. "Sorry about that," I said. Christ, I could not believe that was a topic of conversation . . .

We left the appointment and made our way home. Justin reached over the console to take my hand while I drove. "There will be bragging. I hope she knows that."

I snorted. "Pretty sure she does, yeah."

Chapter Twelve

WE GOT BACK to the shop and Juss wanted to help Sparra with the ATV he was working on, citing he'd rest after lunch. He and Sparra had always been good mates, and since his accident, Juss had easily fallen back into step with him.

It helped that Sparra was easy going and never batted an eyelid that Juss couldn't remember him from before. If he had to explain something again, he'd just tell it like it was the first time.

And I shouldn't have been surprised when Juss had said he and Sparra were going to walk down to the corner takeaway shop and grab us some burgers. Sure, they delivered, but Juss and Sparra wanted to walk and chat, and after all, they'd done it a hundred times. But not since the accident.

"We'll be fine," Juss said to me. "I'm using the scooter."

And what could I say? He was an adult, for crying out loud. I couldn't tell him no. I wasn't his keeper.

"Okay then, well, be safe. And if you need me, call me."

Juss rolled his eyes but he smiled. "Dall, I'll be fine."

I nodded, because yeah, sure, I knew he would be. And he was cautious about overdoing it, and I knew he wouldn't push himself. But damn, I could still worry.

I watched the front gate as they left and I watched it every minute they were gone.

Davo clapped me on the back. "He'll be fine."

"Hmm."

"You gotta let him do stuff."

"I know. I just . . ."

"You just worry. I get it. And I don't blame ya. But it's just down the road, he has his scooter, and Sparra won't let anything happen to him."

"Hmm."

"He needs to be able to go into a shop and order and pay for stuff, Dall. He's gotta start doing that shit some time."

"Yeah, I know . . ." And I *did* know that. "But God, if something were to happen . . . if he falls or gets dizzy, or hears a car screech its tyres and freaks out, or—" I shook my head. "I can't bear the thought of him having another setback."

Davo's tone softened. "I know, mate. And I'm not downplaying anything that he went through or what you went through with him. But you can't be there every minute of forever. He needs to start doing things on his own again."

I sighed. "I know."

"How're you gonna be when he starts to drive again?"

I shot Davo a look that probably bordered on panicked and wild. "Christ. I dunno. I'm going to not think about that until I have to, is what I'm gonna do."

He chuckled. "You've got a bit of time yet. But you're gonna have to think about it eventually."

"Hmm." Fucking hell. "I don't want to wrap him up in cotton wool, and I know he's not made of glass. But he's not *un*breakable either. When you come so close to losing someone, something inside you changes. You'll do anything to protect them. And when you watch them struggle every day, you want to make sure they never have to struggle again. The smallest thing to you and me could see him on bedrest for a week." *Or in hospital, almost catatonic.* I shrugged. "I'm always gonna worry. It's just part of who I am."

Davo nodded to the front gate. "Well, you can stop worrying for now."

And sure enough, Juss and Sparra were back. They were laughing at something, and he looked so happy, a pang of guilt lanced me. He should be doing things with his mates, and I felt bad for maybe shielding him a little too hard.

My face must have said as much, because Davo gave me a nudge. "It's all good, Dallas. He needs someone looking out for him."

"Haven't you two done any work while we've been gone," Sparra joked as they came in through the roller door. "I leave for thirty minutes and the work ethic goes to shit."

Davo threw his oil rag at him and we laughed as we headed into the breakroom. And all the worry aside, Juss' smile told me all I needed to know.

He needed to enjoy the good times while they were good, because Lord knew he'd had enough bad times.

We ate our lunch and Sparra gave us a rundown of how things were going with Carissa, and I'd just finished my burger when the phone rang.

I left them to keep talking for the rest of their lunch break and took the call in my office. "Muller Mechanical. Dallas speaking."

"I need to speak to Justin Keith, please."

The voice was horrible and familiar and it took a second for me to place it. It was Justin's mother. I stopped cold; anger ran like ice through my veins. I wanted to do evil to this woman, but I remembered all too well that my temper and yelling at her were partly to blame for Justin's meltdown. So I kept my voice calm and neutral. "Janet."

"Hmm, Dallas," she said, and I could just picture her sneering as she spoke my name. "I assume you're the reason he won't answer his mobile when I call it."

"I don't care what you assume."

She was quiet a second and decided to try again. "Don't suppose Justin's calmed down enough to speak to his mother?"

"Calmed down?" I asked incredulously. *Don't yell, Dallas. Don't yell.* With a deep breath, I tried to be composed. "Do you have any idea what stress and high blood pressure can do to someone with a brain injury?"

She was quiet for a second. "What?"

"Justin went to hospital in an ambulance after your little stunt last week. He couldn't speak or do anything. Ever seen someone you love catatonic like that, Janet?"

"I don't know what you're talking about," she snapped.

"I'm talking about brain injury. You know, what Justin has, if you even care. Something he has to live with forever, something that is affected by high levels of stress. Like you turning up demanding money."

"I deserve that money."

"You know what you fucking deserve?" I began, my jaw clenched.

But then I noticed Juss standing at the door. His smile was rueful. "Is that my mother?"

Goddammit.

I nodded, and he held out his hand for the phone. "Are you sure?" I asked.

"Yeah. I'll be okay, Dall."

I handed the phone over and he put it to his ear. "Mum," he said. "I'm sorry."

I shot him a look. What the *hell* was he apologising for?

"Oh no, don't misunderstand," he said. "I said I'm sorry. Sorry I missed your head when I threw my cane at you. I thought I had better aim."

Shocked, I snorted out a laugh, but Juss wasn't done.

"If you call me again or if you turn up here again, I will call the cops. I will take a restraining order out against you. You're not my family. You disowned me." Then he smiled at me. "I have a real family, Mum, and he chose me. He chose me twice."

My heart just about burst to hear him say that. I could hear her tinny voice squawking through the receiver but he was done. He'd said what he needed to say. While she was ranting away, he simply disconnected the call and slid the phone onto the desk with satisfying finality. *He was done.* I stood up and stepped around my desk to throw my arms around him in a crushing hug. I whispered into his neck, "Baby, I would choose you a hundred times."

"And I'd choose you," he replied.

I pulled back and put my hand to the side of his face and thumbed the scar above his eyebrow. "I'm sorry you had to go through that. I know your mother's been horrible, but it still sucks that you had to do that. Do you feel okay?"

"Dall, I'm fine." He smiled sadly. "I actually feel good about telling her that, like a weight has been lifted. I think when she just showed up and started yelling, I was shocked and I wasn't prepared at all. But I am now. I know what she's after, and I know you'll protect me."

"I will."

"And like you said, we find our own family."

I kissed him. "I like the sound of that. You and me."

"And Squish."

I snorted. "And Squish."

"Who is probably wondering where I am and why I've missed our nap time."

"Then you better go let him know you're okay."

"I am tired," he murmured. "And I need all the rest I can get for tonight."

"For tonight?" Then I remembered as soon as I'd said it.

"Oh yeah, and don't think you're getting out of it. It's doctor's orders."

"Pretty sure it was just a recommendation."

He gave me a lopsided smile, full of cheek and daring. "Well, it's my recommendation that you don't hold out on me." Then he was serious. He whispered, "It's my first time, Dall. My first proper time without a condom. Not just with you, but ever. I've never done that before. I mean, I have, we have, obviously. But I don't remember it. Well, I can remember that time at Hallidays Point, but I want to feel it now. I want to experience it, firsthand, and make new memories."

I lifted his chin and kissed him softly. "I have no intention of holding out on you." Then I winked at him. "I just hope your expectations and my *actual* capabilities are on par."

He chuckled. "I hear practice makes perfect."

"I might need it," I said with a laugh. Then I sighed. "You sure you feel okay about your mum?" I needed to be sure . . .

"Yeah. Actually, I feel good about it. I needed to say that to her. Whether she listens is up to her, but I said what I needed to say."

I studied his eyes for a moment. They were a clear brown, tired, but there was no blankness, no sadness. "Okay, baby. I'll just be here. If you need anything or want to talk, I'll come straight up."

He glanced around to make sure no one could overhear. "What if I need help watching porn?"

I laughed and gave him a light smack on the arse. He smiled as he made his way upstairs, and I got back to work, grateful for the distraction. I didn't need to be thinking about what we might be doing tonight. The last thing I needed was to be working with a semi.

But between bikes, ATVs, and the never-ending phone calls, I was more than distracted. It was good, though. It felt . . . good.

Like maybe—and I didn't want to jinx myself—that life was beginning to look up. Maybe we could plateau for a bit and find our new normal. Now that we'd identified some of Justin's triggers, we could avoid them and manage them. Hopefully, his mother would now leave us alone, and he could just concentrate on getting better.

I knew it had only been a week since his last episode, and I knew it could all be different in another week. But I wanted to believe the worst was behind us.

I wanted to make sure it was.

Juss came back downstairs just before closing. I was finishing up some paperwork and heard his laughter in the workshop. God, it made me smile. He helped the guys clean up and lock everything down for me, and Davo said he'd lock the gate as they left. Juss pulled the roller door down and came to lean against the doorframe to the office.

"They said they'd see you in the morning," he said.

"Oh, okay. I'm just getting things ready for Toni. It's her first day tomorrow."

"Yeah, the boys were talking about it. Davo reckons you're too much of a control freak and you'll still be trying to do everything and driving Toni mad."

I laughed incredulously. "A control freak?" Then I thought about that and how I'd run everything my way for years. "Yeah, okay. So maybe he's not entirely wrong. But I gotta say, Juss, I'm looking forward to handing things over."

"You are?"

"Yep. The creditors, debtors, inventory, phone calls . . . my God, the phone didn't stop ringing today. Now I'm used to the idea of someone doing all that for me, for us, I think I'm really gonna like it." I sat back in my desk chair and sighed. "I just want some time to breathe, ya know? So it's not a madhouse every day, trying to get everything done. I'll still have all my responsibilities, of course, but I want to be able to enjoy working on some bikes, having a laugh with the boys, and spending time with you. We've talked about cutting back on stress for you, and it's about time I cut some stress from my life too."

He smiled. "That sounds really good to me."

"We ready to go upstairs?"

"Babe, I'm so ready for you to take me upstairs."

I barked out a laugh. "Right, then."

"No, I mean it. I'm *ready* ready. I took care of the pipes, if you know what I mean."

It took me a second. "Oh my God, right."

He chuckled and raised an eyebrow. "Are you having second thoughts?"

"Hell no."

"Then what are you waiting for?"

I shut down my computer and stood up. "Absolutely nothing." I walked to him and kissed him soundly. "Get your arse upstairs."

He grinned. "That's more like it."

I followed him up, getting a perfect close-up view of his arse, and it didn't take my dick long to notice either. The anticipation was going to kill me. He'd wanted this for weeks and I was beginning to think I might not live up to his expectations.

When we were inside, he took one look at me and laughed. "Dall, you're overthinking this."

"You have expectations now. You're probably thinking this is gonna move both heaven and earth, and I'm seriously thinking it's gonna be over in like, five minutes. Maybe four."

He laughed again and took my hand, pulling me close. "Babe. You know me, right?"

I nodded. "Yeah."

"You know what I like, and you know how I like it. You've had years of experience with me, and I have none with you. It's the only time I'll let you use my amnesia against me." He chuckled and pulled me down for a kiss. "I have no expectations, honestly." Then he made a face. "Well, that's not true. I have two expectations. One, that you'll take it easy on me. My body isn't as flexible as it used to be. And two, that you will come inside me. I need to know what that feels like."

I gasped, his words sending a jolt of desire to my balls that almost buckled my knees. I crushed my mouth to his, using his surprise to claim his mouth with my tongue. But he was right . . . I knew him. I knew his body, what he liked, and how he liked it.

His smile broke the kiss. Grinning now—because he knew he was getting what he wanted—he pulled on my hand and led me to the bedroom. He stopped inside the door, where I could see the bed.

Which he'd already prepared. There was a pile of pillows across the middle of the bed, covered with towels. The perfect height for me to bend him over. The lube was lying on the bed covers.

Justin smiled proudly. "I told you I was ready."

I laughed and kissed him again. "First, we need to get you naked."

The days of ripping our clothes off and fucking, rough and demanding, were done. I couldn't even pull his shirt over his head without considering his arm, and getting him out of pants had to be slow and careful because of his leg.

But I didn't mind one bit. It gave me time to kiss every reveal of skin, to savour every moment. And getting him onto the bed was an exercise in caution. Once upon a time, I'd have just thrown him on the bed and crawled on after him, but not anymore.

He needed to trust that I would take care of him and make this good for him. But I also knew he couldn't endure too much for too long, so timing and endurance were important. There was a happy medium in there somewhere, and I was determined to find it.

Once I had him into position, bent over the pillows with his arse high up in the air, I rubbed his back and skimmed my hands over his arse. I poured lube onto my fingers and ran them across his hole.

He moaned.

I pushed a fingertip inside him and slowly worked him, getting his arse ready for me. Yes, I'd been inside him since the accident, but I hadn't fucked him. I hadn't thrust and stretched him like I was about to.

God, just thinking about it . . . My cock ached to be in him right now.

I worked in another finger, and then I added my tongue. He gasped and gripped the bed covers. "Oh fuck," he groaned. "Dallas, what . . . oh God."

I chuckled. "I know what you like, remember?"

He groaned, a deep guttural sound as I tongue-fucked him some more. When he began rocking his hips back and forth, I knew he was ready.

I lubed my cock and poured more over his hole, working it in with my thumb before lining my cockhead up and swiping it over his slick entrance, pushing just a little. "You ready, baby?"

"Yes. Dallas, please . . ."

So I pushed inside him, slow, so torturously slow, and he fisted the blankets and whined as I pressed in. He gasped as he took me into his body. I stilled, holding myself right there while he got used to the intrusion. I leaned over him, lay down on top of him with my cock fully seated inside him, and whispered in his ear, "Breathe, baby."

It took a moment but his breaths deepened and he relaxed, then began to roll his hips. I followed his tempo, slow and intense. He began to groan, gruff and gravelly.

That sound, so familiar and so new, told me he loved it, told me he was ready for more. So I listened to him, to his body, and set my pace in tune with his grunts, his groans, his mindless pleas for more.

I thrust in deep and pulled back slow, gently gripping his hips and giving him every inch. Giving him exactly what he wanted. Slow, tender, and so fucking good.

He was tight and hot, slick and welcoming as I took him. Pleasure building so thick and strong, I could taste it. My cock felt like steel, so hard, my balls needed release.

"Baby, I can't hold on," I ground out, my hips thrusting of their own accord, seeking more, more, more.

"God, Dallas, do it," he panted. "Come inside me."

I thrust in one last time, every inch, and my orgasm barrelled through me. Pleasure and love overwhelmed and consumed me as I came, spilling deep inside him.

He gasped and cried out as I groaned through my release, thrusting with every pulse. I collapsed on top of him, still inside him, while the world around me spun. He gave me time to catch my breath before he began to rock his hips.

This was what he loved.

He loved my spent cock inside him, my come inside him. He loved to stay joined, coupled and close. He slid his hand underneath himself and began to fuck his fist. "Dallas, I need . . ."

"I'll give you everything you need, baby," I murmured, reaching under him. I replaced his hand around his shaft and gave him a few hard strokes.

"Oh, God."

I kept my semi-hard dick buried in him while I jacked him off, and knowing which words would send him over the edge, I whispered into the back of his neck, "Can you feel my come inside you?"

Juss stilled; his cock surged and swelled in my hand before spilling onto the towel beneath him. He cried out, trembling and convulsing with the power of his orgasm until he collapsed on the mattress.

I pressed my weight on his back, still in him. I never wanted to leave. But he'd probably overdone it and was going to be sore tomorrow. So I slowly pulled out and he whined. "Stay."

I chuckled and kissed his shoulder and behind his ear, but I kept my length pressed against him. "Baby, I don't want to hurt you."

"I can feel how hard you are."

"Because you just jerked off with my cock in your arse. It's hot as hell."

He ripped the pillows out from underneath him so he was flat on the bed. He spread his legs wider and raised his arse. "I'm not kidding, Dallas. I want more."

Fuck.

There it was. That demanding, sexual side of Justin that had been absent for so long. So I gave him what he wanted. I knelt between his thighs and gave myself a few long strokes before I pushed back into him in one, sharp thrust. He was so slick, so inviting.

He was home to me.

He moaned as I thrust in and out of him. I kissed the back of his neck, his shoulder, as I drove into him, balls deep and rocking, and I was at the edge already.

Being inside him, making love, was everything familiar and brand new all over again.

His eyes went wide when I came, and he gasped as he felt it. "Oh, God, yes. Dallas, yes."

I collapsed on top of him again, and this time I did pull out. Before he could protest, I rolled us onto our sides and wrapped him up in my arms. I kissed him, deep and with all the love and passion I had in me. And for a long time, we just lay there, kissing, holding each other, basking in what we'd just done.

He was tired though, and when he nuzzled into my neck, I

stroked his back, his hip. "You're going to need that massage," I murmured. "And a hot shower. And dinner."

"Mm." He was almost asleep. "Just wanna stay right here."

I held him a bit tighter. "I love you so much," I whispered.

"Love you too, Dall." After a few moments, I felt him smile into my neck. "Love what you did to me, love how you did it."

I chuckled and traced lazy circles on his back. "You're going to be sore tomorrow."

"Worth it." He sighed and snuggled in some more. "So fucking worth it."

Chapter Thirteen

"ARE YOU SURE YOU FEEL OKAY?" I asked. The guys were about to arrive for work and I was making sure the office was somewhat tidy for Toni before she arrived for her first day. But I needed to make sure Juss was feeling okay after last night. Again.

"Like I told you each of the ten times you've asked me already, I feel great. I'm a little achy in all the right places, but it's a good ache." He leaned over and pulled my chin up for a kiss. "And I appreciate you asking because I know you worry, and you worry because you love me. But so help me God, Dallas, if you ask me again when everyone's here, I will tell them why you're asking."

I chuckled, because that was such a Justin thing to say.

"And I will use the fire extinguisher as a size guide."

I burst out laughing just as we heard Davo drive into the yard. "Okay, I won't ask again. I trust that you'll tell me if there's something wrong."

He was pleased by that. "I will."

He pulled his scooter over and sat down, then made a face. I raised an eyebrow. "I'm not going to ask if that hurt, but if I were to suggest some padding on that seat . . ."

He wiggled on the seat. "No, but I might be in need of another massage by tonight."

"Now, that, I can do."

"With your fire extinguisher."

Davo and Sparra walked in. "What's that about a fire extinguisher?" Davo asked. "Are we due for a safety check?"

Juss chuckled as he scooted out to greet them. "Something like that."

Toni arrived next, and after formal introductions to the team, I spent most of the morning in the office with her, showing her the ropes. I wasn't surprised that she had it all down in no time given she was answering the phone and taking bookings in her first twenty minutes on the job. She laughed with the boys at smoko time and could talk shit about bikes with the best of them.

She was a perfect fit.

After lunch, Juss called it a day and went upstairs and I followed him up. "I'm not going to ask," I began.

"I'm fine, Dall. Just tired. It's nap time for me and Squish. I'll come back down later."

"Okay then."

"Toni seems to be working out all right?" he said, getting himself on the couch.

"Yeah, she's great. She's already reorganising stuff and making spreadsheets to streamline our ordering process."

Squish came out of the bedroom and joined Juss on the couch, and Juss started flicking through channels. "Sorry, Squish," he said. "No fishing shows today. The Spanish motocross championships are on. We can watch *Fishing Australia* later."

I laughed and leaned down to kiss Juss' forehead. "Call me if you need me."

His eyelids were getting heavy already, but he gave me an easy smile. "Mm, doing booty calls now? 'Cause I think I'm gonna need more of what you did to me last night."

I laughed as I went back down to the shop, and I spent most of the afternoon working on a Honda bike that had picked up dirty fuel.

It was weird that every time the phone rang, I reached for my back pocket to take the call. Davo laughed at me a few times when he saw me, and he nodded to the office. "Wondering why you didn't hire someone years ago?"

"God, yes."

Toni still had to come and ask me questions now and then, but she mostly had it all under control. Which meant I got my work done so much quicker, and without the interruptions, I could do a better job.

Juss came back down at 3:30 and he and Sparra finished up the job they'd been working on, and I stuck my head in the office to make sure Toni was going okay. "How's your first day been?"

"Good!" she said. "Just getting things organised. I'll attack the filing cabinets and stationery cupboard tomorrow."

"Make a list of anything you need, and we'll get it."

"Oh, there's an email that came through a little while ago," she said. "About a replacement van. If you read it and tell me what you want me to say, I can draft up a reply for you."

"Oh man." My gaze automatically went to Justin, where he was talking with Sparra. "I guess that's a conversation I need to have with Juss first." I gave her a smile. "I'll let you know tomorrow, thanks."

That was a conversation I'd put off long enough.

When everyone left for the day, I locked the gate behind Toni and headed back into the workshop. Juss pulled the roller doors down and went to head into the office. "Babe, it's home time," I called out.

He stopped. "Don't you have paperwork to do for a bit?"

"Nope. Toni's got it all under control."

His eyes lit up. "So we have an early mark?"

I smiled at that. "Yep."

"I do believe there was talk of a massage."

I led him to the back stairs. "I do believe so too."

I followed him up, noting how his steps had improved. He used his leg with much more ease now, taking each tread with more confidence. I doubted he'd ever again be sprinting up them two at a time like he used to, but seeing his improvement made me smile.

We got through the door and he headed straight for the

kitchen. "I was thinking we could have veggie stir fry for dinner," he began.

"Sure. Sounds great. But, uh, Juss, can we talk for a second?"

He stopped to stare at me and his face fell. "Did I do something wrong?"

Oh, baby. "No. Why would you think that?"

"I don't know. You just have a line between your eyebrows that you get when you're worried or thinking about serious stuff. Or when you don't want to tell me something. Like you don't want to tell me something right now . . ."

"And you thought you didn't know how to read me," I said with a smile. I took his hand and we sat at the table. "There's nothing wrong. I just wanted to talk about the van and whether or not we should get it replaced."

He sagged a little and put his hand to his heart. "God, is that all? Shit, Dallas, you freaked me out."

"I'm sorry. I should have told you it wasn't anything about us." We'd learned the hard way that freaking Justin out didn't end well. "I'm so sorry."

"It's okay. I just panicked for a second." He took a deep breath and let out a sigh of relief. "What about the van?"

"Oh, it's just the insurance company has requested some information about whether or not we want the van replaced. And I wanted to ask you."

"Me?"

"Well, yeah. I guess I need to know if you want—not now, but when you're ready—to replace the mobile mechanic van, and if you wanted to do it again."

"Me, drive?"

"When you're given the all-clear."

He frowned. "I don't know. I haven't thought about it."

"Yeah, and you don't need to answer right now. You certainly don't have to do it if you don't want."

Juss thought for a long few seconds, then shook his head sadly. "I don't think I could. Be a mobile mechanic again. I mean, not on my own, for a long time. I can't lift a lot of things, and physically, I just don't think I could."

"It's okay, baby. You don't have to decide right now. You don't need to worry about it or stress over it. You can say no now, and in a year's time or five years' time, if you want to think about it again, that's okay too."

His gaze locked to mine and he nodded. "Thanks. I just . . . I'm not ready. I can't drive yet anyway, and . . ."

"And?"

"And I don't know how I feel about driving." He put his hand to his forehead. "I mean, I'll probably drive again at some point, but I can't . . . I get so tired and I can't concentrate too much for too long. My reflexes are kinda slow, and the idea of being in another accident scares the shit outta me, if I'm being honest. Or causing one. God, what if I hurt someone?"

I cupped his face and kissed him before pulling him in for a long, hard hug. "It's okay, baby. You don't need to worry about it right now. I just need to tell the insurance people what we planned on doing and wanted to ask you first. The mobile van was your idea, and it was your thing."

He was quiet while I held him and I rubbed his back, giving him time to think and relax.

"What do you want me to do?" he asked eventually. "As my boyfriend? And as my boss? Are they different things here?"

I pulled back and put my forehead to his so he had to look at me. "Boyfriend first, always. We've never had an issue with lines or boundaries, and I don't want to start now. I would never make you do something you weren't comfortable doing, as a boyfriend or a boss, okay?"

"I know. I'm sorry. I just wasn't sure . . . I didn't know how I should answer."

"The truth, Juss. Whatever you feel."

He gave a small smile. "You don't want me to do it, do you?"

I sighed. "And you said you couldn't read me."

He smiled at that. "Guess I'm learning."

"Baby, I don't know how I feel about you driving at all." I admitted. "I'd be happy to scrap the van altogether. I don't want to risk any more accidents, and as a boss, I have to think about those things. It's just not worth anyone else going through this. But as a boyfriend, the idea of you even driving on your own scares me right now. I know I can't wrap you up in cotton wool, and even small things like you walking to the take-out shop with Sparra was enough to freak me out. That's something I have to work on, I know that. You have to have your independence, and you can do whatever you want. But the thought of you being hurt again just terrifies me. The thought of you being hurt and me not being there to help you terrifies me even more." I sighed, long and loud. "I know I can't be there all the time, and I know I can't fix every single thing. But . . ."

"But you're a control freak and you can't help that."

I snorted. "Exactly."

His gaze flickered between mine. "Remember when Doctor Chang said fear of more pain stopped me from wanting to have sex? Well, it's a bit like that for you. Not the sex part, obviously. But after the accident, you went through hell too. And you're just trying to do whatever you can to never experience that again. I get that. Believe me."

I got a little teary, and I nodded. "Yeah. But like you said; you'll probably drive again someday and we'll have to work on that. I don't want my fear to stop you from doing anything."

"Small steps is what she suggested."

"Small steps." I nodded. "I can do small steps."

He smiled and relaxed with a deep sigh. "So we can agree on maybe one day but not right now."

I kissed him. "Agreed." He slotted in against me once more and wrapped his arms around me, giving me one helluva hug. "Hey, I thought I was the resident best-hug giver. Are you trying to take my title?"

He chuckled. "You smell like petrol, grease, and dirt. And sweat."

"Sorry. I should shower."

He held me tighter. "Absolutely not. I love that smell. A mechanic smell, my favourite kind. You could bottle it." Then he ran his hand down to my arse and gave me a squeeze. "Or we could be naked and you can rub that scent all over me." My dick twitched and, of course, he felt it. He laughed. "Someone liked that idea."

I nuzzled into his neck and whispered against his ear. "How sore do you want to be tomorrow?"

He chuckled and moaned as he craned his neck, giving me more skin to kiss and nip. "You'll just have to massage me all better."

I scraped my teeth along his jaw before capturing his mouth with mine. He moaned into my mouth and melted against me, so pliable, so giving.

I led him to our bedroom, stripped us both naked, and laid him face down on the mattress. He wanted a massage, so that's what I gave him. I worshipped every inch of him until he was begging me to fill him. So then I gave him that too.

***

THE NEXT FEW days were blissful. Work was great: having Toni in the office was a godsend and everyone was less stressed all round. The new hoists were delivered on Friday and I ordered pizza for everyone at lunch, and Juss and the boys had more races on the new stools. I don't think we stopped smiling all day.

And the next few weeks were much the same. Justin's appointments with Doctor Chang were now only once a fort-night, and Megan only had to do one homecare visit a week. He met his new therapist and was pleased they'd worked on a long-term plan together. He kept doing his physio exercises and he was walking more and more. His strength was increasing every day, and although he still only worked until lunchtime, he was doing a lot more. He'd still take his nap with Squish every day, then come back down and help us finish up. That schedule probably wouldn't change for a long time, and that was perfectly okay with me.

He didn't get any new memories or flashbacks, and given he hadn't had any in over a month, it was becoming less likely he ever would.

And that was okay too.

Somewhere along the way he'd made peace with that. He had all the memories he needed, he'd said. He was more focused on living in the present, making new memories here and now, and planning for the future.

I certainly couldn't argue with that.

Jimmy and Nancy had invited us again to their next family lunch, and Justin had enjoyed it just as much as last time. The same familiar faces were there, plus a few new ones, and Juss wasn't so tired this time. At first, I might have thought it a little odd that he and Jimmy had formed some kind of bond. He was the driver of the truck that hit Justin's van, after all. But Juss bonded with Nancy too, and all their kids who were all our age, or a bit older. Then it occurred to me what it was . . .

Justin had found himself a part of a family. And me too, I guessed. But maybe they were like the parents he'd never had, the fondness and affection he needed from his own mother and never got.

When Juss had told Nancy what had happened with his mum, she'd hugged him fiercely and basically swept him under her wing with all the other kids like a clutch of chicks. And Juss had just positively beamed.

"I really like them," he said as we got home. "They're just such good people."

"They are," I said, getting out of the ute. "I bet Jimmy was a real looker in his younger days."

Juss had smiled at that, but then he was quiet a while, which I put down to his being tired. He parked himself on the couch but didn't fall asleep straight away. He stared at the TV, though he wasn't really watching it, while I folded the clothes from the dryer. His brow furrowed, which told me he was overthinking something.

"Everything okay?" I asked, sitting down beside him.

"Yeah." He took my hand and studied his fingers as they threaded with mine. "Just thinking about something Jimmy said today."

"What was that?"

"When he toasted to family and all that."

I thought the whole family thing had been on his mind and it would seem I wasn't wrong. "I think they include you in their family now."

He smiled, tired but happy. "I think so too. I like that."

"I do too. I know it means a lot to you."

"It does. I mean, I have Becca and the girls. And I have you."

"You do."

"And you said something once about found family."

"Yep. The people who choose you. They love you because they want to, not because they have to."

His hold on my hand tightened and a worry line formed between his brows.

"Juss, what is it? What's the matter?" He tried to swallow and struggled, and for a heart-stopping second, I thought he was having another turn. "Juss?"

"I'm okay, I just . . ." He let out a shaky breath. "I don't know how to ask this. It kinda feels wrong to ask, like I'm asking too much. But then it feels so right . . ."

"Baby, you can ask me anything. Anything at all."

His soulful brown eyes met mine. "Would you marry me?"

I stared at him, shocked, stunned, speechless. I was not expecting that, and it took me a second to form words. "Marry you?"

"Yeah, sorry. I know it's a lot to ask, given—" He waved his hand at his head, namely his scar. "And I probably should have asked a better way, like more romantic, but I'm pretty sure if I tried to set something romantic up, I would've freaked out trying to organise it and keep it secret from you. Probably would have had another meltdown, actually. And today, all that talk about family . . . I mean, you're my family. You're my everything. And I want it to be official and real, and we can get married now; you said we could—"

I kissed him quiet. "Yes."

It took him a second. "Yes?"

"Yes." I nodded and my eyes burned with tears. "My God, yes. I would love to marry you. Nothing would make me happier." I kissed him again. My heart was thumping against my ribs, I was so giddy! But he'd said something first . . . "But before I get too excited, why would you say it's a lot to ask?"

"Because of my injuries," he replied like it was obvious. "Because chances are, I'm gonna have some cognitive issues later in life. Around Jimmy's age, probably. And asking you to sign up for that probably isn't really fair."

"Justin, I love you. Nothing's gonna change that. In sickness and in health, or however it goes. That's what love means. Please don't ever doubt me."

"I don't doubt you, Dall. You're the one true thing in my life. Out of all the fog and fear and loss, was you. I can't imagine my life or my future without you. I want to marry you and wear your ring and be yours in every way I can. Maybe not just yet. I mean, I'd marry you right now if you wanted, but just knowing is enough for now. I don't want to overload my brain, but just knowing we're a kind of family is all I need."

"We were already a kind of family, Juss."

"But this makes it real." He shrugged and made a face. "In my head. I don't know why. But legally too. The government can't say we're not a family if we get married. And hospitals and insurances can't say we're not a family either."

"Oh, baby."

"If something were to happen, Dall," he whispered. "I need you with me. But it's not all just doom and gloom. I want to be yours for all the fun stuff too, I want to be married to you, to be your husband."

I kissed him again. "And I'll be yours."

Juss' eyes filled with tears and he began to cry. "You'll really marry me?"

"Yes, baby. A thousand times yes." I thumbed away his tears. "Why are you crying?"

"All I ever wanted was a family of my own."

"Oh, Jussy." I pulled him into a hug. "We are a family. Married or not, you and me, we're a family."

He sobbed and sniffled. "And Squish."

"Yeah, baby. And Squish too."

He inhaled deeply and settled into me, like he could finally relax. I held him until he fell asleep, and even then I still didn't get up. I let him sleep with his face smooshed into my chest, his hands tucked in between us, and I wrapped him up in my arms and let the realisation of what just happened settle over us like a warm blanket.

We were gonna get married. He wanted to marry me, to make it official, to make it real. He still seemed to think he wasn't worthy, so obviously I would need to spend the next fifty or sixty years proving to him that he was.

He asked me to marry him. And no, I didn't need any fancy proposal or grand romantic gesture. That wasn't who we were. We were just two knock-around blokes trying to make sense of life, together. All we needed was each other.

Squish chose that very moment to join us, jumping up onto the couch, already purring and looking for the best place to curl up with Juss. "Yes, you too."

Two Years Later

JUSTIN

"ARE YOU READY?"

"I am so ready."

Dallas grinned. "Me too. You nervous?"

I inhaled deeply and let it out real slow. We were dressed in matching navy dress pants and white button-up shirts and shined dress shoes. It didn't hurt that Dallas' shirt was tight and showed his muscly chest and biceps. And how his pants hugged him in all the right places. His hair was freshly cut, his beard trimmed, and he was handsome as hell. "Nope. I'm excited. Why? Are you nervous?"

"A little bit. Just about speaking in front of people, that's all."

"Don't be. We've got this."

He shook his head, smiling. "Since when did you become the expert?"

"I had a good teacher."

That was true. The last two years had been amazing and sometimes hard, but mostly great. If we could call it a climb, then the view from the top was spectacular. It hadn't all been easy. I'd had ongoing physio but my leg was as good as new now, and there'd been ongoing neuro follow-ups, scans, appointments, and therapy sessions. I still had to watch stress levels, and doing too much and overworking my brain would put me back on my arse for a while. And, of course, the headaches were still a thing.

I never did get all my memory back. I got some random bits and pieces, some flashbacks that hit me out of nowhere, but there were still holes in my timeline, but there was nothing I could do about it. I had to accept that. I could either spend time and energy being mad about it, or I could put that time and energy into making new memories. It wasn't really a choice.

I hadn't had another episode. I hadn't had any worrying downfalls or major setbacks. And that was, without any doubt, for me at least, because of Dallas.

He'd disagree with that and say it was because we knew how to address stress now, but we all knew it was the truth.

My prognosis was good, though I would always be a traumatic brain injury survivor. The likelihood of me having issues later in life was always a possibility, but we were aware and proactive with my health. The truth was, Dallas was right, like he usually was. We were in this together, always, no matter what life threw at us.

I'd come up with a plan for my money, and that was to let it sit earning interest until Dallas and I were ready to sell the business and move on. That wasn't going to be for a long while away, another twenty or thirty years, God willing. We debated over buying a house somewhere close to the shop, but we loved the flat upstairs. We loved being close to work, and it meant I could easily go home if I needed to rest, without driving. But maybe one day we would move, when we were looking to retire, and the money was my safety net. And if that had to include funds, should I need medical care later in life, then so be it.

It was just what we'd have to do. Like everything, we'd do it together.

Together, forever.

"I think they're waiting for us to start," Dallas said.

I held out my hand for him to take and looked down at myself. "Do I look okay?"

"You're sexy as fuck," he said, stepping in for a kiss.

"Okay, you two, Jesus H Christ," Sparra said, interrupting us. "We're all over here waiting and you two are here making out."

He said it loud enough so people could hear, and, of course, they laughed. I chuckled and took a deep breath and held out my hand. "Okay, Mr Muller. Let's do this."

Dallas grasped my hand, holding on tight. "It is my honour to walk down this aisle with you."

He made my heart skip a beat, or ten. God, we were finally getting married. And yes, we chose to walk each other down the aisle. We didn't exactly have willing parents, but we also wanted to begin our married lives as equal partners.

We'd asked just our closest friends and family to attend our wedding. Becca and the girls were there, of course, but my mother most certainly never received an invitation. I don't even know if she knew about the wedding.

I'd seen her once since I'd cut her off. I ran into her downtown and she was as surprised to see me as I was her. She looked around for Dallas and smiled when she realised he wasn't with me. "Boyfriend not leeching off you today?" she'd sneered.

"You mean fiancé?" I'd replied with a bright smile. "He's always with me. He, unlike you, would never abandon me."

Her expression turned sour, but I was done with it. I was done with her. I was about to remind her that I'd call the cops if I had to, to keep her away from me, but instead I turned and walked away.

I hadn't seen or heard of her since.

Becca hadn't spoken to her much over the last two years either, so it was more than likely that my mother didn't even know I was getting married.

And for that, I was glad.

I had my found family, and today I was making it official.

Davo and Lauren sat at the front with little Elliott on Lauren's knee. Elliott was dressed in a little vest and pants outfit that matched Davo's as if it wasn't the cutest thing ever. Davo becoming a dad was the best thing to ever happen to him, and he was full of advice for Sparra, because he and Carissa were expecting their first baby any day now.

That made me and Dallas uncles, and I'd be lying if I said I didn't love it.

Kids weren't something Dall and I wanted, but that didn't mean we couldn't love and spoil them rotten.

Jimmy and Nancy were in the second row, dressed up all fancy and beaming like proud parents. Dallas' dad and step-mum were there, and Mark, one of his brothers. They didn't have an overly great relationship, but the fact they'd come today meant a lot to Dallas.

Our wedding was on Dixon Park Beach, overlooking the Pacific, where Dallas had brought me a few times since the accident to relax and soak up some sun. When he'd suggested it as a location, I couldn't think of anywhere better.

There was a small congregation of white chairs and a celebrant who stood at the end in between two tall stands of white flowers. Everything looked so simple and perfect, and admittedly, I'd had a lot of help from Toni with everything. I think she took pity on us and did most of the organising.

But the whole thing was perfect. It was a beautiful spring day, the ocean was sparkling, the sun was shining, and some passers-by had gathered a safe distance to watch. We met the celebrant at the front and the ceremony began.

"I'd like to thank everyone for coming today to witness the union of Dallas and Justin," the celebrant said. "And don't worry, everyone. I've been told they wanted the ceremony short and sweet because, and I quote Dallas on this, 'No one likes that drawn-out, boring stuff.'"

That earned us a chuckle, but honestly, it was true. So the celebrant gave a quick spiel about the sanctity of marriage and love and acceptance, and before we knew it, it was time for our vows.

Dallas and I turned to face each other, our hands joined between us, and I'd never seen him so nervous! I rubbed the backs of his hands with my thumbs and he gave me a thankful smile. "I'm supposed to be going first," he said. "That was a bad idea, oh my God."

I chuckled. "You're okay," I whispered. "Just breathe."

He held my gaze and he must have seen something in my eyes because he nodded. "Justin," he began. "The last two and a half years have been a helluva road we've travelled. Some would call it hell, and some wouldn't have survived. But not us. We've come out better, stronger. Because steel has to go through fire to come out stronger." He let out a shaky breath. "Every day with you is a gift, and I promise to cherish you always. I will never take you for granted, not for a single second. I love you, Juss. Always have, always will. And I am proud to call you my husband."

I got a little teary and had to wave my hand in front of my face so the tears wouldn't fall. A few people laughed, and then it was Dallas who squeezed my hand.

God, now it was my turn . . .

I took a deep breath in and let it out slowly. "Dallas. You have been, without a doubt, a mountain of strength. Through everything, every procedure, every ordeal, you never took a backward step. And because of you, every step I've taken, no matter how small, has been forward. And I'm more in love with you than I thought was ever possible." I smiled at him. "After my accident, I spent a lot of time wishing for my memories to come back. I was missing pieces of my life, and pieces of myself were gone. But there was always you. And through it all, I realised the pieces of us were what kept me together." I squeezed his hands. "I promise you, Dallas, that I will love you forever. You are the reason I get up in the morning and the reason I try to be a better man than I was the day before. And I am proud and honoured and lucky as hell to call you my husband."

The celebrant smiled. "Dallas, do you take Justin to be your husband, to love always—"

"Yes," he blurted. "Yes, I do."

I laughed, and our guests laughed too. But then he slid my wedding ring over my finger and another piece of my heart slotted into place.

"Justin, do you take Dallas to be your husband—"

"Yes! I do."

The celebrant laughed, and I took Dallas' ring and gently put it on his finger. His smile, the tears in his eyes, stole the breath from my lungs.

"Okay then," the celebrant said. "I now pronounce you married. You may kiss your husband."

Dallas cupped my face and kissed me, not like we'd planned and not like we'd practised, but there was so much emotion in that kiss . . . his hands were trembling, and when he pulled back, his eyes were glassy.

I nodded, because I knew. I felt it in my heart, in my soul.

We were married. Legally, our very own little family. I was so happy, so full of love and hope, I just could have burst.

We were hugged and congratulated and hugged some more. We had a casual reception at the surf club, which was basically just lunch with our nearest and dearest. We didn't want anything super fancy. We just wanted it to be official.

And as I sat with Dallas by my side and listened as he talked and laughed with everyone, the weight of the ring on my wedding finger settled something deep inside me. I turned the silver band with my thumb, feeling the smooth glide against my skin. It felt so right. It was as though something lost was found. I couldn't explain it or why it made me feel so content.

"You okay, Juss?" Dallas asked.

I must have zoned out. Everyone was looking at me. "Yeah, I'm great. Just . . . happy, daydreaming."

Sparra shot me a look as though he'd been trying to get my attention. Shit. I leaned in and spoke in Dallas' ear. "Babe, can I have the keys to the ute. I want to get a pill."

He was immediately concerned. "Are you okay? Today's been a lot . . ."

"I'm fine, Dall. Honestly, never felt this good."

He studied my face for a second, as though he was looking for a tell or sign that I had a headache. Seeing none, he handed over the key and went back to the conversation. Sparra followed me out, and not a second later, Davo joined us.

I handed them keys. "Be quick, but be careful. Drive safe."

They grinned as they ran off and gave it a few minutes before I went back to the table. Carissa and Lauren smiled because they were in on our little plan, and I took my seat. Dallas put his arm around my shoulder as he laughed with Jimmy and Toni's husband, and he was none the wiser at their absence, and thankfully he never asked for his keys back.

But, about forty minutes later, it was time for us to go. Dallas paid the tab while I thanked everyone for sharing our special day with us, and I saw him looking around for Davo and Sparra. He'd noticed they were gone.

When he was done, he made his way to Lauren and Carissa, no doubt to ask them where the boys had gone, and I was beginning to think something had gone wrong. They were taking too long and Dallas was going to find out . . .

"Where's Davo and Sparra?" he asked Lauren and Carissa. "I thought they must have been at the bar. Or in the bathrooms? Did something happen?"

"No," Lauren said quickly. She tried to smile and her gaze darted to me, something Dallas didn't miss at all.

"Juss, what's going on?"

And just then, thank God, Dall's blue ute came around the corner. And not only that, but our bikes were loaded onto the back.

Dallas spun to me. "What? Justin? What the hell?"

"Surprise," I squeaked. God, was his reaction good or bad? "I booked our honeymoon."

"Our bikes?"

I nodded. I'd ridden a little over the last twelve months. I'd even driven the ute a few times, but I was ready to get back into it. Starting now. "Yeah. A week at the beach house in Hallidays Point. The one we stayed at years ago. It's all organised. The boys are taking care of the shop, and Toni's got everything sorted."

Dallas looked over at Toni, and she gave him a bright smile and a nod. Then he looked at Lauren and Carissa. "You all knew about this . . ."

Oh God. This was going bad. "I wanted to surprise you with something special, Dall. Somewhere that meant something to us. Because I remember that place. When we went there last time. And I wanted to ride with you again. We haven't really had a chance to do that. Not since the accident—"

He took two huge strides and collected me in his arms, lifting me off the ground and kissing me. "Are we really going riding?"

I nodded. "We have a week. No trails, but maybe an easy circuit. Small steps, right?"

Dallas hugged me, tucking me into his side as Davo and Sparra got out of the ute and threw the keys to him. "You're welcome," Davo said, wearing a shit-eating grin. "It was just the one bag by the door?"

"Yep," I answered. "Beauty of having just one wardrobe."

Sparra put his arm around Carissa but he smiled at me. "Oh, and Squish is fed. I'll check on him every day, I promise."

"He likes fishing shows on TV," I said.

"Jusso," Sparra said flatly. "I'll feed him; I'll even pat and cuddle him. But I ain't watching fishing shows with him."

I laughed and looked up at Dallas. "Husband?"

He put his forehead to mine. "Yes?"

"Are you ready to go?"

"We're leaving for our honeymoon right now?"

"Yep. Everything's taken care of."

We got into the ute, waving goodbye to our friends and family, and Dallas took my hand. I brought our joined hands to my lips and kissed the wedding ring on his finger. "Husband. I really like the sound of that."

"I really like you saying that," he said with a heated look in his eyes.

"Then we better get going. There's a certain sofa I remember in that beach house, and I remember what you did to me on it. I want to see if it's still there."

He laughed and started the engine. "I can't believe you planned this without me knowing."

I smiled as we began the drive north. I turned my wedding ring with my thumb and watched as the sun caught the gleam. "I can't wait."

"Can't wait for what?"

"Everything. Being married, beginning our lives as husbands, being happy forever."

Dallas grinned. "Me either, baby."

Exhaustion settled over me. A tiredness I hadn't felt in a while. I yawned and tried to shake it off. "Dunno why I'm so tired."

"Because you can finally relax," he offered with a smile. "After all the build-up and excitement of the wedding, it's over. Have a nap, baby." He gave me a wicked smile. "You're gonna need your energy later."

"Hmm, sounds promising." The truth was, I *was* tired, and a nap sounded pretty good. Especially if he intended to wear me out later . . .

I kept hold of his hand and closed my eyes and allowed the warmth through the windscreen and the hum of the tyres on the highway lull me to sleep.

A GENTLE HAND on my arm woke me. "Juss, baby, we're here."

I sat up straight and took in my surroundings. I was still in the ute, but we were stopped out the front of a familiar house.

Oh my God.

I got out and looked around. The trees, the sand, the smell . . . No one ever prepares you for the missing senses of memory loss. It's not just the memory itself, it's how it feels, how it smells and sounds, how it tastes.

But I remembered this place.

I turned to the house and followed Dallas up onto the front porch decking. He opened the glass sliding door and inside was a pale cream kitchen, a dining table, and a sofa . . .

"I remember this," I said. Dall smiled at me, but he didn't get it. "No, Dallas, I remember this. Everything. I remember us being here before, years ago. I remembered this all before, but seeing it . . ."

Dallas came back to the doorway and wrapped me up in his big, strong arms and held me tight. "Oh, baby."

"It's so weird. I remember you coming up from the beach, right there," I said, pointing toward the ocean. "You were wet and freezing cold, laughing. I remember riding our bikes from here. I remember us cooking noodles, and I remember cuddling up on the couch because we got back late and it was cold. I remember that couch . . . Dallas, I remember it."

Dallas pulled back a little so he could see my eyes. "I remember too."

The complete love and devotion he had for me was in his eyes, written on his face. "I meant what I said in our vows," I murmured. *God, was that just today?* "For a long time, there's been parts of me that felt incomplete. Maybe even before the accident. Then I woke up in hospital and the most amazing man was sitting there, already in love with me. Like I was the luckiest guy in the world. And it took a little while as I tried to put the puzzle of myself back together. But Dallas, it was the pieces of us that made me whole. Not me by myself, and not just you, but us."

He kissed me softly. "The pieces of us make me whole too."

Then he bent down and scooped me up, bridal style. "What are you doing?"

He grinned. "Carrying you across the threshold. It's not our house, but it is our wedding day."

I laughed as he stepped inside and put me gently on my feet next to the couch. "I love you, Dallas."

He beamed. "And I love you. Always have."

I sighed, content and safe in his love. "Always will."

THE END

About the Author

N.R. Walker is an Australian author, who loves her genre of gay romance. She loves writing and spends far too much time doing it, but wouldn't have it any other way.

She is many things: a mother, a wife, a sister, a writer. She has pretty, pretty boys who live in her head, who don't let her sleep at night unless she gives them life with words.

She likes it when they do dirty, dirty things... but likes it even more when they fall in love.

She used to think having people in her head talking to her was weird, until one day she happened across other writers who told her it was normal.

She's been writing ever since...

MISSING *pieces*

SERIES COLLECTION

9 781925 886764